WHAT A WAY TO GO

Also by Bella Mackie

Jog On: How Running Saved My Life
Jog On Journal: A Practical Guide to Getting Up and Running
How to Kill Your Family

WHAT A WAY TO GO

BELLA MACKIE

b

THE BOROUGH PRESS

The Borough Press
An imprint of HarperCollins*Publishers* Ltd
1 London Bridge Street
London SE1 9GF

www.harpercollins.co.uk

HarperCollins*Publishers*
Macken House,
39/40 Mayor Street Upper,
Dublin 1
D01 C9W8

First published in Great Britain by HarperCollins*Publishers* 2024

1

A catalogue record for this book is available from the British Library

HB ISBN: 978-0-00-8365950
TPB ISBN: 978-0-00-8559526

Typeset in Adobe Garamond by Palimpsest Book Production Ltd,
Falkirk, Stirlingshire

Printed and bound in the UK using 100% Renewable Electricity
at CPI Group (UK) Ltd

MIX
Paper | Supporting
responsible forestry
FSC
www.fsc.org   FSC™ C007454

For Lizzie. En.

It is the wretchedness of being rich that you have to live with rich people.

Logan Pearsall Smith

ANTHONY

Looking back on it now, I wouldn't change much about the night I died. If you ignore the ending, and obviously I can't, it was a pretty fantastic evening. Given advance warning that you were about to breathe your last, you might run around screaming, pleading with whatever god you think is most likely to hear you, 'I want to live,' thereby wasting your final precious moments. I'm glad I wasn't, it meant I spent the evening drinking Champagne like water and being so fulsomely praised to high heaven you'd have thought I was the dictator of a small but prosperous country. If I had one tiny quibble, it would be that eight precious minutes of my last night on earth were given over to Mary Chambers and her insistence I hear all about her new charitable endeavour.

Of course, she wasn't supposed to be allowed to get anywhere near me. At most, I thought I'd briefly say hello and then allow myself to be pulled away by somebody more important, and nearly everyone was more important than Mary Chambers. The insufferable woman called the office several times a week, without success. I never once returned the calls, not that she took the asteroid-sized hint. She'd been left a devastatingly large fortune by her husband when he died last year. Fell off his yacht in the middle of the night near Portofino – that made the collective eyebrows raise, I can tell you. Especially those of his daughter from a previous marriage, who was incensed to find that her name wasn't in the will, and unsuccessfully sued Mary for her share. I knew how desperate she was to invest with me, and the sheer bulk of her fortune tempted me a few times, but I always ended up resolving to say no. The woman was too nosy, too enquiring. I needed investors who didn't prod and pry - and that was Mary's entire raison d'être. If Mary Chambers had anything to do with her husband's death, as his daughter kept loudly insisting, I would've found her much more interesting, but she didn't have the foresight. Truthfully, John Chambers was a bad drunk, who staggered under the weight of his enormous girth and fell overboard.

Boring, but hardly sinister. No, she didn't have the capacity for it. The woman only excelled in one thing: wittering. But she made the cut, somehow my wife thought it was important she be there. 'She's on the board of the Lamcusi Foundation!' I was informed, as if that made all the difference.

My big mistake was to take drugs *before* the dinner. After was expected, even encouraged. But before? It made me sloppy. In my defence, I'd been as stressed as a person could ever be and I'd felt a burning desire to let loose. I'd looked around at the gardens, glittering and impossibly beautiful, and I'd finally felt a rush. Olivia had gone all out, and as much as I'd been annoyed by the months of preparation, the place looked fantastic. We'd begun down by the lake, decked out to look like a midsummer night's fairytale. Hundreds of big glowing orbs were woven throughout the branches of the trees which surrounded the water. 'A soft light', just as my wife had hissed at an organiser earlier who'd made the mistake of adjusting the bulbs too brightly. Similarly, the jetty, rewaxed just that morning, was festooned with smaller orbs. Even more stood on spikes around the banks of the lake. The crowning glory though, was an enormous glowing orb which had been dropped into the bottom of the lake by ten strong lads that morning. My wife had had a vision you see, 'of water lit up from above *and* below', and given how much we were paying the planner, there was no way to tell her it wouldn't work. The orb was handmade in Italy, and nearly smashed twice as it was unboxed and rolled down the hill to its destination. But it was worth it, the gasps of our guests as they walked through the enormous arches and saw the final result was enough to tell me that my birthday party would be one for the ages. And I was right, though perhaps not in the way I'd imagined.

After the drinks, we were ushered to the marquees by smiling young women in appealingly tight black dresses. As my friends moved from the first beautiful room Olivia had hired an army of minions to decorate and into the second, where dinner was to be held, I'd started to feel almost carefree for the first time in months. You think your troubles are insurmountable and then a waiter hands you a glass of really good wine. You're handed several more, and then all of a sudden you're in the bathroom with George doing a line or two of his best powder and you find yourself briefly untethered from the woes which have been sitting on your chest like a bloody bull elephant. Sometimes a little recreational relief can be a great idea; I can't bear the puritanical society we seem to have become, where the importance of health and longevity have surpassed any notion of fun. But then, I was dead by sixty, so I will concede it's perhaps not wise to follow my advice too closely.

As I walked to the table, men intercepted me to pump my hand and slap my back, women kissed my cheeks and let their fingers linger in mine just a second too long. They all wanted a chance with Wistern; I could have taken my pick in that moment. What a boost for a man on the brink! Maybe it would be ok, some part of my brain began to think. There were hundreds of people here, and that was just the strictly selected A-list. Olivia had fielded calls for weeks from those who didn't make the cut, begging to come and kiss the ring. Surely *some* of them would stick by me. A man can't lose all of this in one fell swoop. Such confidence was the gift of the drugs, I see that now. I might be self-assured to a fault but I'm not usually devoid of all reality. Still, I'm glad I spent a little of my last night on earth with a small semblance of hope. I sorely needed it. But it meant I wasn't focused on who was where, and as I wandered through the room, I saw Mary Chambers standing in front of me, waving wildly as if I was a cab she wished to flag down.

I was never a man who flew into rages. I paid thousands of pounds to a range of martial arts experts to fight with me in a variety of gyms around the world in order to get any aggression out. A guy who trains top MMA athletes once told me my right hook was equal to that of anyone he'd ever met, but must be reined in. So many guys get into finance and think the way to succeed is to ooze raw testosterone. There's a fine line between smoothly intimidating and actually frightening, and I've always been careful to stay on the right side. But upon seeing Mary Chambers eagerly waiting to pounce, I found myself impulsively wanting to punch the waiter to my right. I frantically swivelled, hoping to find someone, anyone, to help me. But it was too late. She'd grabbed my arm, and centred herself so close to me that I could smell her breath. And then a funny thing happened. The despair I'd been holding at bay for weeks if not months suddenly collapsed like a burst balloon right on top of my head. It wasn't going to be ok. Mary Chambers started talking earnestly at me about cats in war zones and I nodded, suddenly feeling like one of them. There wasn't anything else I could do; I realised it at that moment, staring into this dull woman's face as she mouthed the words 'living in their own filth' at me. I'd probably go to jail, I thought, and tried to imagine what that would be like. Would *I* have to live in my own filth? Certainly Mary Chambers wouldn't advocate for me as earnestly as she was for these bloody animals. Like everyone else, she'd gossip about my wrongdoings, and shun my wife at parties, sanctimonious to the last, just like every other guest here. Barely a soul in this marquee had any real moral backbone – I could reel off the list of sins for every person I saw. Rohan, tax fraud. Jeremy, a slum landlord on a gigantic scale. Chuck, beat up someone outside a private members club for brushing past him. And there was Alice Begby walking past. A woman with a lineage going all the way back to the Tudors but who had at one point been so hopelessly addicted to shoplifting that she'd actually been barred from Harrods. None of them hurt their own though, they transgressed against people they'd never actually have to fraternise with. That's where I'd fucked up.

Mary Chambers was looking at me with concern, and I realised sweat was pouring down my neck and causing my collar to stick to my skin. I grabbed another glass of Champagne from a waiter and waved away her offer to get me a seat. After another impassioned treaty about the plight of child slaves, I finally felt my wife's hand on my arm, telling me it was time for dinner. As she steered me towards the head of the table, she whispered, 'God, what a bore, I didn't see her until it was too late.' I felt sick and irritable, and irrationally furious with Olivia for not doing her job better.

'For fuck's sake Liv, it's intolerable to have to deal with these people. I told you this was a huge mistake.' She pursed her lips and looked like she was about to berate me, but I wouldn't give her the opportunity. 'Just spare me. I'm not in the mood for one of your interminable lectures.' I shook her off and reached my seat just as the ridiculous announcer in white tie Olivia had insisted on having declared the dinner was served. I'd successfully avoided a tiresome fight with my wife, but an hour later I was dead. Life is a funny succession of swings and roundabouts.

OLIVIA

The night had gone in a flash. Drinks at seven, dinner at nine and speeches in between. The children gave an appropriately gushy one about what a fabulous father he was. It certainly sounded authentic, but that's what a top-class speechwriter can do if you pay them enough. His mother gave a mercifully short tribute, where she quite clearly confused him with his older brother and kept referring to him as Andrew. It wouldn't have mattered so much if Andrew hadn't died at eight, traumatising Anthony for years, and I couldn't deny it briefly soured the mood. Every other part of the evening went off perfectly, and I felt myself visibly relax once the guests were ushered through into the second marquee.

When the role of charming hostess overwhelmed me, I'd slip out for a cigarette, and at one point before dinner I went down to the lake to show Allegra the lights, since she'd arrived appallingly late and missed the whole show. I saw my husband smoking a cigar on the other side of the banks, in close conversation with Giles, and we nodded at each other, but that was really the extent of our interaction that evening. No doubt a large part of why I enjoyed the night so much.

It was well past midnight when I was made aware of what was happening down at the lake, just as the band was in full swing and most people were on the dance floor. I myself never dance. I have a horror of the drunk and unselfconscious, and find myself cringing whenever I see people I normally respect flinging themselves around a dance floor. Instead, I'd held court at the seating area by the grand piano, trying not to shudder every time Alex Lawson shimmied past me. The woman was one of London's most celebrated QCs and there she was, trying to entice Roger Simons, who just happens to be a high court judge, to do the limbo. I hissed 'dignity' at her as she stumbled by, but she was too far gone to pay me any heed.

I was talking to my dear friend Lou Molton about how well the night had gone. A very talented interior designer, but she's terrible with keeping both money and husbands, and though she hides it better than most, I know she's appropriately jealous of me. She was saying how beautiful the marquee looked when Lyra pushed her way through the crowd and stumbled up to me. I hadn't seen any of my children since we finished dinner. None of them had been particularly excited about attending, but it was a three-line whip. I'd been firm they make an effort until the speeches were done, all with the promise that after that, they could do as they liked.

As usual with Lyra, my first emotion upon seeing my third child was one of annoyance. Despite my pleas, she'd opted to wear a black mini dress with trainers, and enough eye make-up as to render her faintly pandaesque. Clothes are a matter of respect and Lyra always dresses as if she's mocking you. Or perhaps she's merely mocking *me*.

'Something's wrong – Fred and Giles are down by the lake, Dad's hurt.' She said it loudly, breaking through the sound of the music, causing several people around us to turn round. I made a low shushing noise to show that she was making a scene, but as usual, she ignored my wishes, tugging me by the arm until I had no choice but to follow her out. Lou was close behind, keen to be on hand for any potential drama, and by the time we found ourselves walking down the path to the lake, several others had joined us. I glanced round and saw Hamish McWhirter, and several women I knew by sight not name – the younger second wives and girlfriends club – were eagerly trotting behind. The journey only took a few minutes, but it felt much longer because my heels kept sinking into the damn gravel path Fred had insisted on laying. I'd wanted sandstone but he'd frowned and told me it was too violent a material for a garden, whatever that meant. Nobody was supposed to be down by the lake now. I'd organised a beautiful fireworks display on the formal lawns at the front of the house to signal the end of the evening, and I didn't want people splitting off and ruining my carefully curated plan like this. They would light up the folly in a truly breathtaking way. There may be more beautiful houses in the Cotswolds, but everyone covets my folly.

I always knew Anthony was going to spoil it somehow, he never could take anything seriously. I'd thrown the party for him, a celebration of our family and our success, and he'd gone off to play silly buggers down by the lake. I tried to tamp down my annoyance at seeing so many people hotfooting it to see what he'd done now, but the irritation had crept up on me and I couldn't remove the scowl that had taken hold. So ageing, a scowl.

Someone behind me gasped. 'He's in the lake!' The bloody lake. The children had wanted a swimming pool, had begged and pleaded for one, but I find them too ugly to bear. Swimming pools are for villas in the South of France, not the Cotswolds where it rains a lot and doesn't get really hot until July. Instead, I'd had the lake dug, stocked it with fresh water and maintained weekly by the groundsman. If they wanted to swim so badly, I'd told them, they could swim in that. My son, to his credit, rose to the challenge, taking a dip every morning, but the rest of them sullenly refused to go near it. Anthony especially was a wuss when it came to cold water, and only went in twice in his life. I wished I'd gone with my original idea and had a maze put in. I'd always thought a maze would be so chic, but Anthony had muttered that if he wanted to spend a weekend getting lost, he'd do it in Ibiza, and that was the end of that.

The scene looked almost like something out of a Renaissance painting. Giles and Freddy were both standing in the water, hands hovering as if conducting an invisible orchestra. In between them was my husband. He was positioned in an impossible way, almost suspended over the water. His face was submerged, his arms dangling like a child being stripped of his clothes. But his legs, his legs were in the air. 'He's been impaled!' wailed a woman wearing a rather revealing red dress. Hamish hushed her, but she was right. My husband had been lanced by one of the spikes used to hold up the beautiful orbs dotting the lake. Speared, just like a fish.

I stepped closer, noticing the watch on my husband's wrist, the one I'd presented to him just the day before. The salesman had gone on at great lengths about how you could dive to 100 feet wearing it, but a Cotswold lake was nothing like the clear blue waters of the Med. Typical Anthony to treat it so carelessly. Several people were now screaming, and I whipped round and glared them into silence.

'He's dead,' Fred said, as if the bloody spike hadn't tipped everyone off. He's always one to state the obvious. A very literal brain, not quite what I'd hoped for in my only son but then the rest of them aren't exactly Mensa members either. I couldn't take my eyes off the orb, shimmering under the water, illuminating the blood. That was the worst part of it actually. You'd think it was the sight of Anthony suspended like a haunted doll on a metal pole, but the dark red water was somehow much more disturbing. A soft light, I'd insisted to the planners, this was anything but.

Hamish had stepped up to comfort the gaggle of second wives, rather too keenly I thought. Lyra ran towards her brother but stumbled to her knees as she reached the bank. Always the pragmatist, Giles had been doing his best to keep everyone away from the body, but he was quite safe there. Nobody was in any hurry to rush towards this horror. Those bloody orbs had done a marvellous job of illuminating the scene, almost like it was planned.

Lou turned on her heels and headed back towards the marquee, yelling over her shoulder that she'd get help. Coward. And me? I didn't move. Not an inch. I'd wished my husband dead many times in my most angry of moments. I'd even thought about ways it might happen, carefully constructing scenarios where he was dragged into the sea by an angry wave, or burned to a crisp in a gruesome helicopter accident. But they were just the normal fantasies we women have during the many crisis moments of long marriages. After one too many martinis, my mother's great friend Jessica De Palmer once told me she consoled herself that her husband would probably die from a violent heart attack like every other man in his family. She'd joked that she took great pains to make sure the housekeeper cooked the most unhealthy options to hurry the process along. As it happened, William De Palmer outlived his wife, and is now married to a much younger woman who put him on a health kick and doesn't allow him to drink alcohol. I suspect he'd rather be dead.

I am very practical when I have to be. Some might call it cold, more than one newspaper has referred to me as 'icy', but it's useful to be able to shut down unnecessary emotions if they threaten to get in the way of action. Two things went through my mind. The first was a vow not to cry or wail in front of these caterwauling women. I knew all too well how the second wives liked to gossip about those who'd come before them, they'd enjoy going over my unspooling devastation if I showed an ounce of feeling. And at the same time, my maternal instinct kicked in. It might be somewhat slower than some women's, I've never been one to obsess over my children like other women – your offspring don't constitute a personality after all – but it's in me somewhere.

Come here, I barked at Lyra and Freddy, so sternly that despite their shock, they immediately stood up and walked towards me. Back to the house, we're going back to the house, I said, grabbing them by their hands. We pushed through the second wives and girlfriends, many of whom were actually crying now, presumably mourning an opportunity lost, and headed back down the gravel path. I remember seeing the twinkling lights of the marquees and hearing the band start playing 'Oh, What a Night' as we neared. How grimly appropriate.

'Don't go this way,' Lyra pleaded. I understood the urge, the thought of having to go and face hundreds of people, most of whom were drunk, felt almost impossible. But I wouldn't let Clara and Jemima find out from some minor acquaintance, or worse, from one of the wait staff. The therapy bills I'd shelled out for my children were already extortionate, why exacerbate it?

We powered across the dance floor, knocking over revellers as we went. Freddy was still caked in mud, and much of it had transferred onto Lyra, which made her look even more like a vagrant than usual. I was trying to smile as we walked, as though this might assuage my guests in some way. Anthony's PA was dancing with a man I didn't recognise, shimmying her hips in a vaguely obscene way. She caught my eye as I walked, and I saw her expression change from one of seduction to one of surprise. My smile dropped in response. I disliked Lainey intensely and the last thing I wanted was for her to follow us, offering help in that slightly breathless voice which always made my blood pressure rocket. I shook my head at her quickly, and her attention returned to the man in front of her. He was certainly fixated on the woman, staring at her cleavage with the kind of dedication that might leave him with a migraine if he wasn't careful.

Eventually we found Clara. Being the youngest, she was sitting at the bar with her friend Willa, clearly over the party and using the opportunity to try to get drunk as quickly as possible. We've got to go, I told her, yanking her off the stool and ignoring the immediate angry protestations. Finally, Lyra, who'd disappeared as we'd marched, reappeared beside me. She'd brought Will, who was looking unusually flustered. I suppressed annoyance. He was Jemima's husband and as such would have to be included as close family, but I'd never fully accepted it. The man was a drip, and I resented that people saw him as a Wistern, something I'm sure he encouraged.

He didn't know where his wife was, he babbled, and I shot him a look of such annoyance that I actually saw him flinch. At another time, I'd have felt a jolt of satisfaction but it was sadly wasted that night.

I knew we couldn't tarry much longer in the tent. From the corner of my eye, I saw Richard Price stalking towards me, clearly deciding that whatever was going on should involve him in some way. I held my arm up to him and pushed my family out of the marquee. We almost ran the last yards back to the house, Fred with his arms around his sisters, Will offering me a hand and quickly rescinding it when I ignored him. As we reached the French windows to the living room, Jemima entered, wearing a robe, her hair wrapped in a towel. As she looked up at us in surprise, I heard police sirens coming down the driveway.

THE SLEUTH

@thesleuth
197 subscribers

The night it all happened, I was just three miles and an entire world away in my childhood bedroom. When I'd left for uni, I'd been so insistent I wasn't coming home that I'd thrown most of my stuff away. What need would I have for it, as an adult living an exciting life in London? I bitterly regretted it now, especially since my mother made my bedroom into her knitting room and plastered the walls in gaudy wallpaper. Small shells which looked undeniably like penises, impossible not to focus on. I'd been sitting at the desk late into the night, watching a documentary on my laptop about a murderer in Crawley who killed people by putting balloons over their heads. It was imaginatively called *Balloon Beast* and if I'm honest, it wasn't particularly gripping. I'm not sure a balloon is the most effective way of killing someone, he messed it up three times and had to use a knife to finish the job. He should've just been called the Knife Murderer, but where's the USP in that?

The laptop still had a crack running down the screen from when I'd thrown it on the floor six months ago. I'd thrown it in rage, seeing red when the power-hungry moderator of Sleuth Seekers banned me for making too many posts. When I say I saw red, I mean it literally. A bright ball of fire flares in front of my face when I get angry. How do you tell someone they're asking too many questions? Aren't we there to dig deeper than everyone else? Isn't that the whole point? The moderator said it was spam, that I was posting too often and not giving other people a chance. Apparently even on a true crime forum there's a self-appointed leader determined to silence the masses if they go against the grain. Even their most active user, someone other people literally rely on for news of a new case.

After a proper night's sleep, I'd reached the conclusion that the place had got boring recently anyway, too much focus on the same old American serial killers. Everyone followed the trend for gore, the more gruesome the better. Mostly they just wanted entertainment, they weren't really interested in injustice, but in filling their lunch break with something that made them feel better about their own lives. If they didn't value my work, I'd take it elsewhere.

I should've started a podcast; I still kick myself that I didn't do it before they exploded and everyone and their nan decided to do one. Fucking *Crime Kittens* has millions of listeners and makes a ton of money and all they do is rehash Wikipedia articles about murderers from decades ago.

Instead, I'd started a YouTube channel, and taught myself how to use TikTok. My numbers weren't promising to start, but I'd slowly built up a small following – people who actually wanted to help solve crimes rather than just sit on their arses watching badly put together documentaries to scare themselves. But I wasn't happy simply to follow the cases that everyone else did. I wanted to have my voice heard properly. For that, I needed my own story. One, it turned out, that was happening right that very moment, just down the road, to a man I knew all too well.

ANTHONY

It really is the oddest thing to be alive one minute and dead the next. They don't give you enough time here to get your head around it and believe me, when you find yourself at the intake centre, you *will* need a moment. I like to think of myself as a man who can deal with any situation thrown at me, but without any explanation as to what was happening, I thought I must be going mad. That, or one of the chaps had given me some dodgy powder. How had I been at a glorious party thrown in my honour one minute, then in a beige and windowless room the next?

Initially, I actually didn't know I'd died. That took several hours. At first I thought I must be in prison, the bleak interiors rather reminded me of some low-budget drama set in a jail, and I braced myself for the inevitable accusations which would follow. But there were no guards, and my hands were uncuffed. Sitting in a waiting room, I noticed large, laminated signs which said things like 'You are safe. Please keep calm and wait for a member of staff to explain things.' And 'Do not harass our volunteers, they are very busy and will call your number when ready.' I looked down at my hands, and lo and behold, I was holding a

18

ticket with the number 69 on it. My favourite number, I joked, though nobody laughed. The lady next to me was crying loudly, which irritated me no end, while a chap in a raincoat lay slumped on the floor as if he was drunk. Perhaps the drugs really had done a number on me, maybe this was all just an odd hallucination which I had to ride out. Every time I went to reception to ask what was happening, a young girl with stringy hair merely shook her head and told me to wait my turn.

When my number was finally called, I was ushered into another windowless room by a woman wearing a twinset, and where oddly, I could hear the faint sounds of 'Come on Eileen' playing somewhere. The deputy intake manager (for that was what her little laminated badge read) rolled her eyes when she heard it, and told the receptionist to play something more appropriate ('They need calming down, Cathy, it's not a party'), before shutting the door.

A shuffle of some papers, a pointed lack of a smile. Her speech was brief and vague. 'Welcome to the processing centre, I'm Susan. I'm very sorry you're with us and I imagine it will be a shock for you to hear what I'm about to say, but everything will be explained to you as and when needed.' She then waited precisely three seconds before telling me I was dead and currently in the delicate realm between life and the afterlife. I had a lot of questions, as you might imagine. Damn shame for a hallucination to involve this dull woman repeatedly telling me I was dead and refusing to give me details. You'd think there'd be pink elephants and at the very least, some sort of orgy not achievable when sober. But even as I clutched at this, something in me knew it was no dream. It felt bleakly real, from the cheap lino floor to the curling edges of the poster on the wall, which showed a sunrise over an unspecified ocean and the words 'Where you go after death is determined by where you went in life.' In my case, that could be anywhere. Capri, St Tropez, the island next door to Richard Branson's Necker which everyone secretly admits is much nicer than his stubby little rock. Not here. Not a place where they play Dexys Midnight Runners.

After a tetchy back and forth where she told me I had to remember how I'd died before moving on to the 'next stage', and I repeatedly told her to cut out the nonsense, she got rather impatient and said it would be better for me if I accepted my death sooner rather than later, I got up and went over to the desk, searching for a phone. My lawyers would sort this out, I don't pay thousands of pounds an hour for a firm nicknamed 'the hyenas' just to spend time in a middle manager's office with a woman like this. No phone. The woman sighed again and stood up.

'I can see I'll have to show you, Mr Wistern,' she said, and plunged her hand into my stomach. I felt a cold sensation, as if she'd poured water into my abdomen and I looked down in confusion. Her hand was inside my stomach, and all I could see was her wrist going right through my belly button.

'Assault,' I yelled, backing away from her. 'That's assault, right there. I'm not having this. Whatever kind of scam you're running, it won't wash with me. I want to speak to the person in charge.' Instead of apologising or looking scared at my outburst, this stupid woman merely smirked.

'I rather thought that might convince you. I put my hand *through* your stomach, Mr Wistern. Because our corporeal bodies no longer exist, there has been no damage to you, that surely must make you see that you're no longer alive?'

'The manager,' I said firmly, which made her sigh again.

'The manager is unavailable, but I'll be sure to let them know you wish to speak to them as soon as possible. Now I'm afraid I have to admit the next person, we're oddly busy today. A porter will show you to your room.'

I was ushered out, still swearing at her as I went, and shuttled to my new dormitory by a woman in a boiler suit. 'Hopefully you're only here for a short while,' she said, handing me a plastic bag with new clothes and shoes in it. 'Once your death details have been sorted out, you get to go to the next place. Just got to figure it out.' When I asked what she meant by that, she merely winked and walked off.

Sitting on a remarkably uncomfortable single bed, I looked down at my stomach. Not a mark on it. The realisation hit, and it hit bloody hard. So this *was* death. Not, as I'd imagined, a black hole of nothingness, but instead something akin to a rundown hostel. If heaven was going to turn out to be run by some hippy collective, I wanted no part of it.

I picked up the pamphlet I'd been given by the orderly. 'Processing your passing.' The front page had a rough illustration of a person shaking their fist at the sky, with the words 'Why it's so important to accept how you died.' The thing was written in language better suited to an eight-year-old. 'You will be sad to find out you are dead and that's ok! The mind shuts down in the last moments of life, this is to protect you – death can often be very painful. Good job brain! As a result, there's normally a gap of about thirty minutes in your memory, and you've got to play detective and figure out how to get it back. Most people die of illness, maybe that's a route to go down first? Or perhaps you were killed in a traffic accident. Ouch! The meditation sessions provided will be vital in unlocking these moments, they are optional but very important.' Why did I have to figure out how I'd died? 'We appreciate it might seem like a silly thing to have to remember, but thousands of years of practice have shown us that people who proceed to the next stage of the afterlife without this knowledge are often very troubled and angry without it, which causes problems for the whole community! To know how you died is in some way, to know how you lived. We hope you understand that this knowledge, however painful, will help you live your best death.' There was a much blunter list of conditions on the back. 'The memory must be full and complete, a vague guess or half memory will not be accepted. You may submit your answer as many times as you like, but only an accurate and detailed description will be accepted. If your death was traumatic, counselling will be provided but please be warned that the waiting list is currently very long. Do not ask other people for help.'

I threw it on the floor in disgust.

My competitive streak kicked in. Even if this was just about the stupidest thing I'd ever heard, I'd be the winner – it was my nature to succeed. I cast my mind back to the party. A party to celebrate my sixtieth birthday, designed to show off my status, my success and my power. What a night to kick the bucket. Still, if the status, success and power were about to be ripped away, perhaps it was another streak of luck for me. Or, knowing how many people in attendance vehemently hated my guts, maybe I was murdered. Now that *would* be exciting.

ANTHONY

I was shown the viewing room by Vince, a fellow 'inmate' as he called himself, and from the looks of him, someone who'd almost certainly done time and knew of what he spoke. Cubicles with thin partition walls, and spartan desks with just monitors and mousepads. 'You can watch them all from here,' Vince explained. 'See how they're coping now you're brown bread.' I looked at him blankly and he grinned. 'Brown bread, dead. Just a little joke to lift the mood, mate. Be careful though – sometimes you catch them doing things you'll wish you hadn't seen. Married thirty years, didn't have a clue my wife farted so much until yesterday.' He gave a mock shudder and walked off.

There was already a video playing on the monitor. My family. It was very odd to see them all sitting in the living room, my stunned wife and muddy children, knowing that 300 of our closest friends were still just metres away in the marquees, throwing back wine and dancing. Knowing that my body was somewhere nearby. An image of the lake flashed into my mind; had I drowned? At the very least I wanted a little bit of weeping, perhaps even some rending of garments. They all looked far too comfortable with the situation for my liking. I could hear the faint strains of music, and focused on identifying the song to avert my annoyance. 'What a way to make a living . . .' Dolly Parton! The DJ had gone expressly against my wishes, veering away from the playlist I'd had my wonderful mate Johnny put together. A musician who sold out theatres all over the world, he'd never have chosen something so tacky. This was a sixtieth birthday for a successful man, not a hen night in Southend.

My children were sitting in various chairs dotted about the room. Lyra, all the colour drained from her face, had her feet up on a table, almost as if she wanted her mother to remark on it. She's always been my favourite, in part because she's made winding Liv up into an art form. There was Clara with her head bent over sobbing far too loudly, Fred standing by the French windows as if he wanted to get far away from the rest of them and Jemima on the sofa, a towel next to her – its moisture seeping into the cushion. Olivia was staring daggers at our eldest daughter, who either didn't notice or didn't care.

Will, who had been liaising with an officer in the hallway, came back in just as the music finally went off. 'Ah, they're just explaining what's happened now,' he said, wiping his forehead as if he'd been doing manual labour. 'Well, they won't say exactly, but obviously the guests have to know something's a bit off.'

Clara looked up then, incensed. 'Off? Dad's dead, Will. Can you not make out like it's a fucking minor inconvenience?' He went bright red and apologised immediately. My son-in-law has never been able to stand up for himself, but capitulating to a hysterical teenager seemed to me to be a new low. Jemima clearly thought so too, making a face as her husband spoke.

'And Lainey's outside, she's very upset. Should I ask her to come in? I don't think she's got a car or anything . . .' He trailed off when he saw his wife's face. Jemima really had her mother's talent for looks that could make a man crumble to dust on the spot.

'Christ, Will, why don't you invite the caterers in too?'

Olivia didn't even deign to respond, and my son-in-law took the hint.

'What the hell happened?' Lyra now, swinging her legs off the chair and leaning forward. I noticed her hands were shaking. 'How did Dad end up impaled on a pole? It's . . . insane. Like, comically mental. Anthony fucking Wistern, harpooned.' She shook her head and I began to retch. Oh God, I'd been impaled. I remembered falling, seeing the lake rise up to meet me, and then a sharp stab just underneath my ribs. The memory faded but the horror remained. How the fuck had that happened? How does someone in modern times get impaled?

'Really?' That was Will again, speaking in an oddly high pitch. 'To me it feels rather like something Anthony would do. Go out with the maximum attention. Dying in his own bed as an old man would be rather too boring for him I'd imagine.'

You wouldn't think it was possible to stop thinking about being impaled once you'd been reminded, but suddenly another thought popped into the foreground. Will sidling up to me in the garden as I was smoking a fine Montecristo with Rufus Lowe, smiling apologetically. Knowing what he wanted, I'd reluctantly excused myself, missing out on the end of a great story my friend was telling me about how he'd just bought a cash-strapped school on the promise to save it. 'Those kids are sitting on prime W1 real estate, the assembly hall alone will make a three-bed flat!'

As I ushered Will a little way down the lawn, my son-in-law had spoken in a low tone. 'Can we have a quick chat about me cashing out, I know you've been very busy lately but it's pretty urgent I'm afraid.' I should've patronised him, made him feel stupid for asking. But I couldn't always hide how irritating I found him, and I couldn't mask my own annoyance at letting him invest. A moment of weakness after a long Easter lunch when, lulled by a nice bottle of Chateau Ausone and a nap in the sunshine, I'd eventually succumbed to his begging. He'd been squirmingly grateful that day, but hearing him now, I realised just how bitter he sounded. My brain, satisfied at remembering the moment successfully, went back to dwelling on the memory of being stuck on a spike. I felt vaguely sick again.

'You think I spent months organising this party so that my husband could die in an exciting way? He was drunk, he clearly fell off the jetty, William.' Olivia fixed him with a look of cold fury and he bridled and stuttered something about still being in shock. 'There was nothing wrong with him at all, apart from the enormous amount of booze he'd knocked back.'

'Yeah, William,' Lyra said, eager to join in the pile-on. 'For you to insinuate he was in any way suicidal is appalling. He was as happy as ever.' Olivia nodded at this, but she knew it wasn't true. We'd fought more in the month before I died than in our entire marriage. She'd been very cold with me, I'd assumed she thought there was another woman and told her she was being irrational. It hadn't stopped her from snooping. I'd found her in my study one night when she thought I was asleep, scrolling through my laptop, the glow from the computer lighting up her features. She'd never find any evidence there. I wasn't so foolish as to save extra-marital communications on my laptop. A second phone, that's what a smart man has. Sometimes even a third, if you're really on top of it all.

'What the fuck though, what the fuck?' Jemima now, rocking back and forth slightly. 'Fred, were you there?' she asked, almost too quickly. 'You still haven't told us what you saw.' All eyes swivelled to the figure at the window, but he didn't turn round. There was a pause before he spoke.

'I heard Giles shouting, so I ran down from the woods to see what was going on. He'd waded out into the lake; I didn't know why to begin with and then I saw him grab onto a shape. An arm . . .' My son trailed off and exhaled loudly, as if he might combust. Then he yanked the door handle and stepped out into the garden before any of them could stop him.

'Back to his arboreal friends,' remarked Lyra before adding, 'his only friends really.' Will went after him, always keen to show how helpful he could be.

Clara was typing something out on her phone, and I craned my head to see. 'RIP Dad', she'd written, over a selfie of tears running down her face. Our youngest was a complete attention-seeker, she once got a ski lift shut down after she tried to climb out of her seat to take a photo hanging off of it, but using my death as content was a new low. 'Maybe he was was murdered,' she offered, not bothering to look up. *Murdered.* Of course, of course that's what happened! Clara might be an egomaniac, but she was no fool. Who the hell thought they could murder me? I felt thoroughly indignant, aware that the heartburn which plagued me was rising in my chest. Heartburn when you're dead felt like a particularly cruel joke. It's not on to kill a man at his own birthday party. A fair fight is all I ask.

'How absurd you all are.' Left with just the girls, my wife had closed her eyes as she spoke, as if to block them out. It made the atmosphere feel even more poisonous. There's nothing like having three daughters to make you long for sons, even those as odd as Fred. 'He wasn't murdered, this isn't a movie.' Why was Olivia so keen to shut down the obvious? The woman's obsession with not causing a scene was affecting her logic. *Impaled*, Livvy.

'Errr, are you joking? You think he just tripped and fell on a spike? Have you ever seen a true crime documentary?' Clara was paying attention now, staring at her mother as if she were an idiot.

'Oh, stop with your weird true crime obsession. This isn't some hitchhiker in bumfuck nowhere Nebraska. It easily could've happened by mistake,' Jemima shot back. 'The news is always talking about freak accidents, people crushed to death or caught in machinery.'

'Yes, but those people aren't Dad, Jem.' Lyra was pouring herself a glass of wine, and I felt desperately jealous. 'Those people do actual jobs in unsafe conditions. Dad works from a mobile phone. Sometimes even two.' Ever eager to stir that one, Lyra looked pointedly at her mother.

'Well, his job must've made him enemies,' said Clara, who was now reapplying her eyeliner in great winged swoops. 'Like, he made a lot of money, that's the number one reason people get killed. And doing it at a birthday party is so classic. Psychos love to show off, everyone knows that. That lady who killed her husband last year in Bristol, she poisoned him at his own birthday too. Rat poison in an espresso martini.' Lyra shook her head in distaste. 'Espresso martinis are so tacky. Imagine going out like that.'

My wife let out a cry of exasperation I knew well. 'Enough! It was an accident, that's all. A horrible, inconvenient accident.' She paused, looking at our children as if for the first time. And then she said something so ridiculous I almost fell off my chair. 'Who knows? Maybe Will is right for the first time in his mediocre life. He wasn't happy about turning sixty, getting older for a man is sometimes harder than for women. We're irrelevant long before we get there, they fall off the cliff at rapid speed.'

From my wife's expression, I could tell she didn't really believe what she was saying; sixty is when men hit their prime after all, so why was she spouting such nonsense?

'He definitely *was* angrier than usual,' replied Lyra, her wine glass almost empty. 'When I was over last month I dropped by his office and Judy let me go straight in. He was on the phone hissing at someone in a weird way. Like he wanted to shout but couldn't, and when he saw me, he hung up and properly yelled at me for not knocking first.'

I remembered that. She'd wanted money of course, she never came to my office just to catch up. I'd sent her away in a fury, unable to calm myself down and feeling put-upon by all sides. Judy had left early that day, another woman whose feelings I apparently had to factor in when I made any decision at all. *But none of that would make your father launch himself onto a metal pole*, I yelled, to no avail. My family lapsed into silence for a minute, all of them entirely alone with their own thoughts. It was broken by the sound of an explosion, and then from the French windows, the sky lit up in angry red flames. Clara and Lyra screamed like banshees while Jemima rolled onto the floor and crawled under the table. Only my wife remained unperturbed as shots reverberated around the house.

'It's a Catherine wheel. Nobody told the fireworks team to hold off,' she said, almost without interest. Another loud bang, and the numbers 6 and 0 lit up the sky in bright red, before wobbling and disappearing. 'There's another ten minutes of this, we might as well watch the show.'

Jemima emerged from under the table and sat back down on the sofa, looking calmer now. She picked up the towel and started drying off her hair again. It was strange, I suddenly realised, for her to have been at the house having a shower while the party was in full swing, and I willed Olivia to snap out of whatever trance she was in and ask what she'd been doing when the door opened, and two policemen came in.

THE SLEUTH

@thesleuth
203 subscribers

I thought about my life as the sun came up this morning, while I was cleaning up Mum's breakfast and stripping her sheets for the third time this week. I'd got three short years away at uni before being forced back to help Mum. I imagined life would open up and offer me everything, but the most exciting thing to happen to me recently was when a cyclist fell off his bike and flew into our front garden, clipping one of Mum's ornamental fairy's wings off. I'd actually asked him in for a cup of tea, realising afterwards he was the only person other than Mum that I'd spoken to in three days. He'd politely turned the offer down. Maybe he thought I was flirting, but even in my desperate state, a man dressed head-to-toe in lycra wasn't going to do it for me. Still, it was the talk of our house for two days afterwards, that shows you how dull life in Chipping Marston can get.

It doesn't help, spending so much time online, but there's nothing else to do. All my mates post photos showing them living the life I thought I'd have and it guts me, but I can't look away. Tomorrow will be different, that's the mantra I'm always clinging on to so desperately. Something will happen, one of these days. I'd muttered it that morning, as I was doing the bins, desperately holding on to my stupid affirmation for dear life. And then, just an hour later, it did.

I first heard about it on a group chat at 9 a.m., when someone called Openeye822 posted that a person had been killed at a house party in Oxfordshire. The group is entirely anonymous, there's over 1,500 people in it, which can get overwhelming sometimes. The kooks post constantly, usually obsessing over cases which aren't interesting. Lady gets killed by her partner – sad, but common. The police deal with those pretty quickly, and we can't look at every murder, can we? Sometimes I mute the chat, but that morning Mum had gone back to sleep and I was so bored by the day already, I'd got back into bed and started scrolling through it. Of course the post got my attention, it was round the corner from me. It felt a bit like winning the lottery. Just four months ago, a user calling themselves InspectorMadshit found out a woman had been discovered in the canal right by their house and got interviewed on the news after he saw a set of keys under a bridge that the police had missed. He'd taken his mate's kayak out when it got dark and live-streamed it all. As a result, InspectorMadshit (or Darren English as the news called him) had become a bit of a hero on the chat, but I couldn't stand how he acted like he was a bigshot now. No longer needing his anonymity, he'd taken to sending the group photos of himself on 'stakeouts', and once posted a picture of the feature the local paper did about him, framed and hung right above his fireplace.

I'd asked for more details. They'd fired back minutes later, saying it was a big house a few miles away from me, and police were on the scene. 'That's confidential, I can't say more right now.' Annoying, but understandable if they were involved with the case. Twenty minutes later, someone else posted that it was all over Twitter, and Openeye didn't reply again. So much for inside knowledge. Someone had posted a photo of the road ablaze with police cars and I was able to match it up almost immediately to the place everybody called 'millionaire's row'. All the beautiful old houses outside of town, originally built for mill owners and landed gentry, have been snapped up by Londoners who add glass extensions and tennis courts and enormous gates so you can't see anything from the road at all. I could easily get there on my bike.

It might be nothing, but it was too close to me to ignore; a rich heiress pushed off a balcony or a teenager snapping and killing their mum after a row. It happens. Watch enough crime documentaries and you'll see how thin the veil is between civilisation and savagery.

I checked on Mum, who was still fast asleep, and cycled down to the address. I knew the road well; I'd driven down it a million times on the way to my dad's favourite garden centre. When we started passing the gates, he would shake his head and make the same boring remark about how local people were being priced out.

He'd been right though, he just hadn't known just how bad it would get. When I was a kid, it was middle-class types, writers, artists, doctors coming in. Now it's the mega wealthy, the kind who have homes in several places and only descend for a few days at a time before fucking off to the Seychelles or something. It started with a rise in farm shops, and it's ended with the old tea shop in town now slated as a 'curated gallery' where you can buy candles for fifty quid or quilts for eight hundred and nothing in between.

From Google Earth, you can see that behind the large gates and twelve-foot-high hedges, driveways take you past swimming pools, tennis courts and manicured lawns long before you arrive at the actual house. One even had golf carts to take residents around the grounds, that's how big it was.

I didn't have to work hard to find the exact spot, there were police outside the gates, three media trucks and a few other people loitering on the verge. For a second, I felt foolish just pitching up on my bike, and I considered speeding past. But then I saw Mike Grenson and drew up sharply just beyond the trucks. Mike fucking Grenson, a guy I've only met once but can't escape online. He pitches up at seemingly every murder England ever has, hanging around live-streaming for the 'grenlins' as he calls his subscribers. The police are constantly moving him on, even arresting him once, when he overstepped and tried to get on site. That only makes him more popular with people, they think he's a rebel with a cause – though the only cause is his ego. He was holding up his phone and pointing it directly at the officer guarding the main gate. Live-streaming already, at the one crime scene that should rightfully be mine. As far as I knew, he didn't even live round here. There's a code you're meant to follow, and Mike Grenson flouting it was just another reason to hate the guy.

When he finally stopped talking, he turned to me and grinned. 'Not like you to be boots on the ground, you're more of an online warrior, aren't you? Got any information?'

I hesitated, not wanting to give this man anything at all but afraid of looking like I had nothing. 'It was some rich guy, I've heard,' I said reluctantly, hedging my bets. He rolled his eyes and forced an artificial-sounding laugh.

'Yeah, we all know that, darling. Even your nan probably knows that by now. Jesus. I meant info, not the most basic starting fact. There's not much to this one I reckon, low-stakes boozy accident. Good for you to get your L plates, eh?' He smiled and walked off, back towards the policeman at the gate.

I moved away, and hovered next to a journalist getting ready to do a piece to camera. Busy applying powder to his already overly tanned face, he didn't notice me, so I listened to him complain to the camerawoman about being called up on a Sunday. 'Sarah only rang me because she knows we've got a weekend place nearby. My wife was furious, we're supposed to be having lunch with her parents. Given the choice, I suppose I've got the better end of the deal here.' Finished with the make-up, which made him look a strange colour, he turned to the story he'd shortly be covering. 'They're still not saying who, right? I mean, we all know, my boss said she got the confirmation from the DG who was at the party. Surprised she was there, always banging on about how much she hates the super-rich. It's a real fucker we can't say who it is. No doubt it's already online, so we'll look slow as usual. What a farce.' The press in cahoots with the police, holding back information from the public? What a surprise.

'To die at your own birthday party, what a shocker,' the presenter was saying just as the camerawoman finally noticed me and urgently shooed me out of shot. 'My wife's uncle choked on a bit of lamb at his 90th, died in front of everyone. They Heimliched him, but it was too late. The bit of lamb flew out and hit his wife on the forehead just as he took his final breath. Not been a fan of birthdays since. Or lamb, come to think of it.' He adjusted his tie and addressed the camera, his face now a mask of blank professionalism.

I wandered away, back towards Mike, who was now harassing a policewoman. 'Just tell me if it was murder. You lot always say it's not suspicious and then it turns out the guy's been coshed over the head by a brick or stabbed in the stomach with a machete.' The woman was doing a great job of ignoring him, and after a few minutes he gave up and told his phone he'd be back with more news later, 'if the powers that be decide to bother updating citizen journalists'. He shot her a look, which she didn't see, and let out a sigh of disgust.

'Jobsworth,' he said to me as if we were in cahoots and not rivals. 'It's Wistern,' he said, misreading the look on my face. 'Christ, you really don't know anything do you? Have at it, darling, I'm off to the pub, dead old men don't interest me.' The leer he gave me as he walked off made that clear. Apart from a sudden desire to kick him in the back as he walked away, I felt pretty energised. If Mike Grenson didn't think there was anything to go on here, he was as stupid as I always thought. A powerful man dropping dead at his sixtieth birthday party was ringing all my bells. There was something more to this, I'd bet everything on it. And if Mike and his grenlins weren't interested, then I'd finally have my own case, all to myself.

Anthony Wistern, CEO of Wismere Holdings, some kind of financial mega company. One of the *Evening Standard*'s 'most influential Londoners'. If you look him up, you'll find photo after photo of him and his wife at parties, him looking tanned and relaxed, her sort of pinched and distant. There will invariably be a shot of them with their kids, four perfectly dressed children with slightly blank yet confident expressions. The kind of kids who went past our house on their school coach every day on the way to the private school in North Marston. The kind of kids who grow up to treat people like they mean nothing, because I guess they do if you live like that.

I couldn't believe he'd been the one to die. I'd known he lived on this road of course, everyone did, but those large gates were designed to keep people like me out. He might as well have lived on Mars.

The first person to be killed right on my doorstep, and it was Anthony Wistern. I knew all the crime stats for our area, and although there was much excitement when a woman called Margaret Lemming died in the local park a few months back, it soon dissipated when the police realised she hadn't been knocked down by a madman on the loose but by her own dog. CCTV was found showing the moment her labrador got overexcited at the possibility of a stick being thrown and body slammed her right onto the sharp edge of a kid's slide. What a wasted possibility.

I intended to leave, I really did. But as I wheeled my bike past the news reporter again, I heard him gossiping with his camerawoman. 'Famous pig of a man, once tried it on with the CEO of Readell and when she turned him down, he spread it around town that she was an alcoholic. Fucked her career for years. She'll be popping the Champagne tonight.' He paused. 'Although that might just be the kind of behaviour to give that rumour legs.'

'What's right for you will come to you.' One of my mum's favourite sayings popped into my head in that moment. This was far from ideal, but if I wanted to be taken seriously in this job, I couldn't run away from the first big case I got to call my own. And Anthony Wistern was miles better than some no-mark teenager like I'd guessed. Anthony was a somebody, a 'BOI' as we call them. Body of interest. And now he was *my* body of interest. I wouldn't give that up just because I hated the man.

ANTHONY

The police kept them all in the living room, fruitlessly trying to stop people walking in through the French windows to find out what was going on. At 2 a.m., Roger Simons, whose shirt was entirely unbuttoned, pushed past one young officer telling her that he was a high court judge and had jurisdiction. The man was a prick but by god you've got to admire that level of confidence. There was a brief attempt to interview my family, but the house was in chaos, and the few officers they had at the scene were mainly just trying to corral drunken guests who were refusing to go home for fear they'd miss out on a juicy moment. I heard one young chap wail despairingly to his colleague that it was like trying to herd cats.

'The man was skewered like a kebab, Edmonds, you can't blame them for wanting to stick around.' A *kebab*. The shame of it all.

At some point, my wife went upstairs, aided by her old friend Penny, which didn't surprise me. She always retreated to the comfort of her bed when faced with difficulty. The rest of my family sat slumped in various chairs, Rosa bringing in endless cups of tea which nobody touched. I looked around the faces of my nearest and dearest and found a mix of emotions. Clara was sullen, glued to her phone. The hysterical tears had long dried after she'd realised nobody was paying her much attention. If I knew my daughter, she'd now be trying to score grief points on social media – that girl would do anything to be noticed.

At one point Jemima said, 'Daddy's dead,' to nobody in particular, which prompted Lyra to roll her eyes. Fred had been marched back into the fold by Will and was again standing by the south-facing window. My boy looked more defiant than sad if I'm honest. There was very little grief in that broad face, which looks so much like my own but carries none of my character. I guess very few people can have it all. A glint on his arm as he stretched out his hand to scratch his face alerted me to the fact that he was wearing my watch. The watch I'd had on just hours ago. Cheeky fucker must've taken it off me when I was dead, like a grave robber.

My son might've claimed a trophy, but the people who gave me serious pause were Will and Charles. Both men looked the opposite of grief-stricken, but in very different ways. Will was holding it down for the most part, but he was doing something odd with his left hand, clenching and unclenching his fingers and then flicking each nail with his thumb until Jemima grew annoyed with him and firmly swatted his hand. For a chap who has persistently failed to produce an interesting iota of character since Jemima introduced him to us, this was a promising development. Maybe I'd get to witness this preternaturally calm man have a breakdown, that would improve my rotten situation immensely. Skewered. The word kept bouncing around my brain.

Charles was the one who really unnerved me. He was actually cheerful, even smiling from time to time when he thought nobody was looking. The man had never liked me, made no secret that he thought Liv had married beneath her, as if we were living in Dickensian England and his family were born of royalty rather than just being the breed of upper-class people who eke out a centuries-old fortune until there's nothing left but a dusty house and an old name. I'd always been incredibly gracious about this, but only because it was easy, being so much more successful than he'd ever be. Now I had to watch him rejoice in my death right in front of my children. I could almost see the capillaries on his nose burst in excitement at the idea that he was now the head of the family. MY family.

At 7 a.m., the police finally managed to sit down with my family and ask them where they were when I died. That's when, to my surprise, the lies started.

NEWS ARTICLE
Sunday evening, 1 July 2018

Millionaire banker found dead at birthday bash

The Wismere founder Anthony Wistern was pronounced dead at a party for his sixtieth birthday on Saturday night. The wealthy hedge fund manager was found unresponsive by a guest in the grounds of Gables House, the Wisterns' country home just outside Chipping Marston. A spokesperson for the family asked for privacy but gave no further comment. Mr Wistern found early success in his partnership with Giles Greymere, and the banker gained renown as a prominent supporter of the arts. He earned the nickname 'Goldicocks' from some in his industry, who found his approach to business to be overly brash. One guest at the party told our reporter that it was unclear what had happened. 'The evening was unbelievable, my wife thought it was the most lavish party she'd ever been to. It was well past midnight and most people were on the dance floor when it happened. We heard a loud scream, and then Olivia walked through the marquee with her children. She looked twenty years older. After that, the police turned up, held us all for a couple of hours while they took our details and then sent us packing. We were lucky to have the driver waiting for us, some people had to wait hours outside the gates for their transport. It was all a bit surreal – like something out of an Agatha Christie novel. I didn't know the guy that well, but I've long admired his approach to business and recently invested with him. It's not great timing for me to be honest.'

Wistern is survived by his wife and four children. The police are not treating the death as suspicious.

OLIVIA

The policemen who'd turned up were local uniformed officers and they were wildly out of their depth. One of them actually whistled when he saw the marquees, but I couldn't blame him since both were almost certainly larger than his house. Giles and my brother were a tower of strength in those dark hours, handling everything and insisting that I be allowed to go to bed after I'd told the police everything I knew, which was just that my husband was dead and the party I'd so carefully laboured over would now be the talk of London. Everything else was my business. Once I'd finished my brief statement, I hurried to my room, took a Xanax and lay down in the dark.

A tragic accident, that's what Giles had said. Just a freak fall, could've happened to anyone. But it didn't happen to anyone. *Anyone* else and it would've been at best a fun story to tell and at worst, a mild inconvenience. This? This was a gigantic problem. Enough! If I lingered on his death, I'd get too angry and the pill wouldn't work. I determined to focus on the positives. It had been a truly beautiful evening, and I wouldn't let what happened mar that for me. I've organised enough parties now that my friends sometimes joke it's a full-time job for me, and then we all laugh because the idea of me having a job of any sort is patently hilarious. But I have to say, I outdid myself with Anthony's sixtieth.

I'd berated Will for his suggestion that my husband might've liked going out with a bang, but it wasn't so far off. Always the centre of attention, my husband, it was his oxygen. Could it look like a suicide? I'd tell the police my husband had been acting strangely in the weeks leading up to the party – which was true. He even went so far as to ask me to cancel the whole thing. I had a witness to that, I'd been having my hair done by Oskar when he said it, and the hairdresser let out a small gasp, which signalled that he'd be storing up this piece of gossip to tell Maria Cavallo when he saw her. She always commandeered my staff, and it *always* irked me. But then Oskar really does the best blow dry in London, it cannot be denied. In order to dampen down any possible embellishment in the subsequent retelling, I'd laughed and loudly told my husband off for being so modest, 'I know you're more focused on the charitable auction part of the evening, darling, but we must make just a little fuss of you.' Anthony never brought it up again, but he'd been absent a lot in the lead-up and when he was at home, he was often drunk. And belligerent, speaking to me as if I were an idiot. He'd always thought I was an idiot. It's a mistake men often make, thinking their wives are stupid when they're actually just full of rage.

'Business is tricky, there are bigger things going on than your table decorations,' he'd said one evening as if I couldn't hold two things in my head at once. The table decorations *were* important, whether or not he deigned to admit it. Appearance matters, in all forms. Part of the reason he was so successful was because he presented himself so well. The confidence, the charm and the wonderful world he offered up – much of which was my design. Born into a lower-middle-class family and effortlessly elevated by me.

The tables looked divine in the end, Murano glass plates in an array of jewelled colours, with glorious linen napkins and clusters of soft white tapered candles designed to throw a lovely glow on the floral arrangements that dotted the tables. A party fit for Anthony Wistern, financial success and man of power. A Happy Meal dumped on a paper plate wouldn't have quite the same elan now, would it?

His disdain hadn't mattered much anyway, I had my plans in place and would never have relied on him to help with anything so serious as party planning. Anthony proudly told people he didn't know where the kitchen was, had never changed a nappy and joked he wouldn't be able to tell you how on earth the household managed to run so smoothly. 'We must have an army of domesticated fairies,' he'd quipped at a party many years ago, when I'd just given birth to our fourth child. I'd long perfected the art of not giving off a single hint that my breasts ached or my hormones were threatening to spill out of the top of my head and flood the room, drowning every single man in sight, so I just smiled beatifically as his friends dutifully roared with laughter.

It's a pity he died at the lake, because it really was some of my best work. But the interiors were just as lovely. I'm always nervous of a marquee, they often give off a whiff of a subpar wedding on the grounds of a golf hotel with aspirations, but the party concierge found ones with beautifully stiff linen, with enormous glass windows, not a hint of grubby tarpaulin in sight. Forty-foot-high plants lining the sides, a walkway through the centre which was erected over a newly dug tranche of water so it felt like you were on a runway at sea, enormous pendants hanging from the ceiling which refracted warm light into every corner of the space. Best of all were the flowers, not your usual overstuffed vases of garden variety displays, but thousands of arum lilies in slim hand-blown glass vases. My florist told me they express the idea of purity and faithfulness and I liked the idea of sending my husband a little dig like that. It was only when that stupid Nancy Leadbetter walked in and surveyed the marquee, that I found out they also signify death.

I heard voices coming from outside, and I rose to look out of my bedroom window, down to the enormous tents in the gardens beyond, still lit up with thousands of twinkling white lights. Our guests were finally allowed to leave, and cars were snaking up the driveway. I saw Mary Chambers and Anthony's PA standing at the end of the drive. Lainey had been canny enough to glom onto someone for a ride – they were waiting for Mary's driver to reach them. Her dance partner must've decided her cleavage wasn't dazzling enough to drive her all the way back to, where was it? Holloway? Mary was stroking the girl's hair, comforting her in a low voice. Lainey was weeping now, loud enough that I saw Mary put her fingers to her lips and shush her. I opened the window to see what she was saying, but all I caught was fragments. 'Suspicious' . . . 'Who', 'they know', 'Well if not . . . killed?'

The gossip had started, as I knew it would. It's the fuel on which society runs, and the evening had provided a motherlode of it. An impaling certainly stirred the imagination. To be entirely fair to Mary, I was exactly the same when her oaf of a husband belly-flopped off their boat. But at least I had the grace not to speculate before he was even in the ground. Although that's not strictly accurate, since his enormous girth meant he sank straight to the bottom of the ocean, and they had a slightly odd funeral which featured Mary sobbing over an empty coffin. Anthony had leant over to me and whispered that they'd been lucky, a real coffin his size would've taken fifty pallbearers. Lainey joining in with speculation about his death was a disgraceful way to repay everything we've done for her. I'd told Anthony I didn't like her the moment she'd started, but he'd brushed me off with a laugh, telling me my jealousy was 'awfully dull'. He always put my suspicions down to jealousy, a classic Anthony tactic.

I rolled my eyes, closed the window and went back to bed. As I fell asleep, I remembered to practise gratitude. I was immensely grateful that despite the gruesome way my husband died, he'd done it with his clothes on, and not, like Jane Borrall's husband, naked but for a latex trench coat. She was never seen again after the Fashion for Famine charity gala, not after that awkward moment when they sent models down the runway in pleather and she ran from the room in embarrassment. There are levels of scrutiny and gossip one can bear, at least Anthony knew the limits.

THE SLEUTH

@thesleuth
296 subscribers

I wasted no time uploading a video explaining who Anthony Wistern was (mostly info from Wikipedia mixed with some quotes from the papers about his social life) – you've got to go quite straight with the initial details, but I made sure to lead with the fact that I'd known him personally, even if I amped up the connection. Truthfully, he wouldn't have been able to pick me out of a line-up if his life depended on it, but that wouldn't have played as well. And I didn't explain the full connection, it didn't feel right. Not that I wouldn't play the cards I had, it was just all about timing. Once it had gone live, my phone rang. The call I'd been waiting for for months. The council pencil pushers had finally got off their arses and found someone who could help care for Mum. Only two afternoons a week; the bored woman on the phone informed me that my mother 'has an adequate level of independence', which was news to me since she can't go to the toilet alone. But it was better than fuck all, which is where we've been for the past two years. The carer would start as soon as they could find someone, there was 'high demand in your area,' not a surprise since nearly everyone who lives around here owns at least one zimmer frame. There's even a town competition where people decorate them for Christmas. Then it's weeks of bells chiming and tinsel crackling as the locals shuffle up and down the high street. I celebrated by cooking a proper dinner for both of us that evening, even persuading Mum to have half a glass of wine. When she went to bed, I sifted through more search results.

I read about how he made so much money that jealous rivals called him Goldicocks. How the family owned an enormous house in Holland Park and the pile in Oxfordshire, not forgetting the chateau in France called the 'Belle Reve'. Houses that have names, I knew, were serious mansions. There was an archived feature from a magazine called *House & Garden*, with photos of Olivia Wistern surrounded by her children in the garden at their house in France, which included a rapturous 500-word description of a hand carved stone bath. There was a story in the *Evening Standard* about the top 50 Londoners you wanted at a party; Olivia and Anthony were joint number 28. I read every fluff piece I could about them, stories about his addiction to extreme sports, his love of fine art. I saw photos of the couple from every stage of their lives – from their engagement party at a private members' club in London, to their last public shot at a gala for charity raising money for wild mink in Scotland (controversial, seeing as minks are an American import and terrible for the native environment).

According to unnamed party guests, nobody noticed he was missing. 'He wasn't any drunker than anyone else, and Ant certainly knew how to hold his liquor.' Another quote: 'This makes no sense, I cannot understand how he ended up dead.'

But I could. I understood more than these people who professed to be close personal friends. I know about Anthony Wistern, and there was another side to the man than the gushing accounts in the press. There was no way his death was just an accident, I could feel it in my gut. I gazed at a particularly striking photo of him – slightly too tanned, just one too many buttons on his shirt undone – and wondered again why *this* was the case that had landed on my doorstep. It's hard to whip up interest in male victims, even ones as wealthy as him, but it was what I had. 'I'm going to find out who did this to you,' I said to the screen, aware that I sounded ridiculously dramatic but enjoying it all the same. 'Now you're dead, I'm going to be your new favourite person.'

NEWS ARTICLE
2 July 2018

Banker impaled at own birthday

Anthony Wistern, the co-founder of Wismere Holdings and a popular figure on the London social scene, died on Saturday night after being impaled on a metal spike at a party for his sixtieth birthday. While the circumstances surrounding the gruesome incident at his family home are still unclear, police say that they are treating the death as a tragic accident. Lou Molton, the wife of esteemed art dealer Lucian Molton, said that Wistern was dead by the time his body was discovered. 'I'll never ever forget the sight of him suspended like that. It's been a terrible shock for everyone, nobody can understand why he left the party and went down to the lake in the first place. Molton said that Giles Greymere, Wistern's business partner, was at the scene. 'He dived in to save him, it was incredibly heroic. But we still don't know what Anthony was doing down there. There was so much blood.' Sources close to the family say that they are struggling to process the tragedy. 'His wife's inconsolable, I haven't heard from her in days. He was the luckiest man in London, this kind of thing doesn't happen to people like him.'

Anthony Wistern was born into a middle-class family in Barnet and quickly made his way to being one of the most well connected and influential men in London through his company Wismere Holdings. Notorious for his charm, the banker mingled with high society and celebrities, always refuting the notion that finance need be staid. It was said he would turn up to his office in a different car every day of the week, and Piccadilly was once brought to a standstill after he rode a horse down the middle of the road for a dare. Married to his wife Olivia since 1986 (their wedding took place at her family seat, Oddingframe; an alpaca from the family farm acted as the ring bearer), Wistern leaves behind four adult children, none of whom work for his company. Insiders are wondering who'll take on the mantle of CEO at Wismere, with many doubtful that Giles Greymere has the natural flair of Wistern.

'Anthony was a one-man success machine, nobody knew how he did it, not even Giles,' said a rival. 'It wasn't his natural aptitude for finance, any idiot can figure out numbers. Anthony had the confidence of a snake oil salesman. Every success was all down to his charm and capacity for persuasion, the man was a great actor.'

ANTHONY

My body was taken away just as the sun stood high over the lake. I was zipped into a black bag and trundled into a van. It really wasn't as strange to watch as you might imagine, since I didn't look much like me anymore. Death does something funny to the face. I was both bloated and saggy and I felt a little aggrieved at how my shirt had come loose, exposing my stomach in an unflattering way. The bloodied hole just above my navel wasn't even the worst bit. The real blow was that I looked, I'm disappointed to say, my age. Nobody watched me go, not even my wife. When I checked on her, she was actually asleep, lying on her side looking peaceful and undisturbed by the events of the evening. The door to her dressing room was slightly ajar, and I could see several trunks stacked up one on top of another, as if my wife were readying for a long holiday. Had she planned a surprise trip for us as a birthday present? Idiotic to imagine I would take weeks off work on a whim just to sit on a beach while she worked on her tan.

With my body now trundling up the A44, I felt a little bereft. A body made for enjoyment, it had served me immensely well for six decades. The facsimile I had up here was a pale comparison. We were given food, but it tasted of nothing, we had beds to sleep in, but sleep was merely closing our eyes and waiting until the alarm went off. 'These things are in place to make the transition to death easier for our guests,' a smiley orderly had told me when I complained. 'Think of it as a halfway house.' When I asked why it seemed impossible to give myself an old five-finger shuffle, she'd shrieked and stalked off and I'd been given a dressing down by Susan for vulgarity. To lose the carnal pleasures I so relished in life was almost enough to make me weep. I tried to think back to the last time I'd had sex, to try to savour the memory and I suddenly recalled hands pushing me up against a tree, then furiously unbuckling my trousers. Lainey had intercepted me between the main course and dessert, telling me there was an urgent call I had to take. I'd watched Olivia eye me with suspicion, which made me follow my PA out of the marquee with an added level of excitement.

She'd walked me to the edge of the garden and down towards the lake, at first trying to pull me into the summerhouse, but when we got up to the door, the handle wouldn't open, and the sound of laughter told us that some randy buggers had got there first. The summerhouse was always in use at our parties, leading to Lyra christening it the shagging shed. Liv hated that, always emphasising that at a thousand square feet and with a fully functioning kitchen it was offensive to give it such a moniker.

With a sigh of frustration, she'd pounced right in full view of anyone, kissing me in a way that smacked of desperation until I'd shoved her off. She didn't like that, grabbing my hand and attempting to stuff it down her bra. I'd snapped at her then, telling her to sort herself out and she'd yelled at me as I walked away, loud enough that people milling around on the lawn above turned round.

'Arsehole . . .' her language always spoke to her background when she'd had a drink, 'you'll regret that.' She was right though, I did regret it. It was practically unheard of for me to say no to the opportunity, the stress of the weeks leading up to the party really must've got to me. Fool. But now a thought occurred. Whoever was using the shagging shed, might have had a front row seat to my death.

I guess they'd have to wait for the results of my post-mortem to truly work out what happened to me. I was quite keen to know that too. It's not fair to be in the dark about such a big part of your story, is it? A fellow should know how it ends, especially since I was stuck in this no man's land until I figured it out. The detective who spoke to my children rushed through the official line of condolence with a bored look on her face before getting down to it. 'Lainey Goodman said that Mr Wistern had been acting erratically in the week before his death and mentioned to us that before the dinner, he'd told her he didn't trust anyone around him anymore. What do you think he meant by that?' That made me sit up in my chair, I can tell you. Erratic made it sound like I was on the brink of some sort of nervous breakdown, to be found shuffling the streets in pyjamas and raving about aliens, when it was a source of pride to me that my mental health had always been robust. I don't mean to imply that those who suffer are weaker than me, but really, would that be so far from the truth? Besides, I'd never said anything like 'I don't trust anyone around me' to her. Clearly, she was taking the break-up extremely badly, not the first time a woman has lost her head when I've told her we'd reached the end of the road. It made me nervous, her talking to the police like this. If she was happy to run her mouth to them, what might she say to Olivia?

My children all professed ignorance at this information, Jemima in particular vehemently denied Lainey's claims and told the detective 'It sounds like she just wants attention to be honest, my father would never have confided in an employee like that. She barely knew him.' She went on to say that my PA had been 'hideously drunk' at the party. 'She was wobbling around on six-inch heels and a waiter had to stop her from falling into the cake at one point. The woman was an embarrassment, I wouldn't take her very seriously if I were you.'

A nod, and something written down in the policewoman's notebook. They moved on, and I slightly unclenched my buttocks. The police were extremely keen to find out exactly why I'd left my own birthday party and ended up by the lake. None of my offspring seemed too eager to focus on this question; all the conversations I'd seen them have mainly focused on how the unfortunate timing of my death had affected them.

Jemima made a point of sobbing, but no tears were actually seen and she seemed always to wind up making a point about how she was supposed to be in the Maldives next week. Fred, who normally never used entire sentences when grunts would do, went on and on about how the marquees had ruined the grass and railed at a policewoman for hitting a tree on the drive with her car, while Lyra sat in the corner texting her girlfriend in Paris, assuring her she'd be on the Eurostar 'as soon as it's seemly'. I felt a little sorry for the officers, when Clara, completely ignoring their reason for being there, asked them if she'd be able to go back to school the next day. The little madam even used *my death* to bolster her argument. 'Dad wouldn't want me to miss my education, would he?' I'd laughed at that. Clara was about as interested in schoolwork as I was in Gregorian chanting. My daughter was just panicked she'd lose her place in the seemingly ever-changing pecking order of terror that teenage girls create for themselves.

Once they sat down to be interviewed separately though, they had no choice but to come up with an official line. Charles insisted on being present, presumably to make sure my children didn't say anything stupid. He sat in my bloody chair as if he owned the place, that was one thing. But I could barely believe it when I saw him eyeing up the Brancetti statue on the desk. It's a little thing, only five inches high, but it was made by the sculptor in his best period, and formed the basis for his biggest triumph – *The Enforcer* – which sits atop a column in New York's financial district and watches over the workers as they head into their offices every day. Brancetti was a committed socialist, who created the work as a rallying cry to the working man and I bought it because I knew it would've enraged him to see it on my desk. My brother-in-law was looking at it like he wanted to slip it into his pocket – lovingly and with an obvious yearning. Brancetti might have retched upon seeing where it was now, but I'm confident he'd roll over in his grave at the idea of some middling lawyer displaying it next to his bread bin.

I'd heard the detectives question my children while my wife slept on, and cursed her for her lack of presence, but what would she have done anyway? Olivia's motherly instincts were less than stellar, even she'd acknowledge that. But her absence meant missing all of them, to various degrees, lying to the police both about what they'd done that night and their relationships with me.

When asked where they were around the time I died, all my children were quick to answer. Freddy had been checking out a nest in the woods bordering the lake. Apparently the noise from the party was upsetting the red-flanked bluetail he'd been monitoring recently, even the police officer had to stifle a yawn at that. He couldn't deny that he'd been one of the first to find me, but he knew better than to react to any of their needling probes about my personal life, or state of mind. It was obvious he was holding something back, I could see it on his face. The boy could never lie; when he tried, he'd chew his left cheek. It was subtle to someone who didn't know to look for it, but to me it was easy to spot. He told the detective he'd had a great night, repeatedly saying it was a 'normal family celebration' all while gnawing at his mouth to the point where I was sure he'd be tasting blood. Initially I felt a funny swell of pride in my boy for knowing when to keep his mouth shut. Not as stupid as we sometimes feared, that was a comfort. But then I remembered seeing him that night; it came back to me in fragments which shimmied in front of my eyes and then disappeared.

I'd just finished off a cigar, when Fred appeared from behind a rhododendron bush looking mutinous and gesticulating at a tree. Someone must have disturbed a squirrel. I'd laughed at his angry little face, all screwed up like a toddler, and told him to relax. 'It's just a tree, Fred, there's literally millions of them about.' Something was missing in my memory, but it felt like we'd had a fight. Try as I might, I couldn't get a visual image of it.

Jemima was very upset when Detective Chande spoke to her, she always went straight to histrionics when faced with difficulty. But she told them some nonsense about leaving the party because Hugh kept pestering her, which wasn't true at all. Hugh liked a pretty girl as much as the next man, but he wouldn't have disrespected me like that. And besides, Jemima was hardly the most beautiful woman in attendance. Where had she been? I couldn't remember seeing her after the dinner. Will even asked me where she was at one point. The man was almost the opposite of a social butterfly, people barely seemed to notice him even when he was seated right next to them. No wonder he clung to his wife so desperately. By the time the police sat down with Jemima, her hair was already dry. Why had nobody asked her what she'd been doing with her head wrapped in a bloody towel?

Clara had no need to bullshit much about where she was that evening, the girl was almost certainly at the bar all night with her friend, gulping down as much vodka as possible. 'Who's the main suspect?' she'd asked, as direct as you like. 'It must be Giles right? He's creepy, don't you think?' The detective gave a vague answer about the investigation being in its early stages and she snorted with displeasure. Good girl, I'd whispered and for a second her eyes flickered skywards as if she'd heard me. As a test, I said loudly: 'You are not allowed to go on holiday with that horrible Chloe Finestein this year,' but there was no reaction, which deflated me a bit. She told the police that she'd last seen me at midnight, which was just before I went missing and that I seemed happy and relaxed. 'Definitely murdered,' she added as she made to leave, already looking down at her phone, 'whatever they say.'

And Lyra? Well Lyra was interesting. You never knew what was going on with her. As I've said, Lyra was always my favourite, a fact I didn't hide – and really why should you? You can't help who you get on with. It probably toughened the others up a bit, made them vie for my attention a little more. When the detective asked why she'd made her way towards the lake, Lyra looked her straight in the eye and said she'd seen Will going that way and wanted to know what was going on. When told that Will had informed them he'd been going back to the house looking for his wife, she didn't even blink. 'If that's what he says . . .' she'd replied evenly, and even Chande had appeared to lose confidence. 'I saw what was happening from the bank, and went to get Olivia. Maybe Will got confused. It's been a fairly strange evening.' Did Lyra want to get Will into trouble for some reason? Or was she just messing about, as usual.

Will reasserted that he'd been looking for his wife, and claimed not to have spoken to me all evening. 'You know how it is, the birthday boy being pulled from pillar to post. Never got a moment with him, I'm fairly low down in the pecking order you see.' A little hostility there, though nobody seemed to notice it. Mainly, his answers were so bland I could see the detective's eyes glaze over, her brain clearly filing him away as a nonstarter. He was wise not to tell them he'd tried to confront me. How would he explain the conversation to them without raising questions he wouldn't want to answer?

Did the police understand that they shouldn't trust a single one of my children? No, they certainly did not. Too slow maybe; policemen are rarely in possession of staggering IQs, but really it was probably more that they were slightly cowed by my family and our surroundings. No matter how much one swears wealth won't faze them, when a person's confronted with it on a grand scale, it always does. My children have been brought up to know they are leaders, even if they don't yet understand what that entails. They can't help but demand respect, even from a senior detective. Their wildly differing accounts were, I suspected, designed to protect them from any secrets they held and would tie the investigation up in knots for a bit, but I doubt they knew why I'd been down at the lake any more than I did. Ah well, if nothing else, it would be fun to watch. And there wasn't much else for me to do.

In the end, Giles smoothed it all over with the detective, ever the reliable sidekick. The man has always been the definition of responsible, he lives for it. People often wonder how we ended up being business partners, but I always knew I needed someone like him. Forget the absurd saying that behind every great man there's an even greater woman, that's tosh. In reality, every great man has a slightly lesser man standing next to him ready to do the dull stuff. The key to a successful life is to know your own weaknesses and then hire people who will balance them out, that's what Giles has always done so brilliantly. In recent years, I'd strayed from my own rule, which might well explain the trouble I'd been getting into, but here he was, sorting everything out as always. He explained (with just the right amount of detail – not too little which might make them suspicious, not too much which might make him look guilty of something) what had happened to me. Well, a version of what happened to me. Giles was dependable, but he'd lie when he had to. Show me a wholly truthful man and I'll show you a loser.

I was born slap bang in the dull middle of middle class, and I've worked my way up pretty seamlessly, but once in a blue moon small tells of my suburban background creep out and threaten to undermine me. Giles was born into the same realm as my wife, and it shows. I've had to learn that authority, they inherited it. From the look on his face, I could see that he expected the police would believe him, and they did, practically gobbled it up. *Anthony had a little too much to drink you see, officer, it was his birthday after all, and a man might get a little overwhelmed with the celebrations you see. We went for a walk to get some air, that's what you do when you're feeling like the room is tilting, after all, and we ended up by the lake. We had a little toast, just to mark the occasion, and Anthony, being Anthony, followed it up with a little sniff of something – I didn't partake, detective, never touch the stuff. He was gregarious, setting the world to rights – he did have a tendency to go on a bit when he was drunk, and I told him we'd better head back to the marquees. Come on, old man, I'd said, but he shook his head and told me he wanted a minute alone 'to reflect on everything he'd done'. I left him on the jetty and walked back down the path towards the festivities where I bumped into Charles, Mrs Wistern's brother. I imagine Anthony decided to go for a little swim, Lord knows why. Or maybe he simply slipped, certainly he was inebriated enough. I could've stopped him if I'd stayed, I can't stop thinking about it, but you will understand, officer, I was pretty sloppy myself last night. It was about five minutes before I heard the shout. I raced back and dived right in, but he was wedged pretty neatly onto that pole. No budging him; remarkable quality. There was nothing to be done. Then Fred appeared. He must've heard the noise and run down to help me, which will haunt me forever. Just a tragedy for everyone, one of those terrible accidents you read about but don't imagine for a minute you'll ever experience. Can I help with anything else? We're all hugely indebted to you for coming out so quickly.*

He handled it so masterfully that for a brief moment, I felt guilty for the astronomic amount of shit that was about to fall on his head from a great height. But when I took his version of events to the deputy intake manager, she told me I was wrong. When I realised he must be lying, I stopped feeling guilty pretty fast.

THE SLEUTH

@thesleuth
467 subscribers

The papers might have been full of gushing tributes to the man, but older articles told a different story. There were several pieces which showed just how many people hated the guy. There was the couple whose estate backed onto Gables – they'd been in an ongoing feud with him for nearly a decade after he cut down a line of old oak trees and planted 30 fast-growing beeches to block out the view. 'It destroyed our garden,' Ronald Wolney told the *Mail*. 'Our house has next to no natural light anymore and my wife is on medication for anxiety as a result.' After Ronald complained to the council, Anthony clearly decided to fuck with him for fun. He started turning up on Friday nights in a heli-copter, hovering for ages over the Wolney house, which caused their dogs to go 'fully tonto' apparently. Then he applied for planning permission to build a treehouse for his 'children' (who were by then well into their teens), which had a bird's-eye view of the neighbouring house. 'The only person who used it was *him*,' Ronald had recounted to *The Oxford Courier*. 'He goes up there with his mates and they shoot air rifles into the night while making a lot of noise. I know it's all done deliberately to break my spirits, he's got a telescope up there and it's always pointed right into the window of our front room. The man is a monster.' From the land registry I checked, Ronald Wolney still lived there. Alone now, his wife had died a year ago. That might be enough to send him over the edge.

Then there was a former business associate from his pre-Wismere days who alleged that Anthony had stolen his clients and reneged on a deal which would've made him millions. 'The tactics he uses are the most underhanded I've seen in twenty years in this industry,' the man had said at the time. 'One day he'll get what he deserves.' And of course, there were many snippets about beautiful women 'cosying' up to him, in that coy language journalists use when they're trying not to get sued. 'We hear Anthony Wistern had a grand old time at the polo last week. Lily Mannox was draped over his lap at one point. It was a stiflingly hot day, perhaps she was feeling a little faint?'

A womaniser, well everybody knew that. He might have been a big London player, but down here he was known for trying it on with the girls who worked in his pub, some of them younger than his own daughters. I'd been working there for two months before I finally met him. He'd brought ten of his friends down for a shoot, and it was clear we had to impress. They turned up late, just minutes before the kitchen was due to close. All men, dressed in pristine Barbours and flat caps, as if they'd googled how to blend in in the countryside. I was one of their servers, bringing bottle upon bottle of wine to the table without a single thank you. Though the private dining room was some way from the main bar, the noise they made drowned out everyone else, and by 10 p.m. all our other customers were gone. By the time they finally left, it was well past 1 a.m. and I was fed up. I couldn't even manage a smile as they'd stumbled out into the car park. Anthony saw my expression, and put his hand on my shoulder as he passed. I thought he was going to tell me off but instead he asked me my name and then apologised for keeping us there so late. With a smile that made him look a lot younger than his years, he pressed fifty quid into my hand and winked at me and somehow I felt disarmed. He remembered my name the next time he came in, and made sure he always had a generous tip for me. Other members of staff complained about him, but I thought he was all right.

Four months later, Anthony and his son Freddy had come in unexpectedly one lunchtime. We were heaving, and by the time we managed to get a table ready for him, our proprietor was in a filthy temper. His son had winced when he clicked his fingers to get my attention, and cringed as his dad sent back his first course on account of it being 'fucking rabbit food'. My shift ended just before they'd finished their pudding, and I was already in the back room getting my coat on when I heard someone say my name. Anthony Wistern was standing just a foot away, smirking slightly. I assumed he wanted me to apologise for the slow service, and I started to say something about how it wouldn't happen again, but he shook his head and put his finger to my lips. 'None of that. I know it won't happen again, now will it?' And then he'd kissed me, plunging his tongue into my mouth while his hands enclosed my neck. My mum and dad never forced me to do any extra-curricular activities, but they did insist I take a self-defence class in sixth form. 'The world can be a scary place, darling,' my dad had said when I objected. 'At times you will need to fight.' And he was right. I brought my knee up fast and connected with my boss's balls with satisfying force. As he staggered away whimpering, I realised his son was standing at the door. In the moments that followed, I barely heard a word Anthony Wistern was saying. All I could focus on was the look of unconcealed hatred on Freddy's face as he dragged his dad out of the room, mouthing sorry to me as they disappeared.

I'd been fired of course, I suppose that meant even *I* had a motive. But nothing compared to those of his own wife and children, I knew that. Apparently, the police thought none of these people were worth investigating, but I did. I could see something wasn't right here, even if the powers that be wanted to brush it all under the carpet.

ANTHONY

Nobody ever imagines the afterlife to be this dull. The highlight of my morning was watching a man drop his hat, then spend a good minute patting his head in astonishment that it wasn't where it should be. Quite why anyone wears a hat here is beyond me, and nobody talks much so I don't bother to ask. They're not big on conversation, it's all supposed to be reflection and contemplation about your death before you 'move on'. I've got to reflect fast, because I am not getting on well in this place. We might not sleep in the way the alive do, but that doesn't mean a good thread count is suddenly irrelevant. I worked hard to live at a level where the normal discomforts of life were for other people and now I'm wearing shoes made out of plastic. But the emphasis on contemplating is almost worse if I'm honest. I'm dead, so I'm pretty sure there's no such place, but if I'd had to describe my vision of hell, 'reflection and contemplation' would surely be an apt description.

Still, all this thinking has led me somewhere. Almost the moment I relayed Giles's story to the deputy manager, I knew it was nonsense. There's no way I could've died like that. I'm a fabulous diver, I work out several times a week and on a good day, I can still see abs when I do my daily mirror inspection. Women always tell me I look twenty years younger, and god knows most of my contemporaries couldn't do a press up as effortlessly as me. No, there's no possible way I died accidentally, and worse, almost comedically. That's not how someone like me goes out.

The only possible explanation is that someone murdered me. When you're as successful as I was, you can't help but have enemies fuelled by pure jealousy. It's always been motivating, nothing like the look of a man you don't much like when he hears how well you're doing. But the simplest answer is the right one, and going by that, Giles must've done me in. It's so obvious. He'd found out what I'd been doing, confronted me and killed me in a rage. The man's a quiet chap, but you should never trust people who repress their animal urges so deftly. I'd taken his surface calm for strength but maybe there was a simmering rage just bubbling along underneath. No wonder he wanted to smooth everything over with the police, he knew any suspicion would fall on him when everything came out. I told a passing orderly that I needed to speak to the manager immediately, and was promptly told I'd have to make an appointment before being given a lecture on how I was spending my time. I was new here, the orderly told me, and a certain amount of leeway was given as a result, but the rules were in place so everyone could enjoy the afterlife. I protested this loudly, getting right up in her face and raging about how ridiculous her job was. The girl didn't bat an eyelid at this, and straight up told me that if watching my family was upsetting me so much, I was welcome to go and join the admin team who were always in need of more volunteers. That made me back off. I'd successfully avoided paperwork like the plague for forty years, I wasn't about to offer to do it now, especially since there's no financial reimbursement for anything here. Money makes things work, neoliberalism is the greatest thing humans ever did and yet now here I am, part of a society which apparently has no use for it. To say I've been so far unsatisfied with my experience of death would be a dramatic understatement. Feeling impotent and furious, I had no choice but to go back to watching my family. I could only hope that one of them joined the dots and realised what Giles had done, but even combined, their level of intellect didn't reassure me.

I checked in on Gables. Jemima was the most boring choice, but I hoped she'd be doing something inane to calm me down. My daughter can usually be found on a treadmill or at lunch where she and her friends talk in great detail about the most mundane of topics. Twice a week she has therapy, and once a week she has a reiki session to 'help her stress'. Given that she was stuck at Gables, the opportunities were narrowed, but I was confident she'd be doing something dull. And she was, she was in the loo. Not quite what I was hoping for, and I quickly looked away. Then I heard quiet sobbing, and cautiously turned my gaze back to the monitor. Jemima's tears seemed overly dramatic, too loud even for a girl who cries at the slightest sign of discomfort. These weren't the usual sobs of my daughter, who can weep on demand, these were real. I peered more closely and saw she was holding a thin blue stick, which I recognised immediately. A pregnancy test, just like the ones Olivia had waved in my face to indicate we were having our four. The last time I'd seen one was when Clara announced her arrival and I remember groaning audibly, provoking a nasty fight which only ended when I bought her a rather hideous French table she'd been eyeing at Bonhams. The strong lines indicated a positive result. Were they happy tears then? My daughter's scrunched up face and aggrieved expression rather suggested they were not. She wrapped the test in toilet roll and stuffed it into the bottom of the bin, closed the lid and splashed her face with water. Back in her bedroom, my daughter ignored her husband when he asked if she was ok, and headed back downstairs. Will didn't follow her down. Instead, he crept into the hallway and walked along the passage until he reached my bedroom. He gently opened the door and with as little movement as possible, saw my wife lying in bed, and pulled it to again before scurrying back to his room. How odd. What on earth was he looking for?

OLIVIA

I found my oldest friend, Penny Donsmen, waiting for me in the hallway. Loyal, always there for me, ever since we first met at primary school. Last night, when I saw her eccentric drop-waisted tartan dress I'd wondered how it was possible we had maintained our decades-long friendship, but that morning I was pathetically grateful to see her, while trying not to stare at her shoes which were shaped like upturned Cornish pasties.

'I'm so sorry, Livvy,' she said, enveloping me in a hug and remembering not to touch my hair. 'We'll get through this, I promise. Do you think you feel up to speaking to the detective?' I gave a small nod, and she took my hand and led me into Anthony's study. 'They're in here, shall I get you a nice cup of tea?' Penny, like much of the British public, is undaunted in her opinion that a weak milky beverage can fix a myriad of ailments. I ignored the offer and told her she could go. I knew Charles would look after me, he always has.

Detective Chande and a slightly sweaty man in uniform sat in my husband's study. I noticed that while he tried very hard not to look awed by his surroundings, she was completely at ease, leaning back with her legs crossed as if it was her study. It instantly annoyed me. She ushered me in and signalled to a chair.

'Oh, thank you, may I sit?' I asked, but she ignored the sarcasm.

'I'm Detective Chande, this is Officer Granger. I'm very sorry for your loss, Mrs Wistern, and I know this is a difficult time, but I'm sure you understand we have to ask you some questions.' Detective Chande was sent down from London, which I *had* initially assumed was a sign of respect. The London Mayor's office had called that morning to send condolences and offer up any help we might need. The last Labour one was publicly incredibly rude about financiers and had piously declined all our invitations, which I thought was a little rich given that she was later engulfed in a scandal after accepting a ride in a private plane owned by a Qatari businessman who just so happened to want to build a new skyscraper in the city. I was glad the latest incumbent had a little more class.

I'd presumed a London detective would handle the matter with the respect and compassion it deserved, I was mistaken. From the get-go she treated me as a normal civilian, and she had a bluntness about her that felt deliberate. We went through the evening's events, and she rudely interrupted me several times, asking me if Anthony had complained of feeling unwell at all, and whether or not it was possible he'd taken drugs. It took all the strength I had to tell her it was none of her business. Truthfully, my husband did have a propensity to go overboard when enjoying himself, and he had a lackadaisical approach to personal safety which had made me shout at him on multiple occasions. On a yacht we chartered one summer years ago, he'd lost a bet to his good friend Jesse Milgram after drinking at least three bottles of wine. Never a man to renege on a promise, he'd ordered the bosun to erect the waterslide at midnight, and he went down it backwards while dressed in Elena Milgram's full-length sequinned gown. The dress got tangled up and the captain had to dive in to save him, which of course he found hilarious. The dress was ruined and Elena was furious, insisting it was couture, but one always knows from the stitching.

They went on a little bit longer, but since Giles had explained the events of the evening in full, and Charles had backed him up, even Detective Chande had to accept there was little more I could tell her about Anthony's death. Instead, she changed tack, and asked me something I didn't expect. 'Did your husband have any worries, Mrs Wistern? He was a successful man, it must have been very stressful for him at times.' I flashed a look at Charles, who was sitting behind Anthony's desk as though he were preparing for a board meeting. He cleared his throat.

'What are you implying, detective? This was obviously a tragic accident.'

Blank-faced, she waited for my reply. Was Anthony stressed? His job was frantic, but that was almost entirely why he enjoyed it. Men like my husband get bored easily. Finance is just a game for grown-ups, and my husband enjoyed the thrill of winning. Should I say yes? Would suicide be an easy resolution?

Detective Chande tried again. 'Was there anything about his behaviour last night to make you concerned?'

'Quite the contrary. He was having a wonderful time,' I said, looking at her as though the question was absurd. Keep it simple, don't get them digging into matters that don't concern them. Charles interjected then, telling them that I was worn out and asking them if they needed anything else. I rose to leave without giving them time to reply.

Penny was hovering in the hallway, and she rushed towards me like a mother hen, flapping her arms and ushering me back upstairs. I do many things extremely well – my dear friend Lydia Chambon once said I was a master of all trades and a jack of none – but grief has never been one of them. Animal deaths occasionally have the capacity to floor me but humans less so. I've lost many people close to me. My mother fell off a mountain while climbing in Scotland, my father keeled over on Christmas morning while putting the turkey in the oven – we've had goose ever since – and my dear friend Katherine Slake died when a jet ski crashed into the banana boat she was on in Spain. The family told everyone she'd drowned, which was understandable since she'd have been mortified if people knew she'd been near an inflatable yellow banana. I was duly saddened of course, but I find it hard to miss people when they're not around.

Back in my bedroom, I fished a packet of cigarettes out of the drawer and opened a window. I only permit myself to indulge once or twice a month, something my dermatologist assured me would make no difference to my smile lines. Looking back at the room, I caught sight of my trunks, all packed up and neatly stacked in the dressing room. Another life had been waiting for me, gone in a flash. Just like Anthony to one up me like this.

Turning back to the window, I sucked on my cigarette and decided to allow grief in. I tried to picture his body, grey and stiff, but even when I focused intently on that image, the anguish I felt was all for myself.

Still, it was odd to think of him dead. If I'd had to put a bet on Anthony's demise, I'd have banked on 75, given his love of cigars and addiction to stress. But even then I'd probably have been wrong. The worst people always tend to live the longest, don't they? That bastard Jimmy Smyth lived to 102, despite terrorising the whole of Holland Park with his insistence on driving that banged-up old Rolls at 80 miles an hour, or his odd predilection for setting off fireworks inside his house to piss off his neighbours.

Just as I was giving up on the idea of mourning, Lyra appeared, and like everyone else in my family, hadn't bothered to knock. My middle daughter demands privacy in her own life but isn't too concerned about it when it comes to others. But she can keep a secret, which is why she's the only one of my children I am sometimes willing to trust. She kept her own girlfriend a secret for nearly two years, only telling us when she was forced into it by Jemima. Purely out of spite for her younger sister, she'd dropped such enormously clumsy hints about her sister being gay that even my mother-in-law, who barely understands anything unless it's written in bold capitals, gleaned what was going on.

Lyra managed to snatch the very best parts of me and her father. Anthony's dark hair, green eyes and his effortless popularity, my skin and intelligence and then a wit all of her own. Jemima, being older, still feels like these attributes should've gone to her. That they did not, in any way at all, surprised us. She's a slightly ruddy-faced girl with mousy hair which none of her siblings have been afflicted by. Her jealousy is at times, embarrassingly palpable.

Lyra grabbed the packet and launched onto my bed. 'Still smoking Modas?' My daughter examined the slim box and wrinkled her nose. 'Even the old grannies in Montmartre have moved with the times.' She took one all the same. 'I heard you kept the detective waiting until you were fully made up and in the mood. That was bold.' I didn't turn around. 'I have to say, having a lie-in the day after your husband dies is a bit of a weird look, Olivia.' They've all called me by my first name, ever since Freddy started doing it when he went to boarding school. I think he did it innocently enough, but they all picked it up and over the years it sounded more and more spiteful. I hated it, not because it implied a distance between us, but because it made me sound like a left-wing parent in North London who thinks her children are her friends.

Lyra lit her cigarette just as the door opened again. 'Funny how Jemima left the party to have a shower last night. Do you think opting for the most boring life imaginable finally sent her mad? Maybe Clara's right. Maybe Dad was murdered.' She made a little o with her mouth. 'Maybe Jem killed Dad.'

Lyra looked at her sister as if she'd only just realised she was in the room and I must say, she timed it perfectly. 'Oops,' she said, shrugging slightly. Jemima reddened with rage, always too quick to react.

'That's disgusting. You're disgusting for that. I told you I got fed up with that letchy Hugh guy who sells Dad those ugly squiggle drawings.'

Lyra snorted. 'They're Keith Harings you moron.'

'And then someone knocked into him and he spilled wine all down my dress so I decided to call it a night. The fact that you would make a joke about Daddy's . . .' she hastily corrected herself '. . . Dad's death is so fucking tiresome. Not everything is funny, Lyra, other emotions are available, you might even find it healthy to explore them instead of covering up your clear unhappiness with lame jabs.'

'Ok, ok.' Lyra held up her hand. 'Just a bit weird that Will went to look for you at the lake, when he told the police he came to the house, that's all. A little joke, sissie, unclench.' Jemima was positively quivering with anger now, and I must say I always took some small pleasure in their antagonism. They spent so much time throwing jibes my way, it was rather fun to watch them do it to each other instead. Then, as though to drive home the point that my life was now a horrible farce, Clara came in, looking down at her phone, closely followed by Freddy who was still wearing his outdoor clothes and hadn't bothered to take off his boots.

Not for the first time, I marvelled at how many of them there were. With Anthony, I felt I at least had an ally, but now it was just me and four people I had made but barely understood. Let's have a big family, he'd said when we got married. 'I want a rugby team of Wisterns.' I thought it was a show of love, how stupid I was, but later I came to understand that to a man like Anthony, a big family showed the world your success. He wanted that success in all its forms, and providing a team of children was the role I took on.

They bickered. Fred wanted to know when the police would be off the land, Jemima complained that the housekeeper hadn't made the beds, and Clara took it upon herself to announce that Anthony's death was already a hot topic online. 'He's trending on social media – loads of theories. Did he really get carried away with the spike still in him?'

I ignored their complaints and told them I intended to return to London, using the excuse that the house felt too sad to stay in now. Really, I just couldn't stay there cooped up for much longer with only them for company. Gables had never really felt like my house. Bought for Freddy, and loved on occasion by Anthony, I'd attempted to get on board with it, but while we might've been ten minutes away from the finest farm shop in the UK according to *Tatler*, that couldn't quite make up for the isolation. You're never as relevant in the countryside as you are in the city. Even those girls who started the 'move to Somerset trend' and banged on and on about 'how wonderful rural living was' held on to their London houses. You only get good hair colourists in West London, everybody knows that. I understood the house was merely a status symbol, another signifier of Anthony's success. Fragrant wife, tick. Gaggle of photogenic children, French chateau, Cotswold manor, a plethora of mistresses and a penchant for cutting moral corners tick, tick, tick.

My mind was already turning to the funeral, which would take a considerable amount of organisation. Not the way I'd planned to say goodbye to my husband, but they do say when God closes a door and all that. Even as my children were squabbling with each other about what they were going to do, I was thinking about whether or not I could pull strings and get him into The Oratory. We're not Catholic, but I've always thought it to be the most beautiful church in London. Certainly, it would be the last party I'd have the chance to organise for a while, and if Anthony's birthday hadn't quite gone to plan, at least I would ensure his wake was perfect.

THE SLEUTH

@thesleuth
512 subscribers

I didn't *mean* to break into Gables, really I didn't. But what was I supposed to do when I had evidence to find?

I'm not even sure you could call it breaking in actually, given how low the wall between the woods and the Wistern land was. All high fences on the side nearest the road, gates which make it clear to even the nosiest of neighbours that they weren't welcome. But this country has wonderful right to ramble laws, and one such path went straight through the trees behind the property. On that side, there was an old stone wall only about eight feet high. I'd been religiously checking Clara Wistern's social media. She had a private account, but with twenty thousand followers, I chanced it and requested to be one of them. Accepted almost at once, I could watch the girl document every single moment of her life in real time, with endless videos about how sad she was. Clara was polished, looking a lot older than her seventeen years, and I thought back to when I was seventeen, wincing at the pale foundation and black eyeliner we all thought was the height of cool. It was intimidating, even though she was a full eight years younger than me. That afternoon, she'd posted a story showing the family at lunch, surrounded by people I didn't recognise with the caption 'Much needed day at Knebden.' Googling Knebden, I discovered it was an Elizabethan manor house near Banbury owned by some rich guy who owned a railway. The story was only eight minutes old and the drive from Banbury to Gables was 45 minutes. I took my chance, a moment alone at the house where it happened was too tempting to waste. I was over the fence in seconds, landing in manicured gardens which wouldn't have been out of place in one of those period dramas Mum loved so much. It took me a few minutes to find the lake, which made me nervous – I didn't fancy having to face an irate gardener or worse, an angry guard dog. Did rich people really have guard dogs or was that just in films? From what I'd read about Olivia Wistern, it felt more like she had silky lapdogs, but I didn't want to take any chances.

The lake, when I found it, was breathtakingly beautiful. It looked both natural and oddly artificial, like a Hollywood studio had designed it. A kidney-bean-shaped body of clear water, enormous fronded plants, and a wooden jetty with a perfect little boat tied up to the side. On one side there were high trees which shaded the edge of the water, and on the other a bank of lush grass which had been cut into perfect lines. A table and four chairs were positioned on the lawn, and a glass summerhouse almost the size of my actual house stood behind it. The whole scene looked too pristine, as though somebody came and hoovered up any unsightly signs of nature once a day.

With my phone out, I walked the perimeter, trying to use the skills you see in detective stories – Sherlock Holmes figures out who the killer is by spotting a tiny fleck of ash on a waistcoat, that kind of thing. Presumably the staff cleaned up the mess as fast as possible – but that didn't mean something wasn't missed. It was dark when he died, and since everyone seemed to have instantly agreed that his death was an accident, I was pretty sure nobody looked too closely. Lazy and incompetent are two sides of the same coin.

I walked round to the wooded side and scanned the bank. Disappointing. I was running out of things to say. But when I got to the jetty, things brightened up a bit. I could see mud tracks coming out of the water, indentations which looked a lot like they could be footprints, and when I knelt down, a tiny speck of yellow plastic. A police cordon! 'Here we are, friends, right at the site where he died. All that's left of Anthony Wistern is this slightly unsettled ground. Just mud and secrets.' I combed the area on my hands and knees, searching the ground in the hopes of giving my fans something, but no joy. Frustrated, I rinsed my hands in the water, walked back to the summerhouse and tried the door. It opened easily. Inside, it was even nicer than I'd have guessed. A picture-perfect living room, full kitchen complete with marble worktops, and at the back, a long day bed covered in pale pink velvet. A house to escape to when you got bored of your actual house. I walked around slowly, brushing my hand over the surfaces and looking at the books on the shelves. If I'd thought the Wistern family were a smart bunch, their choice in literature quickly changed my mind. From the spread in *The Style Bible* I'd found earlier in the week, I knew the main house had a library stuffed full of old classics, but this selection was mainly cheap-looking romance novels and the odd thriller, including one titled *The Family Secret*, which felt appropriate. Clearly, these were the books the family actually read, and the official library was all for show. It was oddly relatable actually, my dad used to hide his Dan Brown books under the bed.

I sat down for a minute, taking in the view of the lake. I tried to imagine Anthony Wistern slipping and falling into the water as the police said, but I just couldn't. As I sat there, I felt a sharp prodding in my left thigh. Moving over a little, I saw something glinting stuck between the sofa cushions. I pulled out a slim diamond hoop the size of a jam jar lid, so sparkly that when I turned it around, it cast dancing shapes on the ceiling. Sure, anyone could've left it here at any time, but something as expensive as this would've been searched for high and low. Why was it wedged down a sofa and left here? Could it be because someone was in here the night of the party and saw something they shouldn't have? Maybe even saw who killed Anthony Wistern?

I was looking for someone with expensive taste in jewellery then. And there were four Wistern women who fit the bill very nicely.

OLIVIA

Everyone had left, even my brother. I'd felt a little pang when he'd pushed off; the man can be as dull as a night at an interpretive dance show, but he handled the detectives manfully and I've always clung to men who look after me. It's internalised misogyny, Lyra tells me. I rather wish she'd internalise more often.

Before he'd gone, Charles convinced me to stay a few more days at Gables, warning me that the London house would be besieged by press. I still had the staff, which was a relief, but to my slight horror, the children didn't leave at the first available opportunity. It felt unlikely they were staying for me, every single one of my daughters was a daddy's girl despite his complete lack of real effort. Oh, he'd turn it on for big events – I would organise birthdays months in advance, usually centred around a theme of their choosing, and he'd be the one to claim all the attention. I hired a full circus to perform for Jemima's tenth birthday, and she'd been in tears when he missed almost the entire day. But he'd walked in eventually, carrying 100 gaudy pink balloons so that you could barely see his face, and made a show of walking a tightrope so badly that all of the children were in fits of laughter, all memory of his tardiness forgotten. Freddy never really belonged to anyone once he was able to walk. We'd bought Gables when he was 18 months old, realising we'd need somewhere in the countryside for him to get rid of his energy. From the main bedroom window, the estate agent had shown me the view of the garden. When he'd said it was sixty acres, I offered the asking price there and then. Sixty acres for him to roam around in without bothering me – I'd have paid double. I rather liked that there was a small church on the grounds, that was a nice touch. Regardless of how much land friends owned, or whether they had their own ancient wood or 18 stables for their delicate race-horses, people were always jealous of that little detail.

Were my offspring devastated? I honestly couldn't tell you. Jemima loved Anthony the most, in a way the rest of us found rather desperate, but in recent years even her adulation seemed to have waned slightly. When she was little, she used to make him promise never to die (I was pointedly never made to swear such an oath) but now he was extremely dead, Jemima seemed less inconsolable than I'd imagined. She spent a lot of time wandering around the house in silence, Will trailing behind her in his ineffectual way. Clara being a seventeen-year-old dramatist meant there had initially been brief bouts of affected weeping, but now she mainly stayed glued to her phone. Lyra has always been a cold fish and barely seemed changed by what had happened at all. She took as much pleasure in being inappropriate as usual, making dark jokes about how Anthony died whenever there was the slightest hint that someone else might be about to say some-thing serious or sincere. She spent a lot of time in her room, and I naively assumed that was when she chose to grieve, until I walked in one morning and found her enthusiastically singing along to 'Bohemian Rhapsody'. That unnerved me, I had no idea anyone in my family enjoyed Queen. As for Freddy . . . I'd say there was some relief there in all honesty. He carried on with his self-appointed chores, fixing the tired old summerhouse door, working in the garden, tending to his damned chickens, the only things my son ever wanted to do. I think he'd have been more upset if one of his hens had died.

When they *were* together, my children would sit around in various living rooms, intent on winding each other up, only straying from this pastime when they bandied together to turn on me.

Comfort came from other sources. One great thing about the Cotswolds is you can have neighbours from London. Honestly, it's rare even to meet a local, every house seems to be owned by someone I'm likely to run into during the week anyway. That meant we had a steady stream of visitors who dropped by with flowers and booze, ready with their condolences, but most importantly, offering me an excuse to spend less time with my family. One day we went over to our friends the Dearborns in Banbury, and my spirits lifted immensely just to be in the company of people other than my own family. In the moments when it was just us, I would inevitably have to confront a demanding or sulky daughter, a mute son or worse – bump into Will and be forced into small talk. It felt like we were all reluctantly stuck, waiting for the first person to break cover and leave before we could do the same. Play-acting as a family in grief, waiting for the moment we could go to bed and breathe a sigh of silent relief.

THE SLEUTH

@thesleuth
587 subscribers

From what I could see from their social media, none of the Wistern kids were exactly high achievers. Fred had a defunct Instagram; he hadn't posted for over two years, but it matched up with what I'd known about him from our occasional chats at the pub. He'd always seemed a bit lonely. Embarrassed by his dad, that was clear from the message he'd sent me the day after I'd been fired, telling me how sorry he was. He must've hated Anthony a hell of a lot to get my number off the manager and send that text. But not enough to walk away from his dad's money, not enough to risk actually standing up for me. Scrolling all the way back, I saw shots of him at school (I googled the uniform, he'd gone to Wellingby, which I discovered was a place for kids who wanted 'the opportunity to focus on non-traditional subjects and physical activity'. This turned out to be code for a school for thick boys who just wanted to play rugby). After he left, it seemed he'd moved to Gables

83

full time to play-act in his farming fantasy. He only followed agricultural accounts for the main part. Didn't follow anyone in his family, that was telling.

Clara was the most helpful in terms of seeing what the family was doing day by day, even if she mostly only posted photos of herself. The photos showed an impossibly glamorous life for someone who wasn't even of legal drinking age. Only one photo of Anthony prior to his death, but since then, she'd posted about him multiple times, each with a crying face emoji. There was even one of her by the lake at sunset, with the caption 'Missing him'. I actually yelped at that. The engagement on these photos was a lot higher than her previous selfies, with comments like 'So sad for you babe' and 'Love you to the moon'. A couple of her stories were more interesting – links to articles which hinted that her father's death might've been more than just an accident, and a slide where she'd simply written, 'I won't stop asking questions Daddy, I'll make this right for you'. The following story was asking if any of her friends would take her riding the next day, so she clearly wasn't too committed, but it was the first sign I'd seen that anyone in her family recognised Anthony's death for what it was. I messaged her then, emboldened by the idea I might have an in with a Wistern, explaining what I did and why I wanted to help. No reply of course, she probably wouldn't even see it. At least I'd tried.

Lyra didn't have Instagram, but she did use Twitter heavily. Her name was 'Lyrawi2' and the photo was blurry, but I knew it was her; people give themselves away online in a million ways. The account said she was twenty-four, a 'photographer' based between New York and Paris, and mentioned being back in the UK. Amazing that some people are so wealthy they're able to 'live' on different continents as if it's just a bus ride away. She'd not posted since her dad's murder, but before that she was on it almost every day. Her Twitter follows showed me that she was interested in left-wing politics, climate change and feminism. A typical twenty-something posh girl, rebelling without really doing anything. She'd retweeted a post about rising house prices which included the phrase 'eat the rich'. A bunch of people had replied, praising her for her 'truth', which made me feel like I was taking crazy pills. Scrolling down, there were photos of her on a march in Paris, holding a sign, which a rough translation told me was 'Power to the proletariat'. A tweet about bankers funding the fossil-fuel industry, and one about cheering on squatters who'd occupied a hedge fund manager's house in London. She clearly hated her dad, but was she really the kind of girl to get her hands dirty or did she just whinge online while happily taking his money?

Jemima's Instagram was much more as I'd expected. Photos of her on holiday, with her husband and their friends, who all looked just like them. They went rowing a lot, which wasn't something I thought people actually did in real life. Jemima didn't seem to have a job, because she posted a lot about brunches and hair appointments, but it turned out she ran some interiors business with her friend Hannah. Business might've been a stretch, given that the services they offered seemed to be something called table-scaping and cushion placement. Do a job you love and you'll never work a day in your life, well Jemima had taken that literally. All the Wistern children lived in a bubble I couldn't burst into without risking arrest. Except, a voice in my head reminded me, Freddy. God, I didn't want to have to get in touch with that boy, who witnessed my humiliation and did nothing. But he was the only lead I had, so I would grin and bear it. I felt supremely nauseous as I wrote him a message outlining my suspicions, but I sent it. I'm nothing if not professional.

ANTHONY

Olivia had gone to bed early after a particularly trying evening where Lyra and Jemima got into an argument about whether or not the family should be putting out a statement about my death. Never one to miss an opportunity, my PR had been on the phone and persuaded my eldest that a gushing tribute would be heartily appreciated by the papers. Lyra thought it was tacky – 'He wasn't *murdered*, we don't need to stand in a huddle holding his favourite jumper, weeping for the cameras. We're not those kind of people.' Jemima got huffy at this, accusing Lyra of being 'freakishly cold', and arguing that everyone else seemed to be paying tributes but them, which was true. Clara was thrilled by the idea, offering to do it alone, which the rest of them immediately vetoed. If I knew my youngest daughter, she'd wear something entirely inappropriate, flirt with the cameraman and try to drop her Instagram handle into the tribute.

'A written one then, we can just say how much we loved and cherished him,' Jemima had countered, which everyone grudgingly agreed to. Olivia, who had chosen not to say anything at all throughout the conversation, suddenly announced she was going to bed.

'Let the PR people do it, darling, that's what they're paid for. Whatever you come up with will make us sound idiotic.' After she'd left, the discussion quickly descended into farce.

'Strong,' suggested Jemima.

'Meaning he would drive a truck over your grandmother,' shot back Lyra.

Clara: 'A leader in both business and family.'

'Would drive a truck over your grandmother *and* her bank manager.' That, from Freddy, made them laugh. We were always surprised when he spoke, and to hear him be funny for perhaps the first time had them almost wheezing in delight. But it only got worse from there. 'A visionary in his field', 'Saw you as a mark a mile away.' 'A devoted husband' was translated as 'Bought his wife diamonds every time he shagged someone half her age.' I left after Lyra suggested 'A family man,' and Clara, with ferocity, replied, 'We don't know how many other kids he had.' That one went too far. I'd always been very careful about that. God knows you don't want to be pushing sixty and suddenly find out you've got a toddler running round somewhere with a mother who's engaged a rottweiler of a lawyer who knows a big payday when he sees one.

I went off to see Olivia, who was halfway through her absurdly laborious night-time routine. The lengths women go to is mind blowing. Lotions, massage, tweaks. And if they don't give the desired results, sometimes full-on surgery. Even Lyra, who professes to be above all of that, had something done to her eyes which makes her look slightly feline. She didn't like that I purred every time she came into a room for weeks afterwards, but I'd paid for it. My family never understood that the breadwinner has certain privileges.

When she'd finally gone to bed, I went back downstairs, not quite ready to go to the dormitory and spend another night listening to an assortment of strangers cry. You'd think they'd be happy to be here. I was really the only person who had taken a demotion in death – the guy two beds down worked in insurance! This place was nirvana compared to his old life.

The girls were sitting in the living room we'd designated as theirs, mainly to keep them at the other end of the house as much as possible. Jemima was talking animatedly, a large glass of wine in her hand. That pregnancy test was clearly being ignored for now. 'We all need to talk to her about it, not just me. And definitely not you' – she was pointing at Lyra – 'you'll just piss her off.' I stood for a minute, waiting for them to elaborate, and it quickly became clear that my children were discussing how my death would affect them. Not emotionally, that much had been made clear. No, they'd finally got down to what really mattered – money. The girls speculated on whether or not the trust funds I'd set up for them would now be unlocked, something we'd decided wouldn't happen until they were thirty and unlikely to fritter it all away on handbags or rare breed animals.

Clara dragged her eyes away from her phone. 'If we don't do something now, she'll spend it all, she's got no idea about money.' She was talking about Olivia with an air of resigned reason, as if Clara hadn't spent 2,000 quid a month on taxis to ferry her around West London over the past year. The others nodded in agreement, all except Lyra who smirked like she knew a secret.

'Not as clueless as you might think. Don't underestimate Olivia.' She refused to elaborate, even when Jemima kicked her firmly in the ribs, and they moved on, but I wondered what she meant.

'All I want is this place,' Freddy said in a flat voice. I hadn't even noticed him, sitting on the floor as if the very idea of furniture was too civilised for him. 'None of you really care about it, but it's my *life*. I'm not going back to London, and I don't need anything else.' How modest of him. 'Just the trust, so I can expand on rewilding, it's vital to restore a healthy ecosystem. I want to be able to live off the fruits of my own land.' Ah yes, my self-sufficient son, doing it all by himself with nothing but a large country pile and a bank account at Coutts opened for him by his father, a true man of the soil.

They carried on, the girls agreeing that none of them wanted to take over the business and weighing up whether or not to ask Giles to buy them out before or after the funeral. Before might look tasteless, Jemima pointed out. Who cares, Lyra had replied, 'it's not a charitable endeavour. Giles is probably already thinking about it, trying to figure out how to get a bargain off Olivia.' They moved on to squabbling about various art works they might like. I'd been a voracious connoisseur and we had one of the finest personal collections in London. After listening to my children discuss in heated tones who would get the Modigliani, I felt furious. Not a single second had been spent talking about *me*. You'd think at least one of them would've at least pretended to miss their father, the one who provided and raised them. The parent they all repeatedly professed to love more, as if pledging their loyalty to a leader.

Jemima was now saying that she'd take the bulk of it since she was the one with a house big enough to fit it all.

'You didn't even know who Keith Haring was,' Lyra shot back. 'According to you, Will is the most wildly successful man in the whole world. You should be happy to let your destitute siblings take your share, dearest.' Quite right too. When I'd presented Jemima with the mews house, she'd hugged me with such gusto, whispering into my ear that I was the best father anyone could dream of, and here she was, with me not even in my grave, using it as an opportunity to get more than her sisters.

They might've taken my death as a win, but they were in for a nasty surprise when the will was read out. Even though I'd lost my life, I'd still come out on top. It takes a special kind of man to do that.

THE SLEUTH

@thesleuth
597 subscribers

I don't trust the mainstream media. Journalists literally went to the same schools as the people in power, you think they're going to risk exposing their own? If you really want to learn about the world, you've got to do your own research. And besides, everything's online now – why pay for something that's already a day out of date? It's still hard not to sneak a look at Mum's tabloid every morning knowing all that. The headlines are designed to reel you in.

When I'd come home to look after Mum (what was the alternative? Dad would've wept if I'd put her in a home), I spent six months obsessed with one particular case. You'll know the one I'm talking about – that poor girl murdered up by Lake Murrough, and what did the police say? That she'd driven her car into the water by accident. Did they listen to the parents who said Sally Gentle had been stalked for weeks before by a neighbour? Did they hell. Too intent on making it a nice clean case they could wrap up quickly. It felt like everyone in the country knew it was bollocks except the force, and it drove me nuts. People even named the man who'd been harassing Sally on crime forums. I spent hours trying to figure out how to get the bastard we all knew had done it.

I can accept now that I'd got obsessed, but that's how I cope when I'm miserable. My mates from uni had all moved to London whereas I'd had to come home, and it felt like the opportunity I'd been given to start my life for real was over before it had begun. One day, after fixing Mum up and making sure she had everything she'd need for the afternoon, I'd told her I was going to a job interview in Woodstock. Instead, I'd taken her car and driven the three hours to Lake Murrough, my hands shaking the entire way. A bunch of the online gang had decided to see if we could find anything that might make the police pull their finger out. When I arrived, I had a brief moment of doubt, wondering if this was going a bit too far, but I was soon put at ease by the self-appointed leaders of the gang, Geoff and Marnie.

They were an odd pairing. Geoff looked a lot like my dad, decked out in a cagoule and sensible shoes, a thermos of tea under one arm. Marnie had a streak of pink in her hair and a tattoo of a bow on her knuckles. They did this a lot, Marnie explained to the rest of us.

'We call ourselves the crime collective and we like to say we're the fourth emergency service,' Geoff said. 'Nobody respects our forces more than I do,' he'd added hastily. 'I was in the Territorial Army for fifteen years. But they have one way of doing things, and we have another.' Someone asked if the group had ever solved a crime, and Marnie shook her head defensively.

'No but we *have* pointed investigations in the right direction.'

Geoff butted in, his face slightly red. 'And we don't take the credit when that happens. Remember that glove we found in that lay-by off the M40 after that girl was kidnapped? That was entirely missed by the police.' A lady behind me gasped, and Geoff looked suitably gratified.

'Did it belong to the perpetrator?' she said, and his face dropped.

'Well, no it didn't, but *they* didn't know that did they? Imagine if it had and they'd missed out on such a massive clue. It meant they had to review their procedures, and that matters, Leslie.'

In the end, we'd spent a fairly miserable 90 minutes on the shore; even Geoff conceded it had been pretty fruitless. 'But we rally, folks, we keep on showing up!' That might have been it for me, had it not been for the fact that three days later, the police announced a dog walker had found a small hammer lodged under a rock just five minutes away from where we'd been searching. The coppers finally got in gear and executed a search warrant of Wayne Deon's house, where they found . . . a fucking life jacket. The bastard had drugged her, driven her into the lake, smashed the window with the hammer and swum away. He might've got away with it, had it not been for one beady-eyed citizen who saw something and said something. The dog walker ended up doing a few interviews off the back of it, where he repeatedly denied being a hero, but he *was* in my eyes. Despite our little group's failure (and ignoring Geoff's clear jealousy of the dog walker, which felt a little sour) I'd felt a sense of purpose that day I'd not experienced before. What if social media meant we could solve crimes ourselves?

I began to spend more time on the forums, zoning in on cases I thought I could help with. Sometimes that meant tracking the local area on maps, or checking where the CCTV was. I even volunteered to go to sites and do a thorough search. I liked that part of it, it felt more useful than just sitting in my bedroom online. I've read a lot of crime fiction, I was obsessed with Agatha Christie novels as a kid, and I've got the knack for it. A great detective questions everything and trusts nobody.

After bringing Mum's breakfast tray down, I sat in the kitchen and scanned the local paper to see how they'd cover the biggest story to happen to Chipping Marston since Derek Crosby drove his minivan into the front of his wife's hair salon after he found out she'd given their dog away. In fairness to the woman, the dog kept biting her and Derek didn't believe it – even when she called him from the hospital and told him she needed stitches on her ankle. He'd told her she must've provoked it, and after the divorce, he managed to get his pet back. People gave him and the dog a wide berth on the high street after that.

The paper didn't have it on the front page, which bizarrely went with a major change to recycling in the area, but they had it on page three.

'Local man dies in tragic accident at birthday party'. Local was a bit of a stretch. Anthony Wistern was about as much a part of this community as a Martian. The paper praised him for 'saving' The Golden Badger, making it sound like he'd stopped a local pub from going bust, as if The Badger hadn't been a thriving hub before he took it on. When Anthony took it over, he fired the landlord. The locals stopped going in protest, and a couple of the bar staff resigned in solidarity, which was how I got a job there. I'm sure that raised some eyebrows, but I didn't feel much loyalty to the town, not after how they'd turned their backs when Dad died. It was a good enough job, and the evening shifts meant Mum would be asleep while I was out. But even before he fired me, I saw it for what it was. A vanity project for a man who had no care for anyone but himself.

There was a quote from Ritu Gupta, who ran the kids' theatre. Anthony had donated £60k last year to prevent it from being closed, which sounded like a nice gesture, but I knew it had strings attached. With that donation, he was 'given' the land at the back of the theatre, prime real estate and right beside the pub. Perfect for the walled garden he added just six months later. Never mind the theatre no longer had a car park or disabled access, Anthony Wistern got what he wanted and that was all that mattered.

After I'd finished with the papers, and washed up Mum's dishes, I lay down on my bed and checked my phone. A new email, from an account I didn't recognise. I got a lot of random emails, usually people sending me crackpot theories. This one was different. Just three lines: 'You think someone killed my dad, so do I. If you want a suspect, read *this*.' There was a link attached. I buried my head in the pillow for a second. Someone had insider knowledge, someone claiming to be a Wistern. Freddy hadn't replied to my message, but I'd added all my professional contact details. Could this really be him? Was he on my side? My heart was pounding as I clicked on the link. When I read the headline, I nearly yelled out in shock.

NEWS ARTICLE
5 July 2018

He was leaving his wife, we planned our Island paradise future

Lainey Goodman is a petite woman, just 5ft 5 in heels. Her long blonde hair is expertly blow-dried, and she's dressed in a blue dress with capped sleeves, delicate gold jewellery emphasising her fresh tan. 'A much-needed holiday,' she explains. A holiday it might've been, but her week away in Malaga was also a time to grieve, to mourn the man she calls 'her soulmate'.

Goodman was the mistress of Anthony Wistern, the investment fund wizard found dead in the lake at his countryside property last Saturday. Much has been written about Anthony Wistern's wife Olivia, a glamorous woman renowned for her parties. The couple have four children, and doubtless they will all find it hard to read about Ms Goodman, who spares no detail about her love affair with Mr Wistern. But she insists she has a right to tell her story, and it's undeniable that Goodman, who weeps often during our interview but bravely carries on despite the pain, has an interesting story to tell. In this honest conversation, Lainey Goodman often reiterates that she doesn't want to hurt anyone, but explains that the truth must come out about the man she lovingly calls her Antman.

'He was more than the media has made out,' Lainey says, smiling at the memory of him. 'Ant was a rich and powerful man, that's all true, but he was also a soft and kind soul in many ways. He helped my mother after her hip replacement, sending over a team of nurses to look after her round the clock so that I could go to Rome with him for three days – so thoughtful of him.'

That trip to Italy was where the couple first said I love you, 'on a roof terrace overlooking the Spanish steps. He brought me a promise ring, a lovely emerald which once belonged to Princess Margaret because he knew how much I loved the royal family. I cried with joy.' We talk for a long time about how happy they were together.

'When we were at my flat he wasn't this big man of business, he was sweet – he used to wear my dressing gown and let me give him facials,' but she is naturally chastened when asked about his family, insisting she tried

96

very hard to deny her feelings 'He was persistent and after a while, I had no choice. Ant always got what he wanted. I'm a firm believer you can't take someone away from a happy marriage.' Goodman raises her eyebrows, as if to signal a truth she's too polite to say out loud. Did she think Anthony Wistern's marriage was a bad one? She sighs, pausing for a second before choosing her words carefully.

'I worked for his wife unofficially too, mainly to help her organise domestic affairs. She was an unhappy woman and often took that out on her staff, including me. I think they married too young – she was only twenty-two – and fundamentally wanted very different things. Anthony needed someone with drive and passion, and Olivia was very comfortable being a society lady. He didn't care about all that, he loved that I worked and praised my independence. I think he just found himself in a situation he couldn't get out of.' Warming to her theme, Goodman adds that the Wistern children were often a point of contention for the couple. 'They were spoiled, frankly, always asking for more. Ant had trust funds set up for them, but they couldn't access the money until they were thirty. That was always an issue – they'd call and say they needed holidays, cars, clothes. He bought Jemima and her husband a house when they got married and she actually complained that it wasn't south facing when he handed her the keys! It caused Ant a lot of sadness, he felt his wife had raised them badly and it was too late to do much about it.'

As keen as she is to discuss what she sees as their epic love story, Goodman is less forthcoming about the night he died. 'All I know was in recent months, he was incredibly stressed out. Not sleeping much, drinking a lot. He told me he was having cash flow problems because his wife was out of control with spending. He even mentioned that he was thinking about selling Gables, which shocked me. His birthday was obscene, she'd spent at least £200,000 on it, and it wasn't for him at all, she just wanted to look good in front of her fancy mates. They had a fight about it that night. He took me out of the dinner for a moment, just so we could be together, and I could tell he was upset. It killed me to see him like that.'

As if aware that she now sounds angry, rather than grief-stricken, she leans back and puts a hand to her forehead as if to calm herself. 'I don't want to be written out of his story.' She corrects herself, 'Our story. I don't understand how things went so wrong that night, how a man as strong as him could just die like that. It makes no sense if I'm honest with you.'

I ask whether or not she's been in touch with the Wistern family since that fateful evening, and she winces slightly. 'I had to find out what had happened with everyone else. The family were already back at the house, and I ran there, I think I was in shock. Anthony's son-in-law (Will Fortesque, a prominent antiques dealer married to Jemima Wistern), he was always really nice to me. I waited in the hallway like I was a nobody while he asked if I could come in, but he came out and told me I wasn't welcome. He looked embarrassed, like he knew it was wrong, but nobody stands up to those women. So no, I haven't been in touch with them. And . . .' she says smiling through the tears, 'I doubt I will now, but that's ok. I know my Antman loved me at the end, that's all that matters to me.'

And with that, we say our goodbyes. Ms Goodman will go back to her flat alone, a place she hoped would be a home for her and the man she loved. A sad end to this very modern love story. And one which will no doubt cause a stir in the elite circles the Wisterns move in.

OLIVIA

I saw the news first thing. Rosa always leaves the papers with my coffee when she comes to wake me up. I read the piece with increasing fury – it was no surprise that she declared they were in love, she was far from the first person to be duped by Anthony – but to learn he'd given her the ring I'd had my eye on for months stunned me. When I'd seen it in the Bonhams catalogue, I'd told him explicitly how much I'd loved it, even sending him a photo so he'd remember. In the end, I went to the auction myself, annoyed at his lack of interest but determined to make it mine. When I walked in, I'd spotted my husband immediately, he was sitting right at the front with his friend Raj, both of them enjoying the attention they always drew. I stayed at the back, thrilled he'd actually listened and keen to ensure he bid aggressively. My husband did well, holding back initially, waiting until the buyers in the room thinned out and there were only two others bidding – one on the phone, you always have to watch out for them – and a prim-looking woman who was all wrong for the ring. After a few minutes of feverish back and forth, Anthony walked away victorious and I slipped out before he could notice me. I walked down Piccadilly in a fug of delight, surprising myself by smiling at tourists as they fussed over directions.

That evening though, he came home in a filthy temper and went straight into his office without even saying hello. The next day he was in a better mood, yet still there was no ring on my finger and I began to think he must be keeping it for my birthday. When that came and went, I knew exactly what was going on. I hadn't confronted him, knowing too well he'd accuse me of following him and tell me I was being irrational. He wriggled out of arguments so deftly you'd think he was coated in olive oil, and I was always the one left looking foolish. But I'd *known* that some other woman was wearing *my* ring, even if I'd not guessed who it was back then. And now, in the pages of that rag, Lainey was flashing it for the photographer as she ran a steam train over my character.

Antman. How people would laugh. I threw off the bedcovers and stood up, marching across to the window and back. Too frantic, I realised, I must calm down. I'd never played the scorned wife when he was alive, and I wouldn't waste my time doing it now. I gathered myself with some slow breathing as my good friend Emily Matlock had always told me to do when I was stressed. She would know, she once had a very uncomfortable six months when her son drove their boat into the pier at Capri, mowing down an old local man whose family then went to the papers the moment they got a sniff of how much she was worth. Then I went downstairs, intent on acting as though nothing had happened. I walked through the entertaining kitchen, where we'd have casual Sunday suppers with friends, and heard noises from beyond. Usually, breakfast was served in the dining room but decorum had gone to hell since he died. The actual kitchen was strictly the domain of Rosa, Mary and the weekend chef, but my children were all in there as Mary cooked. I watched them from the hallway, not quite ready to face their inevitable demands.

Lyra was hunched over the countertop, reading the paper out loud to the others. I'd shielded them from his philandering, which had done me no good. He was always their favourite, even though he did very little to deserve it, and I often wished I'd thrown it in their faces when they'd been dismissive of me. Why should I have hidden my hurt in order that he continue to be the fun one? From their faces, I saw my efforts had been in vain anyway. Not one of them was surprised by this latest affair.

'I saw them together at the pub about three months ago,' Jemima said, when Lyra finished reading. I stiffened. 'I went down there that weekend Will was on his brother's stag do. Olivia was in Florence, and Dad said he'd take me to the races so I drove down the night before on a whim, but when I got to Gables, he wasn't there. I was bored waiting around with just Fred for company, so I decided to go to the pub. One of the waitresses said he was in the office.' She paused, as if trying to push away a bad smell. 'I didn't knock.' Of course she didn't, it was practically family law. 'Dad was leaning back over the desk, hips thrust out for balance. And Lainey was on her knees, enthusiastically doing something that was a job but was decidedly not *her* job.' A perfect blend of oversharing and prudishness from my daughter, all in one sentence. Lyra laughed far too loudly, while Clara made retching sounds. So they knew what he was like and *still* they favoured him. Bastards.

'I stood in the doorway for a second, just feeling like I was going to be sick, and I must have gasped, because he jolted forward and looked straight at me. He didn't move though,' she said, and shook her head in what I assumed was distaste. 'Didn't follow me, or call after me. Maybe he stayed and finished, what does that say about him?'

I almost snorted at that, I couldn't help it, stifling the instinct and moving quickly away from the door. Anthony always prized his own pleasure above all else; the idea he'd continue on with his office fumble after his daughter had caught him wasn't at all fanciful.

Now even Fred was chiming in, though with less mirth than the others. 'I saw her and Dad down by the summerhouse the night of the party . . .' He trailed off and the others pounced.

'What were they doing?' That was Lyra. Another retching sound from Clara, who was overdoing it now and then Jemima, slightly indignant.

'Why were you creeping about down there?'

From my vantage point, I could see my son redden. 'I was checking on the fish. They dropped a massive bloody orb in the lake, even though I *told* Olivia how distressed it'd make the koi. I gave her more respect than she gave them though.' He looked furious for a minute. 'Four of them died and *still* I didn't want her upset, so I didn't tell the police about it.'

I waited for the heartless joke that Lyra would inevitably make, but it never came. Instead, she turned to her sister. 'Why so annoyed Fred was down by the lake, Jem? What are you worried he might've seen?'

Jemima replied with a huff, and a brisk 'Oh shut up, Lyra, I was just surprised Fred saw them, that's all.'

'A bit of a downgrade from that model,' I heard Clara say, the others making noises of agreement. God, they'd known about *her* too. Clara would only have been about eight, one of her sisters must have told her, a family tradition of sorts, passing down the news of your father's adultery. What a tribute to the man. She was right about Lainey being a downgrade, that much was certainly true. But after thirty years with Anthony I'd come to learn that he'd have shagged your grandmother if bored enough.

He'd have been proud of it too, made it into a joke and somehow left everybody impressed rather than shocked.

'It's hardly the surprise of the century, is it? At least it wasn't one of her best mates again, she was a nightmare for at least six months after that.'

And again! Perhaps they knew about women I hadn't even suspected. Maybe they sat around with Anthony laughing at my blithe ignorance. Perhaps that's how they bonded, and there was me thinking their clear preference for him was only about his money.

'What will Lainey do now Dad's dead?' That was Jemima again, sounding idly curious. 'Presumably shuffle off to a rental in zone 5 and cast out for another man who'll fill her father figure fixation, that sounds like her best hope. The wives will be on full alert now she's told all. It's like putting your resume in the *Daily Mail*.'

I retreated from the hall, walked up the stairs and shut myself in the dressing room. Once again, my children had placed their father above me in the pecking order. I felt very tired, too tired to have an argument with them about it. Staring at the trunks stacked in front of me, I reminded myself that his deep failures no longer mattered to me at all. I had a plan, and despite the undeniable spanner thrown at me, neither his death nor this latest revelation would change that.

ANTHONY

She left for London without telling the kids, just got in the car and hotfooted it the next morning before anyone woke up. She didn't even let Penny know – her oldest friend woke up to find Liv gone. That's the thing about Livvy; if someone shows the slightest disrespect, she'll cut them off until they beg for her approval. All this time she'd been hiding away up in our bedroom, acting the role of devastated wife and the moment she heard the kids discussing Lainey in a less than censorious way, bam! She's up and gone. It was the same with how she hated everything until someone she admired proclaimed it good. She refused to go to the opera with me for twenty years, saying it was 'like cats howling' but the moment she discovered a new surrealist production of *Madame Butterfly* was 'the latest sold-out show, attended by only the most discerning', suddenly she'd booked us a box. It was five hours long, mostly silent apart from some random lines of song which were yelled in Finnish and by the end I was banging my head against the wall in desperation to leave. Liv insisted it was one of the most delightful evenings she'd had out in years.

It wasn't fair, this retelling of my life by people like Lainey Goodman. I wanted tributes from the great and the good, obituaries from world leaders and perhaps even a bust of my head placed in a nice central London square but instead I'd been called Antman in the national press. The love of my life? Hardly. The article made out like we were going to be together forever, when in reality, the last thing she'd said to me was, 'God must be a man, because there's no way a woman would let another woman have the misfortune of meeting you.' More eloquent than 'choke on it' I suppose. I'd broken it off with her three weeks before the party, growing bored with her clinginess, but she'd played her cards well. She knew what I'd been doing, she informed me, and would feel morally bound to tell officials if I decided we were really over. That was a bit of a doozy, I can tell you. I'd never been blackmailed before. Extortion! By someone who was now shamelessly singing like a canary to the media about our love story. Women were too much! I wondered whether to add her to my list of suspects. But what use was I to her dead?

If my wife had stayed on and listened to our offspring for a little longer, she'd have perked up. The mild mockery was merely an amuse-bouche, the real meat came later. They wanted my money, of course they did. My children might be many things, but they're not communists. That didn't stop them from discussing my apparent shortcomings as a father.

Remarkably, all of them had wildly different reasons to resent me, which I suppose at least meant I'd offered a range of options. Always keen to lead a conversation, Jemima was talking about my brief indiscretions (and mostly I was very discreet) as if they somehow mortally wounded *her*. I believe she actually used the word 'trauma' at one point. I had a business which demanded a huge amount of my time and a family who grabbed most of the rest. If I occasionally needed a little respite, well, Olivia understood . . . mostly. To see Jemima babbling on to her siblings about how I'd damaged them all with my actions would've been funny had it not been clear that she was a chip off the old block. At least I'd done it with style, and always made sure to pull the escape cord when needed. I didn't blame her for looking elsewhere, not with the human equivalent of sliced white bread occupying her bed, but she'd picked appallingly.

Even Lyra was united with her sister. I could've paid a therapist a million quid and they'd still not have brought those two together as effectively as their hatred of me did. Lyra worked herself into a lather about how I only cared about money, 'no matter the means of acquiring it'. Apparently, I was so intent on hoarding my wealth that I'd turned into some kind of tyrant in her eyes. 'It's capitalism. As Balzac said, "Behind every great fortune lies a great crime."' I knew I shouldn't have paid for her to live in Paris. You don't send a child to live in a country where they celebrate killing their rulers and not expect some blowback.

Fred came last, as usual, telling the others I'd threatened to sell Gables. You'd think a house could never mean that much to a person but to my son, Gables meant the world. I never cared much about where I lived, if a place got boring you could always buy somewhere new, but Fred never wanted to be anywhere else, as much as we cajoled, threatened or tried to bribe him to go to uni. As it turned out, his grades would've required more than a mere one-off donation, I'd have had to build a new library. So Fred moved down to Gables, and we tried to ignore the ever-growing vegetable patches and occasional escaped chicken. When I'd let slip I was thinking of selling the place, he'd gone ballistic. Quite frightening actually, to see your son's face contort like that, rage seeping through every pore. He'd picked up a log and thrown it in my direction, without saying a word, before storming off down to the lake. Now I was dead Freddy clearly thought the house was safe. Pretty convenient, eh?

After that, they took turns recounting the ways in which I'd bullied them. Clara piped up with a story about how she'd always been scared of me.

'I showed him my art project – the photos of me on top of the lions in Trafalgar Square – and he just shook his head and muttered something about how I might as well have been home-schooled. I threw that stupid ashtray he had on his desk at the wall and cried so hard that my eyes puffed up and I couldn't go to Bella's party the next evening because I looked like I'd been attacked by bees. That meant Louis ended up getting off with Sara Milton and she *knew* I liked him.' Knowing my youngest daughter as I did, it sounded like young Louis had made a lucky escape. 'But even then . . .' she said, with a dramatic pause, 'he didn't deserve to be killed.' The others rolled their eyes.

'Oh my god give it a rest, Clara. Jesus.'

'Do you know about the four Fs of trauma?' This was Lyra, of course it was. She was always spouting new therapy buzzwords at her mother and me at any available opportunity. She once told me I wasn't 'doing the work' because I didn't want to accompany Olivia to a three-hour charity tea party in aid of some long dead queen's boat which she solemnly informed me 'had a ball-room in dire need of rehabilitation'. 'Flight, fight, freeze and fawn. I took flight, Clara always fought him, Jem kissed his arse and Fred froze.' The girls looked at their brother with pity, he was undoubtedly the weakest of the bunch and they all knew it.

'He dominated everyone in his orbit. Especially Olivia. Yes, well, I know she's a nightmare . . .' That was Jemima, hushing the others as they made sceptical noises.

'Just look at her. The woman doesn't really have an identity without him. He sort of designed it that way, right?'

Lyra chimed in. 'She's a very nice vessel, like a beautiful objet d'art he can display. Empty though. Hollow.'

'Do vases make withering comments you'll remember forever? I didn't know that they had that kind of autonomy.' They'd swung back to slagging off their mother, certainly a more comfortable place for me.

An uncomfortable idea was forming somewhere in my brain, one I nearly didn't engage with. If Charles had alibied Giles so quickly, had one of *them* killed me? Had my own progeny conspired to off me for their inheritance? I can't lie, it's something I've had uncomfortable thoughts about before. When you've got a lot to lose, your trust in people diminishes, family members aren't exempt from that. After all, they do say you're most likely to be killed by someone you know. It crossed my mind a few times as the kids got older, usually when they were being particularly greedy. Lyra used to narrow her eyes at me in an unnerving way whenever I mildly suggested she might want to pay me back for the apartment in Paris if she thought my money was so distasteful. Jemima had recently caught me with Lainey, and clearly still had a lot of anger about that. With Fred, it was more recent. That rage I'd seen when he found out I might have to sell Gables, it was unnerving. If I'd mentioned his outburst to Liv, she'd have rolled her eyes at the idea of our son being violent. 'That boy is so wet. If he wasn't so keen on the countryside, I'd think he was a Liberal.'

When they eventually went to bed, I tried once more to force the memory of my death to come back. The drinks, the dinner, the toasts which even I'd thought got a little effusive at times. The dancing, whirling around the floor with Rick's delightful new wife Melissa until an icy stare from Liv caught my eye from across the room and forced me to hand her reluctantly back to her husband. Things got blurrier after that. More drinking, an ill-advised shot handed to me by someone . . . who was that? All I can see is a hand outstretched, a drink spilling onto my arm. Then a cigar outside the marquee. And then, nothing.

THE SLEUTH

@thesleuth
2.6k subscribers

I'd never had so much positive attention in my life. People were constantly messaging me with their theories and their pleas for me to keep going and it felt great, but I needed to maintain the momentum. I decided to go down to The Badger once Mum was asleep.

Even though lots of people online were still stuck on Giles, I'd never really been interested in him as a suspect. The guy wasn't going to kill his business partner, not when they were making money hand over fist. And if Giles had shoved him like that, do you think he'd be the first person on the scene when people heard the commotion? Of course not, he'd have scarpered up to the marquees and blended in with the crowd. First rule of murder, get away from the scene. After reading what Lainey Goodman had to say, I'd been more sure than ever that his death was a personal thing. That meant the family. Ticking off what I knew – that I'd found an expensive earring at the scene, which meant a woman had been there around the time he died, and that Anthony enthusiastically cheated on his wife, I knew I was looking at one of the family. Who else would be in the summer-house? I'd messaged my anonymous emailer back several times, only to be met with silence. Freddy hadn't replied either. And as all crime experts know, there's no such thing as coincidence. Why was he hiding behind an anonymous account instead of just helping me? He might have been on my side but he clearly wasn't willing to do the work. Classic trust fund kid.

It was a rare night out and I had to psych myself up to cycle the few miles. I'd been fired just over nine months ago, and hadn't dared show my face since. Nobody had even texted me, not even Karen, and I'd thought we were close. I'd bought her a book on houseplants when she moved into a new flat, only to see it in the Oxfam on the high street a few weeks back. Who knows what Anthony had told them, but they clearly wanted to keep their distance.

I opened the camera app on my phone, and pulled my hoodie over my face. I'd made it a rule to be anonymous on these videos from day one – you never know who's watching. And besides, it ramps up the tension well – these true crime podcast presenters all seem to make the decision to dress super feminine as if the gory content feels less scary when the host is wearing Hello Kitty earrings and bright pink lipstick, but I think my approach is more appropriate. I recorded a bit about what I was doing and then locked the screen. Later on, I'd splice the videos together for a quick TikTok hit. The crime purist in me doesn't like watching a case recapped in 30 seconds but I can't deny the numbers.

I ordered a drink and sat at the bar next to an elderly pair in matching anoraks who were fussing over whether or not to use the loo before they set off. It wasn't exactly the glamorous gastro pub Anthony Wistern hoped he'd own. In the early days it had been rammed full of his mates, men called Henry and Charlie or worse – one night I actually served a Rollo. But now it had an air of neglect, as if management had given up, which I suppose he had in a way.

Once the old biddies had left, I was the only one at the bar, and I worked up the nerve to ask the girl at the till, who was clearly my replacement, how it was going. She looked at me with confusion. I stuttered something about the owner dying and her face cleared.

'Oh right, yeah. Erm, I mean, he wasn't here day to day or anything . . .'

I slipped my hand into my pocket and pulled out my phone, keeping it below the bar. I hit record, wincing slightly at the angle. I was anonymous yes, but it made me look as though I had two chins, and I already disliked the one I had. Still, vanity had to be sacrificed for the truth. I read that on a fortune cookie once, never thought I'd be spouting it as genuine wisdom.

'Not the most popular guy,' I said. 'I bet you were glad he wasn't here much.' The girl shrugged, and I began to feel embarrassed. A few minutes passed while I drank my vodka and thought about leaving and then suddenly she leant towards me.

'I didn't like him very much but it feels rude to say that now he's . . .' she mimed a slumping over, 'y'know, dead.'

Cheered, I nodded a bit too vigorously. 'Oh yeah, the rumours about him weren't great.'

She rolled her eyes. 'I'm only here till I can go to uni, and he never really spoke to me. But he sure was interested in Karen.' I already knew about what he'd tried with Karen but for the recording, I had to be clear.

'Oh, did he harass her?'

'He used to text her sometimes, telling her she was beautiful or asking her to work late when he was down at weekends. She can handle herself, but it was so gross. The wife only came in once. She ate about four lettuce leaves and spent the whole time looking uptight. But the kids came in here sometimes when they were down at their country house.' She said the words in a mock posh voice. 'They were the worst.'

I knew that from experience. I'd once had to hold Jemima's dog while she ate dinner because 'Lola finds stone floors too cold.'

She was still talking. 'The brother tried to be one of the locals, he worked so hard to get Luke on side with chat about land management, as if we've all got acres of our own. Heard he had a bit of a crush on the girl who worked here before me. But she got fired for stealing, so that was a non-starter.'

I leaned forward and gripped the bar when she said that, she was in her stride now.

'And the oldest one, she hired the pub the night before her wedding and her guests trashed the place. One guy started smashing wine bottles on the floor and then chucked ten-pound notes at me when I told him to stop.' The door opened, and she straightened up, seeing a group of young guys coming in. 'They didn't always come in with their dad. Jemimaah,' she drawled the name 'got pretty friendly with Luke – supposedly they had a thing a few years ago, before I started, and she bitched about her dad all the time to him. He was there the night Anthony died actually, working as a waiter at the dinner.'

I felt a jolt of excitement. 'Is he around?' I asked quickly, before the new arrivals grabbed her attention. She laughed. 'Not tonight, but he'll be on shift tomorrow. What are you? Some kind of journalist?'

'Oh, much more than that,' I said as I finished my drink and handed her a fiver. 'I'm a detective.'

OLIVIA

What a relief it was to be home. From the moment I arrived, the staff and my friends rallied round me. The house was festooned with condolence flowers and thoughtful cards from far and wide. Someone even sent a balloon display shaped like a Champagne bottle, which was so entirely inappropriate that I burst out laughing at the sight of it. No note, perhaps it was from an admirer testing out the waters? I used to have rather a lot of them, even if Anthony insisted that men only flirted with me to get closer to him.

Leandra came over with her breathwork master, and though I always rolled my eyes at her penchant for woo-woo therapists, I must say that we had the most calming hour together. He told me, very perceptively, that I was carrying the weight of the world on my diaphragm and urged me to exhale any toxic energy I detected in my body. He wasn't to know that I'd left the toxic energy behind at Gables, in the form of my offspring.

I didn't feel it appropriate to take up dinner invitations or be seen out publicly before the funeral, especially as there was still so much press interest, but I couldn't simply sit in my house with the curtains drawn like a less begrimed Miss Havisham, could I? Life must go on. Some people revel in grief, don't they? Mourning someone who's been gone for decades to the point where it becomes their entire identity. Not me. I decided to let my close friends know I was available for some much-needed fun. That was giving Anthony more respect than he'd have given me, let me assure you. If I'd been the one to die, he would've forgotten I'd ever existed within a matter of months depending on which woman turned his head next, and months is optimistic.

As a result, I had as many friends over as possible, the highlight being when Margot Lemaire and her husband stopped by for lunch with their adorable American friend Bruce Patron who apologised profusely for intruding at such a sad time. I usually find Americans to be slightly crude, and the mysterious insistence so many of them have on wearing attire more appropriate for the golf course was always troubling, but Bruce was charm personified and lightened the mood immensely. It didn't hurt that Margot told me about his wonderful Art Deco mansion in Newport Beach at the same time I noticed he wasn't wearing a wedding ring. When they left, I told him to get in touch when he was next in town and he looked very pleased indeed.

Clara returned to London in order to go back to school (the only one to insist she would never go to boarding school, and back then, I'd foolishly agreed) but I didn't hear from the others and nor did I want to. Normally Clara would rarely emerge from her room when at home, but something had changed, and it felt like she was now watching me the whole time. I wondered if she was waiting for the right time to sneak into my dressing room and 'borrow' some jewellery. Her glowering presence didn't stop my mood getting a little brighter each day. It was the little things, like a special painting sent over by Lucas Bergoni, a thank-you for Anthony always championing his work. Roberto even offered me his villa in Sorrento if I needed to get away and regroup. I was sorely tempted. It's known as one of the finest houses in Italy, with several Canalettos lining the staircase. But Charles reminded me that there was a funeral to be planned. He didn't add, but I could see it in his eyes, that it would look bad for me to flit off to the sunshine mere days after my husband had died. Bucket of cold water poured over the offer by my brother notwithstanding, it helped me see that I was not, as I had always been told by my husband, merely his plus one.

In an odd way, I felt as if I'd been released from a job I'd hated. Being married to Anthony was a round-the-clock gig with no days off. It certainly hadn't been advertised like that in the beginning. He'd come into the shoe shop I worked in one quiet afternoon, and found me trying on some vertiginous velvet yellow platforms. I didn't notice him at first, too entranced with how I looked in the mirror; my god I was lovely. When I turned round, he was leaning against the door, arms folded, smirking. He wanted some ballet pumps for his mother, he'd told me, only he didn't really know what they were. Even after I fixed him up with the style she'd requested, he lingered. The shop was never busy, and I found myself sitting down with him and laughing as he mocked the people walking by. Of course, I gave him my number, he was strikingly handsome and incredibly charismatic. Always has been, which helped cover his multitude of flaws. The first year was a dream, he was so different from the men I'd grown up knowing. They were endlessly polite but always just a little dull. Slightly pink in the face and with little of what my mother would have called 'spunk'. Anthony was ambitious, aggressively so, and he made things happen. We travelled endlessly and spent excessively, everything was just for fun – not a minute was wasted on anything he considered dull. And he was so generous and complimentary that I quickly allowed myself to believe my life was always going to be that easy.

Both of our mothers disapproved. His because I imagine she'd wanted him to marry a homely Irish girl and mine because Anthony was 'too brash', as she said once. I knew what she meant, but that was exactly what I wanted. The two women barely acknowledged each other before or after the ceremony, just stared at each other in deep suspicion. We laughed about it at the time. 'Like two old cats wondering whether or not to hiss first,' Anthony had said.

You marry a man like that at a cost. He always put himself first. With work, with his penchant for risk and with his inability to refrain from pursuing other women. All the time meanwhile, I was expected to stay looking as I did when he met me, which takes up an increasing amount of time and is a hard thing to get right (my good friend Clarissa Montello is one more facelift away from looking like a Renaissance baby) while also running three houses, raising the children and acting as the perfect companion whenever required. I was at every function, game for every adventure, and I would listen to his rants whenever work got hard, or a rival became more successful. Great men have egos the size of planets but skin as thin as silk, and you learn to your cost that the combination is always a disaster.

THE SLEUTH

@thesleuth
8.8k subscribers

Some evenings can drag on forever, and the only way to make them less dull is to have a drink and fall down internet rabbit holes. Find a good one, like researching whether or not the *Titanic* really sank, and you can go for hours. That night, I'd stumbled across a Victorian poisoner who drugged people with wedding cake, before I fell asleep on the sofa. By the time I'd drunk three cups of tea and scarfed down some toast the next morning, I felt pretty much human again. I browsed the day's news stories. The media still couldn't get enough of Anthony Wistern, covering everything from who he'd dated (some super-model who painted the word 'prick' in red nail varnish on his car when she found out he was married) to how much he'd once spent on Champagne (£100k, at a bar in Monaco for the Grand Prix, spraying most of it on the diners below). The tell-all from his mistress had been excellent for my view count. If he really had been planning to leave his wife, then that certainly put her

119

in the picture as a suspect. Scorned partner, it's a classic true-crime trope for a reason.

I couldn't avoid taking Mum to the doctors and then ferrying her to a coffee afternoon at the respite centre, where I was told repeatedly by a woman called Melanie in a scarlet jumper with the word 'Strong' written across the chest that I must carve out time to have fun too. When I finally sat down and checked my inbox, there was still no response from my 'source', which was so frustrating. What did Freddy have going on that was more important? I thought about messaging the crime collective – there was normally a text group in daily use – but they were currently all on a brief hiatus while Geoff had a hernia operation, and a small voice told me not to offer anyone else the chance to get credit. Being part of a group meant following a leader, and I felt like I could do better by myself. It was time to confront Freddy.

ANTHONY

My wife got the call about my post-mortem results midway through a Pilates session with her trainer. I used to join them occasionally before work, until Liv realised I was spending more of the sessions eyeing up Lara than I was stretching. After that, she'd moved the time of the lesson. No slouch, that woman. She'd answered mid-pose, her head between her legs, and given a brief smile.

'Accidental death, inquest to follow, but that'll be months away. We can bury him as soon as possible,' she'd told Lara, before going straight into a rather aggressive plank.

She didn't seem at all fazed by this momentous news, even keeping up her lunch plans while I sat by the monitors eating a sausage sandwich and seriously considering vegetarianism for the first time in sixty years. My chauffeur Ryan picked her up, he'd been with us for over ten years and the man knew all my secrets. Well, nearly all of them. A good driver is a godsend, someone who can get you from A to B *and* provide a sounding board with no judgement. Of course he'd signed an NDA, but even without it, I'd trust the man more than most of my close friends. I think he was probably sadder about my demise than most of them, even if I couldn't list a single personal detail about him.

As Olivia walked towards the car, her phone rang and she stopped to answer it. I was taken aback by how much younger my wife looked, not just in her face but in her demeanour. She was lighter somehow. I didn't have a chance to dwell on what that meant, because in that moment I saw her, the girl loitering just feet away from our house, almost sunk into the neighbour's hedge. Holland Park is often awash with stray tourists from Notting Hill and the market, seeking out the beautiful houses to use as backgrounds for their photos, but this girl was different. She looked faintly familiar - a journalist? No. The stories were still running, but the freelance photographers had somewhat dissipated in the days since my death, currently captivated by the news that some old pop star died while having sex with a woman young enough to be his granddaughter. He'd had a heart attack while orgasming and she was happy enough to give them constant pap walks and tell reporters every single detail. My story was dull by comparison, which made me feel a little sad. When they found out I'd been murdered, I reassured myself, there'd be a certain boost in attention – a murder was sexier, perhaps even more so than a man dying during actual inter-course. The girl was looking intently in the direction of my wife, eyes wide like she'd seen a celebrity. Olivia gabbed away on her phone, noticing nothing. After a minute, she walked quickly towards Olivia, holding up her phone and pointing it straight at my wife and I suddenly had the feeling that Liv was in terrible danger. But nothing happened. She slid into the car without a glance at the girl and they drove off. But as I followed Liv's journey, I swivelled my head back and saw her running towards the car for a second. She gave up as they rounded the corner; Ryan never took seriously the patronising '20mph is plenty' signs dotted around London, and the girl never stood a chance. But the look on her face had suggested intense feeling. I didn't like it at all. Had she been sent by one of them? Was she going to tell my wife everything?

THE SLEUTH

@thesleuth

18.7k subscribers

The video of me confronting Anthony's wife netted me 95,000 views on the first day. I'd like to say I planned it perfectly but it had all been a spur of the moment thing. I'd messaged Freddy again, telling him I'd turn up at Gables if he didn't reply, and that got his attention. At 3 a.m., I got a response – not by text, he was clearly intent on covering his tracks – but from the anonymous email account. Freddy wasn't particularly subtle. 'Why does Olivia keep talking to Charles about "sticking to the plan?" Why is she having meetings . . . Another one this afternoon, what's it about?' I knew Charles was Olivia's brother from news reports, Fred must be in London after all. I'd sent several messages back but again, no response. Gables could wait. I had to go to London and see what was going on for myself.

The Wistern house was the grandest place I'd ever seen, if you disregarded the old National Trust properties my mum used to drag me round when I was little. Even as a kid, I remember thinking it was a weirdly humiliating thing to pay to have a peek at how the ultra-rich had lived. I'd have given a lot to see inside this house though. Six storeys, with multiple balconies on an impossibly picturesque square where every single property was painted a different pastel shade. The Wisterns had opted for pale pink. Did the neighbours have meetings to make sure they coordinated? What if someone painted their place bright orange? This wasn't real life, it was a place for rich people to escape real life. A man in a hi-vis jacket brushed up beside me, slowing his pace, and I flinched, thinking he was a policeman. He paused, eyeing me up as if storing my face in his mind. As he walked on, I noticed the back of his jacket said 'Private Security'.

When I reached the house, there was a lone photographer waiting around outside who seemed happy to answer my questions. 'I've been waiting to get a bit of footage of one of them looking weepy, always money in the bank.' He'd laughed before adding forlornly, 'People keep coming round, but she's not been out yet.' I asked whether or not he thought Anthony Wistern's death was really an accident, with a meaningful look he completely failed to pick up on. 'Don't think there's anything nefarious, darling, he got sloshed and then spiked. To be honest, I'm only here cos I'm meeting my mates in Shepherd's Bush later.' The British press, taking the official explanation hook, line and sinker.

After thirty minutes, he pushed off. I took out my phone and started recording, speaking quietly in case the security guard came back and stopped me. 'I'm standing outside the home of Anthony Wistern. As you know, he died at his sixtieth birthday party. *Apparently* he walked down to the lake, jumped off a jetty and impaled himself on a spike placed there to hold a giant glowing orb.' I made sure to make this sound sarcastic. 'The police say it's an accident. They think we're stupid. We're not. Anthony was a problem for someone, clearly. But who? That's what we don't know yet. But we do know a woman was in the summerhouse that evening, don't we?'

I heard a door slam, and then, like I'd conjured her up, Olivia Wistern emerged onto the street. 'Anthony's wife is just yards away from me,' I managed to say, 'she's clearly going somewhere important with this guy.' Then something amazing happened. She laughed. The woman let out a fucking melodic titter and her face lit up with what looked a lot like glee. I was filming her at an angle where you couldn't quite see she was on the phone and it made her look a bit unhinged, which I was pleased with. 'That's the look of grief, everybody,' I managed to say as she got into the car and drove off. Without thinking, I started running, chasing the car like I was running a race. I thought it would look so good on camera, everyone loves a bit of live action. Unfortunately, my body took offence at this sudden burst of movement, and I only managed to get to the end of the street before I had to stop.

After the wheezing subsided, I managed to croak out a few words for the video. 'Something's not right here, I can see it, I know you all see it. We're fed up with crimes going unpunished. If they can do it to each other, just imagine what they can do to you.' Still feeling like I might keel over, I signed off with a flourish. 'This has been The Sleuth, subscribe to my account for new updates coming soon.' I felt pretty proud of the name. It made me sound commanding. On the drive home, I rehearsed possible catchphrases, trying to find one that felt right. I settled on 'uncover everything' but suspected I could do better.

The numbers were slow that evening, but when I checked the news the next morning, it turned out the autopsy results had been made public and someone had linked to my video in a true crime forum, making the numbers go mad. I'd had 200,000 views overnight and the comments were pretty amazing, all from people who got what I was doing and wanted to support me. They praised my bravery and told me to keep on digging. I even got a private message from a fan offering me money. 'You nailed that, showing her living it up before her husband's even in the ground. Don't let them get away with it.' It felt so good to be recognised for my work, and for a while I just refreshed the screen, watching the view numbers go up. Then I shook myself out of my ego trip and realised what it this meant. They'd somehow managed to fudge the autopsy – accidental death? There was no way. Just like with Dad, the powers that be had seen all the red flags blowing in the wind and turned their heads the other way. I'll admit, I gave serious thought to kicking my laptop off the bed in that moment, stopping only because I knew I was already pushing my luck with the existing crack. Instead, I got to work, renaming the video – 'Olivia smiles at autopsy result'. The audience clearly thought she was guilty as sin, and it was never a bad thing to give them more of what they wanted. But the crime community moves on quickly if there's no new information. I had to feed them constantly and for that, Freddy needed to step up.

OLIVIA

Things were coming together fairly nicely, all things considered. The post-mortem result was a huge relief, allowing things to move forward without the shadow of scandal. Anthony's lawyers had met with Charles and me to apply for probate and appoint my brother as executor. In truth I was surprised my husband had chosen Charles for the role, given his dislike of my brother was no secret. Anthony would often start snoring the moment Charles walked into a room, leaving my normally unflappable brother red in the face. I suspect it was done to bog Charles down with hours of unpaid work. But my brother would be able to deal with everything in a speedy manner, and naturally I wanted nothing to do with it given what was about to happen.

Once probate was granted, I'd arranged for the family to have dinner at Tanners where the will would be read. Anthony always waved me away when I told him he had to get his affairs in order. And not the fun kind, I'd added, which made him blanch. Like most men, he didn't like to think of himself as anything other than immortal. When he turned forty and had a wobble about the newly emerging greys in his hair, he'd spent a few months seriously looking into cryogenics – 'death is a human weakness, Liv' – only deciding against it when I showed him an article about the company whose refrigeration had failed one long weekend, leaving all 89 bodies not only still dead but now distinctly soggy. He'd looked a bit green at that, and the idea had never been mentioned again.

He had made a will in the end, and while he'd never explicitly said where he intended his fortune to go, I'd always assumed it would be me. But that was before I knew the truth, and of course he never suspected I would have that information. Instead, he'd drop little jokes about how I'd be a very happy widow when the time came. He dangled it in front of the children too, playing them off against each other for fun, promising one of them more than the others just to see them all turn on the chosen one or suddenly spend more time with their father in a naked display of desperation. We were all tied to the man, dependent on him to maintain the only lifestyle we'd known. And didn't he just revel in it?

In some ways, I was almost relieved that there was nothing for the children now. None of them had ever worked seriously or made any attempt at independence, which meant they'd have only frittered an inheritance away in a variety of absurd and inane ways.

The cautionary tale was that of Alice Russell's son Max. When Tom Russell died, he left the bulk of his fortune to their only son, an odd boy who seemed to spend his entire childhood making model boats. He'd brought down his latest effort to show his parents at a dinner party one night and Anthony didn't endear himself to Alice when he pointed out there was no way the thing was watertight, causing Max to flee the room in tears. But even a hobby should be done well, this was papier-mâché and had gaping holes in the hull. Much worse was to come. After spending years making larger and larger models, at 24, Max built a new type of floatable which he announced he'd be sailing across the Atlantic to raise awareness of rising sea levels. The thing cost nearly four million quid to build but as far as I could see, had mainly been constructed out of water bottles. His voyage was followed avidly on social media, right up until it sank. The last message from Max was one asking his mother to charter a private plane to pick him up, which caused considerable mockery on the internet and even made him into a meme. I would die if one of my children became a meme. I'd rather they were destitute.

I knew it would be very hard for my children to learn they were on their own. And for that reason, I wanted to be there when they were told. Of course I wouldn't be *openly* triumphant about it. I even intended to tell them that my own will would benefit them, but only if they acted with respect. None of them had ever treated me with anything beyond mild disdain, and if it took money to get them to behave better then I'd happily wield it over their heads for the rest of my life. Just as Anthony had done to me. We would convene at Tanners, and my children would have a nasty shock. Thinking about it made me feel more optimistic than I had in years.

ANTHONY

If you ever find yourself at the corner of Waldon street and Lyon mews, you could do worse than spend a few minutes watching the patrons of Tanners as they enter and leave. It's one of the oldest and stuffiest restaurants in London, and the people who frequent it are an interesting bunch to observe. It felt good to be back at Tanners, you just know where you are at a place like this. They served King Charles II and some of his many mistresses in the Salon Vert. They opened every day during the Blitz, even as the buildings next door collapsed. Nothing can shock this establishment, not even the time Hugo Lowestoft tried to bring his pet goat into the dining room one afternoon. The manager had greeted both Hugo and Jeremy, since that was the goat's name, welcomed them calmly, and then took the bemused creature to the back offices where a Waldorf salad was delivered to him personally by the head chef.

As Ryan drops Liv off outside, I can see Sir Llewellyn Clark and his wife slowly climbing the steps of Tanners as they have every Thursday for decades. He holds a walking stick topped with an ivory elephant, which feels brave. She is one metre behind

131

him, in a pale lilac skirt suit made by the same tailor Her Majesty uses, I know this because Liv used to wonder why anyone wanted to look like the Queen. 'Take away the crown and she's just an old lady in bad shoes.'

As if by magic, the manager has appeared, hovering by the door to greet such a special guest. As Olivia exits the car, he rushes down with an umbrella. She looks as elegant as ever, her blonde hair pulled back in a low ponytail and fixed with a small black ribbon. She greets the manager as though he were an old friend, placing her hand over his in a slightly regal way.

Olivia had told the children that attendance was non-negotiable, but the edict wasn't necessary. None of them would've missed the will reading. Five minutes after my wife entered the restaurant, my eldest daughter turned up. Jemima lingered on the bottom step for a minute, her phone to her ear, striding back and forth in a slightly agitated way. By the time I zoomed in on her, she'd hung up and walked up to the entrance, raising her eyes at the elderly doorman who took just a fraction too long to open the large oak door. Jemima looked, I'm sorry to say, dull. She certainly had expensive tastes, but unlike Olivia or her sisters, never seemed to know what suited her. Will turned up just a couple of minutes behind her, which felt odd. Why hadn't they come together? Normally I wouldn't pay him much attention, the man was a black hole of charisma. But today he looked harassed, and I wondered whether he might cause any trouble. Unlikely of course, his nature almost forbade it, but perhaps he was in a worse position than I'd thought.

Ten minutes later Clara strolled up the steps. As was her wont, the girl was wearing an entirely inappropriate mesh dress. I waited for the manager to say something, but of course he didn't; a Wistern didn't need to adhere to the dress code. She was texting furiously – no surprise there – and I was quicker to zoom in this time, catching a glimpse of the conversation. The name meant nothing to me, but the message was intriguing. She stopped to take a selfie on the steps, throwing up a peace sign and pouting in front of the famous doors. The notorious womaniser Charles II would surely have approved.

Freddy was fifteen minutes behind schedule. London had always overwhelmed him, which baffled me – a boy should revel in all the city offered – and every time he returned, he dealt with it by wearing ugly noise-cancelling headphones and keeping his head down. I could see by the doorman's face that he imagined my son was going to ask for directions, and had to tamp down his surprise when Fred told him he was there for the Wistern dinner. That night he was wearing a shirt I recognised. It had been given to him by an ex-girlfriend, one who'd stuck around longer than any of the others, until she realised his world promised less glamour and more composting than she'd imagined and gave up. Secretly I'd been pleased. It took more than a keen eye for a fortune to claim a seat at our table.

Last to arrive, well over half an hour late, was Lyra. Living in Paris for so long had apparently changed her body clock, and my middle daughter constantly underlined how suburban it was to think about having dinner earlier than 9 p.m. She'd dressed down, clearly to annoy her mother. Trainers would certainly do the trick. Since Lyra was the last to arrive, I followed her inside, feeling an excitement at watching what would inevitably be a family punch-up. A stooped old man in a plum red waistcoat took her through the main restaurant and ushered her into the private dining room, heaving the oak door open with a huge effort to reveal my family. All seated in near silence.

The room was undeniably beautiful in a fusty sort of way. The staff always made a point of telling you about the ancient silk wallpaper, artfully illuminated by the candles flickering on every surface available. Thick red curtains were closed to cancel out noise from the busy Soho street, giving the room a claustrophobic feel. It was a place undeniably designed for the old money crowd, though more recently I'd noticed a suspicious number of loafer-clad men and women in branded clothes coming in for dinner. This clientele brought with them their new money, and were tolerated, but never given the best tables. Instead, they were seated over in the left-hand corner of the dining room, and the lights were dimmed ever so slightly in that part of the restaurant. 'Hopefully that'll dull the shine of their watches,' shuddered my wife, when she'd learnt of the new approach.

I was under no illusion that we were old money. Nobody is truly old money now, apart from a vanishingly small number who inherited their fortune and didn't piss it away in pursuit of pleasure. The rest of them have receding chins and large cold houses they can't afford to heat, venerated simply for their name, much like my son-in-law's parents. In a way, our union had been the best of both worlds – Liv's family were well respected and I made the cash, and that meant we could bypass most of the snobbery which normally surrounded such recent wealth accumulation. We never made it all the way up to the highest ranks. There were certainly some people who would always see us as middle class and gauche to boot, but I think we juggled it well. Liv might've longed for an elusive invite to Launsingham Castle, but we'd been on holiday with tech billionaires and angel investors, and as I always told her, they were the new global royalty.

It was a sign of our success that she'd managed to book the private room at such short notice; I'd overheard the manager reminding an underling to send flowers to the people we'd taken the booking off and was amused to hear it was Rohan Puri and his wife. I wished I could tell Liv, she'd have been thrilled to know she was more deserving of a table than the man who bought a yacht so large, a bridge in Denmark had to be dismantled in order for it to sail freely.

My eyes went straight to Olivia, sitting right between two of our daughters. She was ignoring all of them, her eyes on the door. As if on cue, Charles walked in, holding a leather binder and looking, as usual, like he'd just been to a three-day conference on workplace safety. I'd made Charles my executor just a month before I died, when I knew what was coming down the pipeline and wanting to make him suffer a little, but I didn't expect him to appoint himself head of my family. I didn't like the way he put the binder down on the table slowly and precisely, just so they couldn't fail to miss his role here.

A trio of waiters came in silently and formed a ring around the table, pouring Champagne into crystal flutes. You don't even ask for Champagne at Tanners, they just bring it and you're grateful. Olivia almost manages to drain her glass before anybody else has picked theirs up – the woman has a remarkable capacity to drink without the godawful hangovers I'd come to expect as I aged. There's nothing of her, I've never understood where she puts it. Perhaps her liver, like the rest of her, is steel coated.

She offered up her glass to the waiter for a refill, and lifted it in a toast. 'To your father, a brilliant man.' I knew better than to think she'd leave it there, and I was right. 'A selfish, steamroller of a man. A man who made me feel like I was queen of all I surveyed but who also had the capacity to treat me as if I were an irritant, a barnacle, a shackle he couldn't escape. He never made it easy. Who knows? Maybe easy would've been dull.'

Once again she refused to treat my death with the solemnity it deserved. Some wives of powerful men used to throw themselves into the freshly buried grave and get interned with their husbands when they died. But here she was, smiling just a little too brightly for it to be comfortable. And she was wearing the bloody ring.

For Christ's sake, Olivia, I bellowed, only to be shushed by an officious woman in a grey suit who happened to be walking past and who reminded me that speaking when watching the living is not allowed. They delight in referencing the rules here. You'd think death would be the one thing to free you of bloody red tape, but if anything, there's more here.

She'd worn it on purpose, she wanted them to notice it. No regard at all for safety that woman, any number of nefarious chancers would slice off her finger to get that stone, but here she was, just waving it around proudly. Jesus, sometimes I think she *lives* to make my life harder. Had any of them noticed it yet? The only person I saw lock eyes on the ring was my son-in-law. Will was practically twitching, such was his reaction. It made me nervous.

They raised their glasses. I looked at my children and saw Jemima drinking water. I was not the only one to see it, Clara pounced the moment her mother had stopped speaking. 'Are you fucking *pregnant?*' she squealed, jabbing a finger at her oldest sister, who suddenly looked uncomfortable. 'OMG, you are! You're going to get so fat. Are you going to have a C-section? You should, you don't want to push a baby as big as Fred out of you, disaster for your vag.' Once Clara had finished her night-marish teenaged screed, Jemima turned to the rest of the table and gave what I think was supposed to be a smile but looked more like a grimace. 'Obviously all of this tragedy has been incredibly stressful – I've been very worried about the baby, but he seems to be doing well. A little bruiser, like his dad.' All eyes apart from Jemima's doubtfully swivelled towards Will. Why was Lyra smirking? My son-in-law, having finally managed to tear his eyes away from my wife's finger, looked dazed. He might be many things, though none of us could ever tell you what they were, but a bruiser he was not. Staring at him a little closer, I could see just how tired he looked. There were dull green circles under his eyes, and his normally bountiful hair was now markedly thinner. A sign of low testosterone, I've always thought, nothing I've ever had a problem with. Practically overflowing with the stuff, could start a donation bank for it.

He plastered on a smile as the family congratulated him. 'All very exciting of course. New life, even as we mourn those we've lost.'

Jemima intercepted, not keen for the attention to be on someone else. 'It's certainly a surprise. We weren't totally sure Will was firing to be honest, but here we are. Maybe Dad is watching over us and wanted to send us all a little hope in the form of this miracle baby.'

I chuckled at that. Apart from the naked cynicism of her marking a pregnancy that clearly began before I died as some kind of gift from the afterlife, she obviously didn't know how little power I had up here. I couldn't even work out how to get warm. You'd think I wouldn't have to think about such things, but I'd been freezing for weeks now, and nobody seemed to care. The girl with the clipboard just rolled her eyes when I asked her. 'Did I know how many people she was processing that morning? Four hundred apparently, since the Herefordshire centre was on strike. In life, I'd have given her a wad of cash and told her to get me a solution, but here, I had nothing to offer. The idea that I couldn't even get warm was further proof that none of us have any idea about what happens after you die. And that's probably for the best, people would develop a pretty serious death phobia if they knew about the drones which turned up when you least expected, their red eyes glowing as they made sure you weren't trying to do anything untoward.

Olivia was clearly peeved at the attention being wrenched away from her speech, and also from the rock the size of a quail's egg on her left hand. 'That's lovely news, darling,' she said, smiling but not making eye contact with anyone. 'It'll be a nice change for you to have something to do all day.' Despite constantly insisting her table-scaping business was on the verge of success, she hadn't truly done a single day's work since her ill-fated attempt at a jewellery line she set up right out of university and which I'd bankrolled. She'd launched with a decent fanfare; Olivia made sure her necklaces were featured in the right places, and for a few months the jet set wore 'Jems' enthusiastically. But nobody actually bought the stuff, she just gifted it all to people she thought would be 'great brand ambassadors' and the company was never out of the red. I closed it down the moment it became clear the factory she was using to manufacture her designs used child labour. I appreciated their reasoning, the kids had small fingers, perfectly designed for working with fiddly gemstones, but while you can get away with most things if you claim ignorance and pay the inevitable fine, for some reason child labour is still a big no-no for most people.

They talked a little more about the impending baby, but even Jemima could tell none of them were truly interested. There's nothing much to say about a baby, even when it's your own. I much preferred it when they were old enough for boarding school. Gave us a proper chance to miss them. People criticise the upper classes for many things, but sending their kids away to school was a genius idea. Clara ended the conversation with a risky crack about my wife now being a grandmother. Luckily for her, the main courses arrived mere seconds later, and Olivia pretended not to hear it. I realised my daughter and Will had barely exchanged a look or a word throughout the baby discussion. How strange.

Nobody ate much. The food at Tanners is not the reason people come here. Apart from the risotto, a reluctant modern addition, the menu was almost identical to that of a hundred years ago. Stodgy, dated and swimming in sauce, much like the clientele. Will is sitting with his head bowed, eyes unfocused. Charles, who has looked doubtfully at the overcooked piece of unidentifiable meat on his plate and decided to speed-eat bread rolls, lets out that awful cough of his and suggests he start reading the will. Everyone nods a little too eagerly.

My brother-in-law goes through the formalities with an enthusiasm that only he could have for terms and conditions. Then comes the smaller stuff, the items none of them will want but will be forced to pretend to be grateful for. They endure twenty minutes of this, Charles reading out a variety of ridiculous gifts I chose for each of them, and I watch to see how long they can bear it before one of them breaks and asks about money. Oddly, it was Fred who crumbled first. As Charles was detailing the precise number of ties my son would inherit (406, with the condition they be boxed carefully and steamed twice a month), he shoved his chair back and walked over to the window, pushing it open and gulping fresh air. 'How long do we have to do this? He's fucking with us, can't we just get to the main event and stop pretending any of us are here for anything else?'

I was grudgingly impressed; Fred didn't normally show any sign of a backbone. This first act of bravery by my son galvanised the others, and Charles reluctantly agreed to send over an itemised list of everything I'd bequeathed to each family member. I was disappointed not to see Clara's face when she discovered I'd left her my father's collection of encyclopaedias.

Fred returned to the table and more wine was poured – they were certainly getting through it. Charles pushed his glasses slightly down his nose and continued. 'Now the post-mortem has been done, hopefully it should be smooth sailing from here on.' He broke off as Clara let out a snort of derision and muttered something about a cover-up, but the others shushed her, keen to get to the good stuff. 'I direct that any outstanding debts be paid by my executor, Charles Holdwood, and authorise him to distribute my assets as I have set out. For my children Frederick, Jemima, Lyra and Clara, I have left trust funds to be accessed only when they reach their thirtieth birthdays. Lainey Goodman is to receive £500,000 as thanks for her hard work and dedication.' There was a collective hiss around the table, Olivia trying very hard not to look appalled, and failing. I think I actually saw teeth being bared.

'All other assets are bequeathed to my wife Olivia Wistern.' I looked over to my wife, expecting to see pleasure. Instead, she was leaning back in her seat, twisting the ring around her finger, her face entirely blank. Where was the gratitude? Charles produced his familiar cough, which made everyone wince. 'Well, at least he had good intentions.' She said nothing, smiling in a rather unnerving way. What *was* going on?

My children on the other hand, were going mad. They were talking over each other, peppering Charles with questions he couldn't answer. Jemima's face was screwed up in disbelief, her hands balled so tightly her knuckles were white.

'So we get nothing but the trusts? And we can't even touch them yet? That's insane.'

Lyra looked angry now, her usual affected nonchalance all gone. 'How much have we got? Dad was always vague about it, but I assume it's generous given Olivia's been promised everything else.' She looked at her mother in a sort of accusatory way, as if she'd been cheated somehow.

'Olivia, what's the plan until then?' Jemima now, whose eye was twitching. 'Your first grandchild is on the way, he'll need a lot of support.' Will was nodding fervently here, a sheen of sweat visible on his forehead. This set Lyra off, telling her sister that a baby didn't make her claim any stronger, and the two of them wasted no time in beginning to tear strips off each other. Freddy got up abruptly and walked over to the window again, breathing heavily. My wife just sipped her wine as if bored by the thought of inheriting millions. I had the odd sense that Olivia was one step ahead of me somehow, not a feeling I was used to, and it made me very uncomfortable. *What do you know?*

The dessert is being brought in, which demands a brief silence. My family will not debase themselves by arguing in front of service workers, but they are all itching to get back to the money, to make sure they get what they think they deserve. Will's hand is actually shaking slightly with anticipation.

Once the geriatric waiters leave, Olivia holds up a hand, the hand with the ring on it of course, why waste an opportunity? This time I see the desired reaction in each of my children's faces. Lyra is frowning, jealousy emanates off Jemima, and pure lust is all over Clara's face. Fred has left the room and I hadn't even noticed. Neither has anyone else. 'Now that his wishes have been read out,' Olivia says with an acid note, 'there's something you all need to know.' My wife looks at her brother, who gives her a short nod. 'Despite what the will *so generously* sets out, there's no money, not for any of us.' A single gasp from Jemima, her hand over her mouth. Olivia smiles at her, almost sympathetically. 'Your father was always a little too relaxed about ensuring your future security – did you know that? I had to sit him down when Clara was ten and tell him he needed to make sure you all had the funds you'd need, I *insisted* on it. He took the credit of course, reminding you all at any opportunity that he was going to leave you all extremely comfortable. But I'm afraid the money is gone, all gone!'

She said it with a flourish and dusted her hands together as if to drive the point home. I realised my mouth was as dry as an AA meeting. She knew. How did she know? Christ, what else did she know? She must be angrier than she'd ever been in her life, and I once saw her make a builder cry after he made the mistake of leaving his coffee cup on the floor. Why wasn't she throwing the table over and tearing down drapes with her bare hands?

I can't bear to watch but I can't look away. They are laughing now, telling her it's a poor attempt at comedy. Lyra is saying she can't spend the first 52 years of her life refusing to develop a sense of humour only to open with this. Now they change tack and yell at her but she refuses to answer their desperate questions. Charles takes it upon himself to handle the situation, with what appears to be a not insignificant amount of relish.

'Direct your anger at your father. Anthony was a careless man – with feelings *and* with finances. It looks like he emptied the trusts about six weeks before he died, all in one go. Obviously he's not here to tell us why, and as usual Olivia is having to deal with his poor choices.' He was in his absolute element here, almost vibrating with pomposity. Again, I racked my brains to try to figure out how they knew, but it was hard to think over the caterwauling coming from my offspring. Even Fred, who had reappeared, joined in, muttering about how much he hated me. As Will comforted Jemima who had broken out the inevitable waterworks, Lyra sidled up to her mother and was whispering something in her ear.

I could just about make out a snatch of it. '. . . and you had the *foresight* to sell all the good stuff. What a neat coincidence.' What was she banging on about?

The strange calm that has accompanied Olivia throughout the dinner slowly seeped away as I watched her listen to our daughter. She is gripping her wine glass so hard her knuckles have gone white. I lean in, trying to hear more of what's being said but it's hopeless while the others shout. My wife suddenly sinks to the floor, glass still in her hand. It shatters as she goes down.

One of the waiters comes in with coffee. He drops the tray and kneels down with difficulty to help her. Is she dead? I knew the news would be bad but even I didn't think Olivia would keel over. As a waiter who looks to be as old as Methuselah croaks out that she's breathing, my wife slowly opens one eye. She's fine. I stand up in a fury – this was supposed to be fun for me and she's ruined it. Before I turn off the monitor, I look at the scene one more time and realise that all four of our children have stayed exactly where they are. They sit with their arms folded, faces thunderous. And not one of them has gone to help their mother.

THE SLEUTH

@thesleuth
21k subscribers

I got a text from Freddy at 5 a.m., which woke me up *and* pissed me off. 'He was a prick, dn't waste ur time mourning him.' Was everyone in this family stupid or were they just utterly convinced of their own importance? Did he really think I was doing all of this because I missed his dad?

Texting me instead of using his stupid email address suggested he was blind drunk, and he didn't reply again until lunchtime, a little embarrassed and with only marginally better spelling. Why had he been so angry, I'd asked, why text me at the crack of dawn? A pause, and then a short reply. 'Been at the will reading.' Christ, it was like speaking to a teenager. And what? I pushed, did you not get eighty million pounds in gold bars delivered in sacks? 'There's no money,' he wrote back. And then another ping. 'Something fucked up is going on.'

OLIVIA

The funeral was organised with a precision that even I didn't possess. We'd engaged Reynauld & Sons, one of the oldest funeral firms in the city, who came highly recommended by Katherine Slake's husband. Her funeral had been lovely, and really only slightly dampened by the number of banana jokes floating around. I was given a wonderful planner, and though initially put off by her name and youth – nobody would instinctively have high hopes for an Amy-Anne – I'd been impressed from the first meeting. She instantly understood the need for security – telling me that a decoy hearse could be arranged to put the most zealous of journalists off the venue – and when I emphasised the need for an elevated atmosphere, she nodded vigorously. 'Don't worry, there won't be any carnations, I've got you.' I cut the Anne off her name and liked her more immediately.

The day before the funeral I awoke to blazing sunshine. Louisa brought in a cup of coffee and told me that my children were downstairs, which drastically dampened my mood. None of them had spoken to me much since the dinner at Tanners, not since they ascertained I wasn't likely to die anytime soon. Do you know, Jemima actually *asked* the doctor that very question? He'd answered with sympathy, thinking the question came from a place of worry and not one of sheer hope. No chance. Just as Jemima can cry on command, I trained myself to faint when the moment requires it. I started as a child when I wanted to stop riding, but really refined it when Anthony started going out later and later at night one summer before we got married. I've not used it in recent years, my husband became upsettingly immune to it, but it worked very well at Tanners. Stopped Lyra's nasty little comments immediately, she looked quite frightened when I began to keel. One night at the Princess Grace hospital where I was 'closely monitored' (given a glass of wine, a nice hot bath and eight hours of blissful sleep) before being discharged the next day. It was entirely worth it.

I had children because that's what you do when you're raised to get married and be a wife. Maybe if I'd not rushed down the aisle at twenty-one, I'd have found another life more appealing, but I knew nothing back then except that Anthony expected me to be at home. I vaguely appreciated that many women before me had fought for the right to work and pay their own bills, but deep down I thought that was like a turkey rooting for Christmas. The first two came in quick succession, Irish twins, as Anthony's mother used to say far too frequently. A plethora of nannies smoothed the path of motherhood and Anthony seemed to love me more than ever. Hence Freddy following Jemima so quickly. A boy! We all pretended we didn't mind what it was, but of course Anthony wanted a boy, men need to make things in their own image – just look at all the ugly phallic buildings rising up in London these days. He was a nightmare from the beginning, refusing to sleep and when he did, doing it with his eyes open so that you could never truly relax.

We took a break for a few years after that, scarred by the experience, but then Anthony fell in with Bijou Chabon. She was the one woman I think he might've left me for, a woman much like me in many ways but with one key difference – she was new. Then whoops! I was pregnant again, a clichéd way of making sure your philandering husband doesn't leave but effective nonetheless. Lyra's arrival meant hiring another nanny, since I wasn't about to stay at home in a baby bubble and let Anthony go about unchecked. I accompanied him to every party, every dull charity gala, wearing more shapewear than is advisable for your respiratory system and I dazzled, even when all I wanted to do was to spit venom in his face.

To dazzle was my only option. He always loved me most when I was a prize he could show off. That commitment I made to my marriage is the only reason Clara exists. By then I would happily have never clapped eyes on another baby again, but she was remarkably determined to make her way into the world regardless of my wishes. And now the four people I gave birth to were waiting downstairs. Four people I find in order demanding, strange, intimidating and annoying. Carrying on after one really was the perfect example of the sunk cost fallacy.

I took my time getting ready, I didn't need an upset right before the funeral. At our wedding, Anthony had commanded the attention, falling to his feet theatrically as I walked into the church, which ensured all eyes were on him as I made my entrance. What bride wants to be met with laughter as they go down the aisle? It didn't get any better as the day went on. He picked me up as we left the church, throwing me into the air. As a result, the first photos of us as a married couple are of my husband looking like a body builder while I'm a blurred mess somewhere above him. Our first dance was mainly him orchestrating a number of very dramatic moves around me which ended in him jumping on a table with a flourish to loud applause. People still talk about it: 'Is there no end to that man's talent?'

The funeral was to be *my* day. He'd have no chance to commandeer the attention, not unless he burst from the coffin in song, which I couldn't entirely rule out. 'Anthony survived weeks in a mortuary and surprised us all with a perfect rendition of "Nessun Dorma", even near death couldn't dim his light!'

Since Anthony's main assistant had made it known that their *relationship* was slightly more informal than it should've been, I'd had to call in our household PA to help organise the day. Agneta was decidedly less glamorous than Lainey, but I guess even my husband had felt he couldn't have his head turned by two employees, which was Anthony all over. Calculated risk. Hire two assistants, one for pleasure and one to actually do the job. Agneta once took in our old dog for six weeks when he'd had an operation and Anthony got tired of the incessant barking as he recovered. Even the bloody dog knew what it was like to fall short of his standards.

We'd been lucky to have a fast-tracked post-mortem. I'd tried everything to avoid having one at all, worried the procedure would delay the funeral, forcing us to spend even more time together as a family. Better to bury in haste and lament at leisure, as my father once quipped when his old trout of a mother died. But the officious detective had insisted on it, telling us there was no way to circumvent procedure. I didn't say, though she should've known, that there's always a way. It might not be fair, but only a fool with no life experience would deny it. If you have even a small degree of power, then fixed lines can easily be bent, into enormous squiggles if necessary. Our good friend Roger Simons had a word with the chief of police and though it still had to go ahead, it was done just three days later. We had to wait for the results, but the body was released to the funeral home immediately.

With a look of practised solemnity, the pallid director (from my limited experience of funeral directors, they always look like they've got one foot in their own grave) asked me if I wanted to see my husband and I said no immediately. Open caskets are appalling. When someone's gone, they're gone. I'd rather the coffin was nailed down, just to be certain it wasn't all some enormous joke he was playing. Like I said, it wouldn't have surprised me. My husband once spent eight months playing a game with his friend where they moved a small Picasso drawing between each other's houses, hiding it in increasingly absurd places until the housekeeper found it in her underwear drawer and brought it to me in tears, worried I would think she'd stolen it. Every joke went too far.

I teased my hair into its normal bouncy style while mentally ticking off the last details I needed to check with Agneta. The Oratory had been more than happy to accommodate us, thanks to my wonderful friend Renee, whose husband knew the friar personally and had emphasised my husband's strong Catholic roots and many charitable endeavours. In reality, the last time I'd seen him step foot in a church was for Clara's christening and we only did that because his mother insisted upon it. The woman lived in mortal fear that babies who weren't christened would end up in purgatory and it was easier to do it than to listen to her endlessly drone on about damnation over Sunday lunches. Fantastically, there'd been a cancellation, some wedding between a racing driver and a society girl got called off after, as Renee put it, the bride found out the groom was shagging his old nanny, and we managed to get a prime slot at 3 p.m. for the ceremony.

Satisfied with my appearance, I finally went downstairs to face my offspring. Louisa was in the hallway, hovering by a table festooned with flowers. She looked nervous as she hurried over to me. 'Your mother-in-law is in the garden room. With the children. She is very upset. I stopped them coming upstairs but . . . I'm sorry.' I frowned, and rubbed my temples. I'd not had to deal with Anthony's mother since he died, which had been an unexpected bonus of it all.

I entered the garden room and found my family in a state of what I can only describe as panic. I despise panic, it's so self-indulgent, and despite raising my children to internalise strong feelings, all of them except Freddy had completely disregarded my advice.

The girls were crowded around their grandmother, who was bent over, leaning against a chaise longue and breathing raggedly. For a moment I thought she must be dying, an idea which induced a tiny flicker of hope. But she looked up when she heard me come in, and I could see from her face that there was nothing wrong with her that a glass of her favourite gin wouldn't fix. Jemima was bright red, blotchy marks all over her face as though she'd been stung by bees and Lyra, who normally finds everything amusing, was slightly wild about the eyes. None of them seemed able to actually explain what was happening. It was down to Freddy to cut through the hysteria. Saying nothing at all, he walked over to me holding his phone. And then I understood.

NEWS ARTICLE

1 August 2018

Goldicocks and the bare-faced lies

Anthony Wistern, the wealthy banker found dead at his sixtieth birthday party last month, had been running a fraudulent fund which may have lost millions of investors' money, a police spokesperson said on Monday. Wistern, who was the CEO of Wismere Holdings, had reportedly set up a private fund for friends and acquaintances, promising them much higher returns than his legitimate business. Police said they'd begun investigating the fund several weeks ago, after an investor raised concerns about her money.

'We can confirm that we are looking into Mr Wistern's secondary business and would like anyone who may have given money to this man to get in touch with us as soon as possible. It's too early to say how many people might be affected by this, but it's certainly looking like fraud on a large scale,' said Superintendent Mark Rally, speaking to reporters this morning. A police insider told the *Daily Mail* that the initial list of those potentially affected is already past fifty.

'There will be many extremely wealthy people who've woken up today to find out they might have lost it all,' the source said. 'It'll be catastrophic for some. In a way, it's lucky for him he's already dead, you can see why there might be a few people who would've wanted to take on the job themselves.' Any suggestion that Mr Wistern's death was connected to his business dealings has been publicly dismissed by the investigations team, who reiterated that his death was being treated as an accident.

Mr Wistern was a well-known figure in the financial world. Two years ago, *The Sunday Times* rich list estimated his personal fortune at £54m and he was famous within wealthy circles for collecting both art and wine. Reporters at the family home in Holland Park this morning were told by a housekeeper that there would be no comment from the family, but Olivia Wistern's brother Charles Holdwood was seen entering the house alongside several other men.

Wistern's death and the subsequent news of alleged financial impropriety curiously echoes the story of Robert Maxwell, himself a larger than life character, who fell off his boat shortly before it was found that he'd stolen millions of pounds from his company's pension funds. An auction of his wine collection made $161,000 in 1992, the proceeds going to pay off his enormous debts.

See pp. 8–12 The Goldicocks Banker – how Anthony Wistern was raised in a two-bed semi and went on to mix with high society.

THE SLEUTH

@thesleuth
35k subscribers

The howl I let out was so loud that other shoppers in the self-checkout queue actually moved away from me. What did I fucking tell you? He *was* murdered, I knew it from day one and now here was a motive – clear as blue sky. I'd been waiting to pay for Mum's crumpets when I saw the headline. You've never seen anyone in my town move so fast – most of them *are* over seventy, mind – I dropped the basket in shock and ran into the street as if I was expecting the world outside to have changed somehow. When it became clear nobody else was paying attention, I turned to my phone and hit the go live button. My community would care, they'd be waiting for my take on the news. Looking back on it, the video turned out really good – I was so energised and raw and I think people really fed off that. None of it was polished like the mainstream media reports but I asked the most important question.

'Did anyone in his family know what was about to happen

153

to their cushty lives, because I don't know about you lot, but that feels like a pretty good motive to me.'

After my initial excitement died down I remembered to tell my fans to go and rewatch the Olivia video. 'Look closely at her face, guys, and ask yourselves – does that look like a woman who's really grieving? I've known loss, I'm sure you have too. When my dad passed away I could barely get out of bed, but this woman is dressed up to the nines and out and about a week after her husband dies? And what about the earring, gang? Someone left it there, are they panicking now?'

By 9 p.m., I'd had nearly a quarter of a million views. My videos were being reposted on every social media platform, and although some newbies were trying their luck with their own coverage, mine was the clear winner. I'd visited the scene, found new evidence, got raw footage of an actual suspect – nobody else could compete with just Wikipedia facts and an aerial shot from Google Maps now.

The phone buzzed. A message from Fred, telling me he'd be back at Gables right after the funeral. Boy, they were rushing that through, weren't they? I'd been trying a new tack, checking in on him and acting like I was concerned about his well-being. It seemed to have worked. 'Will be hiding out there for the rest of time, bring sustenance', which was actually kind of funny considering what he'd just learned about his dad. 'Name the date,' I'd replied. Finally, he was coming round.

ANTHONY

Oh Christ. If there's a good way to learn that your family now know what you've been up to, I'd like to hear about it. I found out when my name was called on the tannoy and I was summoned to the director's office. Good I'd thought, a chance to tell the head honcho what a terrible job he and his team were doing up here. I would read him the riot act, list every complaint I had about the place – and there were many. I arrived at his door and went straight in without knocking, to be greeted by Susan. She sensed my disappointment, perhaps the large huff gave it away.

'Yes, just me again. The director is tied up.' She smiled at me in a slightly disconcerting way, and instructed me to sit down, which I did with a grumble. 'I hope your stay here is progressing nicely. I know it's not at all what a man like you is used to, my apologies, but hopefully it won't be for too long, eh?' I nodded, and wondered why I was behaving like an obedient child when faced with this woman. She unfolded a pair of glasses and put them on. It still confused me as to why glasses were needed post death. You'd think your physical ailments would somehow correct themselves in the afterlife, but I still had a niggling pain in my ankle from a bad rugby tackle thirty years ago up here.

'We seem to have a little problem, Mr Wistern, but I'm sure you'll be relieved to hear I've taken care of it.' She spoke in clipped tones, and I realised she was attempting a power play. Perhaps Susan was a worthy opponent after all. 'It appears some news broke about you an hour ago. Normally we don't concern ourselves with living news – who wants to hear about the polar ice caps melting or listen to reports about how badly fucked the economy is?' She laughed at this, and I found myself joining in even though under the most recent government, the UK was doing very well indeed with their 'bonus austerity plus' campaign. She stopped laughing just as my chortles had reached a peak, leaving me feeling a little foolish. The smile had gone, replaced by a blank expression. She tucked a braid behind her ear and stared at me, right in the eyes. 'It seems you've been unmasked, Mr Wistern, getting up to things you shouldn't have been. I suppose a man as smart as you knew it was coming, didn't you? Lucky timing on the old dying thing it seems?' The smile was back, but I saw it for what it was, a taunt. 'You know what I'm talking about, don't you?' I nodded, unable to speak. 'I thought that might be the case. Thank you for being so cooperative, it'll make this all a lot easier.'

She pressed a buzzer on her desk and spoke. 'Melanie, can you bring in the form?' The smile had gone again. 'As I said, normally we wouldn't bother you with such things, after all, your misdeeds hardly concern you anymore, do they? You got away with everything scot free! Clever you.' This didn't sound like praise somehow. 'But we have a guest staying with us at the moment . . .' 'guest' was how they referred to us, as if this was Claridges and we were free to leave at any time. 'And he's put in a complaint. It's delicate, Mr Wistern, I'm sure you understand, but we don't like to have people share a living space with their victims. Or the family of their victims, I should say.' She giggled slightly at this, and I felt a little afraid of her. Women her age often hide madness, you rarely discover it until it's too late. The door opened and the woman called Melanie came in and handed my tormentor a clipboard with a sheaf of paper on it before going out again.

'Well, what's the problem?' I asked, crossing my arms, feeling petulant now. Susan leant forward and almost purred at me.

'I won't name names. Everybody has a right to privacy here. But this person is one of our longest-staying guests. And he saw the news today while watching his wife. He hadn't realised you were here you see, a bit of the old "dementia" going on and somehow he'd missed it. That's why he's been here so long.' She mouthed the words 'gaga gaga' at me, which even I thought was a bit much. 'He's very upset, I'm sure you understand. So for the sake of harmony, Mr Wistern, we're going to move you to a solitary room for the time being. Think of it as an upgrade, like I'm sure you've been waiting for.' Smiling again, she gestured for me to leave. I stood up with dignity, and managed to hold my tongue for once as I opened the door.

'Oh, by the way . . .' I looked back over my shoulder. '. . . Rather unsporting of someone to leak it to the press the day before your funeral, don't you think? I imagine the church won't be quite as packed as your wife's been expecting.' I slammed the door – I couldn't help it – and heard her laughter follow me as I stormed down the hall.

OLIVIA

Apparently you can't cancel a funeral with just a day's notice. The thought of having to sit through a ceremony for him while everyone around us whispered and judged felt impossible, and I begged Charles to bin the whole thing, let him be cremated at a suburban public facility and really show people we'd washed our hands of him. But Charles stood firm, telling me it would look entirely worse if we went into panic mode, and that righted me. Fairly quickly, the cancellations began to roll in. Two members of the Greek royal family (I'd always found their brazen insistence on using titles that had been binned off 50 years ago charming) pulled out the fastest. They were followed by the usual riff-raff of West London, titans of the finance community, several major philanthropists, and a tech giant who apparently owns half of San Francisco. Then came the close friends, who left gushing messages of support while apologising profusely for not being able to make the ceremony after all. 'Tabitha is really quite unwell, we don't feel comfortable leaving her.' 'I've got to fly to Rome first thing in the morning, something ghastly is going on with the office there, it's completely unavoidable.' Only one person told the truth. Isobel Duncan, who texted me to say she couldn't risk being photographed. 'It's terrible, Livvy, but I work too closely with investors.'

I'd phoned Giles almost immediately, wanting to know what he was doing about it all. Do I like my husband's business partner? The answer is complicated. I admire the man for putting up with Anthony all these years which I know from long personal experience is no easy feat. But he's dull. Sensible, serious and slightly reminiscent of a history teacher, albeit one with a mansion in Surrey and a collection of classic cars Anthony used to call his model railway equivalent. He picked up on the first ring, sounding clipped and formal and before I could even get a word out, told me he couldn't speak to me. 'There's a criminal investigation, Olivia. This isn't appropriate.' Then, in a lower tone, he hissed 'You *knew*, didn't you? Fucking hell,' before hanging up and leaving me standing in my dressing room almost reeling from the shock.

My children all slept over at the house. There were already a barrage of photographers outside and none of us wanted to be the first one on the front page with the inevitable 'disgraced family member breaks cover' headline attached. Charles told me the police would want to speak to me as soon as possible, but he'd managed to persuade them to hold off until after the funeral.

'It seems someone went to the papers before the investigation really got started. So they're on the back foot a little bit here, which helps us.'

I'd taken several sleeping pills and gone to bed, right after I'd called a cab for Anthony's mother. If I let her stay even just one night, I feared I'd be saddled with her forever and in the grand scheme of things, that would be the worst thing my husband had done by some measure. It helped that the press thought she was a staff member and didn't bother to take any photographs, the only time her beloved frumpy grey dress served any of us well.

The morning of the funeral I woke up feeling groggy and ancient. After an extended morning routine, which included icing my face until it stung, I dressed. A crepe black dress, spiky patent court shoes which looked faintly menacing, a cashmere coat and sapphire earrings which warmed my skin. I'd wanted to wear my diamond hoops, but one had gone missing at some point and despite making Louisa and Rosa turn both houses upside down in search of it, there had been no sign.

I went downstairs and greeted Amy-minus-the-Anne. Without any attempt at sympathy, she told me the cars would be ready in five minutes and stalked off, muttering into an earpiece. I could hear sobbing coming from the piano room. Clara.

'They're such bitches,' she cried, when she saw me come in. 'I asked Lyra if I could go live with her in Paris and she laughed at me.' She wasn't actually crying, I noticed, just shuddering with rage at being mocked, and hoping for pity.

'Calm down right now. Your eyes go horribly puffy when you get hysterical.' That only set her off again.

'None of my friends have texted me all morning and I'm supposed to go to a party tonight but how can I if I'm a social outcast?' She gave a snort of frustration and shook her head. The teenage narcissism was strong in my youngest child. I yanked her up from the sofa, and she yelped in protest. 'It's ok for you, you're old, but I'm just starting my life – if nobody wants to associate with me cos of this family I'll die.'

I lost my cool now, and Lyra must've heard me shouting, for she suddenly appeared at the door. 'We are burying your father today. There will be photographers, so you better go and fix yourself up. I will not have a single member of this family look anything less than perfect. They will *pounce* on anything, do you hear me? Do you *hear* me?' Clara shook my hands off and fled the room. I glanced over at her sister in some fanciful expectation of support, but Lyra just shrugged and followed her out.

I kept my head up as we left the house, leading my family down the steps and onto the street. A gaggle of shabby-looking journalists were swarming the cars despite the best efforts of the security team, yelling at us in the hopes we'd turn around.

'I'm sorry for your loss, Mrs Wistern,' one man wearing stonewashed jeans shouted, as though I'd turn and thank him for his worthless condolences. 'Did you know he was a crook?' 'Are you living off stolen funds, Olivia?' Nobody replied. We were doing so well until one of them shouted 'Give us a smile', and to my eternal regret, I whipped round and found myself practically snarling at the baying mob. I regretted it the moment I heard the cameras clicking at double speed. You might water-board a woman for her secrets to no avail, but tell her to cheer up and you'll meet a banshee.

At the entrance to the church, there were security guards in black suits on either side of the doors. It made Anthony's funeral look like a particularly exclusive night club, which I suppose he would've liked. As we walked down the aisle, I looked around to see who was in attendance. Just two days ago, we'd been fielding calls from people who hadn't made the cut, desperate for an invite, but most of the pews were almost entirely vacant.

As we neared the front of the church, I spied a tabloid news-paper editor, a singer Anthony once spent the evening with hitting golf balls off the stage at Wembley stadium before a concert, and finally our former prime minister. He only lasted 90 days in the position before resigning after a scandal engulfed him that even Anthony couldn't defend. Salad dressing, I ask you. If you must have a fetish, pick something that at the very least doesn't have an expiration date. Even before his downfall, neither of us had contemplated voting for him (he's fucked a jar and he's fucked the business community, my husband remarked after it all came out) and I felt my entire body shudder. The grubbiest of people still came, of course. He was one of them now.

Despite everything, the service was lovely. I'd wanted a ceremony which would be sombre in tone, but with some soaring touches. Our dear friend the conductor Matthew Baron, gave up his time to fly over and oversee a chamber music group. I left the music up to him, and he did a wonderful job, though the Shostakovich piece he chose turned out to be nearly 36 minutes long. I could see Clara looking down at her phone without any subtlety, and I have to say, the empty space meant the high notes hit rather jarringly. Things cheered up slightly with the cardinal's reading of Tennyson's elegy, which he delivered with impressive vigour. I have to say that one line slightly clanged: 'Let Love clasp Grief lest both be drown'd,' but we rallied well, and only Lyra actually laughed out loud.

After the eulogy from our dear friend Bernard Leon, which was slightly too effusive given the news, but I suppose too late to rewrite, a choir sang the Sanctus and I realised I was crying. The music moved something in me, it reminded me somehow of my old horse Horatio with his big doleful eyes. Still, one must show a little sadness at a funeral, it's expected. I was outdone though. As we left, I saw Lainey sitting in a pew at the back, sobbing her heart out. She'd looked up at me as I passed by, with a smile which almost conveyed understanding, as if we both shared a unique grief. The moment was broken by a hysterical laugh echoing right through the building, and I whipped round to see that Lyra had torn her ridiculous fascinator off her head. I nodded at my daughter in a way I hoped showed approval.

The after-party, as Clara had dubbed it, was a much grimmer

affair. I'd insisted it be held at Lyall House, a grand sixteenth-century building just off St James which used to belong to Charlotte Stanley, who had once been incredibly rude to me at a charity auction. Since the family were forced to bequeath their home to the National Trust after squandering their fortune on an ill-fated stud farm which never produced a winning horse, I felt no compunction about spending money there that Charlotte would never see. The great hall was decked out with wildflowers and long tapered candles which cast a wonderfully subdued light. In one corner, the string quartet were set up and we had wonderful catering by Romola's daughter Allegra, who only did the most elevated of events.

All of it was wasted of course. Most of the guests who'd braved the ceremony didn't turn up to the wake, and frankly, it looked like a desultory office party which people couldn't wait to escape. Nevertheless, I worked the room with the skill that *Tatler* recognised when it made me one of their top party hostesses several years in a row, making sure to give everyone some attention – even those who weren't strictly deserving of it. At 6 p.m., after a conversation with a woman I only knew a little, and who clearly only came to lord the news over me ('Such shocking news. I think it's fantastically brave of you to show your face today, I don't think I could do it'), Clara came over to tell me she was leaving.

'All my friends have been desperate for me to fill them in,' she said, all memory of her despair forgotten. 'The whole thing makes it even more obvious he was murdered and I literally can't keep up with the texts – most people think it was either you or Freddy. I'm going to the party now, don't wait up.' Somehow, Clara's reputation was bolstered by my disgrace. I couldn't bear it anymore. Humiliation was too weak a word for the day's events, and I fled without any goodbyes.

The only thing keeping me going that day was my brother and my dear old friend Penny. They bundled me into a waiting car and took me back to Charles's house in Richmond where we sunk several bottles of wine he'd boosted from Anthony's wine cellar and tried to brace for what would happen next.

ANTHONY

Shostakovich? Thirty-five minutes of bloody lift music, and all the while people were losing the will to live. George Grosvenor, one of the few real mates of mine to show up, looked like he might actually have fallen asleep, poor fucker; I'd have done the same if my current state didn't prohibit it. When we go to bed, we just lie there for eight hours as if that's a normal thing to do. And nobody questions it! Apparently it's 'processing time', whatever the hell that means.

I knew turnout would be bad after the news had come out, but I was still surprised at just how bad it was. Giles was obviously absent, no doubt trying desperately to save the legitimate branch of Wismere and cooperating with the police like the good boy he was. Nobody from the office came, none of the old boys I'd partied with since university, not even a handful of mates from the art world – and they *love* a scandal. I only managed to get through the service by keeping my eyes on Lainey, the only person to properly put on the waterworks. It didn't hurt that the dress she had on made her cleavage look fantastic if I viewed it from the right angle. I was impressed she showed her face truth be known. I'd have put good money on Liv having security dart her and drag her sedated body off site, so it was a big risk.

After the ceremony, Olivia had made the remaining mourners (not so much mourners as gawpers at this point, the kind of people who slow down when they drive past a car crash) go stand in a dusty old hall full of flowers and candles as if I was a Victorian ghost they were hoping to summon. Honestly, if you hadn't seen the tiny photo of my face on the order of service, you'd never have known any of it was for me. Choral singing for Christ's sake!

My kids took the opportunity to get stupendously drunk. Even Jemima, supposedly so focused on impending mother-hood, had a few large glasses. Lyra was in the gardens for most of the wake, smoking endless roll-ups like a gap year student. Jemima joined her at one point, sitting down on the step and sighing loudly.

'What a shitshow,' she said, waving away the fog of smoke surrounding her sister. 'Do you know I haven't had a single text today? Not one. Nobody wants to catch our disgrace.' Lyra turned towards her, a strange expression on her face.

'Well, that's not entirely true is it, dearest? I'm sure at least one person has been in touch.' Jemima's face was rigid, her jaw muscles working overtime. Lyra was enjoying herself, leaning back against a step and stretching her legs out. 'Share with your sissie. It's not healthy to keep secrets you know, the baby will absorb all that guilt.'

Jemima stood up and kicked her sister squarely in the thigh, producing a yelp of surprise. 'If you have something to say, then say it. But you don't want to have a real conversation, do you? No wonder your girlfriend stayed in Paris.' Then she was gone.

So Lyra was holding certain information over her sister's head, smart girl.

When things wound up at the wake, I realised I didn't yet know where I was going to be buried. Amy-Anne helped answer that for me. 'They're not even going to watch,' she said in a low voice to Agneta as they said goodbye to the remaining guests. 'He's being buried in Cockfosters tomorrow morning and she just told me none of them will be there. *Goodbye, Mr Morday, mind the stairs; it's a bit slippy out.*' Agneta had raised her eyebrows and let out a whistle.

'Ooh, that's cold. But I guess better to get as far away as possible from the stink coming off him – she's always been all about her reputation.' Another goodbye and then Amy-Anne again.

'I should've got her to pay upfront, trying to invoice Mrs Wistern is going to be a nightmare.' Poor Amy-Anne, if she got even a penny out of my wife now it would be a miracle.

Liv left before the final mourners had even got their coats on. I followed her out of a side door and into a waiting cab. Then it was off to her brother's house where I finally learnt just how much she knew. The ability to watch the living and do nothing was often excruciating. Your presence cannot be detected by the living, however much you try. It worked out well for my wife however. If I'd been able to let her know I could hear her talk about how long she'd been planning on leaving me, she'd have been fucking terrified.

THE SLEUTH

@thesleuth

42k subscribers

I'd checked in on the funeral details the moment they'd gone online. A few photos of the family looking stiff and panicked, headlines like 'Family breaks cover for funeral' and my favourite: 'Wistern's wife worn out', alongside a pretty unflattering picture of her looking like she was growling. The paper had extensive details on how much her outfit cost (£89,000, most of it jewellery) – nothing like a story about people in nice dresses to divert you from what's really going on. I'd toyed with driving up to London for it but told myself it was pointless, there's no way I'd have been allowed in. And what was there to see anyway? Just a bunch of hypocrites pretending to cry over a man most of them despised.

Instead, I posted a video showing some images from outside the event, including one of Jemima where she appeared to be wrenching her hand away from her husband's. It was weak stuff, but you've got to keep up the content if you want engagement. There'd been a stabbing in York two days ago and

168

it was getting a ton of attention. It's always women with kids who get the biggest headlines. Motherhood elevates some victims to martyr status.

Fred wasn't back yet, so I returned to the pub to try my luck with Luke. I was so keen to know more about this supposed relationship with Jemima that I turned up before The Badger opened and sat outside for twenty minutes in the rain feeling like an idiot. Eventually a car pulled up and Luke got out. With a big smile, I explained who I was and what I did, slightly exaggerating my credentials ('I present a top crime show' was a stretch, but you've got to sell yourself) and he looked a bit unsure.

'But didn't you used to work here? I remember, you got fired for stealing.'

Christ, was my self-confidence so low I'd assumed he wouldn't know me? We hadn't had any shifts together as he mainly worked lunch, but of course he'd remember the girl who got fired. I stammered out something about how Anthony made that up after hitting on me. There was silence for a second, then he nodded. 'Sounds about right.'

Eventually he agreed to chat but told me he couldn't while he was at work, which burst my bubble a bit. Reluctantly, I agreed to meet him back at the pub at 11.30 p.m., and spent the next ten hours with my mum, clock-watching in front of TV programmes about bored retirees looking to buy holiday homes in countries where they usually professed to find the food inedible.

The pub was closed when I went back, and he let me in through the back door. Luke was polite but guarded, and I had to really work to get him to agree to be on camera.

'I love a bit of true crime, mate, but I don't want to get in trouble. No disrespect but you're not exactly a pro, are you?'

I attempted confidence, telling him the only person he'd get in trouble with was dead, which made him laugh.

'I guess you're right. But only from the neck down, ok?' Deal made, Luke opened up. He'd worked at the pub for six years, and knew Anthony Wistern 'very well, the man wasn't shy about making himself heard'. We chatted about what it was like working for him – 'he veered between charming and fucking rude' which was my own experience too – but I wanted to dig deeper.

I asked him how he'd come to be at the party.

'Anthony asked a few of us if we wanted to help out with the booze. They had their own bar staff obviously, but he asked me to serve a local beer. I think he wanted to look like a country squire – all the rich fuckers who come down here cosplay like that. Tweed and wellies and labradors they can't control. It's like Disneyland for posh people, the Cotswolds. Never mind the kids round here who live in poverty, they couldn't care less.'

'So you agreed?' I asked.

Luke shrugged. 'Two hundred and fifty for the night, wasn't going to say no to standing next to a keg. Nobody really wanted it anyway, not when they were serving Champagne on tap. It was a pretty easy gig.' He paused. 'Well, apart from the fact that my boss died at it.' He lit a cigarette, and blew smoke at my phone, clouding the frame for a minute.

'Was there an atmosphere that night? Knowing what we know now, there must've been people there who hated him.' Like his family, I thought. He didn't answer for a second, smoking furiously.

'The whole evening was completely insane, mate. Two marquees, I'm not talking about those ones you freeze your bollocks off in. These were mansions, real glass windows and carpet, chandeliers hanging from the ceilings. The wealth on display, it was unlike anything I'll see again – some people had their own security, on top of the event security. But it was one of those nights where the vibe felt off, you know? Like, it was all about being seen, not having fun. Old boss man *was* having fun, that was obvious. Plastered from the start, like a man trying to drink away a hard day, you know?'

I knew that feeling. 'You agreed to talk to me, does that mean you think someone might've killed him?'

He smiled. 'You're really on that, huh? I watched one of your videos, mate, I'm curious why you're so adamant he was killed.'

It sounded patronising, and I bristled slightly. But I had confidence in my opinion, and facts to back it up, so I explained that a rich, healthy man like that doesn't just fall into a lake onto a conveniently placed spike while hundreds of people roam about.

'Did you know his family rushed to have him buried before any of this came out? You've got to dig deep, you've got to question everything you saw that night.'

Luke sort of smirked at me in a way I didn't like, and I felt as though I was losing control of the interview. So I pounced, knowing this was building to my killer question. 'Were you having an affair with Jemima Wistern?' The guy leaned away from me and waved his hands so vehemently he knocked a glass over.

'What? I dunno where you got that idea from.'

I held the camera steady and zoomed in on his face. 'Let's just say I've got information from a stand-up source. I've got to ask these questions, Luke, people deserve the truth.' As I spoke, he got up from the bar and pulled me off my seat. I carried on filming as he pushed me towards the door and out into the dark night. 'You've got a responsibility to clear this up. Did Jemima have something to do with her father's death?'

He shook his head again furiously. 'Anthony said you were a nutter after he fired you, stay away from me.' The door slammed so loudly a pheasant flew out of the bush in shock. It made for a nicely dramatic moment actually.

I turned the camera back towards me, angling it so you could only see my silhouette. I was panting slightly. 'He told on himself there, didn't he? I think we're getting closer to the truth even if our eyewitness won't tell us what happened. Is he scared or is he in someone's pocket? He might want to run away, but I won't. Not even if this gets dangerous. I've got a feeling we might be making some people feel very uncomfortable.'

OLIVIA

I couldn't sleep well at my brother's house, I never understood why he had such short curtains over the windows, which were both tremendously ugly and ineffective at blocking out the light. As I lay in the cramped bed, I thought about how Anthony had always misjudged me, thinking that I didn't know about his affairs – both business and pleasure. I was merely a wife to him, and a wife holds a necessary but nowhere near top-level job for men like him. I imagine he saw me at the level of one of his junior analysts, very useful but entirely replaceable if needed. If asked, he would joke I just shopped, socialised and whiled away my days in a variety of meaningless ways. He was partly right, I'll give him that. But his low valuation of me made him careless with his secrets.

In the beginning, he'd hide things with a level of effort I respected. It took me a year to find out about his first affair, but the lengths he went to slipped pretty dramatically over time. After all, I'd forgiven him once, why not do it again?

Eight years ago, something snapped in me. Charles heard from a lawyer friend that Anthony had met with him several times to look into how he might best protect his assets in the event of a divorce, and for the first time I'd felt there was a real possibility I might be cast out into the wilderness where the first wives wander. I've seen them out there, a dazed look in their eyes as if they still cannot understand how thirty years of service ends up in a vicious alimony battle which, even if you win, results in your carefully cultivated social status falling off a rocky cliff. They get bad work done, start going on increasingly bizarre retreats where they learn the benefits of ecstatic dance and orgasmic woodwork, and eventually they buy somewhere in Hampshire and are never seen again. As much as I resented Anthony, I couldn't bear that. If we were going to divorce, it would be on my terms.

My brother planted the seed that I should start a get-out fund, and with his help I began moving money into an account he'd set up. Our household finances were all my domain. For all that my husband seemed to live for his work, accumulating wealth was never his main interest. Of course money was a huge part of that drive, but really I think he liked the adrenaline and the machismo of *making* it more. He liked to spend it too, on art, on cars, on fine dining and the parties he encouraged me to throw. His ostentatious instincts came from his upbringing, I was sure about that. I'd grown up in a family which thought excessive displays of wealth were a horror, but somewhere deep inside, though he'd never admit it, he thought it demanded respect. So every month, a considerable amount landed in the 'domestic account' as Anthony called it. It was to cover everything my husband found too dull to think about but imagined I enjoyed. I didn't, I always palmed it off on whoever our domestic PA was at the time.

But now I began to handle the finances myself. I set up a new household account which Agneta could access. Then I would move the rest to the one run by Charles. It wasn't hundreds of thousands, even I couldn't claim our monthly domestic output was that high, but it *was* substantial, building up every month. I became thrifty, slowing my shopping habits over the months and years to the point where I rarely bought new things. I didn't stop entirely of course. I was committed to my goal but I was hardly going to start wearing hessian and wooden beads like a teacher. Instead, I tailored everything I owned, became an expert in vintage, and sold things I no longer wore instead of having the housekeeper take them off to charity (I'd always suspected she kept the best for herself; I once saw her going out in a jumper which I knew from eight paces was a Loro Piana). My ally in this was, of all people, Lyra. She was visiting one weekend and walked into my dressing room when I was packing up some bags ready to take them to a designer resale shop in Kensington. My middle daughter refused to countenance my claim that I was merely having a clearout. She wouldn't let it go, asking if Anthony was keeping me on a short leash. So I told her. You're the feminist, Lyra, well I'm doing something for myself, isn't that what women's empowerment is all about? I want to keep some money aside for myself in the event that your father decides to have another midlife crisis and start a new life with a willowy blonde who'd presumably give you some new siblings pronto. That swung her pretty quickly. Nothing like dangling a stepmother who'll leech away your inheritance to conjure up some solidarity. She started taking my stuff back to Paris and selling to auction houses. The jewellery was her idea, you get a lot more for it of course. I kept stuff I really loved, but honestly one diamond becomes much like another if you look at it long enough. I even sold off some of Anthony's smaller art pieces that he'd fallen out of love with. Over the years, it all added up very nicely.

I started to notice something was off again six months ago.

At first I thought it was another woman; I'd had my suspicions and they were usually right. It started with an increase in gym visits where he would get irrationally fixated on his waistline, before cutting back on the booze and then finally becoming much more affectionate with me, that was the real tell.

In my wildest dreams, I hadn't thought it could be something worse than an affair, but then Anthony never failed to surprise me. It turned out he was running some kind of scam. I'd listened one night when he was in his office at home, heard him talking to a woman about how well her money was doing, reassuring her that she'd get it back very soon. 'Anita, you know you're my priority, darling, now let's get that lunch booked in so I can shower you in Champagne and show you how much lovely money you're making.' Not that odd, if it hadn't been for me immediately recognising the name and knowing something was off.

So not for the first time, I went through his computer when he'd gone out. Usually I was looking for women he was shagging, not women in their late eighties who walk with a stick. It took a while to wade through all the interminable spreadsheets and inscrutable financial terminology, but I eventually found that he had different email addresses and was in touch with a lot of dubious people, the sort we obviously didn't fraternise with, but who had money to burn. Then some people we knew socially. Mostly, they seemed happy with his services. But one wasn't. I'd been right, it *had* been Anita Vasher on the phone and the old woman was insistent that she get her money back. Anthony assumed I didn't understand a jot about his business, as though it was rocket science. Men in finance always try to make out that their jobs are complex but it's just nonsense. They convince themselves of it because otherwise they'd have to admit they're merely hopped-up gamblers, playing with other people's money like it's Monopoly.

I knew all about Anita Vasher, of course I did. The woman was almost legendary in London for her eccentricities and, of course, her money enabled such strange behaviour. She would put on extravagant events for her favourite charities and then not turn up at all. If she did attend, she wore a tracksuit and would wave people away if they dared approach. She ate dinner at the same Austrian restaurant every evening, the same meal every time. People would go and watch her sometimes, this tiny old lady eating a chicken schnitzel the size of a flat screen TV, just to see her in the flesh. She'd never RSVP'd to any of the parties I'd invited her to, but I never gave up asking. Against all my better interests, I liked the idea of her very much. I once saw her sitting on a bench in Hyde Park and went over to say hello, whereupon she told me I could only sit down if I solved a riddle for her.

'What disappears as soon as you say its name?'

I'd smiled at that, Charles had been a great one for riddles as a child. 'Silence,' I said, thrilled to avoid looking stupid in front of her.

'Just what I was enjoying right until you turned up,' she shot back as quick as you like. The woman lived exactly as she wanted to and people paid her her dues. The idea that Anthony had been stupid enough to try to get one over on Anita Vasher was unbelievable. Idiotic fool.

'The four most dangerous words in investing are: 'This time it's different . . .' That's what my brother said when I went to him with what I'd seen. He looked through Anthony's home computer (the man always made a show of telling me the password, as if I'd ever need to use it when I had my own. It was all smoke and mirrors – as if he didn't guard his phone like a lion. That had a password I'd never been able to guess) and after a few hours of sifting through its contents, he took off his glasses, wiped his forehead with a handkerchief and told me sombrely that my husband was running a Ponzi scheme. God bless Charles. He'd never liked Anthony, but he managed to disguise his glee with a mere smirk before quickly moving into full brotherly concern mode.

That's when we doubled down on the savings. Anthony would go to prison for this, Charles was adamant about that. Nobody ever ran a scam like this without being discovered. 'You know I've never taken to the man, but I didn't think he was an idiot. Man must've had a breakdown or a brain tumour, any headaches recently?'

Charles was wrong, this was just the ultimate result of my husband's addiction to the chase. We had more money than he even noticed, my theft was proof of that, the pursuit of success was what led him here. He'd grown bored, even I'd noticed that, and this must've given him the greatest thrill. The stupidity lay in not thinking about how quickly his life would blow up as a result. Then again, Anthony would probably do very well in prison, he'd no doubt end up being the leader of some faction. Men always followed him around like puppies eager for fun.

The game had changed. The fund was no longer a theoretical safety net but a very real one. I *would* need it. We ramped up the transfers. The nest egg was coming along beautifully, Charles always assured me. He'd invested a lot of it, and though I knew my brother to be a cautious man who'd never choose anything with the words 'high risk' attached, I had close to seven million in an account which didn't bear my name, wasn't located in the UK and couldn't be discovered by my husband, even if he was smart enough to look. Which, based on his recent judgement, he wasn't. Not enough to live as I was used to, and I'd be on a tight budget for the rest of my life, but more than I'd ever see once Anthony was arrested. All our shared accounts would be frozen, Charles explained, and the likelihood of getting nearly anything back would be minuscule.

'You're also going to be implicated,' my brother told me solemnly. 'Caesar's wife and all that. It might be worth getting out now, they'll still want to talk to you, but you'll be at a distance from it all at least.'

I was reluctant. Despite it all, I was attached to the man. My entire adult life has been spent in some kind of service to him and though sometimes it didn't feel like it, I did love him. But four weeks before his big birthday celebration, we were having dinner together and he was on the phone the entire time, chewing with his mouth open, ignoring me. Gazing at him, red-faced and jowly, a bubble burst, I decided it was time. Let an optimistic 25-year-old deal with his old age, if he got out of prison in time to find one desperate enough to take him on.

I was going to do it after the party. Give him one big night of glory and then leave in the morning, that seemed fitting. I'd packed my trunks and had booked to stay at the Mayr clinic for a couple of weeks until the shock of it all dissipated. Stern-looking women in white suits feed you half a cup of broth and make you get up at 4 a.m., you come out looking ten years younger. But he could never let me have my big moment, always had to rush in with one of his own. The day after Freddy was born, he bought a plane. Visitors who came round to see the baby ended up looking at image after image of this six-seater death machine he'd decided to bid on while I was in labour. He sold it a year later, chastened at how small it was compared to those of others he knew. So of course he chose to die the night before I told him I wanted a divorce. I should've expected it really. The greatest display of one-upmanship ever seen, bravo, Anthony.

Charles had reassured me every day since that everything I'd squirrelled away so carefully was still safe, but now Anthony's fraud had been revealed, he was clear that I'd have to meet with the police as soon as they requested it.

'Better to do it all straightaway, it'll look less as though you've got anything to hide, Livvy.' Everything might've felt as if it was falling apart, but I still had my fallback plan. I clung on to that for dear life. Eventually I drifted off to sleep, and dreamt that I was on a boat with that charming American, Bruce Patron. I woke up feeling somewhat cheerful, despite so many of my friends dying at sea. Dreaming of water signals good luck and I was sorely deserving of some.

ANTHONY

She made it back to the house at midday. The photographers were back in position, our road was a good spot for them. A retired footballer and his fashion designer wife had moved in six months back which meant there were always a few cameramen skulking around trying to get a shot of them. A few neighbours had winced at their arrival, but were happy to accept the housewarming invitation when it came, delivered by a man dressed as a Victorian butler and served on a silver salver. I couldn't work up much disdain, a gormless footballer was really the least of our worries.

The tone of the scrum gathered outside my house had changed. Freed from the pretence of being respectful now that I wasn't just a rich dead guy but a rich dead criminal, they surged around Livvy yelling the most awful things. After hearing the true extent of her betrayal at her crisis meeting with Charles the night before, I was furious with her, but I still bristled at another man disrespecting her like this. One greasy-looking scumbag asked her if she was going to apologise for living off stolen funds, as if my wife was some gangster's moll draped in a cheap mink. She stumbled through them, rushed up the stairs and faced an excruciating wait for the housekeeper to come to the door. Olivia went straight downstairs, not making eye contact. I knew she couldn't have borne any sympathy from the staff.

My wife headed to my wine cellar, angrily punching in a code and slipping quickly into the cool dark room. After Jemima had wound up drinking £17,000-worth of Brunello one evening with her friends, I'd laughed until I'd wept, and then promptly decided my collection needed a little more security. Sloppy mistake to give Liv the code.

I watched her drink two glasses of a nice Montrachet in quick succession. It wounded me to see her drink it as though it was just cheap plonk. Just another stab in the heart from this double-crossing witch of a woman. Leaving her husband of over thirty years the moment the road got a tiny bit rocky? Do you know, last night I was so incandescent I tried to find the exit here so I could get back home and give Liv what for. I walked around the building looking for a door which might let me escape this place, yelling that the joke had gone on long enough. Eventually a woman in a porter's uniform had thrown a *net* over me as if I was a wild animal, before two others came and marched me over to the deputy director's office where I was met with a lecture about how the afterlife was not a place for violence or aggression and that I was to learn to solve my emotions with maturity.

'Concentrate on remembering how you died, Mr Wistern, not on why your wife was leaving you,' she'd said, smiling at me. But what if that was exactly *why* I died?

Olivia's phone rang.

'Did you know?' It was Giles. She didn't answer him immediately, instead she leaned back against the glass door of the refrigerator as if considering it. Tell him you bloody knew, I hissed. She couldn't get away with stealing my money and then washing her hands of me.

OLIVIA

Did I know? A stupid question from Giles really. As if I'd break down and confess that I was in on it. For all I knew, the police were listening in, hoping to hear my confession so they could have someone alive to pin it on. And besides, a more interesting question would've been, what did I know? I knew the man I married was stonkingly ambitious. At his first job, he'd reported a colleague who'd been impressing the bosses for insider trading and felt no guilt whatsoever. In fact he'd taken me out for dinner the night he got fired, toasting his own plan with pride. I knew my husband was . . . morally agnostic, shall we say. Taxes were a sporting challenge to work around, regulations stifled innovation, speed limits were merely a suggestion, human rights made everyone soft and the concept of loyalty held people back.

I was never in doubt that Anthony would do as Anthony pleased. Some women drive themselves mad fighting never-ending battles about clothes being left on the floor or the uneven division of childcare. My old friend Poppy Hammond was in the Priory for six weeks after she saw her husband take his socks off while they were having dinner and casually flick them onto the floor.

When she came out, he was on his best behaviour for an entire month before he broke and left his muddy riding boots lying face down on the carpet. She's on quite strong medication now.

I knew early on that I wouldn't win on any front with my husband and so I never ran myself into the ground trying to. If he wanted to do something irregular at work, he would come up with a reason which worked for him. And the thing was, everything always worked out for him. Never once did he face the consequences for any of his actions.

I'm no tiresome moralist, I've known a fair few people who've ended up tangling with the law – when you're dealing with enormous sums of money sometimes mistakes are made – but for god's sake, have the skill either to hide it well or get away with it. Instead, my husband had the affrontery to die before I'd cut all ties with him, and now I had to deal with the fallout. It made me want to dig him up and kill him all over again. He'd known I'd be screwed and hadn't even bothered to protect me.

'No, I knew nothing, Giles,' I said, suddenly feeling tired. 'I'm devastated he'd do this to you.' Throw in some empathy, make it sound legitimate.

'That bastard,' came the anguished reply. 'Everything's fucked, Olivia, he's sunk us. I wish I'd . . .' and then he hung up.

I walked back upstairs and poured the rest of the wine down the kitchen sink, hoping that if there was an afterlife, Anthony was screaming in despair at the waste.

My phone rang again, and looking at the screen I saw it was Lyra. A thought occurred to me in that haze of medication and Montrachet. If I couldn't trust my husband, how could I trust my children?

ANTHONY

Charles turned up shortly afterwards, thank god. At the rate she was going, she'd have finished off all the good wine by the time the assets were seized. He was walking a little taller than usual. Pompous arse even greeted the housekeeper with a consoling pat on the shoulder.

'Anthony's mess won't affect you, dear.' As if he was some Dickensian master of the house.

Olivia's real lawyer, Benjamin Bottle from Bottle, Blum and Bowlers turned up five minutes later, looking exactly as a man whose father, grandfather and great grandfather, all lawyers who carried the name Benjamin Bottle should look. He coached her extensively on what to say when the guys from the serious fraud unit arrived, summing up with a clear brief: 'Say nothing; it may be helpful to cry a little if you can.'

I hated all of them in that moment. Giles, calling my bloody wife as if his hands were entirely clean. The front of the man! I'd had a jolt of recollection when he called me a bastard so angrily. We'd fought that night down by the lake. He'd been suspicious, accusatory, asking me if I was doing anything 'in an unorthodox way'. He'd said it so pompously that I'd laughed, hoping to convey how absurd I found the question. We'd stood by the edge of the water in a standoff and I'd turned the tables on my business partner, accusing him of not trusting me and demanding to know why he was asking such outrageous questions.

Giles had told Liv that Wismere was screwed and he was right. I knew investigators would already be locking down the office and removing every single computer, piece of paper and bloody stapler in the place. He wouldn't even be allowed to step over the threshold, and it was all because of bloody Anita Vasher. I've not made anywhere near enough mistakes to actually rank them, but she was undoubtedly my biggest.

The woman inherited a lot of money from her father, who owned diamond mines back when owning a diamond mine actually meant something, and I'd been introduced to her at an exhibition of Jingdezhen porcelain where we bonded over a particular blue vase that even I couldn't afford, though she could've easily bought the entire lot without blinking. Anita looked like a nice old grandma, that was what blinded me. Stooped, a little doddery and a tendency to lose her train of thought. I'd latched on to her immediately, everyone knew the Vasher name, and offered to take her out for tea. People said she was curmudgeonly, unwilling to suffer fools lightly, but she was charmed, I'm catnip for old ladies, even the ones in tracksuits who only eat schnitzel. All you've got to do is put on an excessive display of good manners and have the odd self-deprecating joke up your sleeve. It helps if you wear a smart suit too, good tailoring hits that nostalgic sweet spot.

After a little wooing, I took some money from her very happily, writing her off as someone who'd be content with a small return and some attention from me. Crucially, she had no children, they're always the prying ones, keen to make sure their inheritance is safe. But the wandering mind was a bloody act, I'd underestimated her hugely. Within weeks the witch was phoning weekly, with specific questions which made it clear she understood finance in a way even most bankers don't. At first I was able to style it out, and when she told me she was going back to South Africa for a while, I thought I was out of the woods. I'd get more investment in the meantime and pay her back later. But something happened. The markets were slumping, making big hitters move their money out of London. I couldn't make the numbers work, and my excuses were beginning to wear thin, even though I offered them with as much obsequiousness as possible. A month before I died, she told me, quite rudely, that she wanted to withdraw her entire investment. I didn't have it. I knew then the writing was on the wall.

I'd always done so well at recognising rich dummies, those who make it quickly and don't fully understand it, or the trust fund kids who want to be taken seriously, desperate to make more and impress their fathers. Maybe I was losing my touch, or maybe I was just getting lazy. The thrill had gone out of it, I accept that now. But I still found it hard to bear that I'd been taken down by a woman who once told me she recommended I wore shoes with velcro because 'your feet swell up in the heat as you age'. Had she gone to the police or had she gone to Giles? And if he'd known, then the question was – did he back down or did he push me? Did he walk away with his tail between his legs like he usually would or did something flip in him?

Soon the accounts would be frozen and Liv's card would no longer work. I prayed (not to God, he doesn't exist, just pen-pushing middle managers everywhere) I'd get to see that moment. It was the only joy I had to hold on to.

OLIVIA

My phone went as I was on the treadmill and I nearly slid off in my haste to answer it. A robo call – I could've wept in disappointment. In the three weeks since the allegations about Anthony had been made public, I'd heard from precisely five people, and one of them was his mother so it didn't count. And even she didn't ask how I was, calling only because she wanted to know what would happen to her annuity. Anthony, unlike my own son, was one of those men who thinks his mother is some kind of holy woman, and never said a word about her drinking or her propensity to make wildly inappropriate jokes. So when she'd asked what would happen to her, I spitefully replied that she'd have to get a job for once in her life, then immediately regretted it. Now she'd have the chance to play wounded, her favourite role of all.

The only other people to call were hardly the A list. Penny, my dearest friend, came up and let me weep into her considerable bosom for three days. But her support held no sway with others. Francesca, Lily and Jamie Mance all phoned, but I could tell they only really wanted to glean insider information to feed back to others for gossip and I would rather have died than give it to them. Mary Chambers sent me a bible verse about redemption, and a note about how she understood what I was going through, as if Anthony was anything like her dullard of a husband. That woman would be sanctimonious to the end, refusing a last meal just so she could make a point of not putting anyone to any trouble.

Even my dear friend Lucinda Emberry was silent – she more than anyone else had experienced salacious untruths being spread about her family. When the MPs expenses scandal broke, Lucinda was at the frontline of falsehoods, with journalists doorstepping her for weeks and I'd called every day. Yes, Andrew Emberry had claimed for a lot, but people don't understand how big an MP's outgoings are. She told the press the curtains weren't owned by Lucretia Borgia, but merely inspired by her. Did they listen? They did not. Privately I thought that expensing for twelve-thousand-pound drapes was foolish given their enormous personal wealth, but I couldn't deny how traumatic the whole ordeal was for them. And yet, she didn't call. I hoped her curtains caught fire and burnt the whole place down.

The only other contact I had was with my children, who were now treating the news with a mixture of hilarity (Lyra) and denial (Jemima). Clara merely asked me whether she'd still get the Patek Philippe he'd promised her for her next birthday. Freddy wasn't in touch at all.

One day I woke up and remembered Roberto's offer to stay at the Villa Borlusti. I must've been mad, because I broke my rule to stay silent and called him. He, of all people, had experience with the law, having been prosecuted several times in Italy for tax fraud. Lucky Roberto, the legal system in his own country was so complex and slow moving that he got off on technicalities every time. When I called, I heard a muffled sound and then the line went dead. So the villa was gone forever. I could almost hear his frantic efforts to block my number before I could call back, in an effort to get away from the taint of scandal.

If he'd just held on another week, I'd have been safe and dry (an unfortunate phrase now I think about it, given Anthony was neither safe nor dry in his final moments). Everyone would've taken my side, understood I'd left him well before the news about his criminality and given me the sympathy I deserved. Instead, I was a pariah, tainted by association.

The men in cheap suits came again and again, no longer concerned with politeness. Did they imagine I was going around like a door-to-door Tupperware sales lady, trying to get people to sign up to a pyramid scheme of some sort? These detectives, who drank endless cups of weak tea and never knew how to sit properly, knew nothing of our world. Charles coached me before every interview, always telling me to 'offer no additional information'. There was a formal interview, held in some grim office with strip lighting which made everyone look ghoulish, and a search of every one of our homes. I fled the London house for that one, which was a dreadful mistake. Journalists swarmed around me, pushing their cameras right into my face so that I reared back like a spooked horse, and yelled the most vile things at me.

'What do you have to say to the victims – will you be giving them back their money?' And worst of all 'How does it feel to be a social outcast?' So outrageously rude, so effortlessly effective.

Most of them left me at the bottom of the road, but two particularly keen younger guys followed me down to the main stretch. In desperation, I dashed into a clothes shop I frequented. It felt like a haven from the moment I stepped onto the thick wool carpet and heard the soothing classical music Lara always played. She was a wonder, Lara, always managing to wrestle the best of the new season from the clutches of bigger and brasher retailers. As she came towards me, I held out my hands in a sort of plea and told her I'd kill for a glass of Champagne. But there was no welcoming smile on her face. Instead, she looked anxiously towards the back of the shop, before ordering an assistant 'to go and help Mrs Tremain'. Then I understood.

'I'm very sorry,' she said, not looking remotely apologetic, 'but we can't help you today I'm afraid. The shop is extremely busy.'

Just a month ago, Lara would have welcomed me in at 3 a.m. if I'd wanted, that's how valued my custom was. And now she was turning me out onto the street with all the grace she might show a shoplifter. Dignity, Olivia, always dignity, I heard my mother say in my head, and I turned on my heel and stalked out of the shop as calmly as possible. Not wanting to go home and face the waiting mob again, I found myself going into the only place that would guarantee anonymity. For the first time in my life, I went to a McDonald's. The residents of lower Holland Park had been up in arms when the fast-food company first announced plans to set up a cafe in the area. But there I was, sipping on a Diet Coke and trying not to cry in public, and I'd never been more grateful for those awful golden arches.

The next day, my face ended up on page three of *The Times*. Wrinkles, stray hairs and bloodshot eyes all there to see, made worse by a combination of high definition and bright natural light. Then even the condescending texts stopped.

OLIVIA

The children came back one by one, all except Fred who refused to leave Gables because he had sheep coming. Sheep! Where he'd decided to put them, I hadn't had the strength to ask. Visions of them shitting all over the parterre garden. Clara had doubled down on her insistence that her father had been murdered, asking questions endlessly about what Anthony had been doing. When I told her to pack it in, she pouted in annoyance, telling me her friends thought it was cool her father was a criminal. 'I always thought his job was so boring, but now it's like the plot of a film.'

Lyra turned up with her girlfriend Camille, pushing through the journalists camped outside the house, and shoving one unfortunate man who tried to push his camera into her face so hard he ended up sprawled on the floor with his head in the hedge. I hugged her for that, which startled both of us. Will and Jemima were the last to arrive, waiting for three days before turning up, presumably to punish me for some oblique reason of their own. I say their own, but Will has no agency in anything. The man is an obliging blank canvas for Jemima to paint all her wishes on. Will's family are truly blue blooded. No money of course, but a surname which still commands respect. Even my mother, so hard to impress, would've approved. It's hardly as though she needed money, all my children grew up with the knowledge their father would provide, but it's Will's one and only plus point that he actually built up his own wealth and doesn't need our assistance.

Antique snuff boxes, faded old plates, who knew? I imagine he sells mainly to Americans who fetishise our history, but I've never asked him – I don't want to encourage him to talk more. Anthony and I once had to leave the dinner table because we were close to hysterics when Will made the mistake of giving a sombre lecture on the history of gilding. Clara had become so frantic with boredom that she actually started to slide under the table and I made the mistake of catching my husband's eye. We always said it was the only time our son-in-law had made anybody laugh.

Now that he had access to them, Charles had been doing a deep dive into our finances with the accountants and it was a fucking disaster. Anthony had signed Gables over to me after the Bijou Chabon debacle, as a sign of his love. We drove down one Friday evening having not been at the house for months, and when we arrived he'd blindfolded me with my scarf and led me out of the car. In our bedroom, he let me see again. There was a new painting hanging above the bed. A Klimt; not the famous kissing one, that's so ubiquitous as to be faintly unappealing now. It was a painting of a woman curled up on her side and looking completely at peace. I pondered it for a minute, as he told me he bought it to show me that I could relax now.

'I hope this shows you how much I value you, Livvy. I know how special Klimt is to you and it took me months to find the right piece to illustrate your worth.' Then he'd showed me the deeds to the house, solely in my name and the first real thing I owned all by myself. I'd been bowled over by this rare display of effort from my husband. But looking back on it, I wasn't the one who liked Klimt. He was. And I never much cared for Gables, he was the one who enjoyed playing the country gent.

When I'd told Charles, he'd been oddly quiet. Coming back to me a few weeks later, on Valentine's day of all days, he'd informed me that whatever document Anthony had showed me was a load of made-up nonsense.

'He must've faked a copy of the deeds, Livvy, it never left his portfolio. He's still listed on the land registry.' The idea of my husband intentionally forging a piece of paper in order to make a romantic, but ultimately hollow, gesture was somehow exactly right. I'd gone ballistic at this, smashing up his horrible balloon dog right at the moment when he walked in with a bunch of flowers so large they obscured the damage for a moment. 'It's a Jeff Koons!' he'd yelled in anguish. The next day, Gables was actually in my name, the one thing I was guaranteed.

I wished to heavens he'd made over the London house instead. Gables is close enough to Jeremy Clarkson's appalling farm shop to make it potentially unsellable. Nobody wants to risk seeing him astride a tractor before they've had breakfast. But it was all I had.

'Everything else,' I was told solemnly by the spectacled accountant who seemed to enjoy imparting bad news, 'was liable.'

Charles did as much as he could, liaising with the fraud goons to try to keep at least one account open 'since to attempt to use your get-out fund is not advisable right now'. I trusted my brother implicitly, I knew he wouldn't let me down. Even if my secret fund couldn't be touched for months, Charles would look after me. He always did.

After a week in the house surrounded by my children, I began to feel a little restless. I'd been monitoring the news cycle and it felt to me as if the brouhaha might be dying down somewhat.

'Millionaire fraudster stole from 80-year-old ex-soldier' might have been the most shameful headline for some people, but my personal nadir was actually, 'Wistern's world: money, deceit and a very expensive wife', which made me sound like the driving force behind his activities and also made the devastating mistake of saying I was 54. Jemima persuaded me against calling them up to correct it, telling me we needed to have dignity, which was a truism slightly undone by Clara who told me I should be glad to be mentioned and moaned that the papers hadn't even acknowledged her existence.

But at least it wasn't on the front page anymore, and the gaggle outside the house thinned every day we didn't give them anything new. The journalists didn't need new photos of us to accompany the twaddle they were writing. There were so many photos of Anthony and me online, every day they had a wide selection.

I decided to venture outside. Waiting until 6 p.m., when most of the journalists seemed to knock off and go to the pub, I wrapped a silk scarf around my hair and put on large tortoiseshell glasses. Looking in the mirror, I couldn't work out whether I looked like a middle-aged Audrey Hepburn or an old Joan Crawford before deciding it didn't much matter if the cameras had gone.

By the time I reached Notting Hill Gate, I realised I didn't have a plan and was in danger of losing my nerve. So I decided to be bold, and scurried down the steps to the Tube station below. I hadn't been on the Tube for at least a decade, and it took me a moment to figure out in which direction I needed to go. The experience was both grubby and exhilarating in equal measure.

At Green Park, I hurried through the crowds and emerged into the street. The rain had set in, and it was bustling with gormless tourists taking photos of The Ritz, a hotel which is now entirely indistinguishable from a gussied-up Premier Inn. I rushed down an alleyway and came to a stand outside Langleys. I first went to Langleys aged fifteen, with my mother. 'A rite of passage,' she told me. She took me for my birthday, explaining that it was the only women's members bar in London. 'It's a haven, darling, a place we can be ourselves for a few hours.' I soon understood that to be ourselves meant to peacock in front of other women of notable birth, which was very much all right with me.

The doorman let me in with a gracious nod, and I walked through the lobby determinedly, conscious that my hair was wet and trying not to lament the inevitable droop in volume. At reception, two young women with impossibly toned arms sat talking in low murmurs, and I had to cough to get their attention. Only one looked up at me, an amused smirk on her face.

'Can I help you?' she said as if I'd walked in off the street looking for a loo.

'I would like a table in the library,' I replied, hating that I sounded a little too eager. I couldn't fail to notice the slight nudge her colleague gave her. These girls who work as hostesses at the grandest establishments around the world, always impossibly beautiful, eminently poised and haughtier than Princess Margaret on a hangover. Of course they knew who I was and how I'd suffered. They were enjoying it.

Eventually the smirking one told me she'd take me to the library. I followed her without thanks, the only way to win the respect of these people is to outdo their rudeness. If you give any sign that you're cowed, they'll have you for lunch.

We reached the library and the hostess pushed open the doors and ushered me ahead. As I walked through, she smiled brightly and said, 'I believe your friends are already here.' Then she was gone and I was left standing by myself. Eight of my closest friends were looking at me, their faces a mixture of confusion and horror.

I have never been a coward. A snob, yes, cold, certainly, and as my children would surely say, perhaps a less than stellar mother. But I don't back down when confronted. I did the only thing I could do. I walked towards the table and made sure to smile as widely as possible without it appearing rictus.

'Hello, ladies,' I said, taking off my sunglasses, 'I didn't know there was a dinner. I just popped in to shelter from the rain; the new exhibition at the RA is divine. Shall I join you?' It took everything in my power to say that last bit without quivering, but I managed it.

Mary Chambers stood up, obviously thrilled to be in charge. 'Olivia, it's a surprise to see you, we assumed you were busy with the investigation – there must be a lot to go over with the police?' She said it as though it were a question, but I could see she just wanted to put the boot in.

'Well, obviously it has nothing to do with me, as I'm sure you know, Mary. I'm a victim in this too.' A chair scraped loudly, and Susannah Luscombe stood up. I saw she was shaking slightly, and I wondered whether she was ill. I looked at her with what I hoped was an obvious amount of concern and she snorted.

'You don't know do you? Christ, I've never met anyone as wilfully oblivious as you, Olivia. Anthony took *our* savings. Christ knows why Guy thought it was a good idea to sign our money over so willingly without consulting me, but he did. It must've been the famous Wistern charm.' She laughed then, so harshly I flinched. 'I've had to make the very difficult decision to take my daughters out of their school. I don't know yet whether we'll be able to keep our house and yet you walk in here and bleat on about how you're the real injured party.' I had my hand up now, as if to stop her in her tracks. 'Have you actually considered that the people your husband stole from weren't all so wealthy that they'd not miss the money? Did you think this was some kind of victimless crime?' She let out a sob, and Mary rather too eagerly leant over to comfort her in a showy way.

'I didn't know about Guy, Susannah,' I said, trying to walk the line between compassion and boot-licking. 'Of course I'm not unaware of the damage he's caused, I've spent the past weeks with police and forensic accountants trying as hard as possible to figure out how to return any and all money to its rightful owners – not that we've found much. Anthony certainly didn't leave me with millions, but I will make sure everything we have goes to helping those he's hurt, that's my one goal now.' I made my voice waver a little as I said this, it needed to sound believable.

'But all this time, you've been peacocking around town and throwing parties with the sole aim of showing everyone how wealthy you are, and it was all from theft. You're complicit, Olivia, aren't you ashamed of yourself?'

That was Mary, clearly playing the crowd, who were all nodding along. How quickly they forgot what they used to say about her.

'I think you should leave now.'

That was Mina piping up from the other side of the table. Susannah had sat down again, her head in her hands, and everyone was looking at me as if I'd just killed the woman's Shar-Pei.

I stood there for a minute, not knowing what to do and boiling with rage at the injustice. This was Anthony, I wanted to shout, but knew any outburst would mark me down as hysterical. I have had no control over anything but the parties you once enthusiastically attended and now sneer at me for holding. At least Anthony was wildly generous with money, barely noticing the amount I spent each month. Natasha has to ask permission to buy anything over £200 even though her husband buys cars as if he needs a different one for each working day. Mina's husband has another family who live four roads away. She knows, everybody knows, but what can she do? The only difference was that instead of just behaving badly to me, which was seen as par for the course, my husband had messed them around now too.

'I was leaving him.' I spoke with a desperation I didn't even attempt to conceal. Several of the women noticeably scoffed. 'I *was*. Ask my brother, it was all planned. It wasn't supposed to be like this!' Nobody spoke for a minute, but I thought I saw a tiny nod from Mina. Of course Mary couldn't let anyone thaw slightly, not now she'd tasted power.

'I have to tell you, Olivia, not a single person believes you didn't know what he was doing. Not a single person.' She enunciated that last bit, with all the relish of a hammy stage actor. 'You would never have left him, however bad he was, he was the one with star power. You were just his wife.'

I hadn't thought her capable of a riposte so devastating. I could do nothing more than nod, too aware of the very real danger that I might scream if I opened my mouth. I nodded at my friends, these women who were looking at me now with unconcealed disgust, and I left the room. As the door closed behind me I picked up my pace, rushing past the receptionists, ignoring the peals of laughter they didn't even bother to hide this time, and stumbled out into the street. Almost immediately, my phone started ringing. Lyra.

'Fred just phoned, someone broke in at Gables.'

THE SLEUTH

@thesleuth
68.9k subscribers

The moment Fred told me he was back, I got on my bike and headed for Gables. When the gates opened, I started filming immediately, before I lost the light. 'I'm here at Gables, where Anthony Wistern was "accidentally" impaled just over six weeks ago. I said at the time something else was going on – check out my video "What are they hiding" – and then well, well, well, we found out he was stealing money from people. I'm talking real cash here – see my last video, "The missing millions".' I zoomed out so my followers could get a good look at the palatial surroundings. I could be the person I wanted to be when I was filming, the person I should've been if life had gone differently. 'It's convenient right? For a guy to walk away from his party and just die in such a gruesome way. But was he so alone? . . . Let's not forget the earring . . . my sources are working on finding out who that belonged to . . .'

As I spoke, I heard someone calling my name. 'That's Freddy, the son. He's agreed to speak to me, let's find out whether he's on our side or not.' I stepped forward, only to hear a loud hiss as the sprinklers went off, practically drowning me. Freddy reached me, his face full of concern.

'Your trainers are wet,' he said, stating the obvious. I pointed out that the rest of me was soaked too and his face brightened as he explained that the sprinkler system was the most powerful on the market. 'Really helps soil nutrition. Olivia has always insisted on lawn, but it really does nothing for the ecosystem. I'm dousing it in hopes I can make it into a wild meadow.' He started off towards the house, and I followed him round to a side door, slightly disappointed not to be going in through the main entrance.

'This way,' Fred called, leading me down one corridor, through a kitchen, past *another* kitchen, and into a boot room lined with pristine wellies and immaculate Barbours. Finally, we came to a stop in the laundry room, and he gestured to the dryer. 'Put your clothes in here and I'll get you something to wear till they're dry.' Then he disappeared off the way we'd come and I dutifully stripped off down to my underwear. A sports bra and black pants – this wasn't a seduction mission.

He brought back a pair of slouchy grey trousers and a white t-shirt. 'My sister's,' though he didn't say which one. We stood there for a minute, not quite knowing what to do, and I seized the initiative.

'Are you ok? Things must be pretty bad.' He smiled then, still not fully looking at me.

'You know, nobody's asked me that but you. I'm fine. You know what he was. I mean, you worked for him.' I nodded. 'I'm sorry about that,' he said. 'Really bad.'

And yet you did nothing, I thought.

'Did you watch any of the videos I sent you?' I asked, watching my clothes whirl around in the machine. 'I feel like you might have come round to my way of seeing things.' I looked at him with meaning, wanting him to admit being my source without being pushed into it.

He sighed. 'I don't know what I think. He died because he was drunk and reckless. He was drunk and reckless quite a lot, and this time maybe his enormous luck ran out. But I mean, what are the chances? An ornamental globe.' He spoke as if this was the most ridiculous thing he'd ever said and I nodded. 'I monitored the organisers as they hammered them down, I had to make sure they didn't damage the trees. Olivia wanted to knock down one of the old oaks because it was "in the way" of where she wanted the marquees.' He shook his head at that, clearly still amazed at his mother's gall. 'The spike could've just been in an unfortunate place.'

I looked down at my phone as subtly as I could. Still filming, thank god.

'But your dad died just weeks before his entire fucking life was exposed. He would've had enemies all over that party, including people close to him. You can't believe it was an accident, you're a smart guy.' He wasn't, not at all actually, but no man is immune to flattery.

I'm very good at reading facial expressions – I did an online course in spotting liars and got a perfect score – and for a minute I thought his face might crack. But nothing is ever easy, is it? Instead, he stepped towards me and put his hand on my shoulder. I noticed the signet ring on his pinkie and the hefty watch on his wrist, signs of the wealth he claimed not to be interested in. I got distracted.

'Isn't that your dad's watch? I recognise it from photos of that night.' He looked down and tugged his sleeve over it.

'This is my watch, your obsession with true crime is making you see clues everywhere.' So he *had* watched my videos. 'I'm sorry, I don't know why I invited you, I feel so guilty about what happened at the pub but I can't get involved with what you're doing. They're still my family.' Disappointment coursed through me. All this set-up, and it would just fizzle out. He pulled my clothes out of the dryer and handed them to me. 'Keep the stuff you've got on. She won't notice.'

He led me out of the house, and I carried on lobbing questions.

'You all hated him, Fred, you've admitted that. If even his family couldn't stand him, doesn't that make murder more likely?' We reached the front door and he ushered me out without a word. The anger reached my throat.

On the steps I stopped and whirled round, putting my face just inches from his. 'There's something you're not telling me. What is it? After what happened at the pub you owe me that.'

A sigh. 'He was going to sell this place.' He didn't stop walking as he said it. 'He didn't tell me, just sent a guy round to value the place. So I confronted him that night, down by the lake and he laughed at me. Told me I was living in a fantasy world, looked me up and down with . . .' he searched for the right word '. . . scorn.'

'And then what happened?' I asked, impatiently.

'I took a swing at him,' he replied, looking down at the ground. 'I should never have done it, I barely clipped him and it just made him angrier. Grabbed me by my collar and shook me, telling me not to try and act like a man when I wasn't one. He only let me go because he saw Lyra coming over.'

'Lyra was by the lake?' I said, trying to figure out what this meant. 'Fred, tell me where everyone was. Think hard.'

He looked uncertain, like a kid being offered candy by a stranger. 'If you want to keep Gables, you'll have to figure this out.' A thin threat, but it worked.

'I saw people. Nobody ever sees me though. I left the party the moment dinner was over, and just walked the grounds, making sure everything was ok. The amount of damage done was just . . .' he looked anguished.

'Focus, Fred.'

'Ok, um, Lyra spoke to Dad for a bit – not very long, I saw her walk off a minute or two later. Jemima and Luke were together near the woods, I saw them when I was hiding out from this girl, Ottelie. Her mum kept trying to introduce us at dinner and I'd run out of things to say to her.' He scratched his beard. 'I didn't even know Jem knew Luke, that was a surprise. Don't blame her though, Will is shockingly dull. And sort of mean sometimes, though I can't explain why. Umm. That's it.' His brow cleared. 'Oh and Giles and Dad had a set-to on the lawn, sometime after our fight, that was the last time I saw him before he . . .'

'Do you know what Lyra was saying to your dad?' I asked, and he shook his head.

'But she told the police she was down by the tennis courts, she wasn't. Everyone was a bit vague on where they were. Well, except Clara, I think she really was just getting sloshed with her mate. She's firmly on your side you know. Thinks he was killed too.'

'Fred,' I said, wondering whether or not I was taking a risk. 'I came here the other day, and I found something in the summer-house. Do you recognise this?' I pulled the earring out of my jacket pocket and handed it to him. He turned it over in his hand.

'You shouldn't have this. This isn't yours.' I shrugged.

'It's not yours either. Do you know who it actually belongs to?'

A different expression now, like shutters had come down.

'No,' he said flatly.

Liar.

'Come on, Fred, this is important. It means something. Does it belong to someone in your family?' He laughed at this, a flash of his father suddenly visible.

'How are you going to help me keep this place? My mother owns Gables, and the only way she'll hold on to it is if all of this goes away. You need to leave, come on, walk.' He propelled me down the drive, with a strength that took my feet clean off the ground. I'd overplayed my hand. In desperation, I wrenched myself free and ran towards the lake, zigzagging so I'd be harder to catch – you learn that in self-defence. I got there well before him. The guy might be fit, but his boat shoes slowed him down. Is it a rule that all posh men have to wear ugly shoes?

He bent over and caught his breath as I stood on the jetty, peering down at the water's edge. Kneeling down, he picked something out of the lake, shaking his head in annoyance.

'Fag butts, they take a million years to degrade. I've actually seen wrens line their nests with them, what a disgusting species we are.' I caught a glimpse of the cigarette before he put it in his pocket. A half-smoked Moda.

'That could be evidence,' I said, 'you shouldn't have touched it.' He scowled.

'Did you not hear me? They're everywhere. The cleaners missed half of them. I even dredged a lighter out . . .' He stopped, frowning at me. 'Look, you've had your lake view, seen the "crime scene", but this is too much.' There was an edge to his voice, and it made me realise I was standing in the middle of nowhere as the light faded with a man a barely knew.

We trudged up through the trees and onto the drive. When we got to the gate, I got desperate. 'Why won't you tell me who was in the summerhouse when your dad was killed?' I said, a little too loudly. 'Why email me with all these hints if you aren't going to help me?'

Freddy pretended to look confused. 'Email? What are you on about?'

Even now, he was lying to me. Idiot. I held up my phone and started to film him. That got him going. With a cry, he swiped at my hand as if to grab it, and I stepped back, holding it aloft.

'You're filming me? For godsake I told you all that in confidence! Give me that phone. Give it to me *now.*'

I'd have rather died. Jumping on my bike, I sped away as hard as I could, only realising when I got home he still had the earring, my one piece of hard evidence.

OLIVIA

My family was gathered downstairs in the den when I got back. It had always been my least favourite room in the house, designed for the children to use as teenagers so that they would keep themselves to themselves. As a result, it was always a smidge too casual for my liking, with embarrassingly oversized sofas and at one particularly low point, a dartboard. Anthony had raised the possibility of digging down a level for a gym and spa, but then a house on the next street collapsed after doing something similar. Imagine the shame of losing your house because you wanted a sauna so badly.

Charles and Will were huddled over a laptop in one corner, while Jemima, Lyra and Clara were nose-deep in their phones on the sofa. It made them look like zombies, chins slack and eyes zoning out.

Camille, as professionally uninterested as ever, was lying on the floor reading a book and smoking. I never saw anyone smoke inside anymore – I only gave up when it became too degrading to huddle outside restaurants like bedraggled office workers – and despite the blatant cheek, it endeared her to me somewhat.

Nobody asked where I'd been, and only my youngest daughter even bothered to look up, idly telling me I looked like a drowned doll. When I interrupted them to ask what the hell was going on with Freddy, my brother was the one to speak first.

'A young woman, seriously quite disturbed by the sounds of things, turned up at the house and Freddy says he found her snooping around the grounds.' He rubbed the bridge of his nose. 'She seems to be making some sort of documentary about Anthony.' Lyra rolled her eyes and snatched the laptop out of her uncle's hands, bringing it towards me.

'It's not a documentary, she's one of those true crime ghouls who's obsessed with murder. Specifically, she thinks Dad was offed by someone at the party. And, it turns out, our moronic brother *let* her in. She rang the bell and he just . . . opened the gate.' Will shook his head as if mirroring my own confusion.

'Did she take anything?' I asked, knowing how lax my son was about security and remembering I'd left a good amount of jewellery there.

'No, Olivia, you're not getting it.' Lyra was smirking at me, her usual penchant for spiteful condescension shining through. 'She doesn't give a shit about your stuff. She's trying to solve Dad's imaginary murder. She's . . .' she waved her finger around her ear, 'fucking mental. Like, never left her village and her parents share DNA mental.'

'You're famous,' said Clara, stretching out her legs and kicking her sister in the back as she did so. She brought her phone over with glee, and showed me a slightly blurry video of me on the street, laughing. 'She says you're the merry widow.'

The video kept playing; I had been escorted into the car by Ryan and driven off: 'Did she look sad to you? Because to me, that looked like a woman who was going out to celebrate. Fresh blow-dry, perfect make-up, a fancy handbag, but most of all that expression wasn't right, was it? Olivia Wistern looks completely at ease with the world. What's the one thing missing here? I'll tell you – it's grief. Keep watching, guys, this case is gathering pace.'

I told Clara to turn it off. She shook her head emphatically.

'Don't you think it's weird that nobody in our own family can see what's staring us all right in the face but this rando can? Nobody gets stuck on a spike by accident, Olivia.'

I shot Charles a look, appealing him to step in and remonstrate with Clara. Unfortunately Jemima took it upon herself. 'She's trolling for attention, Olivia, that's what people do these days, just look at Clara's entire online presence.' Clara let out a whine of protest. 'Plus, she's cuckoo. Fred said she must've been filming him the whole time and she's already posted a teaser video so expect to see some proper footage of your son posted any minute now. Lord knows what he said to her, it's not like he doesn't get a bit conspiracy minded on occasion. Remember when he got obsessed with the idea that pesticides were making men infertile? In another life, they could've been mates. Or maybe lovers, ugh.' Jemima was drinking a large glass of wine which threatened to tip over onto the rug. I took it from her hand, irritated at how little care my children showed for anything.

'Drinking this early in your pregnancy? How nice for the baby to learn about your hobbies so young.'

'She also asked someone from Dad's pub if they know you Jem – like you'd ever be seen dead in The Badger, right?' Lyra looked at her sister, eyebrows raised.

'Stop watching it! It's stressing me out, and the doctors said I've got to keep calm, though how that's possible right now I don't know.'

Clara was still clicking through the videos – there appeared to be dozens. My fury grew.

'When did she film me? Is that even allowed?' It was unnerving that this weird person could just capture me like that without me ever realising. At least, I reassured myself, I looked nice in the footage.

'You're allowed to walk down a street with your phone, Olivia,' Lyra said. 'It's not illegal, even in Holland Park. I can't believe you didn't see her standing there.'

'Well, she's certainly getting the attention she seeks,' said Charles dourly. 'The latest teaser video has 80,000 views.'

'What did my video get?' I asked, and was met with laughter from Lyra.

'Want me to read you some of the comments? "She looks exactly like my aunt who we all hate", "look at that smile, definitely guilty of something".' My daughter's face brightened. 'Why is her hair so puffy, she looks like she's been hit by lightning.' Every single one of my children laughed at that, and I noticed that even Charles let out a small snort. Aggrieved, I tried to reclaim some authority.

'What did Freddy do with this girl?' I asked.

'Haha, he was so lame. He told her to go and then he basically just let her talk for ages and then he yelled a bunch of stuff about how much she'd broken his trust.' Clara flashed the phone in my face again so I could see my son all red and yelling. 'And that coat, my god he looks silly. Someone said he looks like three small children standing on top of each other.' Lyra collapsed at that, and her younger sister looked pleased. 'He didn't even call the police, said he just let the girl leave. What a simp.'

My brother cleared his throat laboriously, a tic which drives me up the wall. 'I must say this is a little worrying, the lady is obviously unhealthily obsessed. I think we have to file a police report, Livvy. If she's unhinged enough to break into Gables we don't know what she's capable of.'

I thought about all the officers I'd had to deal with lately, their unfriendly attitudes and obvious pleasure in trying to take me down a peg, and felt a sense of dread at the idea that I'd have to see them again willingly. 'But if he's admitted to letting her in, there's not much to report, is there, Charles?'

'Maybe she's right though,' said Camille, rolling over and exposing her entire stomach to the room. 'What if he was killed, it doesn't sound so far-fetched to me? You only need one person to hate you enough to do a murder. And everyone hates him.' She looked round at us, her eyebrows wriggling slightly.

Clara clapped her hands together. 'Thank you! That's what I've been saying. I always knew I liked you more than Lyra.'

Will seemed to think he should defend my husband's honour at that point and huffed slightly. 'That's not quite fair, Camilla,' he said, anglicising her name as if it sounded more comfortable to him. 'His family loved him very much. One mistake doesn't make him a pariah.'

One thing my family can bond over is our mutual nausea when Will tries to ingratiate himself. As he spoke, I found my eyes wandering from Clara (miming a gun exploding at her temple) to Lyra (eyes bulging, lip flipped up like a horse so her teeth were exposed). Even Jemima, who as far as I could tell, married him entirely willingly, was looking at her husband with a sort of exhausted embarrassment. Lyra broke the moment, with her impeccable timing for lobbing verbal IEDs.

'I mean, what's love, right? You love your family because that's what you do. You're not raised with another option.' My daughter looked at her sisters. 'I'm not like, *happy* he's dead but I definitely didn't like him.' She shrugged, and went to sit by Camille on the floor.

'He was a bulldozer,' Jemima said, which surprised me. Out of all of them, she was the one who most craved his affection.

'Remember that guy who lived four doors down? The one who parked his car an inch too close to our house for Dad's liking? Thought it was some kind of power move.'

I remembered it well. One day he'd told Jemima to come outside and play with him. From the boot of his car, my husband produced six large custard tarts. Carrying them over to the neighbour's car, he announced they were going to practise her throwing skills. And with that, my husband chucked a pie straight at the neighbour's vintage Porsche. Jemima had gasped, and he'd laughed in delight at her reaction. I watched from the doorway, seeing my daughter experience that frisson of excitement you get as a child when you're doing something naughty. Normally that sensation crops up when the adults aren't looking, but there was her father, authorising the transgression.

Her aim was spot on. The tart exploded into the metal grill. Anthony high-fived her, not seeing the neighbour coming out of his house until he was right in front of them. The man was elderly, wearing a shirt and tie even though it was a Saturday. He looked at his car in abject shock, as Anthony took the last tart and squashed it right down on the convertible roof. Before the man could say anything, Anthony had turned to face him and said, in a tone laden with amused malevolence, 'You think I'm a clown, huh? You think it's ok to park your fucking car right in front of my house? Well, there you go . . . that's my best joke.'

Jemima shuddered at the memory. 'I've been having EDMR therapy to process the bad memories. My therapist says I've already made more progress than anyone she's ever treated.'

'I'm impressed,' Lyra said, sounding anything but. 'You're actually talking about him critically for the first time. Is this . . . growth?' They began to squabble, in the same tired way they had since they were little, the worst barbs thrown without any real effort.

'Oh, sure,' Jemima shot back at her sister, 'only you saw how wildly messed up this family is, I'm sorry I didn't acknowledge your infinitely superior intellect, Lyra. I know it's what you cling to in lieu of having, you know, a meaningful existence.'

Her sister laughed. 'Is getting married at twenty-six and doing cutlery arrangements to fill time a meaningful existence? Then I guess you're right. Follow the ordained path and become our mother, that certainly seems the way to happiness.'

I let out a screech when I'd only intended to mildly shush them. The noise surprised everyone, most of all me. It sounded like a fox calling out in the night during one of their crazed mating rituals.

Finally, they were silent and paying attention. 'Right now, there's not a single person in London willing to say a good word about your father,' I hissed, and Will put his hand up before thinking better of it. 'You can sit here and destroy his character all you want but you will not speak a word of this outside of these walls. Our reputation is all we have in life. At this moment, ours is in tatters, but memories are short, and one day, this horrible month, this *mensis horribilis*, will be a brief blip – if we handle ourselves with dignity.' I paused for a second, wondering if I believed this and deciding I had no choice but to. 'We still have our dignity; let this nasty little person's conspiracy theory burn out, and say nothing about any of this to your friends. We will not add fuel to the flames.'

'Oh look, here's one I missed.' Clara was playing a clip now, and everyone craned to watch it. The shaky footage was dark, and the slightly breathless narrator was saying something about having to take risks like this when the police were doing nothing and then suddenly, I could see where she was.

'She's in the shagging shed!' yelled Lyra. I winced at the moniker, but she was right, it *was* the summerhouse. I hated that damn place. I'd wanted it to be my sanctuary, but found we'd built it at exactly the wrong angle, and the sun made it feel like a sauna during the day. This ghoul was wandering around touching our possessions as if she lived there. She even sat on the couch, her face obscured so that the viewer could only see her legs. Silence, a small yelp, and then an earring hove into view. A diamond hoop. *My* diamond hoop.

ANTHONY

Well, well, well. That set the cat among the pigeons I can tell you. The girls knew full well who that earring belonged to. They might not know that Europe is a continent or be able to comprehend time zones but they recognise precious gems. Clara was the first one to say it, pointing at her mother as though picking her out of a line-up.

'This is ridiculous, I'm often in the summerhouse, I probably lost it months ago.' A valiant attempt, darling, but it didn't wash. The children pounced. Jemima most aggressively, which was an interesting tactic.

'No way, you never went in there, and the whole place was cleaned top to bottom the day of the party. Why lie?'

On the back foot, Livvy stumbled a bit, saying that they all had earrings like that, and she wasn't even sure it was hers.

'If you were at the summerhouse that night, you'd have seen who killed Anthony, *non?*' said Camille, to vigorous nodding from Clara.

My wife was outraged now, asking Lyra if she felt it was ok for her girlfriend to disrespect her so monumentally in her own home.

'Not really your home though, is it? Not anymore.' That was vicious, even for her. Perhaps Lyra felt a pang of guilt for the first time, because she followed up with: 'But to be fair, she wasn't wearing those earrings at the party, was she?' Everybody thought about this for a minute. Honestly, I couldn't have told you what she'd been wearing, even if you'd pointed a gun at my temple.

'I wasn't even wearing earrings, I had an emerald necklace on, I'd never gild the lily like that. Besides,' my wife added, 'those hoops are daytime wear only.' There was a silence, my family looking at Liv with suspicion. 'I was only down at the lake for a minute, Anthony had been awol for too long and I thought he might be down there with another woman, but I couldn't find him, so I left. I never went near the bloody summerhouse.' That was the first time I'd heard her admit to being down there. Then my wife jumped off her chair.

'Jemima! Jemima was wearing them! I noticed while you were all giving your speech, I was furious because she hadn't asked. If she had, I'd have said no. Round hoops with a round face, it didn't work, darling.' All eyes were on my eldest daughter now, who was pointing violently at the door.

'Shut up, shut up, he'll come back and I can't say it in front of him. Please just wait, I'll explain later.'

I hadn't even realised Will wasn't in the room, that glass of water had taken a while, where on earth was he? Lyra looked triumphant, and I suddenly had a memory of her coming up to me at the party, eyes glittering as if she had a tremendous secret to tell. 'Jemima's been snogging the keg man,' my daughter had informed me, 'happy birthday.' She was most disappointed to find out I already knew, that I'd only hired him to make Jem uncomfortable. I was always one step ahead, that's what my family would do well to remember.

They were silent when Will eventually came back in, no glass of water in sight. He comforted her when she explained away the tears. 'It's just all so upsetting to be hounded like this.' Jemima asked him to go and get the car. 'I can't walk past those cameramen again, not looking like this.' Once he'd gone, she told them everything. Well, not everything, but enough to make her sisters laugh like hyenas and my wife force her to show them a photo of Luke. Olivia peered at him for a minute and then nodded.

'Well, everything's a trade-up when you're married to Will I suppose.' They were so busy asking Jemima questions about the affair that they forgot to ask if she'd been in the summerhouse when I died. And Olivia seemed to have completely got away with admitting to being near the lake around the time I died. Women, they waste time on the small details and miss the bigger picture entirely. Only Clara looked unconvinced, staring at Jemima and her mother as though she didn't quite believe either of them.

THE SLEUTH

@thesleuth
97.4k subscribers

My inbox was full. After I'd posted the video with Fred, I had so many messages from viewers that it took me four hours to reply to them. I know how important it is to interact with your fans – that's the great thing about the true crime community. So many people had their own theories, all springing from *my* reporting, and it made me feel great. There was nobody left in my real life to take an interest in what I was doing.

Most people felt a bit sorry for Fred, even though he'd come across as sort of aggressive in the edits. 'Is he single? He's quite cute for a possible murderer.' 'Not him, you need to interview the business partner – Gill.' Giles. I welcomed a range of opinions but it got my back up when people told me what to do, especially when they couldn't get his name right. One person wrote a whole screed about how they thought Anthony had been killed by a local man they named as Robert Hutchinson, all because this man had allegedly killed their cat after a long-running neighbourly dispute about the height of a fern. I deleted that fairly quickly. Didn't want to get sued just because of some personal feud over plants.

I appreciated them all, even the weirdos. I guess the idea that I had people listening to me was a confidence boost, one I really needed. In my head, I realised I was thinking of them as fans, which felt both embarrassing but also kind of great. I toyed with giving them a nickname I could use on the videos, like the podcasts *Crime Kittens* or *Social Sleuths*, but I didn't want anyone to laugh at me. So I held off the idea of a chummy name until I could think of one which blew me away. 'Dirty diggers'? That sounded like they were gardeners. It was harder than you'd think.

One of the final messages was from my 'source'. 'Hi again,' the message read. 'Your latest video caused quite the stir. You need to push Luke on what him and Jem saw that night. Tell him Jemima's pregnant, that might get him talking.' I reeled in surprise. Freddy must have changed his mind.

NEWS ARTICLE
1 September 2018

Fall of the carefree couple

He was a man more used to making the society pages in *Tatler* than the front pages of the red-tops. But in the months since Anthony Wistern's death, he's become a topic of intense interest across the country.

Today, neighbours gathered outside their vast stuccoed houses in London's fashionable Holland Park to watch as many of the Wistern family belongings were carted away.

It's another chapter in a dizzying series of events which have taken place since the financier known as

'Affluent Ant' was found dead at his birthday party in the Oxfordshire countryside. A tragic accident left London society mourning one of their leading men. But before the tears of the glitterati had even dried, it emerged Wistern had been running a secret fund which had defrauded many of the same friends who grieved him. One man's actions have caused an earthquake in London society, and now it falls to his neighbours to watch as his castle is dismantled before their eyes.

As a large marble table is carefully loaded into a truck by eight men, Tabitha Collins looks on sombrely. A petite woman in her fifties, she is determined to watch until the last piece of furniture is gone. For she has a personal connection to the Wisterns, and it's not just that she used to attend their famous Christmas parties every year.

'My friend's father invested with him,' she says, shaking her head. 'He met him at an auction and was charmed by the man. He was good at that, charming the naive. He begged Anthony to let him invest, even going as far as to ask me to call him. I told Adrian it was too good to be true, but he wouldn't listen. And now it's all gone. His family is staying with him now, afraid to leave him even for a minute in case he does something stupid.'

I ask her what she thinks about the family now, as a grand piano is winched through a French window. 'I try not to think about them at all,' she says. I point out that they've lost everything because of the actions of one man too, but Collins shakes her head angrily. 'They lived off other people's money happily for years. To me, they're just as guilty as he is.'

This house was the scene of many celebrations. The Wisterns were notorious for their parties, throwing them at the slightest opportunity and never skimping on the theme or the decor. One neighbour remembers life-size replica safari animals being delivered to the house, a very accurate model of a giraffe going in through a window just as a lion was wheeled through the front door.

It was also home to four children, who grew up on these six floors of prime London real estate. For them at least, the neighbours feel some sympathy.

'They've had their lives turned upside down these past few months. Whatever their parents did, they shouldn't be blamed,' sighed a man who didn't want to be named. 'Although they weren't very nice actually. One of them threw the most godawful parties when the parents were away.'

Her neighbours offer up considerably less concern for Olivia Wistern. 'I was invited over once, when we moved in. When she'd had a good look at me and decided I wasn't quite glamorous enough, I wasn't invited back,' one resident said, staring at a beautiful silk chaise longue which was being wrapped in plastic on the pavement. 'Olivia certainly prized her collection of dazzling friends. She excluded people from events if they didn't fit her narrow criteria – rich, attractive and well connected. If you weren't eligible, you were invisible.'

Many of the people watching the removal men do their work are still convinced she knew about her husband's real business. Her lawyers strenuously deny this.

'Olivia Wistern is a devoted wife and mother, and has spent her life caring for her family. On top of that, she has dedicated much of her free time to charity work, raising hundreds of thousands of pounds for worthy causes. She has never had any role in her husband's business, and was as shocked as everyone else to learn what had really been going on. She asks once again that she be left to mourn, and to look after her children, all of whom are scared and sad at the moment.' It should be noted that Olivia Wistern's youngest child is seventeen. The oldest is twenty-eight.

A large painting is brought out of 9 Ladern Road, covered in bubble wrap, one of many removed by authorities on this sunny day. It's hard to make out the image, but could it be the Chagall Anthony Wistern is said to have paid £2.8m for at an auction just last spring? 'He loved collecting,' said one close friend who asked not to be named. 'But sometimes it felt like he did it just to make other people jealous. If a work was in demand, he'd swoop in with a huge offer, then invite the losing bidder over to see it hanging somewhere silly, like in a toilet.'

That damning assessment shows a dark side to Anthony Wistern. People usually spoke of him warmly, gushing about his charisma and generosity. But as we now know, Mr Wistern was capable of hiding many things. The adage 'Don't speak ill of the dead' is right and proper, but this former friend is just one of many who have discarded it since the financier died. Perhaps most tellingly, an old school friend has made allegations of theft, which if true, show that his shady tendencies were long held. Michael Farthing, a pupil at Stonehurst senior school at the same time as Anthony Wistern (who got there on a scholarship), says his former friend stole a watch from his father's study when they were fifteen. 'He'd mentioned several times how much he admired the piece, it was a vintage Cartier model and my dad had shown it to him one weekend,' Mr Farthing told *The Mirror* last week.

'We had a party two weeks later, a birthday bash for me and my brother, and the next day, the watch was gone. We couldn't prove it was Anthony, so my father took the decision not to report it to the school. It was a generous act, one he didn't deserve. Ant had a look in his eye the next Monday at school, and asked me what the time was on at least three occasions that day. Three years later, when we left school for the last time, he waved at me as he got on the train to go home and I saw he was wearing the watch. Anthony took what he wanted, and clearly he never stopped.'

The housekeeper stands by the door and keeps her eyes firmly on the movers. A man carefully carries what appears to be a large jewellery box down the steps, alongside a colleague who holds a small sculpture this newspaper identified as a Lamenti, wrapped in a protective bag and partially hidden from view. Olivia Wistern is a famous clothes horse, who once persuaded Selfridges to stay open one night for her birthday. She was rumoured to have a room just for handbags, telling people that her husband approved of such extravagance since 'they held their value like nothing else'. A sound investment perhaps, but those purses will now be sold off, the proceeds paying off only a tiny fraction of the enormous debt owed.

As the sun begins to dip behind the elegant roof, it might be of interest to our readers to know a little of its history. Long before the Wisterns made it their base, the house was owned by another couple who fell from grace. It was built in 1885 for a man called George Farland, a successful landowner who wanted to impress his much younger second wife Kitty. The couple spent huge amounts of money on silk wallpaper and antiques from around the world and took great pleasure in holding balls and soirees at their home to show off their success. An account of one of their parties noted that 'Mr Farland is eager to display his good fortune, and those acquaintances fortunate enough to be in receipt of an invite to his home are happy to oblige.' But in 1891, the family found themselves in enormous difficulty.

The details are scant, but it appears that George Farland developed a terrible gambling habit and hid the extent of his addiction from those around him until it was too late. The house was sold, the fine furnishings stripped and auctioned off. Mrs Farland, who had married expecting a certain level of comfort, divorced her husband and he died three years later, staggering home drunk from a pub south of the river and falling down dead in the street.

As the last moving van drives off and the gates to number 9 are closed behind it, it's not hard to think back to Mr George Farland and see echoes of the past. Nothing more was heard of Kitty Farland or her two children. Perhaps they lived a life of quiet reflection and modesty. Or maybe they sank into poverty and despair, left unmoored after George destroyed their standing. It remains to be seen what will happen to Olivia Wistern. Will she learn the lessons of the past or will the actions of her husband stay with her forever?

ANTHONY

Interesting developments today, though it's a low bar in here. The fact that I did press-ups instead of sit-ups is *interesting* when the rest of your day is spent trying to avoid the new intake of doddery old dears who want to talk to you about their grief at missing the village fete. But even by these standards, today was a thrilling one. The morning the house was seized, everyone was resolved to get up early. Lyra back to Paris, Jemima and Will heading to his parents' place and Olivia and Clara to reluctantly head down to Gables. But none of them rose as early as my youngest daughter. 5 a.m., an hour previously undiscovered by Clara. She threw on a hoodie and jeans, and left the house without even a slice of toast. Since the chef had been let go, none of my family appeared to eat very much, occasionally ordering takeaway, eating out of the plastic bowls and then leaving the packaging strewn about the kitchen. The house had begun to look like student digs; these people were absolutely useless at basic survival without me, or more accurately, without my money. I'd once paid Bear Grylls to take me on a survival mission in the Canadian Yukon. Two weeks with just my backpack, and I'd thrived. The whole thing cost upwards of 300,000 what with the guides and the doctor we had on standby, but it was worth it to go back to basics and live off my wits.

I followed Clara as she took a taxi, unable to figure out where she was going until we pulled up right outside her uncle's house. Why in the world was she visiting Charles at 6 a.m.? He was as surprised to see her as I was, opening the door and frowning slightly. Dressed in a three-piece suit (I'd believe you if you told me he slept in it), he told Clara that it wasn't a good time. 'On my way to work,' he said rather brusquely, but my daughter didn't move. It was important, she had to speak to him *right now*. Sighing, he ushered her in and offered her coffee. As he got to work with the espresso machine, my daughter sat on a stool and slumped her head over the kitchen worktop as if defeated by her early start. I looked around the room, wondering if there was a hint of personality to be found here. Everything was in boxes; the man must be preparing a move, perhaps he was finally checking into some sort of retirement village where the pace of life would be more to his liking. They took their coffee into the living room which was only half packed.

'We'll have to share the sofa I'm afraid,' he said as he sat down awkwardly on the edge of it. Clara scanned the room doubtfully. I could imagine what she was thinking – small, beige and boring, the encapsulation of her uncle in every way.

'I need to talk to you about Dad. About how he was murdered.'

Charles put his cup down carefully on the floor and looked at her with obvious disappointment. 'Clara, my dear, Anthony was *not* murdered. It was either an unfortunate accident or, and I hate to say this, he took his own life.' The lying toad. 'We know what he'd got himself into – the writing was on the wall

– and your father was hardly likely to stand up and face the music. I do wish you'd stop this, your mother is extremely fragile. Just this morning she has to leave the home she's lived in for almost thirty years. All this talk of murder is too much for her to cope with.'

Clara wasn't paying any attention. Instead, she was looking keenly at the bookshelf behind his head. That's Dad's, she said, pointing at a copy of *On Liberty* by John Stuart Mill. The early start must've addled her poor mind, I hadn't read a book since Olivia forced me to read *Peepo* to Jemima and I got so bored I let her watch a Bond movie with me instead.

'No no.' Charles sounded like he was spluttering slightly, and I craned my head to look again at what Clara was pointing at. There, right next to some old law books, was my Brancetti sculpture! I let out a roar of rage which sent one of the drones the centre uses when they're short-staffed flying over to my cubicle. Its little eyes flashed at me, and an automated voice demanded that I respect the community rules about silence. Lowering my voice to a hiss, I caught the end of a response from my daughter: '. . . since I was born, Charles, I remember because I once threw it at Lyra's head.'

My brother-in-law was visibly uncomfortable now, loosening his tie and coughing in that irritating way that he does. 'It's not an original, darling, obviously my funds don't stretch that far, this is just a mass-produced knock-off. A little embarrassing to admit, but there it is.' She marched over and picked it up, her face triumphant.

'It still has the scratch on it. I missed Lyra, unfortunately, and it hit the wall. That mark would hardly be on a copy, would it? Why have you got one of Dad's most prized possessions in your sitting room? And where,' she gestured to the boxes, 'are you going?'

I have to say, I was impressed with my youngest daughter. All looks and no books, we'd always said, but here she was, solving crimes and humiliating the oily Charles Holdwood in one go. Charles smoothed his hair and attempted a smile. Then he held up his hands.

'Ok, you're a smart girl, I'll tell you the truth. I took a few things from the house before the asset forfeiture notice came through, some keepsakes for your mother. Rash of me, but I know that however bad things are now, they're only go to get worse. Everything, and I do mean *everything*, will soon be gone. We're trying very hard to save Gables but the rest is . . .' He clicked his fingers. 'I'm the only one looking out for your family now, Clara, and I'm trying my best.' For perhaps the first time, I wished my wife was here, just so she could see what a snake her 'saintly' older brother was. She'd always compared us, holding Charles up as some beacon of morality whenever I did anything wrong and now here he was, nicking from his own family. At least I'd done it to people I cared nothing for.

She wasn't buying it, that much was obvious. Clara was the most suspicious of all beings, a teenage girl. If it wasn't for all the hormones, they could run the most successful interrogation team the world has ever seen. 'I came to see you because all the talk of people being down by the lake last night reminded me that *you* were there just before midnight too.'

He nodded. 'Yes, I was taking some air, the tents had got very stuffy. I saw Giles right before we heard the commotion, I told the police that.' My daughter narrowed her eyes.

'Right. But before that, you were talking to Olivia. I was . . . on my way to show my mate the church . . .' she stumbled on this, what 17-year-old enthusiastically shows her friend a holy site at a party? More likely, they were doing drugs, but who was

I to judge? 'And you were saying she'd need to leave Gables by 9 a.m., why?'

He pursed his lips. 'You'll have to ask your mother about that.'

So they'd been planning her departure for the morning after my birthday party, early enough that I'd still be asleep. How cowardly.

'Yeah ok, but you've been coming over pretty much every day since Dad died and it's been impossible to avoid hearing you talking . . .' she's been eavesdropping like crazy, 'and I know you've got some secret fund set up for her so it's not really private anymore, is it?' He stood up, failing to conceal his shock at this casual revelation.

'I really do need to get to work, Clara. Rest assured I'm here to help you through this difficult time, which, I hate to remind you, was caused by your father. The adults are dealing with things so you don't have to.' He almost marched her to the door, reminding her to be kind to her mother. Clara's faced remained impassive, even though he had her by the hoodie.

'Where *are* you moving though?' she said as they reached the hallway.

'Oh, just somewhere a little more central, nearer to work,' he replied, his confidence returning now she was nearly out of the house.

'Can I see?' He looked like he was about to say no, but he picked up a brochure from the hallway table and handed it to her. A three-bedroom mansion flat in Marylebone, decked out in dark wood and marble with an on-site gym and 24/7 concierge. Asking price – five million and some change. It was about the last place I'd have imagined my brother-in-law living.

'Fancy. I'll take this, show Olivia. She'll be so jealous. Just as she's getting kicked out of her house, you're buying this place. I didn't know you earned so much, Uncle Charles. No offence, but Dad always said you were sort of a middling lawyer.'

He snatched the brochure back. A silence, then: 'What do you want?' Said through slightly gritted teeth. And just like that, my youngest daughter lived up to the name Wistern and set out her demands.

THE SLEUTH

@thesleuth
100k subscribers

I'd finally hit 100,000 followers, and toyed with the idea of doing a video with balloons to celebrate, but forgot all about it when Luke replied to my message, agreeing to meet me again without much persuasion. He even wanted to apologise for brushing me off. People always treat you differently when you're famous. Even Michaela Sturrock, the most annoying girl at school, got super popular after she went on a reality dating show called *Shag, Marry or Kill*, where people either slept together, got married in a fake ceremony or hunted each other with actual crossbows. The producers insisted the bolts weren't lethal, but the show got pulled after Michaela had her arm broken by a shot. She was so annoying that someone tried to kill her on TV, and *still* everyone in town queued up to buy her drinks in the pub. She was even guest of honour at the Chipping Marston fireworks night but had to leave after a particularly loud Catherine wheel went off and triggered her memory of running away from Chad, the trigger-happy crossbow contestant.

We met at the Gloomy Hedgehog, a pub which lived up to its name. Even the beer looked deflated. I filmed him from the neck down again, and the conversation danced around for a bit until I told him we needed to talk about Jemima. 'She's currently my prime suspect; if you know anything that might clear her name, now's the time to say it.' It worked like a charm. He'd been having an affair with Jemima Wistern.

'For years,' he said, looking anguished. 'On and off since she was sixteen. We'd meet up whenever she could get down, even after she'd met her husband. Especially then. Dunno why she married the guy, she was always complaining about how boring he was. She told me we'd be together eventually and that she just had to do what her parents expected for a bit before we settled down. I know we were from different worlds but we worked you know? She was amazing – not like her family at all when we were teenagers. That changed when she went off to uni. I found out she'd got together with Will when they came into the pub with their mates. They trashed the place, not giving a shit because her dad owned it. And while she was being sick outside, she told me they were living together! I'd been saving up so I could move to London and be with her and it meant fuck all to her.' It was hard to try to conceal my complete hunger for more information while I made comforting noises and waited for him to carry on.

They'd stopped speaking for six months, and then seen each other again at the pub. 'She'd walked in on her dad getting a blow job from his secretary and I comforted her, I felt bad she had to see that. That's when things started up again. And that's why she wasn't at the party when everything kicked off that night. Her dad knew I knew what he was doing with his PA, and he also knew about me and Jem somehow. So we were sort of locked in together. He asked me to work his birthday with a mean look

in his eye you know? Not the sort of offer I could turn down.'
He looked embarrassed. 'And besides, I wanted to see Jem. The
girl's a nightmare – she won't be seen anywhere public with me
but she'll drunkenly call me up all the time and tell me she can't
live without me. It messes with your head. I've tried to move on
from her but I can't do it. I'm honestly not even sure what I like
about her. She's not the kind of girl I thought I'd end up with
for sure.' He looked at me as if I'd understand, and I did. Sort
of. He thought he'd end up with a girl like me. But he didn't
want that, he wanted the rich girl who was mean to him. I wasn't
exactly brimming with sympathy.

'So that night,' I'd said, losing interest in the upstairs downstairs love affair he was so intent on describing as a big romance.
'What really happened?'

They'd had a big fight when they finally got a minute alone.
After the dinner, he'd been working the keg at the bar and Jemima
had walked up with her husband. She'd ordered two glasses of
Champagne off his colleague and entirely blanked him.

'I was so fed up. I grabbed a bottle of wine from the tent
and took it down to the lake when I got a five-minute break.
Then I texted her and told her if she didn't meet me, I'd tell her
fella everything.' He looked triumphant as he said it. She'd gone
of course, why would she risk it? Having her secret boyfriend
reveal all at such a big party would be the kind of gossip her
friends would feed off for months.

They'd fought, they'd made up, they'd probably done some
kind of fumbling, but I didn't want to know about that. Call me
a prude but all the sex stuff that intersects with true crime makes
me uncomfortable. Murder isn't sexy, although I know it's a great
selling point. There's one true crime podcast called *Bae or Slay*
which rates serial killers on how fit they are and the hosts get
giddy ranking everyone from Richard Ramirez (they gave him a

seven) to Harold Shipman (a one, and only because they found an old photo where he was wearing a Fair Isle sweater they liked). Their tagline is 'Slaying it, literally' and even in Chipping Marston, I've seen at least two teenagers wearing jumpers emblazoned with it.

At one point during their reunion, they'd heard noises near the house. When Jemima saw it was Anthony with Lainey, she'd snuffed out the candle and made him lie down in the dark. Apparently Anthony had even knocked on the window, slurring about how squatters weren't allowed, before giving up and walking away.

'Close call.' Luke shuddered. After whatever making up they did, Jemima and Luke fell asleep, which seemed insane to me since she was at a black tie event for her dad and he was working, but then I've always been afraid of spontaneity. 'It was really romantic,' he said, his eyes slightly out of focus as if he was back in the moment. 'Until we were interrupted again.'

This time it was from the other side of the lake. 'Her dad was back, and Jemima opened the door so she could hear what was happening. He was with some guy who kept asking why a woman called Anita was harassing him at work, and Anthony was telling him not to worry about it. It got a bit nasty to be honest, the guy took a swing at Anthony and he sort of stumbled backwards like he might go down. I had to stop Jem rushing out to help him – he was just winded I think. She hated him but she always defended him when anyone else slagged him off.'

'And then?' I asked, feeling anticipation rise in my chest.

'He stormed off after a few minutes and Anthony just stood there sort of laughing to himself, which was a bit weird. Jem was about to go see if he was ok, but then her *mum* turned up.' Here we go. 'She walked right up to him and shoved him in the chest! Mental. Honestly, I always worried about Jem meeting my mum, but her family are straight-up dysfunctional. Jem's mum and dad went at it for a bit, and I told Jem we had to go. They were walking nearer and nearer the summerhouse, and I didn't want to risk being caught. We scrambled to get dressed – Jem knocked over the bottle and spilt red wine all down her dress – but we snuck out just in time; when we left they were almost at the jetty.'

He insisted he didn't know what happened next, and looked at me blankly when I suggested he'd witnessed the final moments of Anthony Wistern's life. 'It wasn't dramatic or anything. Just a husband-and-wife barney. And they didn't find him for at least another twenty minutes. That's *ages*.'

Who are these people who walk through the world with such little interest in what's really going on? What did Jemima think, I ventured, but he just shrugged. It turned out Jemima wasn't speaking to him, and hadn't since the night of the party. He'd been calling and texting every day but nothing. It was clear now why he'd changed his mind about talking to me; Luke had worked himself up into a rage and figured out that burning everything down might be the only way she'd respond. Well, I was happy to be of service. All he asked of me was not to use his name.

'Don't want my mum knowing I was still seeing her, she calls Jem a tart with no heart.'

I felt gross doing it, but I told him I'd heard a rumour she might be pregnant and he went quiet.

'Right then,' he said as he got in his car. 'I wish you'd told me that before.' Then he drove off at speed and something told me I'd lost a possible friend there.

I didn't waste much time on Luke's sorrows. This was my biggest win so far. I was literally getting information the police could only dream of – and the net was really closing in on Olivia. I had conflicting feelings about when to post this news online.

Too soon and it might make the Wisterns close ranks even more. Too late and I'd lose momentum. At the moment, I was posting a new video at least once a day, often twice, even when I had no new information. It didn't much matter – as long as the vlogs had catchy titles which drew you in. 'The killer's taunting us' did well, as did 'You won't believe this', which was just a brief post about how much Gables was worth (9 million according to a website I found in 3 seconds). Everything is content, even if it's not relevant. I don't much like this side of it, but it helps drive attention. And attention helps achieve justice. A small evil for a greater good, that's what I tell myself.

Tatler interview, November issue

Once upon a time, a girl with hair the colour of rich cocoa was born in a birthing pool at her family's chateau, set in the hills above Nice. The year was 2001. This baby grew up to be a natural artist, a social whirlwind and a distinguished ballet dancer. She had everything a little girl could dream of, beautiful parents, houses around the world and even her own pony. Aged just fifteen, she was already one of *Tatler*'s 'guests to invite to any party', and her model good looks landed her a modelling gig with Candarge diamonds. Life was good for this lucky girl. But a few months ago, it all fell apart and the life of this modern princess was shattered into a million pieces. For this lucky young woman was the daughter of Anthony Wistern, the celebrated banker who died in July and was later found to have been running a Ponzi scheme which targeted some of London's wealthiest men and women. Since this revelation, the Wisterns have been cast out of a community they once led. Gone are the parties, galas and holidays. Instead, the family has had its assets frozen, their house in Holland Park raided, and their reputations decimated. Clara's mother Olivia is said to have decamped to the family's country home in Oxfordshire and is reportedly 'a shadow of her former self'. A great beauty in her own right, she denies knowing anything about her husband's actions, though many have raised an eyebrow at this. 'They were a team, and she was no fool. Liv spent other people's money with impunity,' said one former friend who holidayed with the couple in Portofino.

For Clara Wistern, life must go on. She is living with an uncle, preparing for her A-level exams next spring, and comes to meet me with a bag full of books just like any other studious teenager, except that the tote is Hermes, out of which she pulls some crystals which she arranges in a circle around us, 'to give us connection'. She's beautiful, with luminous skin and diamond studs all the way up both ears. And she's ready to talk, despite knowing that she's unlikely to garner much sympathy.

'I accept my life as it is now, and that means talking about what's happened. For me, it's important to process this trauma before I can move on.' We talk for a while about what happened to her father as we wait for our coffees (an oat milk macchiato for Clara, who is wary of dairy, on the advice of her herbalist). We talk a little about her studies ('I'd like to help people in the future, that's why doing well in art is so important to me. It helps process emotions.') I ask her what kind of work she envisages doing in the future, but she's not sure. 'Maybe setting up a charity? I'm not really a logistics person, but I could definitely fundraise.' Like her mother, Clara is a fabulous party thrower; she eagerly regales me with the story of how she organised her sixteenth birthday bash. 'I wanted a venue that hadn't been done to death – and in London that's almost impossible – so I made the planner beg the Bank of England to let us use their rooftop. It was amazing, we had fire-breathing tightrope walkers.'

After a long conversation about grief and the importance of self-care (Clara is wise beyond her years and makes sure to maintain regular facial and massage sessions. 'Prevention is better than a cure, that's what I've learnt'), we inch closer towards the elephant in the room. I skirt around her father's death, unwilling to upset this diminutive teenager who checks her phone every two minutes as if hoping for good news. Eventually, she raises it herself.

'I don't remember much about the evening to be honest, I think from shock . . .' She trails off and gives a half smile, before applying lip gloss and checking her phone again. Early reports of Anthony Wistern's death reverberated around London's social scene, with many refusing to believe it was true. Clara says she was one of them. 'I thought it was a joke,' she tells me, a single tear in her left eye threatening to ruin her perfectly made-up face. 'He was an action man, he used to do squats with me standing on his shoulders. The idea that he could die seemed unfathomable.'

And what, I tentatively ask, did she make of the allegations that her father had stolen millions from people he knew, including the uncle of one of her classmates? At this, Clara Wistern displays some of the steeliness her father was known for, telling me that many people were jealous of her family.

'It goes against everything he stood for,' she says, lifting her face up in defiance. 'He worked really hard, he had a talent for business that so many others dreamt of. It seems awfully convenient to pin it all on him now he's not here to speak for himself.' A loyal daughter, it's understandable she would defend her parents in this way, but I feel I must press her on the issue. As I do, she suddenly looks like a frightened little girl, and the mother in me just wants to give her a hug.

'I think him dying in an accident is just impossible,' she says finally, looking at me in the eyes. I ask her what she means, and she shakes her glossy hair vehemently. 'It's just so easy now, isn't it? To pin this all on him and take away everything we have. I just think it's all too convenient and I've never been afraid of asking questions others won't.' She calms down and breathes through her nose (*for more tips on meditation, read our feature on Princess Beatriz of Spain and her spiritual advisor Clemente who teaches 'elite nostril work'*). I ask if she's saying her father was murdered and she shrugs. Her poise makes it easy to forget she's not quite an adult yet.

'I think he wouldn't just have fallen off a jetty like that. There's a person making videos about him, did you know that?' She pulls out her phone and shows me the account. At least fifty videos are on display, all overlaid with text which say things like 'The missing piece of evidence that proves this was a cover-up.' I ask Clara if she knows who's making them and she shakes her head. 'When I saw the first one, I thought they were just some basement loser. But you watch one, then another and it's made me think,' she replies. 'My dad had a lot of power, that made other people resent him. So I think he was killed, and so do all my friends.' I ask what's next for this smart and beautiful girl and she brightens.

'My whole life has been turned upside down. I'll get my exams and probably go travelling or something. Maybe do some modelling to fund it, I've always enjoyed expressing myself artistically like that. Maybe help get the truth about my dad – that would make him proud.' Conspiracy theory, or just grief manifesting in a different way? It's not for me to say (*if you'd like to know more about manifesting, consider our piece on Plum Helly Jones, London's latest mystic who argues we can all manifest our destiny*).

We say our goodbyes as the sun gently dips behind the houses outside, and I have the chance to see her face in profile properly again. The nose of her father, proud and straight. The big eyes of her mother. And a mouth all her own, set in a determined pout. Clara Wistern could most certainly be a full-time model if she wished. For the photoshoot which accompanies this article, the entire team spoke highly of her determination to get the best shot. Draped in diamonds and wearing autumn's most luxurious fabrics, readers will surely agree that the crown might have been snatched away, but the princess remains, even if the fairytale now looks slightly more complicated (for the cosiest autumn looks, turn to page 48 where we suggest you try spun silk cashmere handmade in Orkney by nuns who only use eighth-century looms).

She certainly has an uphill battle to get people to see past her last name, however. The stain Anthony Wistern has left behind will take many years to wash away, no matter how dazzling his youngest daughter may be.

ANTHONY

I watched my wife pick up the magazine with the rest of the mail and walk into the kitchen. Liv was wearing one of my old robes, a silk number I'd always thought made me look like an Italian count, and it drowned her. She'd lost weight; my wife was always someone who ate to live and now she wasn't bothering. Her hair hung limply around her shoulders and to my horror, she appeared to be wearing sheepskin slippers much like the ones I remember my grandmother calling 'baffs'. She needed to get it together. Just because the walls had fallen in, didn't mean she had to go around looking like someone who had finally been allowed out on day release.

Olivia made herself a cup of coffee and took the magazine into the orangerie. What a beautiful building it was, it still made my heart beat faster when I saw it. The double domes made it look a little like a nice pair of bosoms, which had a similar effect on the old pulse. I'd even taught the children to call it the booby room when they were little, which Liv never found funny. Inside, the plants were thriving, which was the only bonus of having a son like Fred. The staff might have pushed off, but he'd never

241

leave them to rot like Liv would've. Plants took one look at my wife and wilted in defeat.

I only had half an eye on Liv, as I worked through a list of people who had motive for killing me. Susan suggested I write one, in a slightly patronising way when she noted how long I'd been at the centre. 'Get it down on paper – the old-fashioned ways are often the best!' she'd trilled, before scurrying off to deal with a heating issue. It occurred to me, as she vanished round a corner, that there was no central heating in the building and I wondered if she'd made up an excuse to get away from me.

The list was impressive, in a worrying sort of way. I'd come up with at least three names before I even hit eighteen. From there, it only got worse. So many people who might wish me dead, mainly because I'd bested them in some way. Johnny Sebold, who'd planned to propose to his girlfriend, until a night at Larizio's put paid to all that. Once she saw my hips on the dancefloor, all thoughts of matrimony to dull Johnny-boy were gone. Then there were men who I'd cut out of deals, still burning with resentment all these years later. One of them saw me at the Cipriani in Venice a couple of months before I died, and sent over a bottle of Champagne. I nodded at him across the bar in thanks, and he mouthed 'choke on it' back. Who else? A fair number of women, I can't lie. Could I name them all? Not a chance. Most of them probably wouldn't actually kill me, despite their many threats. A heat of the moment 'I hope you die a slow and painful death' just because they've found out you're seeing their best friend is hardly a serious worry, is it?

I scanned the list as Liv flicked through the magazine. Giles, the kids, Charles, if only because he was jealous of what I'd achieved. Prince Albert of Monaco, who thought he was better at squash than he was and got taught a lesson – was that a good enough reason? I'd put a lot of effort into this bloody list, but none of them really felt right. Frustrated, I screwed it into a ball and threw it at a passing orderly's head which earned me an hour of what was called 'contemplation' but was for all intents and purposes, detention. It made sense somehow; every decision taken by the architects of the afterlife strongly suggested they'd been failed teachers with a deep yearning for the respect not given them in life.

A scream forced my attention back to my wife. I peered at what she was reading more closely – these monitors might be old (a cost-cutting measure according to the clipboard dogsbody), but I still managed to get a good look at a photo of a beautiful young woman atop a marble statue of a Greek god. In a bikini made of wildflowers, lovely looking bos . . . Jesus Christ, it was Clara. My seventeen-year-old daughter was half naked in Tatler, right under a headline which read 'Wistern Wins Again'.

I cursed my wife for flicking through the piece so quickly and craned my head over her shoulder to see better. A lot of dross about adversity, something my daughter wouldn't know how to spell let alone experience and then! She'd mentioned that strange woman making those videos, praising her for looking at my death and urging others to do the same. Liv grabbed her phone and stabbed at it. If she was calling Clara, she'd be disappointed. Phones were for 'geriatrics' apparently, and the only way you could even hope to get hold of her was through WhatsApp. Even then, she'd normally leave you on read unless she wanted something. And what could Liv offer now? Frustrated, she tried a new tack. Charles picked up after the third ring and she berated him for letting Clara do the interview. I couldn't hear much of what he said, but I gathered he thought it was a good sign that *Tatler* would still print the name Wistern and said something about how my wife should be grateful for that.

'She thinks,' hissed Liv, 'Anthony was murdered. This is

insanity, Charles, the girl isn't well.' My wife's brother was clearly trying to placate her, but she was having none of it. 'I just want to be back in London and for everything to quieten down. I can't do that without money, Charles. I need you to do more, you're my *brother*.' She was pouting as she talked, just as she always did when she felt like she wasn't being given what she wanted quickly enough. She looked so desperate I felt a little pang of guilt but it went away soon enough. I'd given her everything and she'd still been planning to jump ship. Let Charles sink with her.

I went over to see Clara, thinking perhaps that she might be doing something worthwhile with her newfound realisation. She was not. My youngest daughter's deal with Charles meant she got to live in his shiny new flat – how had he got that past Olivia? – receive a hefty allowance, and carry on as though none of this had ever happened. I found her lip syncing to some disembodied American voice saying, 'It's hot girl autumn' and recording it again and again. Feeling slightly on the edge of despair I turned off the monitors and fervently tried not to think about how much I missed the soothing embrace of alcohol in these moments. I looked down at my list of suspects and scored all of them off except my family. I went through what I now knew about the evening and crossed off more names. The only ones left were Jemima and my wife.

OLIVIA

Of course she'd only done it to make me angry. To be stuck in exile while Clara was doing photoshoots at, of all places, my great friend Nancy Meluise's country house, was just breathtakingly galling. Nancy, who spoke to the *Telegraph* just weeks ago and said I was always 'grasping and a little too keen'.

After speaking with Charles, I felt slightly calmer. Charles had rented me a flat in Marylebone, which I could move into once the dust had settled. I didn't love that he was currently living there with Clara, but accepted it made sense while he was having renovations done to his place. My daughter had been insistent on staying in London, and Charles even suggested the idea to me, eager to help lighten my load. I've always held the upper hand over my brother. Smart with figures but no good at emotions, which made manipulating him fairly straightforward. One sign of female emotion and he'd do whatever I wanted in order for it to stop. It was all the easier since he never married, which didn't surprise me one bit. About as much sex appeal as a wallaby, that man.

Freddy drove past the kitchen window astride an enormous

tractor and I closed the curtains. We hadn't spoken since I got here, I was too enraged that he'd spoken to that mad girl so openly. Apparently, she used to work at Anthony's pub, before being fired for theft. I wondered whether I should leak that to the papers, since several of them had picked up on Clara's claims and were now linking to this woman's revolting channel. My idiotic daughter had poured petrol all over flames which had been dying down slowly, ever since the coroner ruled Anthony's death a probable accident.

'Mr Wistern was highly stressed as a result of his criminality, knowing that it was almost certainly about to be unmasked, and the night of his birthday had imbibed a large amount of alcohol. Cocaine was also found in his system . . .' blah blah blah. It would've been accepted by everybody, had Clara not announced to the world that she thought differently. All my children acted like contrarian fools as teenagers. Lyra voted for the Socialist Workers Party when she hit eighteen, though even that was less imaginative than her younger sister's attempt.

My phone rang. Lyra; well I didn't want to talk to her, I didn't want to talk to any of them. It buzzed again. Jemima this time, sobbing so loudly I couldn't hear anything she was saying. How can I help you when you're behaving like a toddler, I asked her, before hanging up. Lyra rang again, and I picked up feeling very aggrieved that I was withering away down here and they only thought to call me when they needed something. At least she was calm, almost nothing fazes that girl. A bomb could go off right next to her and my daughter would probably order another glass of wine.

'There's a new video up,' she said, sounding amused. 'And it's a doozy. Hold on, I've sent you the link.' It popped up on my laptop, and immediately started playing an advert for pest control. This girl was making money off our backs now. The advert came to an end, with the jingle 'Wipe them out with just one swipe', and then a caption appeared on the screen. 'You'll never guess what I've found out.' A headless man was talking, the noise from a pub making it slightly hard to hear. 'It's Luke, Jemima's local boytoy . . .'

I listened to the whole thing in growing horror, and stayed rigid for a second as the screen faded to darkness, followed by another caption. 'Doesn't this point the finger right at a certain person? Post your thoughts in the comments below.' My ears buzzing in a slightly frightening way, I was only vaguely aware that Lyra was still on the phone. I slammed the laptop shut and walked out of the room, desperate to get as far away from it as possible.

ANTHONY

I watched her pour herself a glass of whisky and drain it. The last time Liv drank Scotch was at a Burns night party hosted by a Texan woman called Rose who was fast gaining a reputation for being a fantastic party hostess. My wife didn't say it, but I knew she was almost nose-bleedingly furious that someone had encroached on her patch. The party, a riot of tartan, bagpipes and dancing, appalled the few Scottish people there but was fantastic fun for the rest of us. My wife was furious at this success, downing Macallan Rare as though it was about to run out. Eventually, she was copiously sick into a rose bush (undeniably aiming right there to send a signal to our hostess) and she'd never drunk whisky since, so I knew she must be feeling particularly panicked. Was she worried about someone stalking our family? I doubted it. She might not like this kind of attention, but she had so far shown no interest in listening to this person's theories. It must have been what was said in the video.

The thought crept up on me for the first time. Did Olivia have anything to do with it? She is, after all, the most vengeful woman you'll ever meet. The woman remembers slights from decades ago, she still talks about her oldest friend Penny not bringing a present to her eleventh birthday. Liv could carry a grudge against an inanimate object if she felt it had wronged her. She once made me get rid of a painting of a seventeenth-century milkmaid I adored because she was certain the eyes were looking at her in a 'nasty way'. But I never really thought *I'd* be in her crosshairs; I'd always managed to overwhelm her vast stores of resentment with my abundance of charm.

Casting my mind back again, I tried to remember the last time I saw her that night. It was after dinner, after the speeches, certainly when I was so addled by all the booze that I only vaguely remember her telling me to pull it together in a quiet hiss. Was that it? I groaned, loud enough that the woman in the next cubicle shot her head up and glared at me. Asking to be moved wouldn't help; I desperately wanted to avoid being anywhere close to the guy near the end who sobbed a lot and spent all his time watching his girlfriend furiously having sex with her new partner (who happened to be his much-better-looking younger brother). He'd been offered counselling and advised not to watch, but he refused, and sounds of her moans and his wailing created a hideous cacophony.

Was I remembering a moment with her down by the lake, or was I making it up because she'd now admitted it? The more I pushed, the more I could see her outline, standing in front of me. What she was saying, I couldn't remember, but I knew there was a pit of dread in my stomach. When Liv lost it, she really went for me. I know it's not acceptable to say that women are more emotional, but we all know it's true. Nobody can screech like a banshee like a woman with a grudge. Not for the first time, I cursed this place and its rules. I knew they had the capacity to retrieve lost memories and yet they didn't let us do it. There was an old lady who sat a few rows back from me who begged to be able to remember moments with her husband before she'd died but was told it wasn't 'helpful for her journey'. She'd had dementia, the last thing she could recall was him wiping her arse, and still they turned her down.

Liv must know she was the last person to see me alive. If she didn't tell the police, she must be involved somehow.

THE SLEUTH

@thesleuth
108.9k subscribers

I'd added my own name to Google alerts well over a year ago when I'd been deep in a pit of self-pity. It made me nasty, I can see that now. I guess I wanted other people to feel as bad as I did, but since I never saw anyone, the only way I knew how to do that was to do some light trolling. It was mainly just snarky comments when people came up with stupid theories – the kind of amateur hour crime voyeurs who make the rest of us look bad. Then I'd get paranoid and worry that someone would unmask me – it happened sometimes, people's lives could be ruined with just a little digging.

My name never came up anywhere. The only mention of me online is a photo of me in the *Chipping Marston Chronicle* aged eleven, dressed as an elf in a Christmas pantomime at the theatre Anthony Wistern helped to fund funnily enough. Sometimes I wonder if it wasn't a mistake to do all of this anonymously. I've seen some of these amateur TikTok sleuths make a ton of money while I do all of this for next to nothing. It's all about the victim of course, but it would be nice to get a real salary for my work. When I solve this murder, I'll ask the *Crime Kitten* girls who their agent is.

The alert showed one mention of the name of my channel – I'd added that when I started getting proper views and wanted to check people were crediting me properly. It was in *Tatler*, a magazine my mum used to read at the hairdressers. I scrolled through the article – an interview with Clara Wistern complete with about fifteen photos. After flipping past an image of her in crystal jodhpurs astride a fountain spraying water out of a stone lion's mouth, I found it. She'd been watching my videos. She believed what I was saying. I mean, she didn't say it outright but that's clearly what she meant. Fred had said she believed me but I'd barely listened because I'd been so intent on trying to convince him instead. But here was someone inside the family who didn't need convincing, and she seemed to think her mother was the strongest suspect.

I guess I'd always known it was his wife. After reading about Lainey Goodman, I'd never really suspected a wronged business partner or an angry neighbour. It was way too obvious his death was a personal thing. Our next-door neighbours were close friends, and to me, they were infinitely more interesting than my own family. Lee had a motorbike and Marian dyed her hair funny colours and the kids were allowed all the sugar they wanted, while my mum thought a sweet treat was a fig roll because she was terrified white sugar would kill me. But one morning I woke up to the sounds of metal screeching. When I looked outside, Marian was in her car, reversing over Lee's motorbike. It turned out Lee had been having an affair with a colleague of Marian's; our family were firmly team Marian, and when she was charged with destruction of property, Mum even testified in court that Marian hadn't seen the motorbike in the driveway. A nice try, but didn't explain why she'd reversed over it eight times, and Marian was given a pretty hefty fine. She kept the exhaust pipe mounted in the hallway as a trophy for years. Marian was the most peaceful person I'd ever met, and if she could almost flatten a motorbike with her rage, I could sort of understand how infidelity could make you kill a person.

Olivia was the obvious choice then. But even with my connections to Fred, I couldn't see how he would willingly put me in a room with his mother so that I could confront her. It's different with the rich – you can't just knock on their door or ask their neighbours what's gone on. It would be easy for her to use her influence to throw the autopsy, she probably paid someone to say it was an accident. People are so bloody naive, they think money just enables you to buy nice things. But the real advantage wealth brings is how brilliantly it can exempt you from the normal rules that everyone else has to follow. I still had a few cards to play though. I knew about Jemima and Luke. Maybe it was time to pay poor old Will a visit. According to my research, he owned a china shop. I guess my presence there would make me the bull. Good title for a video that, guaranteed numbers.

ANTHONY

Introspection isn't something I used to give much sway – onwards and upwards, don't look back, that was my philosophy – but there's not much else to do here. I was a young man with a drive to attack the world. It was a shot in the arm to me, starting my first job in the city. I climbed the ranks at Jerrard's pretty fast, always wanting more than the guy sitting next to me. I worked harder but I also learnt how to work better. Most importantly I learnt how to charm people, how to make them want to give me their money and then stay and buy me a drink. The win was all I sought, I was a competitive man and it didn't matter much what the prize was, I just wanted to be victorious. In business, and in life. The money, as hard as it might be to believe, was never the end result for me, and maybe that's why I was so good at making it. The desperation some people give off in the pursuit of it is a stench you try to avoid – I knew that better than most.

When Giles and I left to start our own fund, I was confident it would be a success. Giles wasn't quite as aggressive as me, but we both knew enough of the right people and he lent a serious-ness that I needed. Our tactic was not to solicit, you see, but we

254

knew how to hustle. The trick was to make out like it was so exclusive that we didn't need your custom, and that makes people rabid. I remember back in the early days when we weren't making any proper money, the owner of one of the oldest auction houses in the world practically begging me to let him invest, and me turning him down in front of his wife just because I didn't like the shoes he was wearing. That kind of story became almost mythical, and only heightened the interest. We were the disruptors, we saw ourselves as the modern pirates of finance, upturning the stuffy corporate environment and taking whatever we wanted. The *FT* once ran a feature about us with a photo of Giles and me lounging on a bright pink sofa wearing jeans, calling us the 'new guard'. I framed it and hung it over the toilet.

Nobody wants to hang around with finance guys, they're the people you body-swerve so hard you give yourself a hernia, so I made a concerted effort to be accepted into the higher echelons of society. The sweet spot is the arts crowd, enough inherited wealth to do what they liked, enough creativity that people don't see them as idle trustafarians. It's a tough scene to break into, but you can be welcomed into any circle if you throw enough money at them. Liv's name helped with that, it blunted my new money sheen somewhat. And we donated heavily; I encouraged my wife to put on parties for fashion types, writers and musicians. We collected new artists' works and made a name for ourselves in a new social circle and my star kept rising. I was respected and wooed by this chosen clique, but when you reach a certain level you learn a secret. All rich people are dull, it doesn't matter if it's money passed down through the centuries or cash made by some wheeler-dealer in the last five minutes. They assume their money makes them interesting, in the same way a model thinks her beauty is enough to get her through life. And for the most part, it is. But by god, it doesn't make for fun.

There are only so many events where people line up to kiss your arse before you want to punch someone in the face just to mix it up a bit. How many cars can you realistically buy before you start forgetting where you've left them? For me, the number was seven, and I got rid of all but one when I realised I'd left a Bentley in a garage off Piccadilly for eight months without ever thinking of it. We had so many staff at one point that it felt like our house was a hotel, and there's only so many holidays in far flung places you can take before you realise the experience you're buying is so cosseted that you might as well have stayed home.

I began to take more risks. I bought a hang glider and when that got boring, started training with MMA champions. I went cave diving, and only stopped when a chap I knew died and Jemima made me swear I'd never do it again. Same with drugs – as fun as they were, I knew my limits. Dying from stupidity wasn't my thing.

But I was just so bloody bored. Even women, my greatest weakness, weren't captivating me as they used to. One night I took a gorgeous woman out for dinner before taking her back to Claridges for the inevitable after-party. In the early hours of the morning, after what I'd assumed had been a fantastic night for both of us, she rolled over and asked me if I'd get her boyfriend a job at Wismere. 'We want to buy a house somewhere out in Godalming,' she said eagerly, 'a job with you would put us on the right track.'

Instead of a glorious repeat performance that morning, I spent an hour talking to her about the prospects of some no-mark named Ludo. That's when I realised that to her, *I* was the dull finance guy. When I'd started out, we'd been fresh-faced young men who'd shaken up an ancient industry, but now suddenly, we were establishment; it shook me to my core.

That's when I started my little bonus fund, thinking if I just went back to basics, I might find the drive I had for it all those years ago. I barely had to do anything at Wismere by then, Giles and I were figureheads mostly, our reputations pulling in the cash and our team of younger and hungrier lackeys doing the long hours for us. I probably surprised everyone by announcing I was going to do a little side dealing, but nobody would've dared object. I took on a few select clients, although I guess really you'd call them marks. I was bored of strategy, bored of playing nice, bored of throwing in my lot with people I'd never really liked.

It was supposed to be a little game, see? To make life feel interesting again, and perhaps just a little more risky. I'd made my name as the man who could charm the pants off nearly anyone, often literally, but I'd got too good at it. I thought it might be fun to take a fortune off the people I'd never have given a second look, even those who I actively hated. I started off by having lunch with Shane Logan, a guy who'd made his money from discount sportswear shops. He was desperate to be part of the establishment – the man wore red braces for Christ's sake – only the establishment made it clear it didn't want him anywhere near. Even the Tory Party declined a donation from the man, on account of his undeniably murky connections to certain countries where he may or may not have dabbled in some light arms dealing. He was so brash he could've given you a contact rash, and yet I took him out for lunch. Not anywhere someone might see me, I wasn't that willing to blow everything up. At his suggestion, we went to a steakhouse off Piccadilly where the waiters wore gold-buttoned blazers. I almost turned on my heel and left when I saw him, wearing a trilby and a waistcoat, but I steeled myself and endured possibly one of the most absurd meals of my life. By the end of it, I had walked away with a million quid of Logan's money and a promise that I'd be the proud owner of a racehorse called Glamazon by the end of the month.

I'd laughed the whole way back to the office, energised by the grubbiness of it all. Three weeks later, I'd gone to see Tanya Simons. She'd finagled her way into the elderly arms of Sir Benjamin Forte almost twenty years ago and stayed there until he died aged ninety-eight. The general assumption was always that he kept going for so long because she had the most extraordinary bosoms and to die early would be to waste them. When the will was read, it turned out he'd left a cool 45 million to his mistress, which can only mean the woman had magic nipples. I agreed to take her on too, what can I say? She made me laugh – not many women can do that.

Within a few months, I'd amassed a rogues' gallery of clients and made friends in places a man shouldn't find himself after the sun goes down. No actual gangsters, nothing so incendiary. I might have been bored, but I liked my life too much to fraternise with people who'd take out your teeth and call it a greeting.

After six months I had fifty new investors who nobody else would've touched with a barge pole. That number hit sixty-six by the end of the year. I always told people to hand over the cash direct; I wouldn't deal with financial managers – corporate stiffs who pored over every transaction were not my friend – and they did, because they knew I could make demands like that.

I stopped at seventy-six. For no real reason other than that it was the age both my dad and grandfather died and it felt auspicious. The money went into an account offshore, and I wasted no time playing with it. I invested in high-risk, high-reward funds, in companies Wismere wouldn't have gone near in a million years and in countries that took a laxer view on 'ethics'. At the start, it paid off. Of course it did, I wasn't some newbie trader who'd shit his pants at a market wobble. I heavily rewarded the investors I knew were the most demanding, and played hardball with the rest. 'You're here because you know what I can do, so just let me do it.'

It would've been ok if I hadn't met Anita. I had stuck at 76 and then I blew past my own limit. The only truly stupid thing I'd done in sixty fantastic years. Was it worth it? Blowing up my life for a cheap thrill? I'm not a man for regrets. My dad always told me you've got to defend your own actions in life or else what's the point in anything? The billionaire philanthropist Andrew Carnegie once said that 'the man who dies thus rich dies disgraced'. I guess he'd never considered the possibility that you could die *before* the disgrace. That lightens the load somewhat, I have to say.

On balance, I went out on top. But now I'm stuck here, trying and failing to remember whether or not my wife killed me and sometimes, when someone much stupider than me figures out how they died and we have to stand as an old lady vigorously plays them out with a rendition of 'So long, farewell' from the *Sound of Music* on an old bugle, I wish I'd lived a more careful life. Whatever's coming next, it must surely be better than the South Gloucestershire processing centre.

THE SLEUTH

@thesleuth
114k subscribers

Life's a funny one. I'd spent three years bored out of my skull, and then in one day, more happens to me than ever before. I'd got a message from the producer of *Crime Kittens*, the biggest true crime podcast in the UK, asking if I'd come on to talk about my work. Obviously, I jumped at the chance, the show is mega. Carey and Bim, the girls who host it, have their own brand deals and drinks ranges. They're basically celebrities – not just in the crime community but in the actual world too – they even went on *Newsnight* to talk about that guy who kept murdering cats a few years ago. Imagine deciding to be a mass murderer . . . of cats. What a waste of talent.

It was fixed for the Tuesday morning, when Mum's carer would be round and I'd have the time to concentrate properly. Luckily it was all on Zoom, and I could tell the producer was impressed that I had all the right kit. Bit patronising, since I was a presenter myself, but I let it go. Being on *Crime Kittens* would boost my audience massively, and I really wanted them to like me.

I wrote up all my thoughts, and jotted down the relevant timelines and potential reasons for murder before remembering to pull up some stuff about Ponzi schemes and Bernie Madoff so I'd sound like I knew what I was talking about. The girls were really nice, but a bit too giggly for me; I'm not one to discuss disembowelment with a laugh. I have to remind myself I'm better off doing things my way when I feel jealous of Carey and Bim. I want the stories to speak for themselves.

I was only on for about fifteen minutes, the show wasn't all going to be about the Wistern murder like I'd thought, which pissed me off a bit. And I didn't really get a chance to dive into all my information with them, since they were more interested in my own motivation for doing all of this research. Bim actually asked whether I'd call myself a conspiracy theorist, which I thought was a bit of an overstep and led to a discussion between the two about whether the moon landings were faked which made the producer step in and tell them off for getting hysterical, but overall, I enjoyed myself and felt like I'd put my theory across well. Nice girls, as I said, but hardly going to trouble Mensa. Once we'd wrapped, they disconnected immediately, which was rude, but their producer stayed on the line and told me I'd done a brilliant job.

Without saying goodbye to Mum, I told the carer (this time a man called Steve who behaved like his job was the last option on a very long list and sometimes hinted he'd like to ask me out) I'd be out until the early evening and to put her to bed early. I took a bus to Oxford and then a train to London, where I spent the journey researching Will's business. A quick check of his Companies House record proved very interesting. The business was in massive debt, the man was swimming in it. Their spending for the last financial year had been over six million quid, which was a hell of a lot of cups and saucers, but they'd posted a loss of three million. How the hell was this gallery still going? When the train got to London, I decided to walk the rest of the way. As I went, I did an impromptu Q&A with fans about the case. They weren't the most highbrow of questions – one person asked if I thought Anthony's death might've been a sex game gone wrong, but there were a lot of people watching and I arrived in Pimlico feeling pretty boosted.

The shop was one of a row, all with awnings and muted signs. A florist, a candle 'emporium', a place which sold cast iron baths, one which seemed only to offer tablecloths and Will's antique shop. I told myself not to be intimidated, shops like these are a dime a dozen near me, all hustling for the Chipping Marston pound.

I pushed the door several times before realising that there was a bell you had to ring for entry. A woman about my age finally opened it a crack, looking at me with mild uninterest. She asked whether or not I had an appointment. An appointment to see crockery; I had to stop myself from asking whether I should've brought a gift too. Reluctantly, she let me in, and told me she'd be at her desk. I felt a little surge of disappointment – was Will not here?

I walked around hoping it looked like I had purpose, sort of nodding at objects as if they were telling me interesting secrets about the universe. There was an assortment of bowls, mostly pretty well worn, and some jugs which must've looked good five hundred years ago but now looked a lot like the crockery shelf at my nan's place. The woman looked up every time I moved, as if I might be about to grab something and make a run for it. I felt my face flushing at the awkwardness. If Will wasn't here, this was a pointless exercise.

I moved towards the door slowly, but as I did, a man came out from a corridor behind the desk. It was him! Tall, with the kind of posture my dad would call 'the stoop and droop', wearing a cardigan over a checked shirt and looking, to my eyes, a lot older than his 31 years. I moved a little closer so as to hear what they were saying; something about receipts; a quip about a politician being interviewed on the BBC that morning 'his house looks like it was designed by Laura Ashley's camper cousin, not what I'd expect from the law and order minister'; and then finally, in a more serious tone, 'Henry called again.' Will looked uncomfortable when she said that and told her to hang up if he rang back.

'I'm not sure that's the sensible course of action, Will,' the woman said, staring at him as if he were being absurd. 'He's clearly got it into his head that we've done this deliberately and nobody gets where he is without being as dogged as a dodo.'

Will frowned at that. 'They died out, Liz,' he said, but she ignored him.

'He'll come in again if you don't call him back. With his lawyers next time – he threatened to get them involved this morning. Why don't you just let him have this one? Whether he's right or wrong, you don't want him talking. We can do something with it later on.'

He shook his head vehemently at this. 'Because I don't respond to this kind of bullying. The man's a chancer, Oliver Ferrand warned me, but it was such a good offer . . .' He sighed and put on his jacket. I moved to the side of the room and pretended to be interested in a vase which was safely behind a glass screen and looked like it pre-dated Jesus. He was going to get lunch, would the woman like anything? She said no rather rudely, as though she was the boss and not him. He must like difficult women, given the family he married into. I wondered who Henry was and whether Will was in some kind of trouble beyond his enormous debts.

The door slammed, and I lingered another twenty seconds before following. He was a few metres up the road, striding towards a coffee shop. I went slowly, filming him as I walked. I did my usual commentary, 'My source tells me Will might know more than he's letting on, let's find out, shall we?' I waited until he'd bought his lunch and sat down at a table in the corner. Then I swooped.

He looked up as I sat down, clearly surprised a stranger had chosen the chair right next to him. Propping my phone up against a pepper shaker and trying to stop my hand from shaking, I told him I was investigating the murder of his father-in-law and wanted to ask him some questions. No point in trying to go in soft, my online persona is one of action. He looked confused for a second, before his face cleared.

'You're that nutter with the YouTube channel, aren't you?' He made to get up, but I'd wedged him in by sitting down, and after a few attempts he gave up and leaned towards me.

'You need help, seriously. This is an illness, a mental problem. My second cousin's wife's father suffers, but with the right meds—'

I cut him off. 'I know more than you think, Will. I know all his kids hated him. I know people lied about what happened that night. And I know you're in the shit financially. Murder is always motivated by one of three things, Will – sex, revenge, or money.' He closed his mouth then, and frowned. Even his frown was pretty mild, almost like I'd disappointed him.

I pushed on, knowing how good it would look on camera if I was aggressive. 'Why are you covering up a crime, Will?' He shook his head.

'Anthony wasn't murdered. Deep down you must know that.

Not every death is suspicious, even if it seems like too big a coincidence that his business was going down the tubes. I can't have a conversation with you about this, it's completely inappropriate.' He stood up again, this time with a bit more conviction.

'I know your wife wasn't where she said she was that night,' I said, cutting through his fake concern. 'And that means you weren't where you said you were either. Now tell me, am I really the one who needs help?'

He grabbed his coffee and pushed past my chair, forcing my chest into the table. It pissed me off. I was investigating a crime, he had no right to treat me like that. I stood up and spoke louder, cutting through the noise of the cafe.

'You can see how it looks, can't you? Lying about where you were. Not great, Will. The true crime community defends you, they say you probably had no idea what was going on, but that's not entirely true, is it?'

Without warning, he grabbed my arm and led me out of the coffee shop, dragging me down a side road. He turned to me, close enough that I could feel his breath on my face.

'Turn off that camera.' He barked it, pointing at my phone. 'Now.' I began to tell him I had a right to film on public land but he shook his head. 'If you want me to talk, you'll turn it off.' I hesitated. If I left it running, I might get some amazing confrontation which would stir things up online no end. But if I missed something vital? I could ruin this whole case. Reluctantly, I made a show of closing the camera and locking my phone. Immediately, his shoulders dropped a few inches.

'Right. Who's spreading lies like that? Do you know how much shit this family is dealing with? *Do you?* This isn't a game for your internet friends, this is a real situation involving bloody bankruptcy. Every video you put out only prolongs this misery for everyone, did you ever think about that? Do you think about anything but this fantasy life you've created where you impinge on people's grief?' This mild-mannered man looked like he was unravelling in front of my eyes and for a second, I felt a bit afraid. I stared at Will, trying to show him I wouldn't back down, and he released my hand with a sigh.

'How far are you going to go with this?' It sounded like he might be bargaining with me, and I answered boldly.

'As far as I need to get the truth. The truth is all we have in this world.' I realised it sounded corny the moment I said it, like a slogan your mum might have on a throw pillow, next to a sign which read 'This house believes in hugs'. My own mum was a sucker for a sign, there were three in our kitchen alone. It's hard not to feel like you're being mocked when you make up your mum's meds at 6 a.m. underneath an italic banner which reads 'This family runs on laughter'.

'You're mad,' he said, but without any real effort. Mad, just a word used to make you shut up.

'I help solve crimes, that's a pretty logical thing to do if you think about it. Part of a healthy society involves confronting injustice and holding powerful people to account. You might not like it, but I'm not going to stop just because you want me to.' I was hitting my stride now. I felt confident and uncowed.

Will ran his hands through his hair. Floppy, but thinning. Posh men either have amazing hair or they go bald before they hit thirty-five. You see them driving through Chipping Marston all the time, and there's always one sad-looking bald guy who looks ten years older than the rest.

'These bloody documentaries, these podcasts, they've got a lot to answer for. Making tragedy into entertainment. Christ, you filmed my mother-in-law just days after her husband died. Where will this end? Do you actually have any evidence of anything nefarious or is this all just a fantasy you've come up with to make your life more interesting?'

Appealing to my better angels felt a bit rich, given what his wife's family were like. 'I won't stop until I know who killed Anthony Wistern.' He rolled his eyes at this, and I felt the familiar flicker of anger. 'I told you, I know your finances are in the toilet. Did *you* invest with your father-in-law, Will?' It was a reach, nothing I had any proof of, but he flinched and I knew I was on to something. 'I know something else too,' I said, feeling adrenaline shoot through me. 'The reason you couldn't find your wife was because she was with her lover.' The word lover sounded weird the moment I said it. We stared at each other intently for a few seconds, and I tried desperately not to blink in case I lost the upper hand. And then all of a sudden, his demeanour changed. He exhaled loudly, shrugged his shoulders and put his palms out in some kind of pleading gesture. Will didn't look surprised at all, just sort of defeated. Even his cardigan wilted.

'Come back to the gallery at 5.30, and we can talk properly about this. Liz doesn't leave until then, so don't come in before, I don't want her asking questions.'

I nearly said, 'Like she was about Henry?' but held back. I couldn't get involved in everything that my brain told me sounded strange. 'Will you tell me the truth?' I said, trying to play it cool.

He was walking away from me by then, and turned. 'I'll tell you everything.'

THE SLEUTH

@thesleuth

149k subscribers

Well, I was arrested.

I'd turned up at the time Will had given me. I believe that a deal is a deal, just like my dad always told me. His life lessons were always about fairness and integrity, nothing which actually helps me in the real world where people do whatever they want and leave you to deal with the consequences. I'd have been better off with a father like Anthony Wistern, one who encourages you to lie, cheat and steal as much as you can.

When I walked in, Will was standing with two men in suits, and I assumed they were clients, so I hovered by the door waiting for him to finish up but instead, they all turned towards me. I had the feeling that I'd been trapped somehow, a sense that only strengthened when the taller one addressed me, asking for my name. I didn't reply. You don't give your name to a stranger, not even if they flash a badge at you like this one did. So he was a cop. Well I'd rather give my name to a kidnapper than a policeman.

Corrupt or lazy. Sometimes both. There was one cop in our town when I was growing up, and the only time we saw him was at the fish and chip shop, the pub, the ice-cream parlour and occasionally the bakery if it was a special occasion. Barely any crime got solved, except for one memorable time when the chippy was broken into and he was on it like a shot. Never seen someone make an arrest so fast. He got fried fish for free every day for the rest of his life, and told my mum it was better than getting his pension.

I parroted what Geoff had always told us to say in this eventuality. 'I do not have to give you my details unless ordered to by a judge.' The shorter man looked at me for a second with a knotted brow, before breaking into a smile and shooting his partner a look.

'Sounds like someone's been on the internet,' the short guy said, looking amused. 'I'm afraid there's a lot of nonsense there. You don't have to tell us your name . . .' I looked at him with triumph. 'But if you don't, we can arrest you. You don't want that, do you, love?' The taller man, who looked to be more senior, shuffled his feet, clearly uncomfortable with the use of 'love'.

'I'm Detective Blaine and this is Sergeant Rashan. Now we've told you our names, why not give us the same courtesy?' I stayed silent. If they were going to carry on with this charade I wouldn't help them. The cop calling himself Blaine sighed, and came towards me, ushering me further into the shop.

'This man says you've been stalking his family. You've been making videos about them, saying they're murderers?'

Will interjected hastily: 'Saying my father-in-law was murdered and making all sorts of allegations.' The policeman nodded.

'As I said. You do know that under the Harassment Act of 1997, hassling people like this is a criminal offence?'

I felt my throat itching, which was a sure sign I was about to start panicking, but still I stayed silent.

'She's been following my mother-in-law. She broke into their family home and attacked my wife's brother. And now she's attempting to blackmail me with nonsense about this vast conspiracy to kill my father-in-law.' Will looked at Detective Blaine soberly. 'My wife's father died in a tragic accident, it's been incredibly painful for everyone and this has made it substantially more trying. She's pregnant, my wife, and stress is so dangerous, I'm sure you both know that more than anyone.'

What a fucking creep, playing kiss-arse to a bunch of cops. The men all nodded at each other, as if sharing some understanding that I wasn't privy to. In any other circumstances, I'd have laughed. These men were supposed to uphold the law of the land and instead they'd shut down any investigation into Anthony Wistern's death, never mind completely missing his years of embezzlement. And now here they were, summoned by a man knee-deep in it to come and interrogate me for doing *their* job.

Will turned to me and tilted his head as if in sympathy. 'We just want you to stop. It's really sad to see you waste your life like this.'

Patronising lies, designed to make me look mad in front of these officers who could easily take me away and have me sectioned if they wanted to. I felt my heart start skipping beats.

They wouldn't call a journalist mad for doing their job, I told them. I wasn't mentally ill, or a stalker. I just wanted my questions answered. People had definitely lied to the police that night; their colleagues! Didn't that bother them, I asked? According to the *Daily Mail*, Anthony Wistern had a personal fortune of over 50 million quid. How much had been recovered? They looked blank, and in that moment I realised they didn't know who he was. 'Not even half of it,' I finished, feeling angry now, panic receding. 'Where's it all gone? I bet he knows.' Will shrugged when the officers turned towards him, and put his arms out at me.

'See what I mean?' he said. Blaine looked at me, and then back to Will and for a minute, I thought I'd got through to him. But instead, he stood up straight and asked for my name again.

'My name is Anthony Wistern,' I said on impulse. 'And I was murdered, why won't you help me?' There was an audible snort of frustration then.

'I am arresting you for failure to give your name to a police officer; you do not have to say anything but it may harm your defence . . .' As the spiel went on, I focused on Will, who seemed to have a grown about a foot taller,

'You know this isn't right,' I said loudly, but he didn't respond. Rashan guided me towards the door as Blaine lingered with Will for a few seconds. I could hear him thanking the detective for being so helpful: '. . . it really is such a relief. We've all been so worried that she might hurt someone,' and then I was in the car being driven away.

In the end it was a bit of a damp squib. They released me three hours later, when I managed to convince them that my mum needed me home for the evening. The police weren't really that bothered with me. A woman called Sandy interviewed me for half an hour but it was pretty relaxed. She even brought me a cup of tea, and it felt more like an informal chat than an interrogation. After some preamble about how bloody cold it was getting (I recognised this from crime docs as a clumsy attempt to get me off my guard), we got to talking about why I'd been arrested. She wasn't fussed by my refusal to give my name, she said, but she'd had a look at a couple of my videos and wanted to know why I was so interested in the Wistern family. Did I know them? Did I understand how thoroughly his death would've been investigated? Was everything going ok at home? Sandy was nice enough, but she hadn't got a clue. I told her about what I'd discovered, simplifying it for her as much as possible but she didn't really engage. Every time I tried to tell her about the earring, or the bartender's story, or the fact that even Clara Wistern was on my side, she just nodded politely. Instead, she kept on asking how my brain felt. Did I feel fuzzy, or confused? Did I hear voices, was I worried people were out to get me? Going on the events of the day, it was pretty obvious that people were out to get me, but I knew not to say that to Sandy. Instead, I told her my dad was dead, my mum was on her way, I had no fun in my life and yet my brain *still* worked perfectly, wasn't that a good sign? In the end, she gave me a lecture on harassment, warned me to stay away from the Wisterns and told me that I would be given an official caution and would be free to go. Relieved at this, I asked her what she'd be doing with the information I'd given her. And just like that, the friendly and sympathetic Sandy was gone, replaced by a blank-faced officer who reiterated that if I kept up my 'harassment' I would be facing a stalking protection order. 'That would cause major problems for yourself, hon, mmmkay?'

Walking out of the station, I felt a little achy and tired but my brain was buzzing. I guess there's nothing like an arrest to sharpen the mind. I was in possession of strong information and the family were running scared. And then it hit me. Jemima was pregnant – that might mean her secret bit on the side was the father! Would Will really keep on protecting the family now that he knew that?

ANTHONY

I went to see the manager to tell him I'd figured out how I died. I hadn't of course, I still didn't know much beyond that I'd fought with Giles, my son and possibly my wife too. The rest was still a blur, but I was so bored in this ghastly place I figured I might as well at least try to bluff it. Once again, I was met with Susan, who intercepted me before I could get to his office. I couldn't be bothered to express my displeasure at this man's lack of respect, so I just launched into a whole spiel about how I'd been very drunk, which was true, and belligerent, which was almost certainly true too. I said I remembered Olivia pushing me, with all the force in her small but vengeful body, straight into the lake.

'She stood there,' I said, making sure to look Susan right in the eyes, 'watching me gasping one last time, and didn't move an inch.' I've always been a good liar, you've got to be in finance. Ninety per cent of it is just the ability to bullshit well. I leant back against the wall, showing her that it was old news to me now, almost boring in fact. All remembered and in order, now please can we start the process of getting me out of here.

And you know what this woman did? She removed her glasses,

273

threw her head back and laughed. She laughed until I saw actual tears fall onto her ugly jumper. I swallowed my annoyance, not willing to give her the satisfaction of a reaction, and waited until she was finished. She dragged it out, wheezing for longer than felt genuine. Eventually she collected herself, and looked back at me, wiping her eyes.

'You gave it a good shot. Everyone does it eventually, some people get so creative they invent the most absurd scenarios – one man told me he thought he'd been attacked by wild boar. In Surrey! At least you stayed on the side of realism. But no, I'm afraid you're not quite there yet. Don't be downhearted. Everyone gets to it eventually, and you're certainly closer than your early attempts, remember you thought it might've been a lady called Anita Vasher initially, and she wasn't even at the party!' She laughed again, and I scowled at her. Men hate it when women laugh at them, it's incredibly unattractive.

'You won't be stuck here forever, but I do urge you to try the meditation. A 98-year-old called Walter came in yesterday, did two sessions back-to-back and he's off on his new journey now. Poor old duck died in the bath, lay there for hours before someone found him, shrivelled up like a prune, he was.'

With an instruction to 'be a little more collegiate' with my fellow waitees – 'Some people have complained that you've been bartering for extra pillows and you know that's a violation of code,' the woman left me in the corridor feeling slightly despairing. It *had* to have been Liv, that's where all this was going. What was I supposed to do now?

THE SLEUTH

@thesleuth
163.3k subscribers

It was 9 p.m. by the time I got out of the station and turned on my phone. An email alert: 'Arrested? God Will is such a tool. He's acting like he saved the family by calling the police. You should probs get a lawyer though.'

It was so breezy, written as if being questioned by police was just a fun little story – so typical of Freddy not to understand real life. Furiously, I wrote back, demanding that he meet me. 'I'm trying to solve this alone, stop fucking about and help me. If you don't, I'm dropping this whole thing. Seriously.' For once, I got a reply almost immediately, 'Can meet you in 45 at Le Jardin, off Marylebone High St.'

So Fred was in London; I wondered whether the whole family had been together when they heard about my arrrest. Maybe they got a good laugh out of it.

I got to the bar ten minutes early and immediately wished I hadn't. It was like sitting in a greenhouse. Tropical plants were everywhere, on the tables, climbing the windows, their tendrils crawling across the floor. There were even plants hanging from the ceiling lamps, and the temperature was so hot the waitress had beads of sweat dripping off her nose when she came to take my order. 'Just water,' I said, taking off my jumper. A room full of plants, it felt made for Freddy Wistern.

I'd drunk two jugs of water, stripped right down to my vest, and was busy fanning myself with a menu when I saw her twenty minutes later. I noticed her immediately – posh girls hold themselves in a way which demands attention – but I didn't clock who it was until she arched an eyebrow and looked right at me. It was Clara. Clara Wistern was walking my way. I wondered if I might faint right then and there, the heat and surprise overwhelming me, and I gulped the air like a fish as she neared the table. I waved, immediately cringing at the feeble gesture, and watched her face fall slightly as she sat down. Don't worry, I felt like saying, I'm disappointed too. Despite the endless hot flush I was experiencing, Clara didn't remove her jacket, and ordered a martini.

'I pictured you differently,' she said, looking down at her phone. 'Like those girls from *Crime Kittens*. But I forgot you're from Chipping Marston, aren't you? I remembered that when I walked in and then it made sense.' An oddly wounding, yet accurate diss. 'All my friends watch your show, none of us know anyone who was murdered before,' she frowned, 'well, except Delilah's aunt but that was in Denmark.' She didn't elaborate, as if being murdered in a Nordic country was par for the course. 'People even started putting bets on who did it,' she carried on, applying a layer of gloss to her lips. 'Most people thought it was Giles when the business stuff came out, but then they came round to it being one of my family; Tilly said Fred cos everyone knows he's quite weird; Lola obviously thought it was Lyra, but that's only because Lola fancies her and she said it would be cool if it was her. Everyone else said Olivia or Jemima, especially after your video with Luke.'

She then proceeded to pepper me with questions about a variety of popular murders, telling me her theories and asking for my opinion, which was flattering. I made out like I knew insider details about a few of them, told her the Canal Creeper was known to be a serving police officer, and could see she was impressed. I was so happy to have a real-life Wistern praise me like this, I realised I'd completely forgotten to ask why she was sitting across from me.

'Are you meeting your brother?' I managed, which earned me a look of derision.

'As if I want to hang out with Fred. Did you invite him?' We stared at each other for a moment, while I figured out what was going on.

'You're the person that's been emailing me, aren't you?'

Clara looked at me like I was an idiot and once again I wondered how teenagers could be so intimidating. Not Freddy. Of course not, he'd made it clear he wouldn't help me. I'd just assumed, but assumption is the mother of all mistakes. What an idiot I'd been.

'Well obviously, how many other people could tell you that stuff?' I laughed then, which she didn't seem to like, curling her top lip as if I'd mortally offended her. Eager to regain her approval, I tried to move the conversation on. The last thing I wanted was for her to think I didn't know what I was doing.

'Why,' I asked, 'why do you think he was murdered?' She giggled then.

'Nobody ever pays me attention cos I'm the youngest, but I'm smarter than everyone. I see things. It was fun to send you tips, it really stirred shit up at home.' The way she said it made me think this was just a unique form of teenage rebellion, but I'd take what I could get.

I began to tell her that while I had Luke's story about Olivia being the last person to see Anthony alive, it wasn't enough, but she interrupted me.

'That made everyone go mental – Miss Morden actually took away our phones for the rest of the day. Hypocrite, I know she's been watching them too. Olivia's really in the shit now, isn't she? I don't know anyone who doesn't think she's the main suspect now.' I nodded, pleased she was still on side. Apparently the idea her own mother might have killed her father wasn't upsetting in the slightest. If anything, she was thrilled.

'But it's all circumstantial. Even Luke's testimony.' I wanted her to think of anything else she might know about her mother which could help cement the story. She leaned forward, excited now.

'Well, I'm currently living at my uncle's place down the road. Wasn't going to go down to Gables and live in the sticks with a murderer, so I managed to do a bit of digging of my own.' The waiter came over with her martini, which was presented in a glass decorated with plants. These guys really committed to the theme.

'Olivia was going to leave Dad, seems like it was all going to kick off the day after his birthday which is so cold right? Anyway, I figured out my uncle was in on it, helping her plan it – for years! So maybe she killed him cos he found out? Dad definitely wouldn't have let her just leave like that, how embarrassing for him. I haven't even told Tilly that, don't want anyone to say they knew when it all comes out.' She sipped her martini as if she'd just said the most normal thing in the world, and I realised legally, she shouldn't even be drinking.

'You're so smart, figuring it all out,' I said, sucking up to her and hating myself for it. 'But I've hit a dead end here. If I go near your family without being invited I'll be arrested again, and there's no way I can prove it was your mum without confronting her. So I need someone to arrange that.' I made my voice softer . . . 'Could you?' She shook her head, obviously finding this suggestion ridiculous.

'*God* no. My modelling is picking up, I've got my exams; Lola's family are taking me to Gstaad at Christmas. Next year I'll be an adult, so I don't really need to talk to her anymore. Charles will look after me, he sort of doesn't have a choice.' She smirked at this, like she knew a fun secret I didn't.

'But couldn't you just see her once, with me – we could film it together?' I dangled this thinking she'd jump at the chance to be in a video but she shook her head and let out a peal of laughter.

'Oh, babe, no way. I've got a certain image, the *Tatler* interview was a really big stepping-stone for me, and as much as I love true crime, it's pretty grubby, you know? Everyone's obsessed with the story at the moment, but it won't be cool in the long term and I want to be known for my own thing, not just cos my dad was murdered.' I didn't ask what that thing was, but I didn't think it would be developing life-saving drugs.

'Ask Fred to arrange it, he's stuck there with her for the rest of time. I'll text him now, and tell him. He'll listen to me, Fred's genuinely scared of like, everyone in our family.' She gave another little giggle and tapped out a message, signalling for the bill with her other hand.

'Let me know when you do though, I want to be the first to watch it.'

I was almost unnerved by how fun she was finding all of this. For me it was a commitment to root out criminals but for Clara, whose own family were at the heart of this tragedy, it seemed to be entertainment. Tentatively, I asked whether or not she'd really thought about what would happen when her mother was arrested. Clara paused for a second and tilted her head.

'Oh, I'm not stupid.' She grinned. 'It'll make me even more popular than I already am.' Then she gathered up her bag and wished me luck. I was left with an overwhelming sense of gratitude that Clara had never been a suspect. I really didn't relish the idea of going up against someone as frighteningly ambitious as she was for herself. The bill arrived just moments after she wafted out. Eighteen quid for one drink. I guess I had to pay extra for the sauna I'd just had. When I emerged into the street, I took a huge gulp of cool air and felt my body give a cry of thanks. I'd walk to the station and psyche myself up to text Fred. Poor guy, I felt sorry for him dealing with all of these women, but he was my only way in.

OLIVIA

As with every other day since I'd moved to Gables, I watched the clock until 6 p.m. when I could make myself a gin and tonic. Time is different when you have nothing to do, and arbitrary moments become incredibly important. 11 a.m. was the first cigarette of the day, 1 p.m. was a glass of wine and some crackers, 3 p.m. was a show on a shopping channel where the hosts hawked increasingly stupid skincare devices and 6 p.m. was when the day mercifully began to end.

Freddy heard the buzzer at the same time I did, and went into the hall to answer it. We'd had weirdos turning up at all hours since that ghoul's videos had gained popularity, and despite my constant calls to the local police, they'd not provided the 24-hour protection I insisted we need. My son was pulling on his jacket when I got to him, and told me he was going to meet a friend. He looked a little odd as he said it, and headed for the door just a little too quickly, so I waited a few seconds, then slipped on my shoes and followed him. Fred was already marching purposefully down the drive, but I kept to the side of the lawn to ensure he wouldn't notice me. I had to check – presumably our house was now on a checklist tour of the Cotswolds. Antiquing in Burford, ice cream in Banbury and a crime scene in Chipping Marston. How ghastly.

Perhaps he was meeting a girl – or a boy – I'm no bigot. A gay son would've been great fun, we could've gone shopping together. But Fred never showed much interest in either sex, and I doubted he'd suddenly met someone when all he does is garden. What then? I rounded the bend where the drive suddenly curves towards the road, and had to stop myself swearing when my left foot sunk into a divot. Standing on one leg and hopping slightly ineffectually, I saw the lights flick on, the gates open, and a person walk through them. I squinted, it couldn't be . . . that lunatic was on my property and my own son had let her in. I could tell from the green hooded jacket she was wearing, did the girl not own any other clothes? I watched as he steered her towards the trees, clearly hoping to get her away from the house so I wouldn't catch sight of her.

I followed my son and this girl right down to the lake. Her voice was getting louder and louder, my son frantically tried to shush her. When they got to the jetty, she paced up and down as though looking for something. From the trees, I could hear every word.

'It was your mum, she murdered your dad. It was her standing just over there, right before he died. She was the last person seen with him. I want to get her to admit it, Fred.'

I fished my phone out of my pocket, and dialled 999.

'An intruder has broken into our home, they have a weapon and they're fighting my son.' I knew how lazy the police could be if they thought it wasn't an emergency – my old friend Sara Churchwell once waited over four hours for them to turn up when someone defaced her front door with spray paint. The words 'blood on her hands' daubed in neon orange, what was not an emergency about that? All because she happened to have a large number of shares in a pharmaceutical business which may or may not have sold opioids. To *help* people. Not her fault people enjoyed the side effects of them.

After I hung up, I walked down to the water, calling out to my son. They sprang apart immediately. Fred was clearly horrified, but the girl, well she looked like all her Christmases had come at once.

She was holding up her phone, I realised too late, pointing it straight at me. Live-streaming, that's what Jemima had called it.

'Can you tell me why you killed your husband, Mrs Wistern,' she said as I grabbed her by the arm and dragged her up the jetty. Instead of helping me, Fred tried to get in between us, protesting that she just wanted answers, and didn't mean any harm. We eventually all came to a stop on the drive and I looked her in the eyes for the first time. Who was this unassuming girl who had convinced Clara and bewitched Fred? Pale-faced, with slightly grey smudges under her eyes. Hair without any volume at all, her tatty green jacket which looked like the kind old women wear for a long walk and a visit to a local tearoom. She was staring at me with anger in her eyes. I felt a slight shiver.

She started hurling the same accusation as before, and I continued to drag her towards the gates, looking straight ahead so as not to be captured on camera, face sans make-up. She was talking to the camera now, saying I was trying to hide my crimes, 'just like the rich always do'. I laughed at that, I couldn't help it. It was all so absurd. The fear I'd felt when I saw her last video dissipated, this girl was just a mad person with a camera phone. No matter how many followers she had, nobody important would ever believe her. Seeing the flash of blue lights beyond the gates, I ordered my son to let the police in. He hovered, putting one foot forward and then back, while both me and the girl yelled at him to help.

'Freddy,' I said, my voice low and quiet, a tone all my children knew to take seriously, 'this person is trying to hurt our family. This is our home, your beloved Gables. This is the only thing you care about. She wants to take it all away from us. Go and let the police in, they can help her.' Finally, he walked towards the security pad. She lost all semblance of restraint at that, yelling that I wouldn't be able to get away with it, which I suspect even she found a little feeble.

'Bit of a cliche,' I said, gesturing to the open gate, 'but have it your way. I murdered my husband and you've found me out. Not the post-mortem, not the police, just you. Now's your chance to tell them all about it.'

ANTHONY

After my disappointing meeting with Susan, I'd gone and laid down on my bed for a long time. Both my neighbours had disappeared that morning, off to the next phase of death. They'd both figured out how they'd gone, one had tripped over his rescue whippet (people always tell you when their dog's a rescue, don't they? Without a doubt the smuggest people I've ever encountered) and had a heart attack. I bet he wished he'd left that dog in the shelter now. The other one remembered falling asleep on a bus only never to wake up. She'd thought about it a lot, gambled on aneurysm and been correct. A death as boring as she was.

After what felt like days (time doesn't exist here, just another incredibly annoying part of this whole experience) I went to watch my wife. The deputy manager might have rejected my theory, but she'd said I was close. That still meant Olivia, no doubt about it. And though I'm aware my wife wouldn't have been described as a friendly face by anyone who encountered her (a hissing snake had more obvious warmth to it), I felt a need to see her all the same.

She was still at Gables, she and Fred living almost entirely separately. It was depressing to see and I'd stayed away for a bit after I saw Olivia watching *This Morning*. A segment about stylish shoes for those with wider feet. Daytime television, how low she'd fallen.

When I rejoined them however, there was a flurry of activity. This girl who'd been following my death with keen interest had turned up at the house, and my wife was confronting her with gusto. I watched as Olivia dragged her up the driveway. She's a small woman, with the bones of a bird, but the steely determination makes her more physically powerful than you'd imagine. As this girl ranted at my wife, accusing her of murdering me and covering it up, I found myself inexorably annoyed by her. This person that only a few weeks ago I'd been so impressed with, absolutely rooting for her to find the culprit, well I realised she'd gone too far. I'd hoped the person investigating my death would be someone with presence and stature (and let's be honest, a man) but this girl was decidedly unimpressive. Squinting, I had the same sense that I recognised her as I had when I first saw her outside our London house. Was that . . . the girl who used to work at The Badger? Jesus Christ, it was! I'd had to get rid of her after she made a fuss when I gave her a little kiss at the end of the night. I've never had any patience for weeds. We had a chap at Wismere who tried to take a week off work when his dog died, and when I found out, I'd ordered him back to the office and had everyone bark at him whenever he opened his mouth.

If my wife was going to be unmasked, I didn't want it to be by this sub-par amateur. I realised I didn't even want my wife to be discovered anymore. I wanted her to know that *I* knew, but that was a different thing altogether. I'd take a lot of joy out of lording it over Liv like that, her crime wiped out any piddling complaints she'd had about me. I'd be the envy of all other husbands the world over – someone with a grudge so large, their wife could never make them feel bad about anything ever again. As a result, I almost cheered as the police took the girl away in handcuffs and my wife ushered our son back to the house. Olivia showed a core of steel I'd always admired and feared in good measure. Fred as usual, let me down.

When they went inside with a police officer to give statements, I thought I'd go and give it another shot with the manager. I decided to try a slightly different tack. I'd say Liv pretended she'd dropped her phone, made me look over the jetty and nudged me in with her foot. If she managed to cling on to Gables, one day she'd die and end up here herself. The South Gloucestershire processing centre was punishment enough if you asked me. She'd never be able to cope in a dormitory.

THE SLEUTH

I was charged under the section 4A public order – stalking involving serious alarm and distress – ridiculous; Olivia Wistern was an ice queen. I got off breaking and entering because Fred had opened the gates, but I was still warned that I could expect a jail term if and when it went to trial. My court-appointed lawyer turned up at 10 a.m. He was young, and clearly daunted by the whole thing, loosening his tie so often it was basically a scarf. I told them I'd been invited to the property, which was true, Fred had said it was ok. They told me I'd engaged in a pattern of behaviour – using the word stalking which I found offensive. I tried to tell them what I knew about Olivia but they wouldn't listen, and even my nervous lawyer told me to pack it in if I wanted to go home. So eventually, I did. I said I was sorry and promised not to do it again. I told them I was depressed 'and seeking help' interjected the lawyer keenly, and needed to be at home to care for my chronically sick mother. The lawyer

288

liked that, kept repeating it again and again, adding the words 'deathly ill' on the fifth time.

Finally I was released on bail, out into the bustling streets of Oxford with a stern warning about being recalled if I went anywhere near a Wistern. But it was all worth it. Two days later, Will texted me out of the blue. The last person I'd expected offered to help me.

ANTHONY

Once the deputy manager had sent me packing: 'Wrong again, Mr Wistern. As much as I enjoy these meetings I fear we're not getting any younger,' I'd flicked through the channels in a sulk, and landed on Jemima purely by chance. Normally she was the offspring I watched the least; now she was staying with her in-laws, her days were even duller than before. But right now, my daughter and her husband were having the most godawful fight; exactly the kind of tonic I needed. Jemima was hurling shoes at Will as he danced around the bedroom in an attempt to avoid them. A boot hit him square on the jaw and he shrieked like a little girl.

'You fucking idiot!' Jemima looked a lot like my mother when she was angry – genes will always fight their way out. 'Investing with my dad AND selling fake fucking plates, are you entirely brain dead?' Will ducked as a stiletto hove into view.

'It wasn't a plate, it was a jug and I didn't know it wasn't legit. Your betrayal was far worse, darling, surely you can see that!' Jemima, who'd run out of shoes, sat down with a sob. Her husband crept cautiously round the side of the bed, and upon

290

seeing the coast was clear, went over to his wife and put an arm around her.

'I know you felt lonely, I was working too hard. But I wanted to give you the life you're accustomed to. That's why I took some risks.' He sighed ruefully. 'I didn't know your dad was running a scam, and I bought those jugs off a reputable buyer. It's just damn bad luck, Jem. But now we've both got our secrets out into the open, we can start a clean slate. We can stay here as long as we need – Mummy loves your garden walks.'

My daughter let out a scream of frustration. 'I can't stand it here, your father whistles all the time – have you noticed that? And they let the dogs eat off their plates, in the middle of dinner! I want to be back in London, I want our old life!' She slumped theatrically down onto the bed, as Will frantically tried to assuage her with promises that he'd make it right eventually. My daughter shook her head at this, sitting up again and pursing her mouth.

'You'll have to go to Olivia – make her hand over some of the money Lyra says she's been stashing. Blackmail her if you have to, just do something effective for once in your life.' My daughter glared at her husband for a few seconds before he gave in and promised to try. However disappointed I was in my children, I couldn't deny that Jemima had just made her husband promise to go into a lion's den with no protection. That was true Wistern spirit.

OLIVIA

I returned to London for a meeting with Charles in order for him to fill me in on what the fraud squad were up to. After explaining the latest developments, he assured me yet again that my fund was waiting patiently for me.

'And you must be patient,' he warned with his most solemn look. 'You won't be able to access it yourself for some time. There can be no suggestion that it's Wistern money.'

My big brother, always so cautious. Anthony hated him for it, but who was the victor here? Charles was even wearing a beautiful new Breguet watch, proof you could do well without climbing over people. He noticed me looking at it, and pulled down his jacket sleeve, embarrassed.

'A silly indulgence,' he said with a small smile. 'We had a good year at the firm and I thought . . . maybe this is my mid-life crisis.'

After going over a few more legal things and asking after Clara, who still ignored my calls and rarely ever texted me, I'd asked to see the flat he'd rented for me, but he'd demurred rather bashfully.

'It's a mess I'm afraid, a bachelor's weakness. Next time.' Charles embraced me with the same hug he'd given me for 50 odd years. Stiff, slightly awkward, and over as quickly as possible.

My next engagement was also stiff and awkward. I was meeting Lyra and Jemima for an early dinner, who'd insisted they had to talk to me. Jemima had chosen a stuffy place off Mount Street, clearly to piss off her sister and in the expectation that I'd be paying. As predicted, Lyra was sitting there with a scowl on her face when I arrived, complaining about the lack of vegetarian options. Jemima, whose bump had grown considerably, was lecturing her sister for eschewing meat. 'Just have a steak for god's sake. The iron would do you good, you're as pale as the moon.'

We ate quickly and mostly avoided the worst kind of sniping until dessert was suggested. Neither of them asked how I was coping, or mentioned their father at all. Eventually I asked what the point of the dinner was, and Lyra put on a show of looking hurt.

'We can't miss our mother?' I raised an eyebrow and she held up her hands. 'Ok, ok. It's about a pipeline problem. The financial pipeline, it's dried up. And we get it, times have been tough, the magic money tree was hacked down to a stump but we still need to live, Olivia.' Jemima shot her sister a look.

'Dad put the flat in Paris in *your* name, you don't need it like I do. I'm having a—'

Lyra cut in, 'baby, yes we know, the first person ever to do it. But you have your knight in shining china, William, the king of ancient pots, he'll sort you out.' She turned to face me again. 'Fred's living in a shed, Clara seems to have forced Uncle Charles to semi adopt her for some weird reason best left unexamined but we're high and dry. So here we are with the begging bowls.'

I wished I could have a cigarette. I wished I had said no to this dinner. I wished I'd decided to breed dogs instead of children.

'I don't know what you expect me to do, I have a small allowance from the financial investigators, and that'll dry up at some point. You know this, why waste all of our time?' The girls looked at each other, suddenly united for the first time.

'Lyra told me about your handbags.'

What a snake that girl was. We'd always favoured her for her attitude, but all that lay behind her insouciance was treachery.

'The stuff you've been selling for years. The getting-away fund.'

Lyra butted in, 'Her fuck-off fund, Jem, you don't have to censor yourself, the baby doesn't understand swears. Must be rather hefty by now, Olivia?'

I recoiled, gripping the table tightly.

'And that ring . . .' My eldest daughter was pointing at my finger, where my lovely diamond glinted. Stupid to wear it, but the idea of getting dressed up for the first time in weeks got the better of me. I twisted it round in order to hide it from view. Magpies, both of them! For a moment I wondered whether I should deny it, but looking at the unconcealed hunger in their faces, decided it might actually be more fun to admit it all. They had no claim to it. So I did, I told them I had some money put away, and that when and if I decided to help them out, it would be on my terms. That clearly wasn't what they'd expected, I imagine they thought they'd been clever to corner me like this after weeks of confinement at Gables, knowing I was at my lowest ebb. Lyra rallied first.

'But surely,' she said, with an innocent expression, 'it's Dad's money. The money he made fraudulently. Wouldn't that need to be seized and investigated too?' Bravo, Lyra, a clever new angle there. But not thought through.

'Of course you're free to tell them, darling. But the money is in Charles's name. And if they did get their hands on it, you'd get nothing at all, would you?' I beamed, relaxing my hands. I'd got them there, both girls looked deflated. I asked for the bill.

'You're right, Mummy, of course you must do with it as you see fit.' Jemima reached for my hand. It was the first time she'd called me Mummy in years, and it marked my victory as absolute. Lyra couldn't bring herself to say anything, but she nodded stiffly.

Of course, my triumph was only short-lived, they always found a way to spoil my fun. Will turned up just as the bill arrived, plastering on a wide smile. Effortless manners that boy, even if they failed to make up for the gaping hole where a personality should be.

'Will's going to drive you home, Olivia,' my eldest daughter announced as she passed me the bill, which I promptly handed to my son-in-law. 'He wants to pick up some of my stuff from Gables, isn't that handy?' She barely looked at her husband as she offered him up, tensing slightly when his hand brushed hers.

I wanted to protest, the idea of spending 90 minutes with my son-in-law was an appalling prospect, but there was no getting round it. Lyra couldn't conceal her mirth, waving manically as we drove away. After some feeble small talk about the travails of staying with his parents for so long: 'Mummy has been so welcoming but of course, it's not our own home and Jemima feels that keenly.' We lapsed into silence which I could see he was finding uncomfortable. The man kept scratching his neck, leaving large red welts every time he did. I lit a cigarette without opening the window, hoping it would annoy him. Another neck scratch, and then a long exhale which to my ears sounded rather shaky. What a weed he was.

We got back to Gables just as the sun was setting.

'Fred here?' Will asked as we went down the drive.

'He'll be in his horrible little shed, you won't see him.' We arrived by the door, and he practically jumped out of the car, coming round to my side to open the door for me as if I were a frail old lady.

I went straight to the kitchen and poured a large glass of wine, not offering him one in the hopes that he'd get Jemima's stuff and make a quick turnaround. To my horror, he began to open a bottle of Côte de Beaune at the counter and swapped out my glass. 'I think you'll find this more agreeable on the old palate,' he said, with a weak smile. Immediately I knew he must want something, this particular vintage was a good one. He'd even brought a little wine cooler to keep it in on the journey, the action of a man who is about to ask his mother-in-law for a favour.

'Cheers,' he said, but without any gaiety, and slumped into a chair. I looked at his face properly now, illuminated by the kitchen light. Ground down, worn out, as if just opening the wine had drained him of all his energy. Why was my son-in-law acting like this? The man usually had one mode and that was polite banality. His greatest skill was being invisible in any room and now I couldn't take my eyes off him as he appeared to shrivel right in front of me.

We sat for a minute, neither of us saying a word. I wouldn't deign to ask him why he was really here, he'd have to sweat a little first. Finally, Will drained his wine in two gulps, and began talking.

'It's a lovely night, isn't it? I wish we came down here more, you've made a proper home here, Liv. I hope we can do the same for the little chap when he turns up.'

He rambled on about how well we've all done to get through the past few months and praised me for keeping the family together. This was so patently absurd a lie that I began to get angry. I wanted to take my wine upstairs and have a long bath, long enough that I wrinkle. As if finally sensing my impatience, Will got up and poured another glass of wine for himself and took a deep breath. Here he goes, I thought, with relief.

'I know it's a bit . . . unusual for me to do all this, Olivia.' He smiled ruefully at me, apologetic even now. 'I won't pretend this was just a trip to pick up Jemima's things, I imagine you can see through it.' He looked past me, to the windows which overlooked the front lawn, scanning the view as the light disappeared entirely. I made a little noise with my throat and he jolted back to attention. 'Right, er, I'll get down to it.' I was careful not to move a single muscle in my face. Why should I make this easy for him?

'I've been very impressed by your sensible approach to . . . what comes next. You've lost so much, but your resolve in the face of society's rejection is admirable, Olivia, truly it is. But I think it's important for you to know something.' Will twisted a piece of cork between his fingers. 'I know you've got some money saved, and I entirely understand why you had to do that; Jemima and I have long felt that Anthony treated you poorly at times. We're both really thrilled you'll be secure.' He was pandering now, and badly to boot. Clearly, I'd underestimated my daughters; Will had been their back-up plan in case of failure. Dazzling stupidity to think this man could ever be part of a winning strategy, they really must be desperate. 'But I think you're – rightly – under the impression that all your kids will be ok. I mean, of course they will, you raised them after all.' Nauseating. 'You think Jem and I have our own money.' Will swallowed, his Adam's apple bobbed quickly. 'But, er, that's not quite the truth.'

I wound my finger in a wrap-it-up motion.

'Sorry, as I was saying. We're actually . . .' He stopped and tried again. 'My business, it's not going well. For a while, Olivia, if I'm honest.' A nervous laugh, then he rearranged his face back into a more sombre expression. 'It's my fault, I trusted the wrong people.' He stood up, running his hands through his hair and it splayed out in a variety of directions. He looked, I have to say, sort of demented. 'Well, anyway. As I say, we're not in a good place. Christ! I'm very close to losing it all.'

Will exhaled, finally letting go of the tension he'd been holding in his body. He walked over to the window, and stood gazing out into the darkness for a while. There was relief there, I could tell. An unloading of a problem, the telling of a secret which has weighed on a person; you feel lighter once you've made someone else bear some of the load, don't you? Unfortunately for Will, the person he told was me. And my instinct has never been to choose unthinking kindness over self-preservation.

'Oh dear,' I said quietly, drawing out my words. 'Jemima won't like that, Will. She picked you for your pedigree, she chose you for what you offered. But it sounds to me like you've done just what her father did, haven't you?' Will looked horrified, his character being sullied like this was too much to bear.

'Not at all! Not at all. I've never stolen from anyone. Of course not, Christ, it's the opposite. I . . .' He was stammering his words now. '. . . I invested with him. Last spring, I'd heard him on the phone to someone about big profits they were guaranteed to make. I've always been cautious with my business, slow growth and a steady profit. But Jemima's got higher standards than Marie Antoinette, and I had a bit of money saved.' He sounded defensive now. 'Why not let the magic money-maker treble it for me? Took him a long time to agree. Told me I'd have to trust him. Trust! I can't think of someone I'd be less likely to put my faith in, god knows what I was thinking. But everyone always said he was the best . . .'

A sigh. I poured myself some more wine and stretched my neck. Must remember to find a local masseuse now I couldn't show my face at the Daylesford spa.

'But then I had some bad luck. There were a few pieces which turned out not to be quite . . . well, genuine. Impossible to tell, an unlucky roll of the dice. I've got to pay people back and well, I can't. There's talk of legal action as a result, one particularly aggressive man who used to work in an auction house.' He shuddered slightly. 'And now I'm at the point where bankruptcy won't be enough. How can I do this to our baby? Where will he grow up?' He clearly expected me to be moved by the idea that my grandson might not be able to live in a palatial townhouse, but funnily enough, I was not.

'He's your only grandson, everyone else is ok – Lyra is doing well, Fred doesn't want for anything and Clara, well she's . . .' Will searched for the way to put this succinctly. 'She's basically Charles's problem now, isn't she? I mean, let's face it, she's never going live with you again, is she?'

I am momentarily distracted by a noise beyond the kitchen. Thinking Fred must have come in uninvited, I got up and walked to the hall but there was nobody. Going back, I wondered how best to play this to ensure that not only was he sure of my feelings, he would also be hurt by my response. He was looking at me expectantly.

'Fred?' he asked, and I shook my head.

'William, you're a nice enough man but you're so weak. You've always been too eager to make sure Jemima is happy, always wanting to smooth the path for her ambitions. Did you ever want the life she demands? You've never really thought about it, have you? If you did, I'd guess that what you really want is a quiet life somewhere upmarket but sedate, where people would go nuts for a few old vases – Somerset would be just right for you, darling. You were never going to be a match for Jemima, we knew it the day she introduced you to us. I'm sorry to say this . . .' I wasn't, I was eager to '. . . but you're a rather insubstantial person.' He was trying to interrupt me then, but I was in full swing. 'Yes, yes, you'd very much like to rush to your own defence, but let's skip ahead, shall we? You want me to give you my savings in order to get you out of a rather big hole and stop Jemima from being angry with you. That's about the scheme of things, am I right?'

He nodded, knowing it was pointless to try to make it sound better than it was. A miserable moment for a man whose family motto is 'Strength through dignity'. I walked over and joined him at the window.

'The way you tell it, you'll use my money to cover up your own failures. It's not a very edifying option for me, is it?"

'Would you like it if our kids had the Wistern name? Perhaps we could make it their middle name if it meant something to you . . .' He reached the begging stage sooner than expected, and I grimaced.

'Let's not do that. Please. You've made several bad decisions, which you must fix yourself. And now it's time for you to go, I'm tired.' Tired of this pity party, tired of everyone in my family wanting nothing but money. Usually Anthony's money, always kissing up to him even though they couldn't stand him. But they'd backed the wrong horse. I was the one with the power now, and I wasn't going to give it up to false flattery. There was a whole new chapter opening up to me. Not the one I'd planned before Anthony went and died on me, but one I could enjoy nonetheless. I hadn't thought much about how my children factored into this new life, but from the evening's events, I wondered whether perhaps I could cut them *all* loose. We'd done more for them than most parents do for their children. But mine?

Mine would always demand more. Enough. I decided that I would call Charles in the morning, and tell him we had to speed things up. He was being too cautious, surely he could give me a little allowance from my account; I needed to start making my way back into society. It would take some time, I knew that. But memories fade and one scandal is always brewing to replace another. Anthony would one day be a footnote. In history and to me. But first, I wanted that nice long bath I'd promised myself.

He nodded, all the fight gone out of him, just as I'd known it would.

'I'll text Jemima.'

'You do that.'

He took out his phone and typed, following me out of the kitchen, through the hallway and up the stairs, trailing behind me like a serf following a queen.

ANTHONY

Liv was enjoying herself immensely, making Will squirm so much he was practically contorting himself. Defrauding people with knock-off pots? Even I wouldn't have done something so risky, especially not selling them to experts who can spot that stuff a mile away. Asking Olivia for money by appealing to her better angels was a terrible tactic. Those angels were no better than they ought to be, and my wife would never have been softened by such amateur flattery. He patronised her, a deadly mistake. Far better to have blackmailed, or threatened, she might've seen the point then. I watched as he followed her up the stairs, he'd be better just throwing himself down them.

THE SLEUTH

@thesleuth

185k subscribers

Will's text had come as a surprise, but it was very welcome. He'd had a change of heart, and after watching my videos, had come round to my version of events. He'd been extremely apologetic, and promised to find a way to get me in the room with Olivia as soon as possible. I didn't fully trust him, not after he'd had me arrested, but that night a message popped up on my phone. It simply said, 'I'm at Gables with Olivia, be here in the next fifteen minutes and she'll talk to you.' I'd dropped the knife I was chopping vegetables with, and yelled to Mum that I had to go out. She could wait an hour for dinner, she barely ate anything anyway. I rode my bike so fast towards Gables that I lost my scarf somewhere along the way, but I got there in under twelve minutes. I let myself in via the code for the gate Will had given me. Apparently, Freddy was here.

'Don't walk across the lawn, don't go anywhere near him.' As if I would. Fred had ended up being one big disappointment.

Once I reached the main house, I crawled on my hands and knees until I reached the third window to the right. After waiting a few minutes, I got a little impatient and popped my head up to see what was happening, only to be confronted by a dark room that was decidedly not the kitchen. I'd miscounted. Too many fucking windows, that kind of amateur mistake could've messed up the whole thing. Lights on, I had the right place finally. I waited for him to give me the signal. Once he put one hand up to the window, I was to go to the door. From there, he'd let me in. I'd come in and confront her then, and he'd told me I could film the whole thing. He even told me *I* could be the one to make the phone call to the police. The excitement was building up in my body to the point where I was actually shivering. I was in control, I was going to take down this woman, and anyone else who hid behind her. One hand went up at the window. It had begun.

ANTHONY

Olivia reached the top of the stairs and told Will he'd need to be gone by the time she'd finished her bath. She didn't turn round to look at him, but she should have. Our son-in-law's expression had changed, his eyes somehow harder and darker than they'd been just minutes before. I felt uneasy, looking around for someone to help. Nobody. Just one other cubicle was occupied, an old man blubbing over a video of his dog. Death really shows up what a piddling little species we are.

My wife was heading towards the corridor which led to our bedroom. She only made it three steps before Will lunged at her sleeve.

'You've *got* to help us, Olivia.' She picked his fingers off her shirt, looking at him with a mixture of naked scorn and downright exasperation.

'Enough! This is pathetic. Go home to your wife, much good it'll do you. I suppose she'll stand by you since nobody else will take her. Not even that handsome barman she's been having it off with for years. Cheer up,' she added, 'the baby might not even be yours.'

They stand there for a moment, Olivia with her jaw set and arms crossed, Will with his fists clenched and his breathing slightly ragged. Nothing good is about to happen, I can sense it. I've always been remarkably good at reading atmospheres. I once realised that Simon Artemis was going to hit Teddy Sloane well before he took that shot which sent Simon's ball into the bunker. I'd not stopped him though, that man was a thug. Teddy got a nasty black eye that day, but Artemis got what he deserved in the end.

I'm broken out of nostalgia by a strange yelping sound. Will is whining like a dog and then suddenly, he shoves my wife with a force you'd not expect such a flimsy man to have. Olivia is catapulted down the stairs, her feet soaring over her head as she takes flight. The staircase is wide and circles to the floor, the focal point of the whole house. Such slippery, worn-out steps.

My wife seemed to hang in mid-air for a minute, before the inevitable happened and she falls three floors, crashing and sliding down the last few steps. It was an uncharitable thought, but I was sure she wished now that we'd had some nice carpet runners put in like the interiors woman had suggested. Olivia's head hit the floor first with an obscenely loud crack. Her legs lay splayed out in different directions. She let out one brief moan, which to me sounded more affronted than pained. Then, silence. I could see the blood oozing across the floorboards. It pooled quite quickly, much faster than you'd think it could. So much blood for such a tiny woman.

The front door opened. That girl stood in the hallway, staring at my wife. She had not yet seen Will, three floors up, frozen with one hand out, as if unaware that Olivia was already lying dead beneath him. I watch as he rearranged his face into an expression of concern, before quickly walking into Jemima's old bedroom. It appears that he found his strength after all these years. I wish I'd known it was in him sooner, the boy could've been a formidable ally.

NEWS ARTICLE

21 October 2018

True crime obsessive kills criminal's widow

Jade Evans was arrested yesterday for the murder of Olivia Wistern. Mrs Wistern, the widow of disgraced banker Anthony Wistern, was found dead by her son-in-law Will Fortesque on Friday night. Evans, a twenty-four-year-old from Chipping Marston, had previously been given a restraining order against the family after waging an obsessive social media campaign against them. The unemployed Evans, who lived with her mother in the house she grew up in, had been fired by Mr Wistern after stealing from his pub The Golden Badger in 2018, and became convinced that Anthony Wistern's death was suspicious, recording videos for her YouTube channel where she espoused a variety of theories about who was behind the alleged murder. In a video seen by our reporters, Evans films herself in William Fortesque's antiques shop, accusing him of covering up a crime. A more recent post alleges Olivia Wistern was the main culprit. Anthony Wistern's death was ruled an accident and our reporter understands there is no basis for Ms Evans' allegations.

Evans has a strong presence in true crime communities online, posting multiple times a day about murder and conspiracy. One moderator of a true crime group told us Evans was always 'going too far with her accusations.

We had to ban her after she started spamming the group with stories she thought we were ignoring at all times of the day and night.' In the small town of Chipping Marston, the news has been a shock.

'She was a lovely girl, but her dad dying really broke her,' a neighbour said. 'He worked for the local council for a long time, and a refuse lorry hit him while he was cycling home. It was just an accident, it was dark out and they didn't see him coming, but she thought he'd been murdered and never stopped talking about it. I remember her putting up posters around town emblazoned with the face of the guy who'd been driving, calling him a killer. But Tony's no murderer, he's a lovely man who brings his pet ferret to the pub every Friday. She wouldn't believe it though, accused the council of covering it up. What was there to cover up? Her dad wasn't some senior official, he worked in the permit office. You don't stage a hit and run for some parking vouchers.'

In a statement, Charles Holdwood – the brother of Olivia Wistern – said that the family needed privacy and time to grieve 'a much-loved mother, who will be missed by her children every single day.'

Wistern had been living at their country house since her husband's fraud came to light. A friend of the family, Penny Donsman, said that she'd been due to visit the day after Wistern was found dead. 'What happened with Anthony destroyed her and she'd effectively been banished from London. She'd been very down for a number of months but when I spoke to her a few days before she was killed, she sounded more optimistic. She was talking about going back to London and rebuilding her life. She wanted to get a Pekinese. I just can't believe this has happened.'

Evans has been refused bail, and will appear in court on Wednesday.

ANTHONY

A deputy manager should not be the first person you speak to when your wife has just died. Naturally I was in a state of shock. Even if I strongly suspected her of ending my life, it was still an outrage. I was keen to know what on earth they planned to do about my son-in-law just going around killing my wife but all I got from Susan was a brief lecture on how important it was to grieve, even in death.

'Many people assume it'll be easier here, when a loved one crosses over,' she told me with the air of someone reading a rulebook, 'but it can still hit you hard.' Surely with all her powers she could call the prime minister and alert him. I even offered to give her his personal phone number, which she found funny for some reason. Then she told me she had another meeting to get to, which sounded a lot like an excuse. Who was more important here? The guy who always wants to talk about horse racing and constantly tries to find a monitor which might somehow show the Derby results? There was nobody here worth having a conversation with but me, and I told her so in very blunt terms only to be met with a yawn. A stringy-haired assistant knocked on the door and came in, giving a small cough and looking at me meaningfully.

'Oh yes, thank you, Tina.' Susan brightened. 'Mr Wistern, I forgot to tell you, your wife will be arriving shortly. It's un-orthodox, certainly not a situation we see frequently, but it happens from time to time.' She then proceeded to look at me sternly and wag her finger in my face like I was a naughty schoolboy. Honestly, this woman was drunk with power. 'I warn you not to tell your wife how she died. It would be very bad indeed, Mr Wistern; I must emphasise that you cannot influence her journey, however much you might wish to. I know a man such as yourself isn't used to giving up control, but do try. It might even be a learning experience for you.' Barely able to speak, I was gently guided out of the meeting room by Susan's sidekick, and led back to my cubicle.

Olivia was coming here. The idea of having to deal with communal dining *and* the woman who murdered me was a pretty bad blow. If I could just remember the details of my death correctly, perhaps I could sneak out before she arrived.

THE SLEUTH

@thesleuth
199.9k subscribers

It turns out doing a proper stakeout is hard work and I'd not layered up properly. Layers are key, my dad hammered that into me. 'There's no such thing as bad weather, only bad clothes.' I was getting colder and colder, and as a result, more fidgety. To top it off, my legs were cramping so badly I keeled over at one point, wincing as I heard the crunch of gravel. Geoff would've trained for this, he'd have knelt in his sitting room for hours on end in preparation, probably while binge-watching *Mastermind*. For a minute, I stayed on the ground, rubbing my knee and wondering why I'd agreed to this. That's when I heard a scream, and all the strict instructions about my cue were immediately forgotten.

I staggered to my feet and rushed round towards the main entrance. A scream like that suggested things were getting dramatic; maybe Olivia was breaking down and confessing to everything without me. But by the time I opened the door, the house was quiet. The hallway itself was enormous, a massive circular space with a round table right in front of me, a large stone vase on top of it. Empty. The flower budget must've been slashed along with everything else. Steps behind the table led up to another vast empty space, with panelled corridors running off it. Everything in this house was ten times bigger than in a normal home, as if it was built for long-dead giants. I looked up, and saw that I was in an atrium, the height of the entire building, a staircase running around the side of it. The light hanging down above my head was shaped like an enormous glowing orb, bigger than a small car and suspended on a steel thread from the very ceiling of the house. I stared up at it for a second, marvelling at how beautiful it was. And then I looked down and saw her. My brain didn't register what was going on for a minute. Despite all my experience, I've never actually seen a dead body. Couldn't even look at my dad's, I was too scarred by the experience of my mum's friend Cathy. The mortician had done her husband David 'dirty', making him look like a puffy Oompa-Loompa and she'd not been able to think of him in the same way since. 'He'll look like a budget quiz show host, darling, it'll only upset you.'

For a minute, I tried to convince myself it was just a dog curled up at the bottom of the stairs. But then I saw a leg, and forced myself to follow the rest of the body, right up to the head. She was twisted in a really weird way, almost at right angles, but it was definitely Olivia. Couldn't miss that hair, voluminous even in death.

My hands were shaking like I'd been electrocuted, but I forced myself to bend down and touch her all the same. Her neck, chest and then finally her wrists, just to make sure. Not cold yet of course, but completely still. A massive diamond on her left index finger glinted at me, and I stared at it for a second, hoping its beauty would erase the horror all around me. I realised I was whimpering like a puppy.

Looking up, I could see nothing but the curve of the stairs leading higher and higher. I stood there for a minute, a hundred thoughts racing through my brain, the loudest of which was screaming at me to run away as fast as possible. But I couldn't just leave, not when I was in the middle of my own crime scene. So I went up the stairs slowly, desperately hoping Will would be there, doing something to sort this, and feeling entirely out of control. When I reached the first floor, I heard a creak coming from above me. I called out for Will, and immediately got a reply.

'Up here!' The voice sounded relaxed, cheerful even. When I finally reached him, he was in a bedroom the size of my mum's entire ground floor, putting a pile of jumpers into a suitcase. He turned round when I entered, and a flash of something I couldn't quite decipher crossed his face.

'What are you doing here? I told you to wait for my signal,' he said, quite calmly as he put the bag down. 'She's still denying it all, so I've left her to collect herself before we talk again.'

The world felt somehow warped and far away. Standing with Will in this beautiful room full of expensive clothes, I knew something was very wrong and I didn't just mean Olivia Wistern being dead three floors below us.

I backed out of the room, but he followed me, asking what was wrong. I couldn't speak, couldn't do anything but point frantically as we went down to the floor below. Then I stopped, and he looked down. He only glanced at her briefly before he looked back at me, almost as if her crumpled body wasn't a surprise. Then he pushed past me and headed towards her.

'Is she dead?'

I didn't reply. Olivia's head was facing in the wrong direction – if that hadn't tipped him off, nothing would.

Will crouched over her body and put his ear carefully to her mouth. After a minute, he got out his phone and punched in three numbers. 999, I guess I should've done that the moment I saw her lying there but I'd lost my bottle. I'd touched her body, freaked out and then I'd just walked away like some kind of amateur.

I forced my attention back onto Will. He was speaking into the phone, confirming that Olivia was definitely dead.

'We have a restraining order . . . she broke in. I found my mother-in-law dead. Please hurry.'

As he said it, he was looking at me right in the eyes. Cold eyes, why hadn't I noticed that before? My mum always told me to look at a person's eyes first. 'Window to the soul,' she confidently said as if she was able to figure out a person just by their corneas. I attempted speech, but it came out too loud.

'I didn't do it, she was *there* when I came in! She was already dead!' Will winced and spoke into the phone again, more quietly this time. Panic was overcoming me and I was yelling now.

'She jumped, she knew we were about to expose her, tell them, tell them what she did.' But he just shook his head at me.

'I can't tell the police that, Jade. Because it's not true, is it?'

I forced myself to breathe through my nose, worried I might pass out if I didn't fix my heart rate. I fainted at school once, after it turned out a boy I liked only asked me out as a dare. The room went wobbly and then bam, I woke up in the nurse's office. He got suspended for one measly day, and I got called swooner for the next three years.

If I wanted to regain control, I only had one option. I pulled out my phone and started filming, live this time. I wanted to be sure nobody could delete the footage.

'I'm at Olivia Wistern's house right now,' I spoke fast, sounding shaky, 'and I walked in to find her dead. Some of you might find it hard to see this but it's important because I'm being accused of killing her.' I flashed the camera towards her body. The view count shot up. 500 people watching me already. Then I focused in on Will, who was still crouched over, talking on the phone.

'This is her son-in-law, Will Fortesque. He's lying, telling the police I hurt her. Record this if you're watching, I need people to get the word out.' He noticed what I was doing then, and got up as I backed away.

'Don't try to do anything, there are people watching – people who are calling for help as I speak.' I stumbled slightly, not noticing a small step which led back down towards the entrance hall, and he caught up with me. As he put his arm out towards my shoulder, I screamed. That's what you're taught to do as a kid, isn't it? He didn't look violent, but you can never tell. Monsters wear normal faces well. In this case, they even wore corduroy trousers.

Will spoke quietly but there was an edge in his voice.

'I want to help you. I'll get you some water, would you like some water?'

Would I like some water? This man was saying I'd murdered his mother-in-law and acting as though he'd forgotten his manners. I kept one hand out in front of me as I spoke, pointing my phone at him in a way I hoped was commanding. 8,000 people were watching now.

'Did you kill her?' I asked. He looked at me with pity. 'Because it's the only thing that makes sense now. You must've killed Anthony, and I got close to figuring that out.' I didn't, I thought it was Olivia, but that could be revised later. 'That's why you were pretending to help me.' He shook his head and sighed.

'The family wanted you jailed for this, but I thought someone with such obvious mental health problems should be given a chance to see how far from reality they'd got.' I bit my cheek so as not to scream again. I couldn't get too hysterical.

'Why did you do it, Will? Did you invest with Anthony? Lost all your money and killed him in a rage? Did Olivia find out? She wouldn't have kept that quiet, would she?' As I spoke, I saw from his face that I was right. 'Look at his expression, guys, read him like a book!' 19,800 viewers. He was talking, something about putting the phone down and getting a cup of tea (a cup of tea with a man who wanted me locked up – not the worst date I'd ever had but definitely up there). I stepped back towards the door and slowly pulled the latch open. When I felt it move, I turned and ran away as fast as I could. As I flew up the drive, I heard a voice call my name. Freddy. He was standing near the house looking confused beyond belief. We both looked at each other for a moment, but then I heard sirens and fled the path. Running by the edges of the trees, I realised I'd never get to the gates before the police arrived so I dived behind a large oak and squeezed into a bush. The police found me there ten minutes later. 76,000 people were watching as they pulled me out by my ankles. I don't know how long the camera kept streaming, I dropped it in the struggle, but I've since been told that the final viewing figure was well over 120,000 people, all watching a still image of some branches. That's how much people believed in me at the end.

OLIVIA

The room I woke up in was entirely beige, decorated like one of those houses you see as you drive through the grim London suburbs as fast as possible. Yellowing carpet, a fake leather sofa which sagged slightly, as if it knew it was merely gussied up plastic, and a hideous picture of a rainbow. So many harsh spotlights everywhere, whoever thought they enhanced a room should be forced to sit directly underneath one for the rest of time; nothing shows off fine lines more. My head hurt quite badly, and my right ankle was throbbing, which made me think I must be in a hospital. Perhaps the waiting room? But we always went to the Princess Helena and they'd never have dared install spotlights. My good friend Diana Latham donated a lot of money to their chemo wing and part of that cash went towards making it a calming and stylish place to stay. Her interiors team did a fabulous job, I remember one doctor saying it was *the* place to get cancer, which nobody apart from me laughed at. He wasn't wrong though. *House & Garden* even ran a feature on how to get the Latham Wing look. Diana had made the sick bed aspirational.

Perhaps I was in an NHS hospital then. Unavoidable some-times. Fred once broke his arm and the nanny stupidly took him to the local A&E, where I endured an eight-hour wait on a plastic chair next to a man who had a lot of blood coming out of a particularly intimate part of his body and who seemed intent on showing me as often as he could.

The door opened, and two women came in. One short and dressed like Anthony's mother, and the other rather beautiful, but wearing an A-line skirt which did nothing for her, shoes with velcro straps and worst of all, an Alice band.

I got up, the fake leather squeaking as I did, and asked when I'd be seen. 'My head is very sore, and I think my ankle might be broken. I can't put weight on it.' I pointed down at my leg to illustrate the point and was surprised to find that both my feet were firmly on the floor. Yvonne, the less frumpy one, gave a sort of mirthless smile at this, and I sensed I wasn't going to get the respect I deserved, although I grudgingly admitted it was a nice touch to be greeted by senior management.

'It's all fine, Mrs Wistern, don't worry. The pain will subside shortly, people often get lingering after-effects but it's completely normal I assure you. Now, what I'm about to say will come as a shock, I've been doing this job for 94 years and I've yet to meet someone who didn't panic a little bit, but you have to hear it.' She was about to tell me there'd be an eight-hour wait, I knew it. I'd have to get Charles to call the Princess Helena, there was no way I was going to sit on that sofa for a minute longer. I started to object but she put a hand out and stopped me.

'I'm very sorry to tell you this, but you're dead.'

After a few minutes of confusion, where I told her that jokes had to be funny and she kept insisting that it wasn't a joke, we then had a protracted argument where I demanded to see her manager, and she grabbed my arm and plonked me back down on the sad sofa quite roughly. I told her I'd be making a complaint to the hospital, started threatening all sorts, but I was stopped in my tracks when the most remarkable thing happened. Yvonne nodded at her underling, and this dull woman in her hideous polyester dress sighed, turned round, and walked through the wall. She walked *through* the wall, and then came back in using the door as she had before.

'We don't like to do that here,' Yvonne said as I sat there with my mouth open. 'In this interim stage, we try to behave as we did in the living world, it gives people a chance to acclimatise. But you obviously needed a little more proof. Please don't try it yourself, it's actually rather painful and you'll end up feeling very nauseous if you're not used to it.'

And then, as I sat there feeling completely loopy, she explained everything. I was dead, I had died, I was no longer on the earth. I'd left behind my family and my house and that lovely Loro Piana coat I'd only just remembered about that I was getting ready to wear all winter. Apparently I was in the South Gloucestershire processing centre, where I would have to remember how I'd died before I could 'transcend' to the next stage of the afterlife. When I asked her what that was, she shook her head.

'You're not ready for that just yet. Figure out how you died first.' I burst out laughing at this absurd bureaucratic system. It all felt ridiculous, so insane and yet so banal. Susan took over, handing me a welcome pack. It even had a name badge included, laminated and to be worn at all times. Why did I have to figure out how I'd died to get on with it? According to this woman, who I assumed could only have died from the sheer boredom of having to live with herself, your mind goes blank roughly 30 minutes prior to the moment of death, so that you don't suffer. But self-preservation means a lapse in time. It's important you recall the way you left the world otherwise you leave a part of yourself behind.

'It's like a healing closure,' Susan said, and I shuddered at the cod psychotherapy. 'Usually you remember within a few days, don't fret.'

'But of course I know how I died,' I said, with annoyance, before realising that actually, I had no idea. What was my last memory? I hazily pictured Will helping me out of a car, and then nothing. I promptly burst into tears, and Susan actually sat down and rubbed my back quite kindly.

'It's a lot, my love,' she said in a whisper, not understanding that I was crying at the thought that my last memory of life was of *my son-in-law*. It was too unfair.

After going through the resources I would be given: 'You can watch your family and join our daily meditation sessions which help unlock memories and nudge you towards the next phase of your journey; I very much recommend you take part. Those that don't find their stay here can drag on a bit.'

Yvonne stood up and told me she'd escort me to the dormitory. I baulked at this. Even at school, I'd managed to make my parents insist I have my own room. My father told the headmistress he wasn't spending good money for me to have nightly sleepovers and somehow a room was found for me. I later found out it belonged to a games teacher nobody much liked, which made the victory that much sweeter.

'The afterlife is not an individualistic society,' I was told, there was no other option. I could only imagine how Anthony had reacted to that.

Before we left for the dormitory, she checked my paperwork one more time and paused for a moment.

'Of course, we haven't covered the slightly unusual situation you're in.' This time she looked genuinely amused. 'Another shock incoming, brace yourself! Your husband is still here. Nobody stays as long as he has usually. Months now, we've had the pleasure.' The word was said with a hefty dollop of sarcasm. 'A bit of a celebrity, we don't get many in South Glos. You hear stories about other centres at the annual AGM, of big names coming in, but usually they're only there a few days. Celebrities are oddly good at knowing how they died; I suppose that's a benefit of narcissism, isn't it?' She paused for a moment while my brain registered that my husband was still here. 'So we'll obviously have to work around that as best we can. Sometimes we have couples who die at the same time. Most recently a lovely pair who died when the model railway he'd made in their garden exploded on its inaugural outing. She was very angry about that when she remembered, bless her. The husband tried to convince her they'd died after a gas leak but the truth always comes out.'

I wondered whether violence worked in this place. Would I be able to rugby tackle my husband when I saw him? Claw at his face? As if she could read my mind (and who knows, perhaps she could. Susan walked through a wall after all), Yvonne quickly shook her head.

'We are focused on your *journey onwards*, Olivia. Not the past. We work together to help each other.'

'Can I help him out by telling him how he died?' I asked, thinking about how that would hasten the end of our time here together. I didn't know whether or not I wanted to do that yet. Would it be a relief to have someone I knew in this profoundly depressing place?

She laughed at this. 'I'm beginning to like you. Look, normally we don't recommend people inform others of the manner of their death. It lessens the acceptance stage and it's left people with some difficult issues when they move on to the next place. But you wouldn't be punished, if that's what you mean. And I can't say you wouldn't be doing us all a favour.' Ushering me out the door, she turned to me and positioned her body uncomfortably close to mine. 'But I wouldn't, Olivia, not if you love him. Where he's going next, well, it would be better to linger here a while.'

ANTHONY

The yell I'd let out when she fell alerted the man in the next cubicle. Tony, who used to be a cab driver and still felt the need to rant about how useless the London mayor was, came over to see what was happening.

'She's dead,' I told him, not tearing my eyes away from the screen. He put a hand on my shoulder in some gruff attempt at condolence and hovered behind me, clearly hoping to watch something a little more exciting than his usual fare. His wife Marie mainly sitting in their kitchen talking to their cats in a baby voice so annoying I often wondered whether he'd felt like the only option was to kill himself. Tony thought it was something to do with a collision with a cyclist, people he hated even more than the mayor, but the powers that be kept telling him he was way off and that meant I spent a lot of time being subjected to rants about how the managers were in the pay of 'Big Bike'.

On the screen, the girl had checked to see whether Olivia was dead but even from here, I could see that she was. She lifted her neck slightly, so as to see her face and then dropped it in panic, which caused a fairly nauseating thud. From that brief glimpse, my wife suddenly looked *old,* a thing she'd spent a lot of money to avoid. She'd successfully staved off the worst of the wrinkles but now they seemed to seize their moment and flood her face. I couldn't have grown old looking at my wife like that, I don't care how callous it sounds. You don't want to be reminded of your slow decline in your own partner's face, do you? That's why second wives are so fantastic.

I must say, the girl looked scared out of her wits. That slightly mad look she'd had before had all but vanished and now she looked like she might start crying right there over my wife's body. I suppose it would be nice if at least one person did. What was Will going to do now, I wondered? Pretend she fell? Kill this girl too and bury her in the garden? Not likely. Fred would probably find her digging up some new vegetable patch. The cook once valiantly attempted to make a soup using his crop of courgettes, and after lunch I'd heard Olivia squealing with laughter when she was quietly told that there'd been an emergency dash to the local grocer's to pick up fresh ones. Lyra had wobbled one of his sad specimens in front of him, the poor thing drooping in shame. 'Don't worry, Fred, it's a very common problem for men.'

The picture on the screen was getting fainter and fainter, and I banged the top of the monitor to try to get it back with no joy.

'It won't work,' said Tony who misses smoking so much he holds an imaginary cigarette between his fingers at all times. Taking a drag on the invisible fag, he summed it up. 'She's dead, so you can't watch what's happening anymore. She died at your Cotswolds gaff, didn't she? That means,' he said with an exaggerated wink, 'she'll be here soon. Any minute, Ant, you'll be reunited with your missus.' Then he shook his head and sucked the air. 'Rather you than me, mate.'

The picture went fuzzy, and finally disappeared as Tony walked back to his own cubicle, all the fun gone for him. He'd be back watching Marie and the cats while I was left with a racing heart and a feeling of dread. Suddenly her baby talk didn't seem so bad. After all, he could switch off the monitor anytime he liked. I marched back to Susan's office, ready to give her my latest theory and hopefully get out of this place before my wife had a chance to greet me.

OLIVIA

I'd gone back to the intake office when I realised I didn't have any clothes with me, intent on demanding that an order be placed. All thoughts of attire were quickly banished when I caught sight of Anthony being told his version of death was incorrect by Yvonne's sidekick. Not for the first time apparently, a little detail which pleased me enormously. For a man as competitive as he, that was a tough blow. At one of Fred's school sports days, the only one he managed to make it to, he ran the 100-metre race against the other fathers, barging two of them right off their feet and making the headmistress get a stress nosebleed after she endured fifteen minutes of him arguing that the guy who came first was cheating because he was wearing running trainers. The children never asked him to attend anything after that, which really was for the best. I was able to watch him storm out, shouting about how he couldn't believe 'such gormless goons' were daring to tell him how he'd died.

'I get to decide!' he'd added as he stomped off, which told me at least his self-esteem was intact even if his appearance was shot to bits. A grey tracksuit, just like an inmate, and bags under his eyes which surprised and horrified me. I assumed you couldn't age after death, and the idea that I too might start seeing fresh wrinkles without the skilled and soothing hands of Dr Snarlman to whisk them away was quite disconcerting.

Apparently, the centre you end up in is all down to where you die. South Gloucestershire clearly not a post-death hotspot, since there were very few people around. The ones that were in my intake were mainly very elderly, wearing an assortment of drab rain jackets and those trousers with elasticated waistbands that old people seem to be the exclusive purchasers of. What a pity I hadn't been in London. Kensington and Chelsea would've been much more fun.

We finally came face to face in the food hall. It was unfortunate that I'd just been given a grey tracksuit of my very own, which was several sizes too big, and so of course I wasn't feeling my best, but I rallied well. Both holding trays, we stood across a table bolted to the floor, neither willing to speak. I contemplated throwing my food directly into his face, a worthy use of it since I wouldn't be touching turkey à la king even if it meant staying under these spotlights for eternity, but decided the high road was the better option. Forcing a smile, I gestured at him to sit down. We eyed each other in silence for a second, my husband holding up a plastic fork as if in self-defence. He looked so pathetic, it made me feel almost optimistic for the first time since I'd checked in. With thirty years' worth of fury in my heart, but a lightness in my chest, I got to work.

ANTHONY

Time is a living world construct. Here, it goes at its own pace. It must've been about three living world days since Olivia first sat down across the table from me and began to list my failures with an enthusiasm I found frankly unnecessary, but it *feels* like it's been five years. The woman does not stop berating me. I go to the monitors, and she's there ready to 'get into it' about the first affair I had. I escape to the dormitory and she's somehow managed to clear it of anyone else in order that we have the room to ourselves, and it's never for what you might hope. No, it's always to insist we go over and over my business mistakes, which she takes great pleasure in calling 'common theft' as if I'm some failed shoplifter instead of the man who managed to cream millions off some of the richest people in the country. There should be some respect for that, especially from one's wife (who did pretty well out of it herself), but Olivia has only fury. I even fled to the meditation room, a place I'd formerly avoided like the plague, but she was there, smiling beatifically, ready to begin again. Even though the meditation is supposed to be of a silent nature, the woman leading it is no match for Olivia, who starts

to list my failings in a chant. She goes on for so long that some
of the older members of the group actually seem to nod off.
Perhaps hearing an angry woman drone on without pausing for
breath is relaxing for some of them, but it's not for me. I've
grown twitchy, nerves aflame, constantly looking round corners
for a glimpse of her. It's been very emasculating, and the powers
that be refuse to do anything. I even went to the HR woman,
thinking an allegation of bullying might make them take a stand,
but she didn't bother to write down my complaint.

'We cannot intervene in marital disagreements, Mr Wistern,'
she'd told me, with a distinct air of boredom. 'The quickest way
out is to remember how you died and move on. I see from your
file that you're currently our longest-staying member . . .' she
shuffled her papers '. . . with nineteen incorrect guesses? Gosh,
that's a lot. The last person to top that was a lovely chap called
Brian who was run over by his own car after he left the engine
running and went back into the house to get a scarf.' She was
laughing now, tears suddenly springing from her eyes and drib-
bling down her face. Amazingly unprofessional. 'It was a little
unusual. The dog was in the front seat and knocked the hand-
brake.' Wheezing now. 'Pinned him underneath the wheels, he
wasn't found for three hours.' As she tried to recover from her
laughing fit, I imagined running her over.

'Best thing about it, the dog had somehow managed to open
the door and jump out, so nobody ever knew his canine
companion had killed him.' Suddenly the laughter stopped and
the woman stared at me with contempt. 'That was understandably a complex case. But yours isn't anywhere near as difficult,
Mr Wistern, so why haven't you got there yet? I'd advise you to
get back to work.'

And on and on it went; Olivia listing my failings as both a
husband and as a person, and me accusing her of killing me. We

330

were at an ugly impasse. I'd gone in with my accusation early, thinking I had the clear moral high ground here, but when I levelled my accusation, my wife simply laughed.

My wife had never laughed at me before, but the alive Olivia was very different from the newly dead version. Apparently my suggestion was so absurd she wasn't even offended by the allegation.

'I didn't murder you,' she said in almost a bored tone. 'Christ, no wonder you're still here if that's the route you've been going down for months. Of course I didn't kill you, what good would that have done me? I was planning on *leaving* you, Anthony.'

Obviously, I was then able to wipe the smug look off her face by explaining that I'd been watching her every move since the night I died, and knew all about her plans. It cheered me to see her look decidedly uncomfortable for the first time, but it didn't last. Soon we were back to fighting about how I'd never done 'a single kind thing for her which wouldn't also benefit me'. It was hopeless.

Despite her constant rage, I believed Liv when she said she didn't kill me. There was no reason to lie now, not unless she was playing some new game I didn't know about. Again and again I went back to Susan with an array of wild guesses about who'd murdered me. I named all four of my children, Giles, Lainey, my mother (though how an 89-year-old woman would manage to impale me on a spike was beyond my reasoning), the husband of a woman I'd been flirting with at the party. I couldn't even remember his surname. I'd just said Tom who works for Staffords bank and wears the most terrible shoes. God his shoes were bad, like the kind of bridge and tunnel brogues you see at Liverpool station every rush hour.

Every time, Susan knocked me back with an increasingly patronising air and an exhortation to 'really think about the kind of death a man like you would deserve,' which didn't help at all. A man like me deserved the death of a pharaoh, dying in his bed surrounded by many mistresses and buried in a tomb the size of Mayfair with all his worldly possessions. Maybe I was looking too close to home. After all, I'd pissed off some seriously important people throughout my life. Perhaps just naming mere family members was beneath me when I could have been killed by MI5 or a foreign government. I like that idea, I must admit. It seemed more fitting for a man of my stature. But when I mentioned it to Susan, she did an exaggerated thumbs down and made a dramatic frowny face. And then laughed far too loudly.

Olivia and I were stuck. I knew how she'd died, she knew how I'd died but not only had we been instructed not to tell each other, it was also obvious we were both holding the information as an insurance policy. Reveal it in anger and I might lose. Hard to see how, since I was now certain I'd been killed by a shadowy and powerful cabal and Liv had just been pushed down some stairs by the most boring man we knew, but if there was a way, she'd find it.

Just as I was beginning to feel really sorry for myself, Olivia offered up an unexpected truce. I'd stopped bothering to watch the monitors after Liv had turned up, but she was new to this, and viewed the children constantly. They'd been behaving terribly according to Liv. Freddy had fallen off the map entirely, Lyra had gone on a bender, crashing at people's houses and ignoring Camille's phone calls. Jemima was talking to anyone who'd listen about how she was going to sue the social media platforms which had enabled Jade Evans, and Clara was giving interviews to the press, portraying herself as a tragic orphan. All of them were calling Charles and asking about money.

From her viewing, Olivia had initially come to me crowing that she already knew how she'd died. She was torn between self-congratulation and horror that some 'nutcase from the village' had been the one to kill her. I must say, I enjoyed watching her almost sashay down the hall to tell the manager about her break-through. I lay on my bed, keenly counting down the minutes until she came back. When she finally returned, I assumed a relaxed expression, hoping to appear sympathetic to the point of patronising. What a face she had on, glowering at me as if it were *my* fault she'd got it so wrong. I consoled her: 'Everyone gets it wrong on the first try, darling,' but she didn't like that one bit, and snapped back that I would say that after twenty attempts. After that, things got a bit ugly I'm afraid to say, and I told Liv her death was so obvious as to be banal.

'A terrible cliche, like something from one of those daytime soaps I always assumed you watched while I was hard at work.' She nearly told me how I'd died then, I saw it on the tip of her tongue but somehow she managed to swallow it. Then, in a silkier tone, she told me the children were having a dinner that night to discuss arrangements.

'At Tanners,' she said, smiling a little too sweetly. 'We should watch it together. A nice family moment.'

ANTHONY

It's a relief to be back at Tanners after the past few weeks. The more I learn about the afterlife, the more I think it really needs a revamp. My own mother is fervently pious, and taught us that there was a heaven and a hell, and no other option. I grew up imagining that if I was good, I would end up in a beautiful cloudy kingdom where one could lounge about being served fruit on platters and if I was bad, I'd end up in a fiery pit where demons bit your ankles. As an adult, I'd lost all faith entirely, and to find out that neither belief was correct has been very disappointing. There had been a whole other option and it mainly consists of drab boxy rooms which smell quite strongly of vinegar and, apart from one instance of a woman putting her hand through my stomach, no magic at all. I mentioned to Susan that she ought to think about making some major improvements, but she was incredibly dismissive of my ideas, even when I offered to put her in touch with Coco Lyons, who runs a major private equity group. They'd turn this place around in a hugely cost-effective way – half the employees here don't seem to do any actual work for a start – but she looked at me like I was simple, and asked if I was labouring under the illusion that the processing centre was a business?

My wife had turned off the main spotlights and found a bottle of non-alcoholic sparkling wine from somewhere. She arranged a blanket over our legs and sat down next to me. On the monitor, the old manager was shuffling towards the door, the tinkling of diners' voices harmoniously welcoming us into the restaurant. I settled back into my chair, took a sip from my paper cup, and for a moment, managed to forget where I was.

OLIVIA

The one good thing keeping my spirits afloat was that I'd figured out who'd killed me. It was easy in the end. One false guess, that's to be expected of course, but then I'd cracked it. It had to be Will. I worked very hard to remember the details of that evening, closely watching my family on the monitors, and meditating diligently. According to the teacher, Anthony had only been once since he came here – and that was just to annoy me. He'd also resolutely refused to do any of the self-hypnosis or deep breathing exercises on offer. Just like him to think he knows better. The man once insisted a gondolier let him take the oar, after deciding we were going too slowly. After much stabbing at the water in frustration, Anthony threw the thing into the air and it landed atop a bridge we were stuck under. A passing tourist chucked it back to us, and it cracked the poor gondolier on the head, knocking him clean out. To the day he died, my husband insisted there was something wrong with the oar.

After putting in the work and piecing together the clues (mainly provided by a rather incriminating video of Will exultantly telling Jemima that he'd had a lovely evening with me prior to my death – 'She'd said she'd help us out, Jem, at least that was a comfort for her.' I knew there was simply no possible way I'd had a lovely evening with my son-in-law, which meant he was covering something) my memory quickly came back. Will, asking me for money. Begging for it, like some kind of Dickensian street urchin. I'd been thrilled to be in a position to turn him down, probably why I didn't give a moment's thought to what he might do next. I hadn't told the powers that be yet. I knew when I did, I'd leave the centre immediately and while I wanted desperately to escape this place, I couldn't go without seeing what happened next. That idiotic girl was clearly the prime suspect, why look elsewhere when she looked so guilty? And Will still had my ring, taken it off my finger before he'd called the police. There was every chance he'd get clean away with killing me and make a huge profit. When the children arranged a meal at Tanners, I was keen to see what might spill out when they were all together.

Poor Anthony, I was always one step ahead of him. Ego gets in the way of most men seeing what's in front of them. It almost made it feel unsporting somehow.

ANTHONY

You know where you are at a place like Tanners. They served King Charles II and some of his many mistresses in the Salon Vert. They opened every day during the Blitz, even as the building next door collapsed. Nothing can ruffle this building's staid and vaunted demeanour. A soothing place to watch my family descend into inevitable chaos.

The manager is hovering by the door, but not because he's eager to welcome my family, the stench of disgrace means those days have long since gone. He's desperately hoping to smuggle them inside without the other diners seeing. The booking would never have gone through if he'd been working, but he was on holiday until this morning and his useless underling didn't see the problem.

'Doesn't he seem stressed?' I asked my wife, who just looked bored. I appear to know things about him I shouldn't, a perk of this whole ordeal I'd not had before. This must be a new phase of death, I'd have to ask Tony about it. I've certainly been here long enough, maybe I can read people's minds now. How do I know he had a holiday? And I knew his wife was barely speaking

338

to him by the end of it, infuriated by his inability to relax properly and spend time with her.

'None of those old Tories will come to your funeral when you die of a heart attack!' she'd yelled as they walked off the flight, and he'd immediately checked his work emails. She's not wrong actually, I can't even remember his name.

A cab comes to a stop and the manager stands up tall. Slouching is distinctly *not* Tanners. Who's that getting out? Fred first, Lyra following him. The manager opens the door and welcomes them profusely, hoping that his enthusiasm will help gloss over the suggestion that he take them to the private room through the service corridor. Even if it doesn't, that's the way they're going, he's screwed his courage to the sticking point and he'll insist either way.

The siblings put up no fuss. They are escorted down the grubby alley to the private room where they are left to wait. The manager sighs with relief. Only four people left to wrangle. Shortly afterwards, Jemima turns up. This should be fun to watch, she'll surely be the one to raise hell at this situation, but even she barely reacts. A slight purse of her lips to express annoyance, but she follows the path as directed and greets the others with a curt hello. If anyone notices the absence of her husband, they don't mention it. If these last guests comply, the manager makes a silent promise that he'll take his wife out for lunch tomorrow. He has a few more minutes to wait. A girl walks up the street, looking down at her phone and slightly unsteady on her ridiculous heels. The manager isn't sure she's even headed his way until the last minute, when she stops by the restaurant and waits for a second. Now he can see she's a Wistern, she has my eyes. Olivia makes a small sound of disapproval, and I assume it's at the skirt which is barely covering my daughter's arse but it's actually because Clara is wearing my wife's favourite shoes.

'I wore them the night you died,' she says, pointedly.

This girl looks a bit vacant, the manager thinks, as he explains the situation and escorts her to the private room. Maybe she's not very bright. I wouldn't agree with that anymore. Clara is canny in many ways, perhaps the most manipulative of my children. I imagine she'll go far in life, as long as she never cares much about loyalty or honour. And why would she? Those weren't the qualities I brought them up with. Clara says nothing at all, even as he wishes her a pleasant evening, she just stares down at her phone as if the secrets of the universe are right there on the glowing screen. In reality, she's watching one of her friends dance around the deck of a yacht in a bikini, but to my youngest, that's as deep as it usually gets.

As the manager goes back to the foyer, he pulls out his phone and texts his wife in delight. He'll buy her flowers on the way home, not knowing it's too late. She packed her bags that morning and left. Took everything but the toaster and didn't even leave a note. I feel omnipotent with this knowledge, stifling a giggle lest my wife know about my new powers.

The children are now assembled around the table. Is it finally time for the truth to be told? With this lot, you'd be a fool to bet on it, except I feel suddenly as though something big is about to happen. I look away – can't have Liv figuring out I know more than her, not when we're this close to the end.

OLIVIA

Anthony keeps gasping at the dullest developments and giggling whenever he sees the manager appear, which is incredibly irritating. Inside the private dining room, my children take their places around the table.

'Oh, there she is. Once in a while you could deign to reply to a text, Clara,' Lyra says, looking slightly irritated. 'I know you think you've really landed on your feet living with Charles, but you're aware that you still have an actual family, aren't you?'

My youngest rolls her eyes. 'A family who doesn't give a shit their dad was murdered, but OK.' That sets Lyra off.

'Are you still on this? Isn't it enough to have one parent murdered? Doesn't that get you enough attention?' Out of all my children, Clara had used the family ruin to the best advantage. Somehow her crowd hadn't dropped her at all, even the friends whose parents had cut me off the moment Anthony's crimes had been revealed. She'd even been invited to Fenella Wyatt's birthday party, and Fenella's father was a baronet. The model agency Foal's Legs had signed her up to their books after the *Tatler* interview, billing her as 'the perfect blend of her naughty father and icy mother'. She and her friends spent a lot of time watching videos about Jade Evans; they'd even started an online petition to have her 'exonerated' which had received several thousand signatures before being been taken down.

'If Jade killed Olivia, it was because she knew she was guilty.' The others rolled their eyes. They've been over and over this, but my youngest will not budge on her conviction that Anthony was murdered. She's not quite come up with a good story for why I was killed though; at the moment I appear to be just collateral damage. It sounds, to use one of Lyra's favourite phrases, rather like she's blaming the victim.

'It's pathetic none of you can see what's really going on. I'm genuinely embarrassed for you.' The girls start speaking over each other, ridiculing Clara, but she gives them no reaction. The bored disdain of a teenager is something to marvel at, and my youngest has perfected it.

'Where's Will? Is he coming or have you finally decided to dump him and make it as an independent woman?' Lyra has changed the subject, smirking as she says it. Despite her newly formed belief that imminent motherhood will make her more important than any of her siblings, it still rankles Jemima when they mock her for being a housewife.

'He'll be here. He's been in meetings all day, business is doing *very* well.'

Even as a child, Jemima would come up with reasons why she was the most successful of them all. Did she really believe it now? Living with her in-laws with a husband up to his neck in debt? Jemima was much like her father, able to gloss over the nasty realities of life in the belief that if you just ignored them, they'd go away. 'I've already signed this one up to Mountbank. I know you got terribly bullied there Ly, and Clara has hardly taken advantage of the academic offerings, but it's just such a lovely little school. They've introduced a form of equine therapy that the new headmistress learned about in Switzerland.'

At that moment, an elderly waiter comes in with Champagne. Tonight, it arrives with another guest, my brother, who looks more animated than I've ever seen him and appears to have lost a little weight. It makes me uncomfortable to see him so changed. I thought there would be more grief, any grief in fact. Charles was my rock, why does he look like he's at a celebration? Clara is too happy to see him, actually getting out of her seat to greet my brother, who embraces her as if she's his own daughter. Next to me, Anthony actually gasps and I shoot him a look which I hope adequately conveys my irritation.

Jemima is smiling brightly now as the waiter hands her a glass.

'To Olivia, an interesting life.' The others dutifully drink, Freddy swallowing almost the entire glass in one. There's a distinct lack of emotion in the room, as if they're talking about an old family cat who died and not their mother. At least Anthony got a few tears, however halfhearted they were. 'Did you know she had an admirer?' Jemima said, smirking. 'When the police gave me her phone, there was a text from a guy named Bruce Patron . . .' I yelped at this, nearly knocking my glass over '. . . asking if she'd like to have dinner. Unfortunately for Olivia, it was sent the morning after she died. He sounded keen.'

'Maybe he had a punishment fetish.' Lyra, of course. I couldn't even dwell on the missed opportunity of Bruce Patron because my children were moving on.

'I still can't believe Will let the girl into the house,' says Lyra, looking pointedly at Jemima. 'An insane thing to do. She'd been stalking us for months, why would he leave the door open?'

'A very good point,' I say out loud, 'why *did* your husband do that?' An orderly walking past points to the sign about the monitor which reads 'All viewing must be done in silence.'

Jemima defends her husband, but it's obvious her heart isn't in it, and talk soon turns to other things. Not even five minutes was spent on the manner of my death. My aunt Eliza never married, and kept a succession of unkempt Irish wolfhounds throughout her life. At one point she had seven, and we dreaded going to her house, which always smelt like wet dog. And yet she died in her sleep aged 96. When they found her, the dogs were curled up around her body, howling. I misjudged Eliza. From where I sat now, she'd had the right idea.

ANTHONY

My family spend the first course going over the contents my wife left behind, that which wasn't seized or sold off. It's a mixed offering, and when I say mixed I mean deeply dull. All the really good stuff is long gone, they're haggling over scraps. The door opens and the elderly waiter shuffles in again. Will is behind him, and I feel Olivia stiffen slightly beside me.

The man is transformed. He's wearing a dark blue suit which fits him very well indeed, and his hair has been cut differently. From this angle, you can barely see the bald patch. Will is smiling broadly, his arms flung wide in greeting. He is, I realise, enjoying himself immensely.

'Family, hello, hello. Apols for the late arrival but business had other ideas. Has everyone got a drink?' He sits down and raises his glass in a toast. 'To Olivia, what a woman!' My wife makes a retching sound.

This bravado doesn't suit him. It's like a little boy trying on his father's shoes. No matter, he's arrived at the entirely wrong moment, and this newly found confidence will soon be ripped away.

'You going to mention the jewellery?' Clara is finally paying attention. Her question was blunt, zeroing straight in on the only real items of value my wife had left.

I suddenly had a keen sense of what was coming, and a little thrill went through my body.

'Why don't we get it valued and then just sell it and split the proceeds?' Clara suggests, and Lyra shrugs.

'Fine by me. None of us are going to wear that stuff anyway. Who wears brooches now?' Jemima looks unhappy at this, clearly thinking that as the eldest daughter, she'd get first dibs. She pouts as she looks back at the list of items.

'Ok, it's two brooches – one emerald and one amethyst. Eight bracelets, her engagement and wedding rings, five pairs of earrings and that nice cross that she only wore when she wanted to look pious. Remember she had it on when Dad was being sued by that neighbour? For six weeks she dressed like a couture-clad pilgrim.' Next to me, Olivia smiled at the memory.

'I knew that judge was an ardent Catholic, bringing my bible into court was a nice touch.'

'I'll have it all checked out by my jeweller,' Jemima was saying, and began to put the list back in her notebook when Lyra frowns.

'The diamond, that enormous ring.' Yes Lyra, yes! 'It looked like it was more valuable than Gables. Where is it?'

All eyes are on Fred. 'Was it there when you found her?'

'I was a bit busy dealing with my mother's dead body to look for rings.'

Tension began to creep across the table. Look at Will for god's sake. I know it's easy to forget he's even here but come on.

'So did that little weirdo take it?' asks Lyra. 'How did we miss that?' She turns to her brother-in-law, and I feel the thrum of adrenaline in my chest. 'Will?' He is still smiling, but it's already faltering.

'The police searched her of course. If she'd had it, they'd have found it. Olivia must have put it somewhere. Or maybe she sold it? That wouldn't be unlike your mother, always rather short-sighted when it came to valuables. I would never speak ill of the dead, but as lovely as she was . . .' a snort from one of my children '. . . she didn't have a lot of sense.' Next to me, Olivia screamed so loudly even the orderly was too shocked to shush her.

I had to give it to him, his performance was very smooth, perhaps he'd learned something from me over the years. But was he really smooth enough to get away with murder?

OLIVIA

Really, I'd despised him since Jemima first introduced him to us, those long cold fingers of his had made me feel quite nauseous when he first shook my hand. I should've warned my daughter off him but really, what would I have said? The man went to Eton, had perfect manners and excellent parentage. He had his own business, spoke fluent Cantonese and to top it off, he seemed to like our oldest daughter which was a surprise to all of us. For a good few months, Lyra joked that it must be some kind of bet he had going with friends, until Jemima found out and set some of her degree photographs on fire in revenge. Lyra exhibited the little pile of ash with the title 'sibling rivalry' which I thought quite clever.

Jemima's eyes were screwed up in concentration.

'Was she wearing it that night at dinner?' Charles thought for a minute and nodded.

'Well she was when I saw her that afternoon. I noticed it, could hardly fail to. It was a whopper. But I admit I thought it must've been costume jewellery. There's no way a ring like that slipped past the investigators.' Lyra patted him on the arm.

'Uncle Charles, when would Olivia ever wear something cheap? The thing sparkled like a disco ball.' He frowned, looking annoyed.

'But then she shouldn't have been wearing it in public. I'm a fool, I should've made her hand it over for safekeeping.'

And that, dear brother, is why I didn't tell you about it. Not everything valuable has to be squirrelled away for safekeeping. Lovely things deserve to be shown off, especially in front of grasping family members who will froth at the mouth when they catch sight of it.

'Oh Christ, this is a mess. We should've reported it missing immediately. If she definitely had it on that evening and went straight down to Gables . . .' A pause. 'Unless you took it off her at dinner?'

She looks at Lyra, who blinks in surprise. 'What, you think I yanked it off her hand while she was eating? Or maybe I persuaded her to give it to me as we said goodbye, in a singular moment of mother-daughter bonding? Yeah, you're right, that sounds just like Olivia.'

'Of course Lyra didn't take anything. You're exhausted and grieving, darling.' Will reaches over to his wife and strokes her hand until she pulls away with disgust. 'Come on now, don't let this awful situation fracture our family. Nothing's worth that.' Lyra's eyebrows shoot up at his emphasis on 'our'. 'Who knows,' he continues, 'Charles might've been spot on the first time. Costume jewellery can be very good quality these days. Maybe she got it to wind you up. She liked odd jokes.' Clara screws up her face.

'Jokes? She wasn't, like, famous for her pranks, and she'd *never* have worn fake jewellery. You might be able to identify a prehistoric plate, but we know diamonds, Will. Anyone with eyes could see that ring was the real thing. I don't know how she managed to hide that from the repo team but it was clearly worth it.'

Jemima nods. 'Worth *a lot*.'

She's right about that. It was the most expensive thing I'd kept hold of, but how would she know? The others also noticed the adamant tone.

'What makes you so sure?'

'I looked after it when she was in hospital. You know, after she fainted the last time we were here.' A pause, this clearly isn't the whole truth.

'No, come on, you said it like you knew more than us.' Lyra is frowning now. Her older sister looks slightly defensive, jutting out her jaw and pursing her lips.

'Like Clara said, you could just tell.' She tries to throw the attention back at her sister but nobody is in the mood to entertain this feeble attempt. 'And when you say "looked after it . . ."' Lyra smiles, showing her teeth '. . . you mean you swiped it off her finger and gave it a proper examination. Did you put it through an X-ray machine while you were there?' Jemima shuffles in her seat, but I can tell she feels no real shame in it.

'I wanted to see it! So did all of you. She was asleep, and I put it back before she ever knew.'

Will looks slightly ashen at this, which is nice to see.

'You took her ring? Why on earth would you do that, Jem? She was in hospital for crying out loud.'

She snaps at him now, angry at what she sees as a lecture on morality. 'Well, if I hadn't I wouldn't know it was a ring once owned by Virginia Burney.' Everyone looks blank. 'She was a mistress of the Duke of Athoring. He had it made from a diamond he brought back from India in 1887. At the time, it was considered one of the finest jewels in the country, and when his wife found out who he'd given it to, it sparked a long and messy divorce case. It's got its own page on Wikipedia. Will, are you ok?'

Her husband is holding his throat as though he has something caught in it. He manages a nod.

'How did you find all this out?' Jem looks triumphant now.

'Credit my good eyesight. There was a teeny tiny snake engraved in the band. I googled it, sifted through a lot of crap to find it, but I did. Apparently, snakes were a symbol of love back then, although some sites seem to think it was a rude joke of the Duke's. It disappeared from public record after someone stole it from a private collector in 1958. So that's murky as hell and Dad definitely would've known what he was buying. Explains why it wasn't listed on insurance and why nobody knew to put it on any seizure list. Anyway, Mum ended up as the lucky owner.' She finishes with a tiny smug bow of her head, and I find myself clapping quietly. Those school fees weren't entirely for nothing if Jemima somehow ended up being the one to solve my murder.

ANTHONY

My daughter got it in one. When Liv gave her a little round of applause I found myself enthusiastically joining in. Was this parental pride? I couldn't quite say, having never experienced it, but it very much felt like it might be. The ring had been a big risk, and that's saying something coming from me. But sometimes public auctions – however exclusive – can be, shall we say, limited? Occasionally the things a man might want to buy are only available unofficially. It's not hard if you have the right contacts – and it can be great fun – but you've got to be smart about it. Nothing stolen from a museum, nothing which could even possibly have been art looted by the Nazis, that really does go down badly if discovered. But something goes missing from a private collection decades ago? Well, that's fair game to me. The owners will have been insured, and if not, more fool them. If some complacent idiot doesn't look after his property, he should expect someone to try to take it. I felt much the same about the money I took, come to think of it.

Once you've got enough money to buy nearly anything you want, it gets dull. Having to work a little harder for something felt much more fun than just going into a store and dealing with an obsequious sales assistant working on commission. Usually I only went down that route for art; there's a fabulous tranche of works if you know the right people. The ring was a one-off. Olivia wanted something which packed a real punch, none of these boring modern jewels you see every other woman in the room wearing, from Cartier, from Tiffany, just high street stuff in a nicer box when it came to it. I'd done well with that demand, it took months of work by my fixer and several large cash withdrawals before I was even given a guarantee the ring existed. They made my guy run ragged for it, blindfolding and taking him to a house somewhere deep in the countryside to see it in person. When he got there, a charming old man with what was described to me as the most fantastic comb-over served him tea and homemade biscuits before bringing out the ring and making him promise to look after it. When I finally presented the box to my wife, it immediately made her forget all about the brief dalliance which had prompted the purchase in the first place.

'It sort of makes sense if you knew Olivia and Dad. They'd have thought it was funny to have this super-secret ring that nobody knew . . .' That was true actually – on the rare occasions I let her wear it out of the house, we'd sometimes catch each other's eye and smile. She shouldn't have been wearing it with such wanton abandon, but my death had meant there was nobody to stop her.

'Foolish,' I said. 'Thief,' Liv shot back. Clara had trailed off, eyeing Will with concern. He was red in the face and gripping the table. Noticing that everyone was staring at him, Will hastily shakes his head and drinks some water.

'Must've swallowed something wrong.' Oh dear, he was falling apart faster than I'd predicted.

Clara looked doubtfully at him before turning back to her sister.

'Very impressive research, Jem. Any idea how much it's worth?' Jemima smiled wider than I've ever seen before, flashing rather too much gum.

'It's hard to say given nobody's officially valued it in decades, but a couple of sites seemed to say at least five.'

'Thousand?' Charles asked, and she looked disgusted.

'Yeah, that sounds like something worth stealing. Jesus, Uncle Charles, no. *Million.*' Even Fred looked up when his sister said that, probably trying to figure out how many ugly shrubs he could buy with his cut.

The waiter opens the door and two young women in knee-length kilts bring in the main courses. Freddy starts on his Beef Wellington before the others even receive their plates; his reaction to stress is always to eat or drink. He told me once he felt like he can't breathe properly half the time. Always such an odd boy. I'd pretended I hadn't heard him and offered to let him drive the Range Rover as a treat. Best to gloss over stuff like that.

For the others, the food remains pretty untouched. Will is sitting with his head bowed, eyes unfocused, and it's the most wonderful thing I've seen in weeks.

'So the ring,' says Jemima, obviously not letting it go. 'We'll have to go to the police. It's the only sensible thing to do, there's clearly been a theft.' Will blinks and holds up his fork, almost stabbing the air around his wife.

'That's a mad idea, darling, baby brain must have come early.' A nervous laugh. 'It was stolen property. And on the slim chance your father bought it lawfully, we don't even have a record of it, no photos or documents. We'd be hard pressed to prove anything. Especially if we didn't notice it was gone the night of the robbery. And what would they do on the slim chance that they found it? Retrieve it and then confiscate it just like everything else.'

Nice try, Will, but it's not going to wash. Not with my daughters.

Charles takes his side, suggesting that it would create more attention.

'I think the last thing anyone in this family needs is more questions, don't you? Perhaps it'll turn up. Things often do, sometimes in the last place you'd think. I found a jar of Marmite in the airing cupboard just last week.' Both Lyra and Jemima shoot him looks which, by rights, should have made him crumble into dust.

The conversation about the ring isn't finished, but Charles has made a big mistake piping up in this moment, just as they're all feeling paranoid and jumpy. The children are about to turn on him, I can sense it. As predicted, it's Lyra who goes first.

'I've called you several times about the super-secret account, why do you never answer the phone?' Fred asks what she's talking about, always the last to know anything that boy. Jemima is quick to explain.

'Olivia had been taking from Dad for over a decade, giving her a pretty sweet nest egg, if a nest egg can be money stolen from someone who also stole it.' He looks blank and she sighs. 'I'm not sure how much clearer I can make it, brother. Lyra found out that our mother, in a rare display of good judgement, finally realised that maybe Dad wasn't the most reliable of men to hitch all her hopes and dreams to, so she siphoned off money from their accounts and Charles banked it for her. There should be a good amount coming to us, unofficially of course.'

All eyes turned towards my brother-in-law, and I raised my glass to the screen.

OLIVIA

The lust in their eyes is quite something to see. Idiotic to let Lyra in on what I was doing in the first place. Nobody ever forgets where money is concerned, no matter the amount. Anthony borrowed five thousand quid off my father in the early days of our marriage and didn't pay him back for four years, despite having the means to. Anthony enjoyed it you see, this tiny sum of money which meant nothing to either of them, wielding it over my father's head as if he'd fought an older lion and was now head of the pride. And now my daughter had the same air of victory.

That money, which was easily made by Anthony but hard won by me, was mine and mine alone. That I never got to spend a penny of it was desperately unfair, but the idea of any of my children getting hold of it before I'd had time to lord it over them was worse.

Anthony was making a funny noise, almost like something was trapped deep in his chest. I looked at him and saw that his eyes were bulging and his face was an odd plum colour. Choking! I yelled for an orderly, and instead summoned Tony who took one look at my husband and asked what was so funny. When I looked back at Anthony, I saw he was giggling like a child, tears running down his face.

'Can't choke here, love,' Tony said as he walked off, 'think about it for a minute.' My husband grabbed my arm and yanked me back onto my seat. Then he pointed at the monitor. Charles was talking, his hands folded on the table, as if giving a lecture to a bunch of remedial students.

'I'm sure she enjoyed the idea, Lyra, your mother often exaggerated for effect, but none of what she told you is true I'm afraid. I don't think she'd have had the nous to plan a scheme like that, do you? If she was selling various items of clothing, I'm sure it was just so she could buy more. A nice little hustle, but small potatoes in terms of profit. I don't have any secret fund to share with you, I only wish I did.' Then he shook his head in a show of mock regret.

I didn't understand, couldn't see why he was lying like this. Charles never lied, not even as a child. The one time he tried, he'd burst into tears and flung his arms around the dog as if to seek forgiveness for the heinous misdeed. But here he was, smooth and assertive, making me sound idiotic to boot. I never exaggerate anything. When I say that Emma Dalton's singing voice is the worst noise I've ever heard in my entire life, I'm being entirely accurate. When I tell you that warm white wine makes me want to garrotte the server, I am being entirely reasonable. And when I say that my brother is doing something so appalling that I'll wait in this place forever to wreak my revenge, I'm telling you the truth.

ANTHONY

Don't ask me how, but I just knew that Charles had stashed all the money Olivia squirrelled away into an offshore bank account in his own name. That was always his plan, her death just meant he could reap his dividend earlier than he'd expected.

Olivia's face was a picture. Shock, confusion, then when she finally realised what he was doing, just unbridled rage. It was like watching the five stages of grief, but sped up. I wiped my eyes in a feeble attempt to show sympathy, but I couldn't stop laughing. It felt so good after all these weeks of soul-crushing boredom and anger. I laughed until my belly hurt, Olivia flapping at me, which only set me off harder, and I slid to the floor in helpless hysteria. Back on the monitor, Charles seemed to have successfully convinced them, which I suppose wasn't that hard given my wife's singular lack of financial expertise and her history of flagrant spending. Clara had backed him up, vouching that he was paying for her studies out of his own pocket. It was clear they'd worked out what they'd say beforehand.

'He's wearing a fucking VACHERON, Anthony!' Olivia was pointing at his arm.

'Nice model too, the Tourbillon, never knew your brother had any taste,' I offered up from my position on the floor. I got a sharp kick for that. I deserved it.

Jemima has a quizzical look on her face, and mutters something to her husband.

'You said she'd promised it to us?'

Will's hand is trembling, as he hisses that they should talk about it later. The rest of them look deflated, and Charles, clearly exultant in his new-found fortune, tries to cheer them up.

'Listen, if Jemima is right about the ring, it'll be impossible to sell on. We can rustle up some paperwork to say it's owned legitimately, maybe we even say it's a very good copy. I'm sure we can find someone who'll vouch that they made it if suitably compensated. The important thing to keep in mind is that if someone tries to sell it, any good jeweller will take one look at the markings and know what it is. Whoever took it doesn't know the provenance, maybe they've already tried to flog it?'

Both Olivia and I are staring straight at Will now, who is as pale as a ghost and gulping at the air like a dying fish. I scramble back to my seat and put my hand on Olivia's. She doesn't move away. In this moment, we are united in the only genuine way two people can be – in hatred for another.

The door opens. It'll be the lemon fucking posset, they always end with lemon posset at Tanners. Apparently, it was the king's favourite pudding back in 1650, and while I can see it might have seemed the height of sophistication then, it always irked me. A fellow wants another option in the modern world, even something as simple as a crème brûlée would've sufficed. Despite my constant efforts, the powers that be at Tanners outright rejected me. Even today, I count it as possibly my most humiliating failure. Understandably, the posset brings back some bad memories for me.

But it isn't the dessert. Instead, the manager walks in. For a second, it seems as though he's going to say something, but as quickly as he opens his mouth, he closes it, looking faintly like he's been stunned by lightning. He doesn't know what to say to the diners, this has never happened before in the history of Tanners, not even when Sir Artemis Barton drunkenly tried to attack a waiter with a silver platter in 1987 and five chefs had to tackle him to the ground in front of a full dining room. As he's remembering the sight of Sir Barton's trousers being pulled off by an irate cook, three uniformed police officers emerge from behind him. They are here to make an arrest.

JADE EVANS

I was released three days later, without so much as an apology. They even warned me that the restraining order was still in place, as if I'd want to go anywhere near that mad family again. It turned out Will had tried to sell the ring I'd noticed on Olivia's hand when I'd found her that night; he'd taken it to one of the best dealers in Hatton Garden, who'd known exactly what it was and phoned the police immediately. It had a plethora of evidence all over it. Olivia's DNA, my fingerprints, and Will's. That might not have been enough to exonerate me entirely, but once CCTV of the jewellery shop was made available, his wife cut him loose and told the detectives all about his money woes. Obviously Jemima realised he'd be of no financial value to her if he was broke, and told him she was leaving. After that, he crumbled and told the police everything. Amateur. You shouldn't kill if you don't have the skill. Now *that* would've been the perfect tagline for my channel.

Too late now, I'm not focusing on true crime anymore, the market is oversaturated. Conspiracy theories are where it's at, everyone wants content on the new world order and videos about how vaccines are making you rot from the inside out. It's too bleak, even for me. I got interested in the crime stuff because oddly, it felt optimistic to solve things; I don't want to exploit people. So I've pivoted my channel to motivational speaking. The story of how a small-town girl was wrongly accused of murder and fought to get herself heard is a really popular one, especially after an agent signed me up and I did the rounds on morning TV shows. Someone in Chipping Marston even asked me for a selfie the other day, which I guess means I'm currently more famous than Michaela Sturrock. And despite thinking I'd missed the boat, I host a podcast now too. Me and this nutritional healer with nearly half a million Instagram followers cover everything from the art of manifesting, to how to be the best *you* you can be. It's doing pretty well, we've even got sponsorship from a yoghurt company that claims to be able to alleviate depression. I'm feeding it to Mum every morning, and she certainly seems brighter, even if she spends most of her time watching TV programmes where people build ugly-looking houses and run out of money halfway through.

I never got any recognition from any of the Wistern kids for my work, not even a thank you from Clara who only posted about her mum's murder twice (never mentioning me) and then announced she was moving to LA to study acting. Her dream, apparently. I heard Lyra changed her surname and got a job managing an artist who makes absurdly huge paintings. According to some puff piece I read, rich people have bigger walls and therefore need bigger art to hang. He's making a killing. The family sold Gables in the end, it was the only thing of value they had and it gave them a nice profit. Mum said the estate agent went around town boasting about his commission. Apparently the buyers were rich Americans, and only plan on using the house for an authentic British Christmas experience. I saw in the local paper that they've put in planning permission to get rid of the lake and put in a swimming pool, which is probably for the best. Freddy used his share to buy 50 acres over the other side of town, and though nobody understands why he's planting trees and hillocks when it's perfectly good farming land, he seems happy. Some of his nervous energy has gone, he managed to look me right in the eye last week when I saw him at the pub. Still hasn't apologised for not telling the police he saw me though, so maybe he's more like his father than he'd care to admit.

I see Jemima around occasionally too, though she always ignores me. She bought a house just down the road from The Badger and Luke promptly moved in. The baby was born last month, a boy apparently.

'Looks just like his dad,' according to Jillian in the newsagents, though who that actually might be is anyone's guess. When Will was finally charged, she'd called Luke immediately, putting on the waterworks, saying she'd been in the process of leaving him, and he just lapped it up. He told me all this in a text message thanking me for bringing them back together, and I'd been so horrified I'd offered him a free life-coaching session. He never replied.

The footage I have of the police pulling me out of the bush by my ankles was made into a meme, I see it all the time on social media. Usually it's accompanied by text saying 'me when my mum finds out I've slept in' or 'me when I run out of my meds' but I don't mind too much. At least people know who I am now. There's talk of my story being made into a TV drama, my agent is fielding calls. Maybe that would be the push needed to finally solve Anthony Wistern's death. I still think about that, despite being officially retired from the sleuth game. Other people got bored and moved on, but I say Olivia Wistern got away with murder, and you'll never get me to believe otherwise.

OLIVIA

All these people who underestimated me, or thought they could predict what I'd do, astonishing really. Even Anthony, the man I'd spent most of my life with, never really knew me. I wasn't the wife he wanted in the end, but then he turned out to be a supremely bad bet himself. There's nothing more shameful than having to bury your husband in a dreary suburb far away in order that angry investors don't deface his grave. His body is interred at the end of the Northern Line, up in Cockfosters which feels rather apt, and his soul . . . well.

Once we'd found out that Will had been arrested, he knew I had my answer. I could go to Susan and tell her I knew who'd killed me. I could leave this place, ascend to the real afterlife, and worst of all for Anthony, I'd win.

'It's not fair you figure it out before I do,' he'd sulked. But that wasn't my plan. Easier, of course, and in many ways, the sensible thing to do. But I had information that my husband didn't. I knew how I'd died, yes, but I also knew how *he'd* died. Not, as he thought, in an exciting or news-making way. Not murdered by a love rival or a jealous businessman. Or even, as we all might have suspected, by one of his ungrateful children. Truly, Anthony had the most humiliating of endings. I also knew, from my many little chats with Susan, that the staff here couldn't stand him. I may not be everyone's cup of tea, but I can be charming when it's needed. And Susan now seemed to have a soft spot for me. She'd been married to a very domineering man, I learnt during one of our moments together, a man who dictated the food they ate and the films they watched and worst of all, she'd confided, the decor in their house.

'It was all red and black, Olivia.' She'd shuddered in the retelling, and I'd rubbed her arm and told her I understood, though I could never truly understand letting that colour scheme into my home. I'd rather live in a tent.

Once the bond was made, she told me that Anthony was the worst dead person they'd ever had in the Gloucestershire sorting unit, by unanimous decree. Even Fred West, she said, had at least been polite. I hammed up stories about how terrible a husband he was, enjoying this new sense of sisterhood, and gradually, I learnt a little about what was waiting for him in the next stage of the afterlife.

'I don't know everything for certain,' Susan cautioned me. 'Very few of our intake have been sent there, Olivia, it's . . . a very specific place.' Her voice lowering a few octaves, she described what she *did* know. And immediately, my plan was obvious. I marched back to the dormitory, where Anthony was sitting on his bed with Tony, the pair of them enthusiastically singing a Duran Duran song complete with air guitar, and told my husband we needed to talk. Reluctantly, the mid-life crisis moment came to a stop, and he followed me to the meditation room.

'Anthony,' I said, speaking as crisply as possible so as to drive the message home, 'We *were* fighting by the lake.' He pumped his fist in victory like a small child, so pleased to be right he didn't see what I was doing. 'You'd been seen stumbling down to the lake with your enthusiastic PA, and I'd offered to take Allegra on a tour of the party just to check you were behaving yourself. I saw you having words with Giles, the two of you drunkenly sniping at each other, which of course I had to put a stop to. Once I'd palmed Allegra off onto Leon Miner, claiming I had to go and have a word with the catering manager, I doubled back, intending to interrupt your tête-à-tête, which had quickly descended into a pathetic wrestling match. Giles stomped off before I got to you, and you turned on me, behaving like a complete oaf, all amped up and saying some truly unforgivable things to me.'

I paused for breath, and realised he was rapt. All you had to do to keep Anthony's attention was simply to talk about Anthony.

'So I made a little mistake. I told you I was leaving you the next day. Stupid of me to let my emotions get the better of me like that, but you'd just said the party was fading faster than my looks and I snapped. You couldn't accept that I'd ever be the one to go, you laughed at the idea. Laughed at *me* for thinking I could "do without you" as you put it. I waited in silence for you to get it, to understand I wasn't making empty threats and eventually, it sunk in. I have to say, it took you long enough. I'd smoked three cigarettes while your booze-addled brain tried to make sense of it. You grabbed me by the hand then, knocking my lighter into the lake, which really made me cross. That was my daddy's lighter, and I really believe you did it on purpose. I told you to go jump in the lake and stomped off up the path towards the trees. When I looked round, you'd taken your jacket off and yelled at me to watch.'

He looked blankly at me.

'Do you not see? You took my flippant remark as a dare. "I'm going to do the best fucking dive you've ever seen." That's what

366

you said. Then you put your arms up, yelled "triple pike" and launched yourself into the water. It was the most hideous belly-flop, Anthony, honestly you looked like a walrus heaving yourself off the beach. My laughter was short-lived of course, when I realised you'd spiked yourself. Nobody tried to kill you. You did it to yourself. A sloppy, sixty-year-old drunk, stumbling off a jetty and disemboweling himself on a spike. I'm sorry I saw it, but it was hard to look away. Just the height of tragic comedy.'

He looked shocked for just a second, and then smiled at me, as if I'd told a clumsy joke.

'I should have raised the alarm, I know that's unforgivable of me but it was such a lovely party, it would've been a shame to end it so abruptly. I saw you were past saving, darling, truly. Once someone's been skewered like that, there's not much anyone can do.'

Anthony was still grinning, and I kept a straight face as he congratulated me on attempting to be funny, though, it had to be said, he now looked rather shaky.

'Not one of your natural talents, darling, but good try.' I repeated the story again, and his smile faded a little. On the fourth go, after I used the word 'bellyflop' again he looked visibly annoyed.

'If you don't believe me, *darling*, go and try it out on the director.'

So he did; he stomped off down the corridor yelling that I was wasting his time. I sat on my bed, practising some calming breaths. Was this the inner peace people waxed so lyrically about? When he came back, he was jubilant, all thoughts of his death being undignified erased. He'd actually managed to massage the story in the space of five minutes so it made him look good.

'I met Yvonne, who was hugely embarrassed not to have given me proper respect before, but it's all smoothed over now. Do you know, I'd seen her around and assumed she was just another civilian, isn't that funny?' It wasn't, but I graciously offered him up a weak smile. 'The whole place is run by women, no wonder nothing works! Anyway, I figured it all out and Yvonne was incredibly impressed. You didn't get it quite right, no change there. What *actually* happened is I spotted your lighter Liv, clumsy old you, and I was going to wade in and get it. Slipped on the damn jetty because you'd had it waxed that day, hadn't you? You insisted on making it look smarter and the guys obviously buggered it all up. I died trying to get that lighter back for you. I don't expect thanks, I know it takes a bigger person to do that, but you could have at least tried not to make your first ever joke out of something so tragic.'

This was our goodbye, finally. Not that he understood that yet; how had it taken me so long to realise how dense my husband could be? Without thinking, I kissed him hard on the mouth, shocking both of us.

'I'll see you soon, Livvy,' he said as he walked down the corridor. 'We'll move on from all of this. I'll do all the hard work to make sure our new place is all set up, just as I always do.'

And then he was gone. By rights, Yvonne should've been angry with me for breaking the rules and telling him everything, but instead, we celebrated in her office with a bottle of Prosecco. I couldn't bear the stuff, a sickly sweet imitation of proper fizz, but I didn't protest. I think that's growth. She knew I was in possession of all the facts about my death, but she also understood there was nothing she could do to make me say the words out loud. And while this place was truly ghastly, imagining Anthony's horror when he arrived at his new home would keep me going. That, and watching my reputation get an unexpected revamp. After a young woman wrote a particularly sympathetic piece about me in *The Times*, people had already been calling the children to express their sorrow. In death, it appeared I had been accepted back into the fold. Instead of the Lady Macbeth figure the press had painted me in life, I was now being recast as a victim.

'Olivia Wistern was in thrall to one man with too much money, and killed by another who desperately wanted it. Perhaps the hateful online discourse about her will now stop, and she can rest in peace.' If I'd known I could've laundered my reputation so easily, I think I'd have come round to Lyra's exhortations about feminism much earlier.

Now I would wait here until Charles arrived. That was another little secret my new best friend Yvonne let me in on. She had the schedule you see, and though she couldn't tell me the exact date ('Death is often off by up to a week – for something so guaranteed, it's a little bit unreliable.') she did let slip it was fairly imminent. And though it was unlikely he'd end up in the South Gloucestershire processing centre, she felt confident she'd be able to swing it and get him transferred here. Poor Charles. A life of dull duty, all for three months of fun. I honestly might've forgiven him you know, had it not been for that brief moment I witnessed on the monitor. My brother, in an uncomfortably enthusiastic embrace with my oldest friend Penny Donsman, on the steps of the flat he'd bought with *my* hard-earned money. They'd been in on it together, right from the start. I hope it was worth it, truly I do. Because I would have my revenge; no man will decide how my story ends. Least of all one who calls a woman like Penny his 'minxy mistress'. Anthony might've have been a terrible disappointment, but at least he had high standards.

ANTHONY

It's a commune. I am to live in a shared yurt with a white family who have dreadlocks and who are teaching their four children to play the bagpipes. Eternity is here, I am told by the woman, in *song*. The baby cries a lot, which they all find charming. The oldest child asks which bunk I want, pointing to a set of hammocks. 'Chanting is at 5 a.m.' I'm told it is compulsory. A man who looks like he considers soap a personal enemy offers to wash my feet if I return the favour. It's not forever, I mutter, over and over until the man puts a hand on my shoulder. He has friendship bracelets on both wrists.

'Oh, but it is, mate' he says, with a wink. I think about Liv's face when I said goodbye, and realise that she set this up. She knew where I was going, she knew about the hammocks. I want to die. Again.

NEWS ARTICLE

10 November 2018

There's something about Mary

In an exclusive interview with *The Times*, Mary Chambers makes the dazzling revelation that she was the person who raised the alarm about Anthony Wistern. As she pours tea in her beautifully appointed living room ('We knocked two houses into one, I just cannot find peace in narrow spaces'), it's hard to imagine that this elegant woman has been secretly liaising with the police for months. But though she looks delicate, Mary Chambers has a steel core.

'My husband always said you'd underestimate me at your peril,' she laughs, offering me a handmade almond biscotti. 'I'm small in stature but I can be fierce. Anthony Wistern didn't reckon with that.' Of all his mistakes, this might have been his most egregious.

Married to the businessman John Chambers at twenty-one, Mary has spent the past forty years as a campaigner and philanthropist. Since her beloved husband died last year, she has redoubled her efforts, raising awareness for everything from the loss of rural hedgerows to the plight of garment workers in Bangladesh. Seemingly no cause is overlooked, and at times she gets confused about which issue she's speaking on, such is her passion. At one point she decries the lack of funding for prosthetic legs for pandas, before correcting herself with a light slap on the forehead. 'The legs are for soldiers, the pandas need IVF.'

Mary is a wonderful raconteur, regaling me with stories – some unprintable – about the great and the good. At one time, Anthony Wistern was one of those people.

'Neither great nor good, as it turned out,' she says, one eyebrow raised. 'John always taught me that if something seems too good to be true, then it probably is. The same goes for people. Anthony Wistern was just a little too charming, a little too lucky. My mother always said I had a second sight about me, and I always felt very uneasy around him. But what could I do? Everybody else thought the man was some kind of financial god.' I ask what spurred her to take action and she takes a moment to think about it.

'At John's wake, he made a terrible joke about the way in which my husband had died. I never let him know I'd overheard him. Anybody who knows me will say I'm famously discreet. I plan on leaving a breathtaking amount of money to a variety of charities and though my friends would tell you it's unlike me to brag, I hope to be remembered as a force for immense good in the world. But nothing else would've happened if I hadn't met Lainey Goodman.'

Goodman was Wistern's mistress, and long-time personal assistant to the financier. 'She came into my local patisserie just as I was about to tuck into a lovely almond flan, and introduced herself. She was in a real state poor girl, that man had treated her very badly, and I ended up consoling her. My husband always said that he'd never met anyone as empathetic as me. It's a gift and a curse.'

The two women struck up an unlikely friendship, and it was Mary that Lainey went to with her worries about Anthony's business.

'She didn't know anything concrete of course, she was just a PA. But she thought something was off; he was very stressed, and always on the phone to one person in particular. So I asked if she knew who it was, and when she said Anita Vasher, I knew what I had to do. Anita is an old friend; we don't see each other very often but I know she holds deep affection for me. A nightmare to get hold of the woman, but I managed it eventually and asked her straight out whether she'd invested with Wistern.'

Mary looks triumphant now, as she well might.

'She had, and she bitterly regretted it. The man was giving her the run around, giving the most ridiculous reasons as to why she couldn't have her money back. I told her quite firmly that he must be stealing from her, which she didn't like very much, but the truth is all we have. Even when I'd convinced her, she wouldn't go to the police, but I've always been braver than most people, so I did it for her.'

Mary Chambers, with the determination that's made her a champion for so many less fortunate than her, reported Anthony Wistern to the National Crime Agency just a week before his death.

'Of course I had to go to the party, my absence would've been noted, but I made sure to keep the conversation as sparkling as he'd have expected from me.'

The investigation took its time to get going, which Mary felt was unacceptable.

'I have high standards for myself, and I expect others to rise to them. Seeing the undeserved eulogies Anthony was getting after his death was too much, so I called an acquaintance at the *Telegraph* and let them know about the investigation just before the funeral. That got the police working, I can tell you.'

I ask whether or not she thought Olivia was involved and Mary is careful with her words.

'I didn't at the beginning, but I could always tell she couldn't much stand Anthony. I even sent her some balloons when he died, not that she bothered to thank me, but I quickly realised she must've known what he was doing – she absolutely ran that marriage. I'm not sure how he put up with it to be honest, men prefer a gentler wife in my experience.'

Ever gracious, Mary *does* offer some kind words for the Wisterns.

'I hope they're together wherever they are. Those two were truly made for each other.'

There's a curious postscript to our delightful interview. As I leave, Mary tells me she's meeting Charles Holdwood, Olivia's brother, that evening.

'We met after he started stepping out with my close friend Penny. Always lovely to meet someone with similar interests.' I'm almost sure I see a wink, but within seconds, Mary's face is as serene as ever, and I leave feeling that you'd never wish to make an enemy of this indomitable, charming and slightly terrifying woman.

ACKNOWLEDGEMENTS

I am so grateful for Kim and Ann, who have been the most wonderful editors. I got so lucky, working with two women with such brilliant brains, endless patience and the willingness to reply to even the stupidest messages I send at random.

Thank you to Philly, Lipfon, Abbie, Claire, Ellie, Jabin, Harriet and the rest of the publishing team at Borough, for doing all you do to ensure a book actually gets noticed in the first place, and without which only my mum would've read it.

Thank you to my agent Steph for being so supportive and always pushing me in the right direction.

Alan and Linds, the greatest parents anyone could ever hope to have. My mother, always my first reader, the person I hope to make laugh. Dad, I hope you finish it by the time you read this.

Greg, for being the most brilliant sounding board on evening walks.

Archie, Maya, Nesrine, Miranda, Benji, Ben, Ruth. None of you have read it (and half of you never will) but you'll check for your names. I love you all.

David, for all your financial advice, which both told me how much I don't understand the system and showed me that's by design.

Finally, thanks to the booksellers who championed *How to Kill Your Family* and to everyone who read it. You gave me a career I could only dream of, and changed my life in the process.